Hostage to Pleasure

NALINI SINGH

BERKLEY SENSATION, NEW YORK

THE BERKLEY PUBLISHING GROUP
Published by the Penguin Group
Penguin Group (USA) Inc.
375 Hudson Street, New York, New York 10014, USA
Penguin Group (Canada), 90 Eglinton Avenue East, Suite 700, Toronto, Ontario M4P 2Y3, Canada
(a division of Pearson Penguin Canada Inc.)
Penguin Books Ltd., 80 Strand, London WC2R 0RL, England
Penguin Group Ireland, 25 St. Stephen's Green, Dublin 2, Ireland (a division of Penguin Books Ltd.)
Penguin Group (Australia), 250 Camberwell Road, Camberwell, Victoria 3124, Australia
(a division of Pearson Australia Group Pty. Ltd.)
Penguin Books India Pvt. Ltd., 11 Community Centre, Panchsheel Park, New Delhi—110 017, India
Penguin Group (NZ), 67 Apollo Drive, Rosedale, North Shore 0632, New Zealand
(a division of Pearson New Zealand Ltd.)
Penguin Books (South Africa) (Pty.) Ltd., 24 Sturdee Avenue, Rosebank, Johannesburg 2196,
South Africa

Penguin Books Ltd., Registered Offices: 80 Strand, London WC2R 0RL, England

This is a work of fiction. Names, characters, places, and incidents either are the product of the author's imagination or are used fictitiously, and any resemblance to actual persons, living or dead, business establishments, events, or locales is entirely coincidental. The publisher does not have any control over and does not assume any responsibility for author or third-party websites or their content.

HOSTAGE TO PLEASURE

A Berkley Sensation Book / published by arrangement with the author

PRINTING HISTORY
Berkley trade mass-market edition / September 2008

Copyright © 2008 by Nalini Singh.
Excerpt from *Angels' Blood* copyright © 2008 by Nalini Singh.
Excerpt from *Branded by Fire* copyright © 2008 by Nalini Singh.
Cover art by Phil Heffernan.
Cover design by George Long.
Hand lettering by Ron Zinn.

ISBN: 978-0-425-22325-3

BERKLEY® SENSATION
Berkley Sensation Books are published by The Berkley Publishing Group,
a division of Penguin Group (USA) Inc.,
375 Hudson Street, New York, New York 10014.
BERKLEY SENSATION and the "B" design are trademarks belonging to Penguin Group (USA) Inc.

PRINTED IN THE UNITED STATES OF AMERICA

10 9 8 7 6 5 4 3 2 1

Craving the passionate and electrifying world created by the megatalented Singh? Your next fix is here! . . . One of the most original and thrilling paranormal series on the market . . . Mind-blowing!"   —*Romantic Times* (4½ Stars, Top Pick)

A sensual, dangerous adventure not to be missed."
                    —*New York Times* bestselling author Lora Leigh

Nalini Singh continues to dazzle and ensnare new readers with each addition to the Psy-Changeling series."—*A Romance Review*

A compelling read with wonderfully developed characters and the strong world-building that has made Singh a star. Readers will revel in this latest installment with two of the most riveting secondary characters from the previous novels."
                                        —*All About Romance*

With a truly inspired mix of passion and danger, this story will keep you on the edge of your seat. [It] will surely earn itself a place among your favorites."   —*Romance Reviews Today*

Delivers increasingly inventive world-building, intrigue-filled plotting, and a complicated and satisfying love story—and will leave readers eagerly anticipating the next installment."
                                                —*BookLoons*

A mesmerizing series."   —*The Road to Romance*
                                          (Reviewer's Choice Award)

This is a wonderful story and I cannot recommend it highly enough!"   —*ParaNormal Romance Reviews*

Ms. Singh is sure to win new readers with this release. I highly recommend the series and *Caressed by Ice* to all fans of paranormal romances."   —*The Romance Readers Connection*

continued . . .

Praise for

Slave to Sensation

"I LOVE this book! It's a must read for all of my fans. Nalini Singh is a major new talent." —*New York Times* bestselling author Christine Feehan

"An electrifying collision of logic and emotion . . . An incredible world where fire and ice mix to create an unforgettable sensual eruption. *Slave to Sensation* is a volcanic start to a new series that'll leave you craving more." —*Romance Junkies*

"AWESOME! . . . A purely mesmerizing book that surely stands out among the other paranormal books out there. *Slave to Sensation* is captivating from beginning to end. It's a must read for any paranormal fan!" —*Romance Reader at Heart*

"Superb science fiction romance . . . Readers will enjoy Nalini Singh's excellent futuristic thriller and demand more tales from this fascinating realm." —*Midwest Book Review*

"You won't want to miss *Slave to Sensation*, the tremendous first book in the new Psy series by Nalini Singh . . . I highly recommend this book and suggest you make room for it on your keeper shelf." —*Romance Reviews Today*

"A sensual romance set in an alternate-reality America with just a bit of mystery to keep readers flipping pages. Character-driven and well-written, it's not easy to put down at bedtime; it kept me reading well into the night." —*Fresh Fiction*

"A fresh, intriguing, and thought-provoking mythology and a very appealing cast of characters . . . I look forward to the next installment from this talented writer." —*BookLoons*

"A must even for those uninitiated in the paranormal genre. The story ends much too quickly, and the author's magical writing conjures up sensual images and intense emotions that linger long after the last word is read." —*Romantic Times*

*I grew up lucky—in an extended family
where the written word was everywhere.
This one's for all of you
who gave me a book as a child,
took me to the library,
or saved a well-loved story to share.
Thank you for those priceless gifts.*

CHOICES

When, in a desperate attempt to save their people from the twin scourges of murder and insanity, the Psy race decided to embrace the Silence Protocol and eliminate emotion from their lives, it was by no means an easy decision. Blood was shed. Innocents and guilty alike died. Hearts were destroyed, and the pain of it split the PsyNet into two.

But perhaps the cruelest aspect of Silence was that it forced people to *choose*. Acceptance or rebellion, parent or lover, sister or child. There was no middle ground. Those left inside the Net would never again reach out to the ones who walked away. And the exiled would live forever with the heartbreak of knowing that those they loved were being taught to devalue love itself.

It hurt.

Like a bruise that would not heal, pulsing with the pain of memory, of loss.

Now, in the year 2080, the hurt has faded, the choices have been made, and those in the PsyNet live a life of cold Silence. Love is no longer something they understand, much less desire. Because to love is to be flawed.

And the Psy do not allow the flawed to live.

CHAPTER 1

To survive, you must become more Silent than the Council, your heart ice, your mind a flawless prism. But never forget—prisms bend light, change the direction of what is known, generate fractures of beauty. Ultimately, prisms create their own truths.

—*From a handwritten letter signed "Iliana," circa June 2069*

In the end, the retraction was deadly simple. The sniper had been given the precise coordinates the car would travel along the sleepy rural road, knew exactly how many people were in the vehicle, where the child was sitting. According to his information, the child was blindfolded, but the sniper still didn't like doing this with an innocent in the vehicle.

However, if left in the hands of his captors, that child would become the unwitting instrument of the worst kind of evil. And then he would die. The sniper didn't kill lightly, but to keep a child safe, he would do much worse.

"Go," the sniper said into the air, the sound picked up by his earpiece and transmitted to those below.

A slow-moving truck veered out of the opposite lane without warning, crashing into the side of the target car with a smooth expertise that forced the vehicle off the road, but would do little damage to the people inside—they couldn't afford to harm the child. More than that, they *refused* to harm the child. But it wasn't the child the sniper found in his sights as soon as the car came to a halt.

A single precise shot and the windshield shattered.

The driver and his adult passenger were dead within the next two seconds, a clean bullet hole in the center of each of their foreheads. The bullets were designed not to exit, thereby minimizing danger to the backseat passengers.

An instant later, the rear doors slid back and two men jumped out, one of whom stared straight at the sniper's location high up in the spreading branches of an ancient pine. The sniper felt a blunt force graze his mind, but the guard had left his telepathic strike for too late. A bullet lodged in the Psy male's throat with fatal accuracy even as he focused his power. The fourth man went down with a silent bullet wound through his chest, having failed to locate the sniper's partner.

The sniper was already moving by the time the last body hit the ground, his rifle in hand. He left behind no trace of who he was and when he reached the car, he touched nothing. "Did they get out a psychic alert?" he asked the unseen watcher.

"Likely. Road's still clear, but we need to move fast—reinforcements will be here in minutes if the Council has teleportation-capable Tk's on hand."

The sniper looked through the open doors and saw the final remaining passenger. A tiny boy, barely four and a half years old. He wasn't only blindfolded. His ears had been plugged and his hands tied behind his back. Near-total sensory deprivation.

The sniper growled and became a man named Dorian again, his cold control falling away to expose the deeply protective nature of his beast. He might have been born lacking the changeling ability to shift into animal form, but he carried the leopard within. And that leopard was enraged by the callous treatment meted out to this defenseless child. Reaching in, he gathered the stiff, scared body in his arms, his hold far gentler than anyone would've believed. "I have him."

Another vehicle appeared out of nowhere. This one was sleek, silver, nothing like the now abandoned truck, though the driver was the same man. "Let's go," Clay said, his eyes a flat green.

Getting into the backseat, Dorian ripped off his face mask and put away the gun before cutting through the boy's bindings with the pocketknife he carried everywhere. Blood slicked his fingers and he drew back so fast, he sliced open a thin line on his own palm. But when he looked closer, he realized he hadn't accidentally cut the child—the boy had been struggling against his bonds for what must've been hours. His wrists were raw.

Biting off a brutal oath, Dorian slid the knife back into his jeans and took out the plugs from the boy's ears, removing his blindfold a second later. Unexpected blue gray eyes looked into his, startling in a face with skin the color of aged gold, a dusky brown that almost glowed. "Keenan."

The boy didn't say anything, his face preternaturally calm. So young and he'd already begun the road to Silence, begun to learn to suppress his emotions and become a good, robotic Psy. But his calm facade aside, he was too young to hide his bone-chilling fear from the changeling who watched him, the sharp bite of it insulting to Dorian's senses. Children were not meant to be bound and used as pawns. It was not a fair fight.

The car came to a stop. The opposite passenger-side door opened and then Judd was sliding inside, his gun strapped to his back. "We have to do it now or they'll track him through the PsyNet." The other man's eyes were a cold brown when he stripped off his own mask, but his hands careful as he touched the boy's face. "Keenan, we have to cut the Net link."

The boy stiffened, leaned into Dorian. "No."

Dorian put an arm around his fragile, breakable body. "Be brave. Your mom wants you safe."

Those astonishing eyes looked up at him. "Will you kill me?"

Dorian looked to Judd. "It gonna hurt?"

A slight nod.

Dorian held Keenan's hand, the boy's blood mixing with his own where he'd sliced open his palm. "It'll hurt like a bitch, but then you'll be okay."

Keenan's eyes widened at the vulgarity, exactly as Dorian had intended. In that moment of distraction, Judd closed his eyes. Dorian knew the Psy male was working furiously to unlock the child's shields and get inside his mind—so he could cut Keenan's link to the PsyNet, the psychic network that connected every Psy on the planet, but for the renegades. Bare seconds later, the boy screamed and it was a sound of such brutal suffering that Dorian almost killed Judd for it. The sound cut off as abruptly as it had begun and Keenan slumped into Dorian's arms, unconscious.

"Jesus," Clay said from the front, merging onto a busy

highway even as he spoke. "The kid okay? Tally will kill me if we get a scratch on him."

Dorian brushed back the boy's hair. It was straight, unlike his mother's curls. She'd had it tamed into a braid the one and only time he'd seen her—through the scope of his rifle—but he'd been able to tell. "He's breathing."

"Well"—Judd paused, white lines bracketing his mouth—"that was unexpected."

"What?" Dorian took off his jacket and covered Keenan in its warmth.

"I was supposed to pull him into our familial net." The other man rubbed absently at his temple, eyes on Keenan. "But he went . . . elsewhere. Since he's not dead, I'm guessing he's linked into DarkRiver's secret network—the one I'm not supposed to know about."

Dorian shook his head. "Impossible." They all knew that Psy brains were different from changeling or human—Psy needed the biofeedback provided by a psychic network. Cut that off and death was close to instantaneous, the reason why defectors from the PsyNet were few and far between. Judd's family had only just made it out by linking together to form the tiny LaurenNet. Their psychic gifts meant they could manipulate that net and accept new members. But DarkRiver's net, the Web of Stars, was different.

"There is no way he could've entered our web." Dorian scowled. "It's a changeling construct." Created by loyalty, not need, it welcomed only a select few—leopard sentinels who had sworn an oath to the DarkRiver alpha, Lucas, and their mates.

Judd shrugged and leaned back against the seat. "Maybe the boy has some changeling blood."

"He'd be a shape-shifter if he had that much of it," Clay pointed out. "Plus, my beast doesn't sense an animal in him. He's Psy."

"All I know is that as soon as the PsyNet was closed to him, his consciousness arrowed away from me and toward Dorian. I can't see your network, but my guess is that he's linked to you"—he nodded at Dorian—"and through you, to your web. I could try to cut that bond," he continued, his reluctance open, "and force him into our familial net, but it'd only traumatize him again."

Dorian looked down at the boy and felt the trapped leopard inside him rise in a protective crouch. "Then I guess he stays with us. Welcome to DarkRiver, Keenan Aleine."

Miles away, in a lab located in the bowels of the earth, Ashaya Aleine staggered under the backwash of a devastating mental blow. A sudden cut and he was gone, her son, the link she'd had without knowing she had it.

Either Keenan was dead or . . .

She remembered the first of the two notes she'd gotten out through the lab's garbage chute the previous week, a note that would have been transmitted to a human named Talin McKade by those who were loyal to Ashaya rather than the tyrannical ruling Council.

I'm calling in my IOU.

The best-case scenario was that Talin McKade and her friends had come through. Ashaya's thoughts traveled back to that night two months ago when she'd put her life on the line to free a teenager and a young girl from the lethal danger of the lab— before they became the latest casualties in a series of genocidal experiments run by another scientist.

It was as she was returning to the lab that he'd found her, the unnamed sniper with a voice as cool as any Psy assassin's.

"I have a gun pointed at your temple. I don't miss."

"I saved two innocent lives. You won't kill me."

A hint of laughter, but she couldn't be sure. "What did you want the IOU for?"

"You're male. Therefore you aren't Talin McKade."

"I'm a friend. She has others. And we pay our debts."

"If you want to repay your debt," she said, "kidnap my son."

With her note, she'd set that very event in motion. Then she'd cashed in every favor owed to her and put psychic safeguards in place to protect Keenan against recapture through the PsyNet. But now Keenan was gone—she knew that beyond any shadow of a doubt. And no Psy could survive outside the Net.

Yet, another part of her reminded her, the DarkRiver leopard pack had two Psy members who had survived very well. Could it be that Talin McKade's friends were cats? That supposition was pure guesswork on her part as she had nothing on which to base her theory or check her conclusions. She was under a psychic and electronic blackout, her Internet access cut off, her entry to the vast resources of the PsyNet policed by telepaths under Councilor Ming LeBon's command. So she, a woman who trusted no one, would have to trust the sniper had spoken true, and Keenan was safe.

Head still ringing from the shearing off of that inexplicable bond, she sat absolutely frozen for ten long minutes, getting her body back under control. No one could be allowed to learn that she'd felt the backlash, that she knew her son was no longer in the PsyNet. *She shouldn't have known.* Every individual Psy was an autonomous unit. Even in the fluid darkness of the Net, where each mind existed as a burning psychic star stripped of physical limitations, they encased themselves in multiple shields, remaining separate.

There were no blurred boundaries, no threads tying one consciousness to another. It hadn't always been that way—according to the hidden records she'd unearthed in her student days, the PsyNet had once reflected the emotional entanglements of the people involved. Silence had severed those bonds—of affection, of blood—until isolation was all they were . . . or that was the accepted view. Ashaya had always known it for a lie.

Because of Amara.

And now, because of Keenan.

Keenan and Amara. Her twin flaws, the double-edged sword that hung over her every second of every day. One mistake, just one, was all it would take to bring that sword crashing down.

A door opened at her back. "Yes?" she said calmly, though her mind was overflowing with memories usually contained behind impenetrable walls.

"Councilor LeBon has called through."

Ashaya glanced at the slender blonde who'd spoken. "Thank you."

With a nod, Ekaterina left. They knew not to speak treasonous words within these walls. Too many eyes. Too many ears. Switching the clear screen of her computer to communications mode, she accepted the call. She no longer had the ability to call out. The lockdown of the lab had been ordered after the children's escape, though officially, Jonquil Duchslaya and Noor Hassan were listed as deceased—by Ashaya's hand.

However, she knew Ming was suspicious. In lieu of torture, he'd shut her inside this plascrete tomb, tons of earth above her head, knowing that she had a psychological defect, that she reacted negatively to the thought of being buried. "Councilor," she said as Ming's face appeared on-screen, his eyes the night-sky of a cardinal, "what can I do for you?"

"You're meant to be having a visitation with your son this week."

She focused on regulating her pulse—an aftereffect of the sudden disconnection from Keenan. To carry this plan through to its completion, she had to remain cold as ice, more Silent than the Council itself. "It's part of the agreement."

"That visitation will be delayed."

"Why?" She had very little power here, but she wasn't completely under Ming's thumb—they both knew she was the only M-Psy capable of completing the work on Protocol I.

"The child's biological father has asked to offer him specialized training. The request has been granted."

Ashaya knew with absolute certainty that Zie Zen would never have taken that step without consulting her. But knowing that didn't tell her whether Keenan was dead or alive. "The delay will complicate the training I'm giving him."

"The decision has been made." Ming's eyes turned obsidian, the few white stars drowning in black. "You should focus on your research. You've made no significant progress in the past two months."

Two months. Eight weeks. Fifty-six days. The period of time since the children's escape . . . and her effective burial in the Implant lab.

"I've conclusively solved the problem of Static," she reminded him, dangerously aware of the growing tightness around her rib cage—a stress reaction, another indicator of the chinks Keenan's sudden disappearance had made in her psychological armor. "No implant would work if we were constantly bombarded with the thoughts of others." That was what the Council intended for the PsyNet—that it become a huge hive mind, interconnected and seamless. No renegades, nothing but conformity.

However, *pure* conformity was a nonviable goal. In simple terms, a hive could not survive without a queen. Which was why Ashaya had been instructed to devise several different grades of

implants. Those implanted with the highest grade would possess
the ability to exercise total control over every other individual in
the hive, to the point of being able to enter their minds at will,
direct them with the ease of puppet masters. No thought would
be private, no disagreement possible.

Ming gave a slight nod. "Your breakthrough with Static was
impressive, but it doesn't compensate for your lack of progress
since."

"With respect," Ashaya said, "I disagree. No one else even
came close to eliminating Static. The theorists all stated it to be
an impossible task." She thought fast and took another precarious
step along the tightrope. Too far and Ming wouldn't hesitate to
kill her. Too little and it would paint her as weak, open to ex-
ploitation. "If you want me to rush the process, I'll do so. But if
the implants then malfunction, do not look to place the blame on
me. I want that in writing."

"Are you sure you want to make an enemy out of me,
Ashaya?" A quiet question devoid of any emphasis and yet the
threat was a sinister shadow pressing at her mind. Ming flexing
his telepathic muscles? Probably, given that he was a cardinal
telepath with a facility for mental combat. He could turn her
brain into mush with a glancing thought.

Ashaya supposed that if she'd been human or changeling,
she'd have felt fear. But she was Psy, conditioned since birth to
feel nothing. Hard and inflexible, that conditioning not only allowed her to play politics with Ming, it acted as a shield, hiding
the secrets she could never reveal. "It is not a case of enemies,
sir," she said, and—making another rapid decision—let her
shoulders slump a fraction. When she next spoke, it was in a
quick-fire stream. "I'm trying my hardest, but I've hit what appears to be a major obstacle, and I'm the only one with the skill
to solve it so I've been working around the clock and I've been
buried underground for two months with no access to the PsyNet
and—"

"You need to have a medical checkup." Ming's stance had
changed, become hyperalert. "When was the last time you
slept?"

Ashaya pressed the pads of her fingers over her eyelids. "I
don't recall. Being underground makes it difficult for me to
keep track." A debilitating condition such as claustrophobia

would have gotten most Psy "rehabilitated," their memories wiped, their personalities destroyed. Ashaya had been left alone only because her brain was more valuable undamaged. For now.

"I think I had a full night's sleep approximately one week ago." Her logs would verify that. She had deliberately interfered with her own sleeping patterns, building her story for this very day . . . on the faith of a human's honor.

. . . we pay our debts . . .

But even if the sniper had kept his word, it was clear that *something* had gone wrong. All her theories to the contrary notwithstanding, it was highly probable that Keenan was dead. She dropped her hand and stared Ming in the face, letting her own go slack as if with fatigue. If Keenan was dead, then she no longer had anything to lose by putting this plan in motion.

"I'm sending a pickup team," Ming said. "You'll be taken to a specialist facility."

"Not necessary." Ashaya closed her hand over her organizer, the small computer device that held all her experimental and personal data. "One of my team can check me out—we're all medically trained."

"I want you fully evaluated by the clinicians at the Center."

She wondered if he was threatening her even now. The Center was where defective Psy were sent to be rehabilitated. "Ming, if you believe me to be compromised, please have the courtesy to say so to my face. I'm not a child to run screaming." Except of course, Psy children didn't scream much beyond the first year of life. She wondered if Keenan had screamed at the end. Her hand tightened, the cool hardness of the organizer anchoring her to reality. *Silence,* she reminded herself, *you are a being of perfect Silence.* An ice-cold automaton without emotion or heart. It was the only thing she could be.

Ming's expression didn't change. "I'll talk to you after the evaluation." The screen went off.

She knew she had mere minutes, if that. Ming had access to airjets and teleportation-capable telekinetics. If he wanted her whisked out of here, she would be. She flipped over her organizer, slid down the cover and pulled out the one-square-centimeter chip that held every piece of data in the device. Not allowing herself second thoughts, she swallowed the chip, her movements calculated to appear innocuous to the watching cameras.

Next, she reached into her pocket, found a replacement chip with enough duplicate data to allay suspicion—as least for a few days—and slotted it in. Just in time. There was a flicker at the corner of her eye. She swiveled to find a male standing there. He was dressed in pure unrelieved black, but for the golden insignia on his left shoulder—two snakes locked in combat. Ming's personal symbol.

"Ma'am, my name is Vasic. I'm to escort you to the Center."

She nodded, rose. His eyes betrayed no movement as she slipped her organizer into the pocket of her lab coat, but she knew he'd noted its placement. Ming would have plenty of time to go through it while she was being analyzed. "I didn't expect pickup by Tk."

It wasn't a question, so the other Psy didn't answer.

"Do you require touch?" she asked, coming to stand beside him. Psy didn't touch as a rule, but some powers were strengthened by contact.

"No," he said, proving her suspicion that Ming had sent one of his strongest men. It mattered little that his eyes were gray rather than cardinal night-sky—exceptions such as Ming aside, cardinals were often too cerebral to be much good at the practical side of things. Like killing.

The male met her eyes. "If you would please lower your basic shields."

She did so and a second later, her bones seemed to melt from the inside out. Part of her, the scientist, wondered if telekinetics felt the same loss of self, the same sense of their bodies liquefying into nothing. Then the sensation ended and she found herself facing a door that existed nowhere in her lab. "Thank you," she said, reengaging her shields.

He nodded at the door. "Please go through."

She knew he would stand guard, make sure she didn't attempt an escape. It made her wonder why he'd teleported her outside, rather than inside, the room. Since, no matter what happened, this was her last day as the head M-Psy on the Implant team, she asked him.

His answer was unexpected. "I am not a team player."

She understood but pretended not to. Was Ming testing her allegiance, trying to tempt her with the kinds of statements used by the rebels to communicate with one another? "I'm afraid I don't follow. Perhaps you can explain it to me later." Without waiting for an answer, she pushed through the door, already able to feel the tingling in the tips of her fingers and toes.

The chip she'd swallowed contained close to a terabyte of data, the result of years of research. But it also contained something else—a coating of pure, undiluted poison. She'd spent hours, when she should have been working on the implant, perfecting the unique properties of the poison for this one attempt.

The calculation was simple: Ashaya intended to escape the Implant lab.

With the heightened security, the only way to escape was to die.

So Ashaya would die.

CHAPTER 2

Amara felt something ripple inside her. Displeased at the interruption, she searched her mind for the source of the disturbance. It took her a few seconds to find it as the majority of her brain was occupied with the complicated task at hand.

The carrier was dead.

That halted her for a few seconds. How very unfortunate. She'd have to ensure she got her hands on some of Keenan's tissue. She had all the test results, of course, but who knew how the protein might have mutated in the years since she'd last taken a sample? It really was a pity the experiment had come to such a precipitous end—Amara had done some of her best work there.

But, she thought, pausing in her examination of the cultures lined up in front of her, it wasn't a total loss in the overall scheme of things. She had ways of getting tissue samples—she'd just have to make sure no one was infected during the retrieval process. She didn't want an inferior strain out there, not when she might yet be able to code a perfect one.

She checked another thread inside her mind, found it solid. Ashaya was still alive. Excellent. Only Ashaya had a mind brilliant enough to comprehend the value of Amara's work. The others, they knew little, understood even less.

Satisfied that nothing was truly amiss, she returned her attention to her work.

CHAPTER 3

I'm certain he almost shot me—the sniper who came to rescue Jonquil Duchslaya and Noor Hassan. He's on the side of good, the side that protects children, but I am ninety-nine percent certain that tonight, in the darkness, he almost pressed the trigger that would've ended my life.

Perhaps that's why I can't stop thinking about him.

—*From the encrypted personal files of Ashaya Aleine*

Ashaya lay down on the tilted examining table, her eyes focused on the ceiling. Though her vision remained sharp, her fingertips were numb. It was her forearms that tingled now, even as her heart labored to maintain a steady rhythm.

Humans and changelings, she thought, as the medical personnel laid out their instruments and began to explain the procedure to her, had it easy. They could fake their deaths any number of ways—crash a car off a cliff, leave a pool of blood for others to find, even write a simple suicide note and fade into the crowds.

But a Psy was tied to the PsyNet by the umbilical cord of a link that was necessary for life, yet also functioned as a shackle. If she ran her car off a cliff, no one would think her dead—not so long as they could see the living beacon of her psychic star on the Net. Even comatose Psy retained the link, their bodies fighting to maintain the life-giving connection.

Ashaya felt her heart begin to stutter, her vision to haze, as the poison spread through her system like a malignant cancer.

But this cancer had the potential to save her life. Because if this worked, she would go into a state beyond a coma.

Some people might call what she was trying to achieve hibernation, but that wasn't technically correct—during hibernation, oxygen did circulate, just so little of it that the individual appeared dead. But it wasn't enough for Ashaya to appear dead. She had to *be* dead for the duration. And there was only one known way to achieve that—cryonic suspension.

While suspended, the body literally stopped. Every aspect of it, even the brain . . . and a psychic link could not be held when the brain ceased to function. A simple, practical plan, except that while it was relatively easy to put someone *into* a cryonic state, no individual, their race notwithstanding, had ever successfully been brought back out—not unless a permanent vegetative state could be counted as success.

Ashaya hadn't made the breakthrough of the century and discovered a foolproof way to reverse the suspended state. Instead, she'd taken the principles of cryonics and applied them in an abstract way. Rather than relying on temperatures well below zero to slow her heart rate and brain activity, she'd tracked down the neurotoxin of a dangerous Australian tick, one that caused paralysis in its victims. She'd then manufactured and remanufactured the neurotoxin, using her abilities to change it a little each time . . . until she had the perfect poison. It would stop *everything* in her body, including her brain—thereby terminating her Net link. If it worked as intended, she would wake from her deathlike state in exactly ten hours. If she didn't wake . . . that was the risk she took.

The real test would come after the waking. As soon as her brain flickered to life, it would instinctively search for, and make, a new connection to the PsyNet. There was no way Ashaya could stop that. She'd be unconscious while it was being made—for a Psy, the Net link was more important than breathing. Those initial moments after relinking would be the vulnerable time. The time when her allies would either protect her or leave her to be recaptured.

Something pricked her elbow. She looked down but there was nothing there. The medical personnel around her were starting to ask her questions at sharp volume, attempting telepathic contact that she deflected with manufactured confusion. Her mind was functioning fine, though her breath was starting to catch, her eyes to close. Even then she knew that this might all be for nothing—for her plan to work, they had to move her.

The PsyNet was a psychic construct, but it had a physical component—a Psy in Europe didn't occupy the same section of the Net as a Psy in the Philippines. If she was far enough away from her last known location when she woke, the link would be made in an area not under blackout by Ming's troops. However, the instant she came to *full* consciousness, her mind would try to resettle her back where she "belonged." But not if things went according to plan . . . except what . . .

Her brain was fuzzy, unable to deal with complex psychic concepts. She became aware she could no longer feel her body, no longer feel the air going into her lungs. Perhaps she might have broken Silence and panicked at that instant, but it was too late.

Ashaya died.

Deep in the Canadian Rockies, Amara dropped a glass vial. It shattered into a thousand vicious points, but she heard nothing, her head echoing with absolute and utter emptiness as Ashaya blinked out of existence. *No!*

Glass cut into her palms, her side, and she realized she'd slumped to the floor. Her blood, she thought, was very red.

Dorian lay Keenan down in a bed located inside the home of DarkRiver's healer, Tamsyn. The original plan had called for the boy to be taken up to the SnowDancer den, located deep in the Sierra Nevada mountain range. But with him in the Web of Stars, Judd had suggested he should be closer to DarkRiver.

Which was how Dorian found himself at Tammy's. Situated roughly an hour out of San Francisco, the house was isolated down the end of a long drive and backed onto a heavily wooded area, but it was still nowhere near as safe as the Snow-Dancer den. "There's more chance of him being seen here." His cat didn't like the boy being so exposed.

Tammy tucked a soft blanket around their charge, hands gentle. "Talin wanted to take him since her and Clay's place is harder to find, but Sascha said no."

"Sascha said that?" The Psy renegade who had mated with DarkRiver's alpha, Lucas, adored children.

"We don't know what the boy can do," Tammy reminded him, "and Talin's got Jon and Noor living with her. Jon would probably be okay, but we're not sure how well Noor can safeguard herself. Keenan could influence her telepathically without even meaning to."

Dorian nodded, his leopard retreating. Keenan was now his to protect, but so was little Noor. "Right." Changelings had rock-solid mental shields; but Noor wasn't changeling, and though she carried some Psy DNA, most of her was vulnerably human. "What about your boys?"

"I'm sending them to stay with their grandparents for a bit." She brushed Keenan's hair off his forehead. "Poor baby's so small—how could anyone have hurt him?" Her tone was on the dangerous side of feral.

He walked over to take her into his arms. "Shh, we've got him now."

"I'll gut anyone who tries to bruise this boy again." She tucked her head under his chin, letting him soothe her. "I don't know who Ashaya Aleine is, but she did something good in getting him out."

Dorian's heart kicked.

I saved two innocent lives. You won't kill me.

"Is Sascha on her way?" he asked, ignoring the flicker of memory. It was far harder to erase the image burned into his brain—of an icy stranger silhouetted against the night sky.

"She should be arr—" They both heard it at the same time. The sound of a car coming down the drive. "That'll be her."

"Hope she can help the kid cope." It wasn't a vain wish. While Tammy was a healer attuned to changeling leopards, Sascha was an E-Psy, an empath, born with the ability to sense and heal emotional wounds.

Tammy drew back, kissing him on the cheek in thanks. "Sascha said he's connected to you. How?"

Dorian had been thinking about that. He raised his hand and showed Tammy the cut on his palm—it was already close to healed. "Blood oaths are powerful things and I promised him he'd be okay. Maybe because of that, when my blood mixed with his, it gave him a choice as to where he wanted to go." And he'd chosen to trust Dorian. It was a trust both leopard and man intended to honor.

Sascha came in at that instant, tall and with worry in her cardinal eyes—white stars on black velvet. "That's as good a guess as any," she said, walking over to stroke her hand gently over Keenan's brow. "He's in the Web, but only through you. You're his lifeline."

Dorian's protectiveness toward the boy intensified. If he had a weakness, it was for the vulnerable, for those who couldn't fight the monsters on their own. "He'll be scared when he wakes." He could still feel those fragile bones trembling as the boy tried to hide his excruciating fear.

"He'll sleep awhile yet." Sascha sent Dorian a worried glance as Tammy excused herself in order to pack for her cubs' stay with their grandparents. "Why don't you go for a run? It's been a hard day." There was a question in her eyes that he read loud and clear.

"No need to worry, Sascha darling." He smiled at her chiding look, knowing full well she had a soft spot for him. "I'm not going to lose any sleep over taking those shots today—they were holding a child hostage." His leopard growled inwardly at the memory of the blood on Keenan's wrists.

Sascha seemed satisfied with that, her attention shifting back to Keenan. "He'll be safe now." Her voice caught and he wondered what emotions she'd sensed around the boy. "Protected."

"Thanks to his mother." Dorian's thoughts turned to Ashaya Aleine, a woman he'd seen as a shadow in the darkness two months ago . . . and hadn't been able to forget since. "You think she can get out?"

"I have my doubts." Sascha closed her hand around one of Keenan's. "From what Judd shared, the Council needs her. And it has a way of getting what it wants."

"I think you're underestimating her." Dorian recalled the freezing tones of Ashaya's voice, recalled, too, how hard and low that voice had hit him. *Fucking two-fisted punch to the gut.* If—

The trapped leopard inside of him snapped its teeth when he bit off that thought, but the human half was in no mood to listen. "So far, she's managed to get three children out of potentially fatal situations—Jon, Noor, and now, Keenan." The woman might be cold enough to give him freezer burn, but she was also smart as hell.

Sascha nodded. "The trouble is, we have no clue as to her motivation. I want to believe that she did it out of love for her son . . . but we both know mothers don't always protect their own in the Net."

Dorian couldn't argue with that. Ashaya was Psy. Psy didn't feel. So why had the Council been able to use Keenan as leverage to ensure his mother's good behavior? It made her a mystery. Dorian had always liked mysteries. What he didn't like were Psy in the Net, Psy who worshipped the cold, unfeeling God of Silence.

Psy like Ashaya Aleine.

His blood thundered with a tidal wave of black rage. It was a familiar feeling—one of the Silent, a cardinal telekinetic named Santano Enrique, had butchered Dorian's sister, using her as a canvas on which to carve his sick fantasies. Dorian had torn the killer apart with his bare hands, but that hadn't quieted the rage in his animal heart, the torment in his human soul.

Kylie's body had still been warm when he reached her.

"Dorian." Sascha's voice cut through the miasma of pain and rage. "Don't."

Don't punish yourself for a monster's crime; don't let him kill you, too. It was what she'd said to him in the months after Enrique's execution, and Dorian had tried to listen. For a while, he'd thought he'd conquered the anger, but it had only been in hiding. Now, it came to pulsing life, triggered by the remembered sight of the blood on Keenan's wrists . . . triggered, too, by the memory of Ashaya Aleine's blue ice of a voice.

He got up. "I'm going for that run. Look after Keenan." Even Sascha, with all her gifts, couldn't erase his guilt. Because that anger, it wasn't all directed at the Psy—*he'd* failed Kylie, failed his baby sister. If he could've split a vein, torn out his heart, given up his soul, and known it would bring her back, he'd have done so in a heartbeat.

But he couldn't, so he'd learned to live with the grief, learned to live despite the guilt, had even fooled the pack into thinking he was getting better. Perhaps even fooled himself. Until *her*.

He'd almost shot Ashaya Aleine at first sight.

Not because she was evil. Or because he'd considered her a dangerous wildcard. No, the sole reason he had almost put a bullet through her was because the instant he'd caught her scent, his cock had gone as hard as fucking rock. The unexpected and unwanted reaction had ratcheted up the raw, angry fury of his guilt until it was an ever-tightening noose around his throat, a burning in his heart. All he'd wanted to do was destroy the cause of his shattering betrayal to Kylie's memory.

Attracted to one of the Silent?

His mouth set in a grim line. He'd cut off his own balls before he accepted that.

CHAPTER 4

He haunts me. The sniper. In my dreams, he is a black
shadow with his eye focused on the scope of a rifle. Sometimes, he puts down the weapon and walks toward me.
Sometimes, he even touches me. But most times, he presses
the trigger. And kills me.

—From the encrypted personal files of Ashaya Aleine

Ashaya returned to consciousness with the realization that
something had gone very wrong. Her mind was functioning, but
her body wasn't. She was paralyzed. A human or changeling,
creatures of emotion, might have panicked. Ashaya lay in silence and thought through the situation.

Unless she had gone blind, her eyes were closed, possibly
taped shut, though she didn't have the senses to verify that.
Closed eyes meant a medical facility of some kind, either a clinic
room or the morgue.

Her body wasn't picking up the sensation of cold or warmth,
so she couldn't verify that either.

Her hearing wasn't working.

Her nose wasn't working.

Her mouth wasn't working.

That was when claustrophobia nibbled at the edges of her
consciousness. She was buried in the most final way—inside her
own body. Her limbs were all completely useless, making escape impossible. No, she thought, dragging her thoughts back
under control before they eroded the cold Silence that had kept

her alive this long. She wasn't human or changeling. She had another world open to her. Inside her mind, she felt for the link to the PsyNet. There it was, strong and unwavering. Whatever had gone wrong, it hadn't affected her psychic abilities.

Following the link, she cautiously lowered her shields and swept her psychic eye across the area she now occupied. Familiar minds began to appear within seconds. She withdrew at once. That was the problem with the PsyNet. Though her initial position was based upon her physical location, because the PsyNet was a psychic construct, the instant she lowered her shields, it began to shift to accommodate her—as if each version of the Net was unique to the individual.

It made no logical sense because the PsyNet followed no laws of physics or math. No one had yet found out what rules it did follow, but one thing was clear—Ashaya couldn't venture into the Net again without taking precautions to ensure none of her "knowledge" of others leaked out. She knew it *could* be done, even knew some of the mechanics of how—Amara had taught her.

She began moving and shifting her mental shields, devising fail-safe upon fail-safe. The next time she opened her psychic eye, she saw everything through a dull haze. Her shields were so bulky as to hinder any attempt to actively surf the Net, but that was fine. Right now, it meant she was an invisible dot among millions of other dots. If she "knew" no one, no one knew her.

Taking a chance, she slit a tiny gap in her shields and listened to the chatter of the Net. Thousands of pieces of information filtered through, but as none of it was relevant, she forced herself to return to the shell of her mind, the claustrophobic prison of her body, wondering how much it would hurt when she ripped the tape off her eyes. Pain was a relative concept. Losing Keenan had taught her that more clearly than even Amara's cruelty.

Tape.

She could feel it now, sticky and abrasive on her lids. Focusing, she began a step-by-step checklist of her body. On the first pass, she found her feet dead but her calves waking up, while her torso remained numb. By the second pass, both her legs were cramping excruciatingly and her stomach felt as if it was trying to crawl out through her throat.

The third pass—her entire body a mass of searing pain.

Agony sloughed away the lining of her gut, flayed the skin from her flesh. And still she forced herself to lie unmoving. She wasn't a trained soldier, hadn't been tortured so she could learn to withstand pain. She lay frozen for one single reason—she wanted to see her son again.

Because if she was alive, then there was a chance that Keenan, too, had made it out alive.

A psychic brush.

Amara.

Ashaya withdrew deep into Silence, fortifying her mind behind another wall of ice, even as her body punished her for the sting of death. The speed with which Amara had tracked her was no surprise, but the connection between them was the weakest it had ever been. Ashaya intended to keep it that way.

She didn't know how long the pain lasted.

When it was over, she lay stock-still and let the world filter in through her senses. She was on a cold steel table. So not an examining or a patient room. A morgue facility of some sort. Air whispered over her body.

Naked. She was naked.

This deep in Silence, that didn't disturb her. She took in the antiseptic smell in the air, the absolute quiet. But tempting as it was to move, she didn't. There had to be cameras. Her body would never have been left unguarded. They had to have scanned her by now. Since she wasn't cut up, it meant that either the chip's protective coating had worked, or something had delayed the normal autopsy process.

Her mind snap-shot to a piece of data she'd absorbed during her peek into the PsyNet.

A virulent flu had swept through several sectors without warning, raising fears of a pandemic.

Unless she'd caught an extremely lucky break—unlikely—it seemed that Zie Zen had gotten the note she'd smuggled out and been ready for her to act. That left the cameras—she'd have to take the chance that the morgue itself wasn't monitored. Why should it be? But just as she was about to attempt to move, she heard footsteps. A door opened, smooth, silent, but for the whish of air. A single pair of feet, boots clicking against the plascrete floor. They came to stand beside her. She lay immobile . . . then realized she was breathing.

"Ms. Aleine, are you conscious? I know you're alive."

It had all been for nothing. Refusing to show any reaction, she raised her hands to her eyes and peeled off the tape, blinking against the stark white light. The russet-haired woman who'd woken her was already taking things out of a small pack and putting them beside her. Clothing, shoes, socks.

She rose to a sitting position. Swallowed. "Liquids?" Her voice was gravel and dust with a topcoat of broken glass.

The woman put a bottle in her hand, nothing but cool efficiency in her brown eyes. "Zie Zen sends his regards." She opened her palm to show Ashaya a small gold coin stamped with the Chinese character for "unity."

There are only ten. Each carried by an individual worthy of trust.

Ashaya didn't need any more proof. "He got my note."

A short nod. "You have a limited window of time," the woman said. "The panic we created with a viral bioagent is starting to die down. Councilor LeBon will be here very soon to take charge of your body."

Finishing the juice, Ashaya got off the table, holding herself steady with her hands flat on the table. Her head swam, and she knew without a doubt that she was about to throw up. Staggering to the sink, she slotted in the plug just before her stomach revolted. What came out was mostly juice, but the spasms felt like muscle tearing and ripping.

"Are you all right?" The stranger passed Ashaya a box of tissues and another bottle—this time of water.

"Yes." Her voice came out husky. "Give me a minute."

As the other woman turned away, Ashaya focused on the contents of the sink and, to her relief, found the chip she'd swallowed—her digestive tract had shut down with the rest of her body, leaving the chip in her stomach. Rinsing it clean as she washed out the sink, she wrapped the priceless object in a piece of tissue and went back to the table.

The stranger had laid out an outfit, and Ashaya wasted no time in pulling it on—underwear, jeans, and a long-sleeved white T-shirt followed by a short-sleeved navy blue one. Spring was heating into summer, but the nights could be cool depending on the location. Putting the chip into a pocket, she braided her hair and stuffed it under the black beret her rescuer held out.

Contact lenses came next. Her pale blue gray eyes were unusual for her dark skin tone. Now they turned brown. That done, she pulled on the socks and sneakers laid out on the morgue slab. Remnants of the poison continued to send twinges through her body, and her stomach was a raw mess, but it was nothing compared to when she'd first woken.

"There's a small stunner in the front pocket—it's a weapon you're trained to use, correct?" Not waiting for an answer, the woman helped Ashaya with the pack. It fit neatly across her back, with straps across her chest and around her hips. "Cosmetics and cheap jewelry in the side pocket. Use them to further your disguise. Misdirection is key. You're not Ashaya Aleine, M-Psy, you're Chantelle James, art student. I'm telepathing the profile."

"I have it." But Ashaya had no intention of using that profile, of escaping one cage only to enter another. To force her child—and he *had* to be alive—into a lifetime spent looking over his shoulder, a lifetime of secrets and lies . . . no, she would not do that to Keenan. He'd been hurt enough.

"Stick to the profile, and keep your PsyNet shields at maximum. We were able to hide your reentry into the Net, but we can't spare the manpower to give you around-the-clock protection."

"I understand." She turned to face her rescuer. "Thank you."

"Keep yourself safe." The woman's eyes were dark, but there was a strange awareness in them. "When this breaks and the war begins in earnest, we'll need your skills to battle the bioagents they use against us."

This. Silence. The protocol that kept them sane while removing their emotions. The protocol that put sociopaths at the top of their hierarchy. But when that Silence fell, minds were going to crack. Emotion could not simply come rushing back . . . not without causing permanent, irreversible fractures in the psyche. Ashaya knew that far too well.

"I'll try my best." But she would not deviate from the path she'd set herself. "How do I get out of here?"

"A teleporter will take you out." She went motionless. "We've run out of time."

The same man who'd teleported Ashaya to the Center—Vasic—was suddenly beside her. An instant later, her bones melted from the inside out and she was falling, falling. She staggered and almost crashed to her knees as they reached their destination. "Where—" she began, but Vasic was already blinking out.

She rubbed her forehead, guessing things had gotten hot very fast. Vasic had most likely returned to get the other woman out. The man had to be the rarest of the rare—a Traveler. Most strong telekinetics could 'port, but not even a cardinal Tk could do so with such effortless speed. Only a true teleporter. A Traveler. Designation Tk. Subdesignation V.

But where had this Traveler brought her?

She turned, hoping to see some indication of her location. But there were no roads. No buildings. No lights. Just trees, what seemed like thousands of them in every direction. A solid wall of green. Realization dawned—Vasic had clearly had to cut her teleport short in order to get back in time to rescue the other woman. As a result, she was alone in the wilderness, when she'd spent most of her life behind lab walls.

Then something growled, the sound so lethal, the hairs on the back of her neck rose in primordial warning. Those reactions, even the Psy hadn't been able to train out of themselves. Another growl, followed by a hissing sound that froze her to the spot.

Dorian was heading back to Tammy's after his run when the call came through. "Yeah?"

"How close are you to the Grove?" Vaughn's voice.

"Maybe an hour at a hard run. Why?"

"Shit." Vaughn muttered something to a third person, then came back on the line. "You're the closest. Pickup ASAP."

Who or what the hell was out there? The Grove was a large tract of land deep in their territory, home to feral creatures with a hunger for blood and tearing flesh. "I'm on my way." He was already changing direction.

"You have a gun?"

"Stupid question." He was always armed, an automatic compensation for his lack of ability to go cat.

"Hope you don't need to use it. Run fast." Vaughn hung up.

Dorian shoved the phone into his pocket and set a brutal pace. Since Vaughn had given him no specifics about the pickup, the target had to be obvious—either highly visible, noisy, or with a distinctive scent. He hoped to hell it was one of the latter two. Darkness had fallen over an hour ago, and, with the moon clouded over, visibility was low. His eyes were cat-sharp, but even a leopard changeling couldn't magically find a needle in a very big haystack. A scent trail would speed things up.

Of course, that might be a moot point.

Because if it *was* a person out there, then he or she was in seriously deep shit. That area was home to a population of aggressive lynx. Real lynx, not changelings. They could be vicious little buggers when provoked. If the subject made that mistake, the only thing Dorian would find was a pile of bones, the flesh stripped off with bloody efficiency.

There were eyes all around her, glowing, stalking. Ashaya stood in place, going over her options for the hundredth time and coming up with the same answer—she had none. She was a Gradient 9.9 Psy, but her power was medical. She had no combat-capable abilities, not even a hint of telekinesis or paralyzing telepathy. Her Tp status was barely 1.1, just enough to maintain her link to the PsyNet.

She could attempt to attack using that paltry bit of telepathy, but even if she gained a few seconds, what could she do? She considered trying to get to the stunner in her pack. But the instant her hand moved, teeth snapped in warning. It made her wonder why they hadn't already attacked.

She found the answer in her next scan of the area—several of the large tree trunks bore fresh claw marks. Something big had passed through here recently, leaving behind enough of a lingering presence that these small predators—judging from the height of their eyes—were hesitating. But that wouldn't last. She was warm, living prey. They wanted her.

Think, Ashaya, she told herself, using the calm fostered by Silence. What would Amara do? The question was a stupid one, something she disregarded in the next instant. Amara had a different skill set, a different way of thinking. What did *she* have?

Medical. Basic telepathy. Basic psychometry. Some other passive Psy abilities. None of them useful in this situation.

The animals—cats?—were creeping closer in a stealthy whisper of claws against the dry vegetation that carpeted the forest floor.

Eliminate the psychic abilities and what did she have?

A quick mind, a body in good condition . . . and the genetic gift of speed.

The only problem was, the predators were faster than she was.

CHAPTER 5

Things to do . . .
. . . people to kill.

—*Front and back of Dorian Christensen's favorite
T-shirt (gift from Talin McKade)*

Dorian smelled blood on the wind moments after he entered the Grove, followed by the angry sounds of lynx fighting over something. His hands moved with lethal grace, throwing knives hitting his palms as he prepared for whatever it was he was going to find. His scent was normally enough to cow the smaller felines, but if they'd blooded a kill, they might be in an animalistic rage.

The scent teased at him, sharp, iron rich. But beneath the spray of blood lay an exotic femininity, intriguing, seductive . . . and cold, so damn cold. "Fuck!" Sweat rolled down his spine as he covered the remaining distance at extreme speed.

She wasn't allowed to die, he thought, his rage a dark red flame. Not until he'd flushed this vicious hunger for her from his system. But when he tracked the scent to a small clearing, it was to discover nothing beyond the slashing aggression of the lynx and the biting iron of fresh blood—no scent of a gut ripped open or bodily wastes expelled during the panic of death. Not even an overlay of sweaty panic. Psy liked to pretend they were cold until death but he knew very well that they screamed, same as everyone else. Santano Enrique had screamed . . . until Dorian had sliced off his tongue.

Knives held with familiar ease, he strode into the clearing. The group of lynx turned, their snarls promising tearing pain. He waited for them to recognize him. They hesitated—long enough to stop mauling whatever it was they had under their claws. He knew what they were thinking. There was only one of him, ten of them.

He growled, letting the trapped leopard in him sound through his vocal cords. It was a growl of anger, of fury, of domination. The lynx cringed but didn't leave. *Damn.* He didn't want to kill them. This was their land as much as it was his. *She* was the intruder, here and in his life—in his fucking dreams. But he'd deal with his crap himself. He wasn't going to take an easy out and stand by while she was being ripped to shreds.

He growled again, putting menace into it. *Get out or die.* They knew him, knew the warning would be carried through. It didn't matter that he was latent, unable to shift into the leopard form that was his other half. No, to these creatures, he was simply another cat. He smelled like one. He ran like one. He hunted like one.

And he killed like one.

One by one, the tufted-ear felines gave disgruntled snarls and wandered off. He waited—knives in hand—until he was certain of their surrender. Then he approached the tree where they had been savaging their prey. He stopped. The concentration of smell was wrong. Freezing, he analyzed what his senses were telling him. Almost smiled. And slipped into the deepest shadows. So fast that he would've been a blur to the eyes watching him.

Cloaking himself in the darkness, he moved as he spoke, well aware a Psy could kill with a single targeted mental blow. "I suggest you come down unless you want me to leave you here. The blood will prove an irresistible draw to the lynx."

Silence. Did she think he didn't know where she was?

"What I want to know is where did a Psy learn how to climb?" He stopped at an angle to the branch where she was perched, able to see one sneakered foot.

"A gymnasium climbing machine," came the cool answer. "I'm afraid I'll have difficulty with the return trip."

He didn't move, fighting his beast's instinctive need to protect. "Clawed?"

"Or bitten. On my calf."

He could hear movement now, knew she was attempting to make her way back down. The cat in him was chauvinistic. It liked to help women. And this woman, it wanted to bite, taste, savor. But that cat, despite its inexplicable and deeply sexual pull toward the icy Ashaya Aleine, was also a cool, calculating predator that knew one of the Silent had killed blood of its blood, heart of its heart. Forgiveness was impossible. "We're even," he said, staying in place. "The debt has been paid."

A pause. "My son is safe?"

No emotion in that. So why had she asked the question? "We keep our promises."

"I don't know who you are. Only that you're Talin McKade's friend." A burst of blood scent, followed by the sound of cloth sliding over wood.

He kept watch, ready to catch her if she fell. "How did you keep the cats from climbing up? There's blood up the trunk, along the branch. Catnip."

She didn't return his verbal volley for several seconds and he heard labored breathing. "I hit them with short bursts of Tp, enough to discourage."

His hackles rose. "Why not just smash their minds, turn their brains to jelly?" Psy had done exactly that in the past. It was why changelings had a policy of kill first, question later, with the emotionless race.

Another pause, more pained breathing. He guessed she'd reached the trunk, and was bracing herself to come down. The scent of iron had become darker, richer. She was bleeding badly. Instinct and anger collided, fought, came away scratched and torn.

"Not all Psy are born equal," she said, her voice taut with strain. "I only have enough Tp to have kept them away from me one at a time. The big burst I tried was barely enough to give me time to climb—even then, they recovered fast."

"You don't have to be a powerful telepath to kill." He was climbing the tree before he'd consciously made the decision to help her.

"No, but you need to have the ability to focus your other abilities in a lethal fashion. It's a talent in itself. One I don't have." Her voice quieted. "Why am I giving away so much information?"

He reached the top to find her with her eyes closed, her legs straddling the branch. "Because," he said, watching those eyes snap open, "you're tired and weak from blood loss." He pulled her toward him. "Shift the leg over."

She obeyed, until she was sitting with both legs on one side. "I may not have the strength to make the climb."

He put one arm under her thighs, the other at her back. And jumped. He landed on his feet, absorbing the shock of the sudden impact with the feline grace built into his genes. He confused medical personnel, had done so since childhood. Everything about him was cat, except that he couldn't become the very thing he was. He'd never run on four feet, never felt the wind rustle through his fur, never bitten down on the neck of prey, taking it down in a furious rush of adrenaline and hunger.

"Impressive."

He glanced down at the woman in his arms but didn't speak as he lowered her body to the ground. She sat up, her hands going to her right calf. From the amount of blood, he knew she'd need stitches at the very least. Grabbing the pack the lynx had been mauling, he began to undo the closures. "Do you have a first aid kit in here?" Made of a durable material, the pack had survived relatively unscathed. If there was no kit, he could at least grab something with which to wrap her bloody leg.

"I don't know," Ashaya said.

The first thing he found was a small stunner. It didn't bother him—he was too fast to make an easy target. And, since she didn't appear to have claws of her own, having a weapon was smart. But—"Doesn't do you much good in the pack."

"Unfortunately, I appear to have forgotten to prepare for a wild animal attack."

Ice and bite. Both sparked along his nerves like wild lightning. When he met her gaze, he realized her eyes were dark. It had been night the one and only other time he'd seen her, but he was certain that wasn't her real eye color. "Your disguise is good," he commented, undoing the snap on the main section of the pack. "It'd be even better if you got rid of those braids. Psy never leave their hair out if it's the least bit uncontrollable."

"Mine is more than a little uncontrollable."

He could feel her watching him as he went through her things. Luck was with her—he found the small kit emblazoned with the globally recognized red cross symbol within seconds. The tube of dry antiseptic was right on top. "Lie on your stomach. It's the easiest way to get this stuff in." He kept his voice controlled and to the point, though his leopard was trying to shove through his skin, agitated by the scent of her blood. "Quickly."

She turned and lay down on the carpet of dry pine needles without argument. Using one of his knives, he sliced away the shredded material above the wound and dusted the antiseptic over it. The fast-acting stuff melted, clotting up the wound within seconds. "This'll give us time to get you to a medic." The antiseptic was an emergency measure. It healed nothing, its function being to keep bacteria from getting in and blood from leaking out. The fact that it was working meant the lynx hadn't damaged anything major.

The kit also came with a stack of "thin skin" bandages. Despite the nickname, the bandages were as tough as stretched steel. "Any pain?" he asked as he wrapped one around her calf, unaccountably infuriated by the damage done to her smooth skin.

"Nothing medically significant."

He sat back on his haunches and watched her get back up into a sitting position. Her eyes went to his handiwork. "You've had some training."

He bit back the urge to snarl at her frigid tone. The ice of it was a fist around his cock, arousing him against all reason, all sense. "First aid." He shrugged, stuffed everything back into her pack, then paused. "You need anything from here?"

"Everything."

"Tough." He did up the straps. "I have to carry you as it is—"

"I can—"

"Yeah, you can crawl," he snapped, "but that isn't going to get me home in time to catch a few z's." And nowhere near fast enough to contain the leopard's enraged attempts at exploding from within his skin. He couldn't shift, had never been able to. But the cat didn't know it was trapped. Right now, it wasn't even sure if it wanted to savage Ashaya or fuck her. "Since I can't dump you here, I might as well get rid of you as fast as I can."

It was a deliberate attempt to provoke, but her face, a face that had haunted his dreams for two months, remained expressionless. Two damn months, he thought again. Endless nights of waking in a sweat, frustrated and hard. And angry, so *angry*.

The sole thing that had kept him from going out and hunting her down had been an enraged defiance against a sexual pull that had begun to turn into an obsession.

Now here she sat, looking up at him with those eyes that were the wrong color—and that blatant lie only stoked his fury.

"You have a lot of antipathy toward me."

No, what he had was a bad case of lust. But he wasn't an animal in rut. And his one stupid, drunken mistake in college aside, he didn't sleep with women who might just freeze his balls off in the night. "I'm going to stash your pack up in the branches. The lynx won't come near it now that it has my scent on it. Someone can grab it for you tomorrow."

Ashaya didn't argue, knowing she had nothing with which to bargain. "Another debt?" She'd recognized his voice at once as that of the sniper. After all, she'd been hearing it in her dreams for eight long weeks.

"Don't worry. We'll collect." With those words, he shrugged into the pack and began climbing.

She couldn't believe the way he moved. It was so smooth, it appeared effortless. He was ten times faster than she had been, a hundred times more graceful. If she'd had any doubts as to what he was, they would've been wiped away by that display. "Changeling," she said as he jumped back down. "Cat."

He raised an eyebrow, his eyes a pitiless blue so true—even in this darkness—that she wondered at its existence. "Meow."

Something hidden sparked to life in her mind, and she found herself thinking that the sniper was beautiful. Darkness, she'd always cloaked him in darkness, but he was a golden god. "How did you know I was here?" Her breath came in pants as she managed to get to her feet, one hand braced against the tree trunk. Her palm landed on something sticky. Her own blood, she realized.

"I'm an F-Psy." A mocking answer. "You're going to have to ride on my back. Try not to stab me while you're at it." He came to her, turned.

The instant she put her hands on his shoulders, she froze. She hadn't had this much close contact with another being for longer than she could remember. Even with Keenan, she'd kept her distance, aware that only Silent coldness would keep him safe. But there was no point of comparison between her weakness where

Keenan was concerned and this changeling who seemed to despise her.

And yet who fascinated her on a level it was madness to even consider.

This close, she could see that his hair was a blond so pure it was white gold, but that was the lone hint of softness in him. The body under her hands was hard, sleek with muscle. She had the sudden, visceral realization that he could snap her in two without thinking about it. Her stomach clenched in dangerous physical reaction, a reaction she should've been able to suppress.

"You waiting for an engraved invitation?" An almost lazy question, but she could feel his intelligence probing at her.

"No." Putting her erratic thoughts down to blood loss, she shifted her weight . . . and almost collapsed. "I can't jump up."

His hands slid around and to the backs of her thighs. "Now." As he lifted, she tried to push upward with her uninjured leg. Her contribution proved unnecessary—he was so strong, he had her legs wrapped around him with one pull.

"Hold on." That was his only warning before he started to run.

Her arms tightened instinctively. She was vividly conscious that he was moving at a pace equivalent to that of a high-speed vehicle. If they crashed into one of the huge trees looming up ahead, their necks would snap. It would've made sense to close her eyes but she couldn't. She needed to see where they were going, even if there was—

A sharp stab at her mind, something . . . someone, trying to claw in.

Amara.

She reacted almost automatically, relying on years of experience to throw up roadblocks created with the impenetrable chill of Silence. There was no way she could hide the fact of her "resurrection" from Amara, but the other woman couldn't be allowed to slip into her mind, could *never* be allowed to learn that Keenan was still alive.

"You asleep?" The sniper whipped around to look at her, barely avoiding a tree trunk.

Every muscle in her body locked, and she realized her trainers had lied. It wasn't possible to suppress any and all physical responses if you had enough strength of will. Ashaya had turned her blood glacial over the years, and still, her body reacted to the threat of pain. "Don't you think you should watch where you're going?"

Laughter that she felt more than heard. It vibrated through the disturbing intimacy of their aligned bodies, threatening her conditioning on a level that could prove deadly. And yet she didn't ask to be put down—it would betray too much, put her entire plan in jeopardy. She gave in to another compulsion instead, one born of the part of her mind that had awakened at fourteen and never returned to sleep. "What's your name?"

He said something that was snatched away by the wind. Deciding to save her questions for another time, but aware he could hear her with her lips so close to his ear, she said, "I think my leg's bleeding again."

He slowed down enough to glance at her. "I can smell it. How bad?"

She heard something in that tone . . . a subtle edge that resonated with the unnamed thing inside of her. "I'm fine now, but in a few minutes, we'll start leaving a trail."

"Then hold on tight." And then he *moved*. If she'd thought he was fast before, that was nothing compared to the whiplash speed of his current pace. She had to close her eyes this time, forced to by the wind that ripped tears from her eyes.

In the ensuing darkness, all she could focus on was the liquid shift of muscle in the body that carried her. Pure power. Incredible strength.

And she was completely at his mercy.

CHAPTER 6

Ming LeBon stared at the empty slab where Ashaya Aleine's body should have been. "Recordings?"

"Blank for a period of fifteen minutes. It went unnoticed because—"

Ming slashed out a hand. "No excuses."

"Yes, sir."

"Send Vasic in."

A minute later, Vasic replaced the security officer. "Sir."

"You secured Aleine's organizer?"

Vasic nodded. "As soon as she lost consciousness. Per previous orders, I teleported it to your desk. Would you like me to retrieve it?"

"No." Ming stared at the other male, one of his most elite soldiers. As an Arrow, Vasic's loyalty should have been beyond doubt. It wasn't anything left to chance—Arrows were all placed on a regimen of drugs meant to turn them into the most unwavering of killing machines. "No alarms were tripped, no other monitors aside from those in this section tampered with. What does that mean?"

"A teleport-capable Tk," Vasic replied, completely unmoved. "Officially, there were none in the immediate vicinity at the time."

"Unofficially?"

Vasic glanced at the recording devices in the room, and "knocked" telepathically. When Ming gave him permission for Tp contact, the soldier said, *The insurgency is gaining in strength. There may be rebels with abilities we aren't aware of.*

A Tk that strong would have been recorded by now.

Then, Vasic responded, still pure calm as all Arrows were, *it was a traitor.*

Open your mind for a scan.

Negative, sir. That would leave me defenseless.

And Arrows never let themselves be defenseless. It was part of their training. Ming himself had taught them that lesson. *Where were you at the pertinent time?*

In Europe. Data flowed from Vasic's mind to his. *After teleporting M-Psy Aleine's organizer to your desk, I rejoined my team as part of an operation to delve into the recent surge in activity within the Human Alliance.*

Ming nodded, having already checked that information. Not only was Vasic the most powerful teleporter he'd ever known, the man was incorruptible—there was nothing left of him to corrupt. However, Ming trusted no one. *As of now you're attached to me. I want you on standby.*

Yes, sir.

Withdrawing from the mental contact, Ming dismissed Vasic and stared down at the cold slab of the morgue table. Ashaya's disappearance could be explained in one of two ways. One, she was dead but her body had been taken because it contained valuable data. That was a real possibility. She'd been behaving erratically the past few weeks—she may even have implanted herself as a test subject.

The second possibility was even more dangerous. That Ashaya Aleine was alive and out of Council control.

She couldn't be allowed to stay that way.

Even as Ming focused his attention on finding Ashaya, several men got off an airjet at San Francisco International Airport. Their job was to blend in and watch—the leopards, the wolves, but most especially, the Psy.

No one noticed them. Then. Or later.

CHAPTER 7

*It's becoming an obsession—my fascination with the sniper.
Today, in the lab, I felt his breath on my nape. It swept like
fire across my skin. I am a scientist, a being of logic and reason, but part of me is convinced that he was real, that I could
have raised a hand and brushed my fingertips across his lips.*

—From the encrypted personal files of Ashaya Aleine

When the changeling carrying her finally came to a halt,
Ashaya wasn't sure he had. Her body felt as if it was still in motion. Forcing open eyes that seemed glued together, she found
herself near a small cabin lit up from within. There was a pine
needle–strewn clearing around the house, and what looked like
wildflowers crawling up one wall, though in the dark she couldn't
be sure.

"Can you keep your feet?" her rescuer asked as he helped
her off his back.

"No." Her legs threatened to crumple when she released his
shoulders, the injured one useless, the other stiff with the way
she'd had to clamp it around him.

One of his arms was around her waist before she saw him
move. "I've got you."

"Thank you."

Quiet. But it was a quiet unlike any she'd felt in the Net,
filled with emotions that battered at her conditioning with unrelenting force.

The door to the cabin swung open even as she fought to

maintain her death grip on Silence. "Dorian? Who's that with you?" The speaker was female, her hair a vibrant red that touched the curve of her spine.

"You didn't get a message from Vaughn?" The sniper—*Dorian, his name is Dorian*—all but carried her inside the cabin and put her in a chair in front of the fireplace. His words might've been harsh, but he was careful with her, almost . . . gentle.

The female closed the door, frowned. "No, I just got back from— She's Psy!"

"Keenan's mother." When he returned his attention to Ashaya, the absolute blue of his eyes felt like flames licking at her, a weapon against which she had no defense. "She's injured. Needs stitches." The words were bitten out.

"Get me the kit. You know where it is." The woman moved to Ashaya. "Name's Mercy."

Ashaya fought the impulse to turn, to keep Dorian in her line of sight. He was dangerous to her in every way that mattered, and though he'd saved her life tonight, she wasn't sure he'd continue to let her live. "You're a medic?" she asked Mercy, even as she listened for the sound of Dorian's return.

"No, but I've had some extra training." She bent down for a quick look. "No use unwrapping that before I have tools in hand. You mind a scar? Can always get it removed later."

Dorian returned, kit in hand. "You're alive," he said with a shrug that was as feline as the way he walked—a grace that held a lethal promise. This man would make a pitiless enemy. "I wouldn't complain."

"No." She wondered whether he'd have shrugged as negligently had he found her mauled body tonight. Likely. "All that matters is that the leg works."

"It will. Dorian, can you . . . ?" Mercy jerked her head in the direction of the sofa.

Dorian moved without argument to expand the compact piece of furniture into a bed. Mercy covered it with a thick sheet, then made as if to help Ashaya. But Dorian was already there, his arm strong and hot around her waist, the heat a vivid indication of his wild changeling energy. "You're not as bony as most Psy in the Net."

She'd studied emotions, understood them better than others of her race, but she didn't know how to answer him, how to comprehend the nuances in his voice, the strange gentleness of his hold. So she stuck to the truth. "Metabolism and genetics." As she spoke, she realized the implications of the distinction he'd made—between Psy in the Net and those outside it.

"On your stomach," Mercy said as they reached the bed. Once she was in position, the other woman gave her a pillow for her head, then placed several towels under her right tibia. "This is going to be rough and ready but it'll get you in shape. You can get one of your people to look at it later."

Ashaya heard something rip, and realized the redhead had torn away what remained of her pants leg from the knee down. "I don't have a people."

"Huh." A quick movement and the bandage fell away. "Lynx. They don't usually attack humans. What did you do to piss them off?"

"I believe they thought I was food."

Dorian made a sound of disagreement. "I think I saw signs of kittens nearby."

"I see." And she did. "They were protecting their young." She pressed her face into the pillow as Mercy probed the wound with a tool she couldn't see.

"Sorry—you want an anesthetic?"

"No," Ashaya said immediately. "Psy bodies don't handle anesthetics well."

"I thought I heard Sascha mention something like that."

Suspicion gelled into knowledge. "You're part of DarkRiver." The leopard pack that had two Psy members, one of whom was Sascha Duncan, daughter of Councilor Nikita Duncan.

"That's no secret," Mercy said but Ashaya sensed a rise in the tension blanketing the room—after a lifetime spent negotiating the cutthroat waters of the Council substructure, her survival instincts were razor sharp.

Dorian's voice sliced through the tension with the lethal efficiency of a steel blade. "Put yourself under." It was an order.

One Ashaya chose not to obey. She was already so vulnerable. If she put herself into the trancelike state that was the Psy version of anesthesia, she'd be placing her life totally in their hands. Preferring to remain conscious, she gritted her teeth and buried her face in the pillow. The choice, she told herself, had nothing to do with the fact that it was Dorian who'd given her the command.

Dorian's eyes narrowed at Ashaya's defiance. "She's not out." He was certain she couldn't hear him. Her withheld screams had to be a solid wall in her ears.

Mercy didn't stop what she was doing. "Her choice. She's keeping her leg immobile, that's all that matters."

"And people call me hard." He shoved his instinctive urge to protect into flippancy, but his hands curled, claws scraping inside his skin. The leopard was still agitated, still trying to break through the human shell it had never managed to shed. The choking need to shift was something he'd learned to live with—he'd had no choice, having been born latent—but the hunger hadn't been this bad since childhood. One more thing to blame on Ashaya Aleine. "Would you like a hacksaw, Dr. Frankenstein?"

Mercy scowled at him. "Let me concentrate. Med school was a long time ago, you know. And I only went for a couple of years."

He grunted but didn't interrupt again. As she worked, he found himself unable to move from his position beside the bed, the leopard insisting he watch over Ashaya. But even that obstinate cat understood she was nothing like the two Psy women he knew and respected. Both Sascha and Faith had heart, had honor. Ashaya, on the other hand, was one of the Council's pet M-Psy, the butcher in charge of creating an implant that would turn the individuals of the PsyNet into a true hive mind.

She was also, a part of him insisted on remembering, the woman who'd saved the lives of two children at considerable risk to her own, mother to a little boy whom Dorian had promised to protect . . . and the only female to have awakened the leopard to raging sexual need with nothing but her scent.

He'd dreamed about her.

Always the same dream. Night after night.

He was in the branches of that tree again, Ashaya's face in his sights. A slight squeeze of the trigger and she would cease to exist, to complicate his life. But then she laughed, eyes sparkling, and he knew it was just a game.

He was standing in front of her now, pulling her braids apart so he could thrust his hands into her hair and crush the electric coils of it in his palms. She was still laughing when he took her lips, such luscious, soft lips.

Such cold, cold lips.

The leopard grew angry, thrust her from him. She stood there, unmoved. Then she raised her hands and began to undress. She was beautiful in the moonlight, her skin gleaming with the night's erotic caress. Entranced, he walked to her. She put her arms around his neck, pressing her lips to his pulse.

As his hands cupped her breasts, the warmth leached out of her. Her eyes filmed over with frost . . . and he realized she was turning to ice in his arms.

What a fucked-up dream, he thought, staring at the back of Ashaya's head. What was worse was that despite the screaming horror of it, he always woke with a pulsing hard-on, his body beaded with sweat, his heart racing a hundred miles an hour. Hungry, he was so damn hungry after two months of those dreams—with no relief in sight.

And that pissed him off, too, that he couldn't go near another woman without his mind sending out sinuous reminders of the woman who haunted him nightly. If he hadn't been utterly certain that no Psy could manipulate a changeling for that long and with that much subtlety, he'd have suspected some sort of a telepathic suggestion.

The compulsion to touch her, *take her*, was a constant beat in his blood by now. It staggered him, the brutality of it. He didn't know this woman, definitely didn't like her, didn't particularly like *himself* around her. But the leopard's craving for her threatened to turn him traitor to not only his people, but to his own sense of honor, a cipher led around by the cock.

Like hell.

He'd become a sentinel despite his latency—stubborn, unflinching will was his trademark. If Ashaya Aleine tried to use the sexual pull between them to bring him to heel, she'd find herself face-to-face with the cold-blooded sniper at his core.

CHAPTER 8

Councilor Kaleb Krychek looked out the window of his Moscow office and saw the trail of an approaching airjet. "Lenik," he said, using the intercom rather than telepathy. His administrative assistant paid more attention when he wasn't trying to protect himself against the rumored twist in Kaleb's secondary talent—the ability to induce madness. "Do I have any appointments this morning?"

"No, Councilor. You're free until the four o'clock with the BlackEdge pack."

He turned off the intercom and considered the possibilities. It couldn't be Nikita, the Councilor with whom he had a quasi-alliance. She was in Nara, Japan, having an afternoon meeting with a man who made his living stealing information from secure PsyNet databases.

Information like Kaleb's training history.

He hadn't eliminated the leak at the source. There were some things he wanted Nikita to know. A small light lit up under the smooth black surface of his desk as the airjet landed on the roof. He passed a hand across another section, bringing up the images from the surveillance cameras that surrounded the landing pad.

His visitor was no one he'd have expected.

However, by the time Henry Scott walked into his office, Kaleb was prepared for anything the other Councilor might throw his way. "Councilor Scott." He turned from the window and nodded a greeting.

"Krychek." Henry waited until Lenik had closed the door behind himself before advancing farther inside. His ebony skin, stretched smooth over the oval of his skull, seemed to soak in the light, rather than reflect it, but it was the aristocratic lines of his face that held the eye.

According to the human media, Henry Scott was considered both handsome and distinguished. That was why he was the face of the Council, along with his "wife," Shoshanna—what the public didn't know was that the marriage was an empty husk, a coldly calculated act designed to "humanize" the Council to the emotional races. In keeping with the fiction, the Scotts were rarely seen separately, and inside the Council, Henry was considered the beta member of the Henry-Shoshanna pairing.

"Would you like a seat?" Kaleb offered, remaining by the window.

Henry shook his head, closing the distance until they were separated only by a short stretch of carpet. "I'll come right to the point."

"Please do." He had no idea why Henry was here. The Scotts made it a point to disagree with any proposal but their own. Shoshanna wanted Kaleb dead, of that he had no doubt. But that was nothing unusual—all the Councilors, but one, were ruthless in their ambition. Anthony Kyriakus was the enigma who proved the rule. "A personal visit is rather unusual."

"I didn't want to chance being trailed on the PsyNet." The other man put his hands behind his back, his stance that of an ancient general. A practiced movement, designed to set the populace at ease, subtly reinforcing the image of Henry as a benevolent ruler. "With Marshall dead, I've become aware that I'm being portrayed as the chair of the Council."

"We have no chair."

"We both know that Marshall controlled things to a certain extent."

Kaleb bowed his head in acknowledgment. "You don't wish to take over the crown?"

"I don't wish to be used as a stalking horse."

When had Henry become this shrewd? The instant after the thought passed through his head, Kaleb realized he'd done the unthinkable. He'd judged Henry on his surface persona, never looking beneath. The man was a *Councilor*. No one became Council without having considerable blood on their hands. Kaleb knew that better than anyone. "You're the most visible member," he responded smoothly, even as he wondered how much Henry knew. If it was too much, he'd have to be taken out of the equation—Kaleb had crossed too many lines in the past two decades to balk at one more. "You and Shoshanna chose that role."

"We both know Shoshanna chose it." Henry's stare was somehow . . . off, but Kaleb couldn't put his finger on why. Perhaps it was simply a case of the man showing his true colors. "I'm giving you warning that that is about to change."

Kaleb realized Henry was talking about far more than media appearances. "Why warn me at all?"

As he waited for a response, Henry's eyes shifted to pure black. The other Councilor was receiving a telepathic message. So was Kaleb. But his psychic control was better than Henry's and he knew his eyes had remained the night-sky of a cardinal.

Ashaya Aleine's body is missing. She may have staged her own death.

Ming, came Nikita's distinctive mental voice, *that's a problem but not urgent enough to interrupt us all without notice. She's a scientist, devoid of the skills necessary to survive on the run for long, even if you are correct about her being alive. I'm more apt to believe that her body has been taken.*

Ming responded on the heels of Nikita's statement. *Her organizer was set to wipe all data if anyone attempted to hack in—*

How is that possible? Tatiana interrupted. *According to my information, Aleine didn't have that level of computing expertise.*

The organizer is at least seven years old. I suspect someone else set up the encryption. But the point is moot—the chip from her organizer is a dummy. Ming didn't bother to wait for the ripples to fade from that bombshell. *We've searched her rooms and lab, as well as Keenan Aleine's room, and come up blank. If she's alive, she's carrying that chip. If she's dead, it's most likely hidden within her body. We need to find her before that data goes public—it could bring down the entire Implant Protocol.*

And Aleine? Nikita asked.

Our priority is to recover the chip.

Shoshanna's icy tone. *Are you giving a kill order, Ming?*

Taking her alive would be the best-case scenario. However, if she resists, eliminate her. But only after she gives up the location of the chip. If you need interrogation assistance, call me.

No one asked why he thought his assistance would make any difference. They all knew that Ming was a former Arrow with an inborn facility for high-level mental combat. He'd made torture into an art form.

CHAPTER 9

Only here, in this journal that I should have deleted years
ago, but which is the sole thing that keeps me sane, can I admit that every act, every movement, every plan, is for him.
For my son. For Keenan.

—*From the encrypted personal files of Ashaya Aleine*

The clock had just ticked past eleven p.m. when Mercy finished with Ashaya's leg and said, "She'll be fine."

Dorian looked at Ashaya's unconscious figure, the grinding
tension in his body slamming into a wave of raw protectiveness.
"That normal?" She looked so damn defenseless.

"You wouldn't have gone out. Neither would I," Mercy said
as she cleaned up. "But she's not a soldier. And I think her body
had another hit recently. Some of the readings I got from her
blood"—she waved a gadget she'd pulled out from the emergency medical kit—"are off."

The protectiveness spiked. "Dangerous? Infectious?" He
breathed in her scent, but found no taint but the familiar chill of
Silence. His leopard opened its mouth in a soundless snarl—he
hated Silence with a viciousness even Sascha hadn't been able to
temper.

"No, nothing like that." Washing off her hands, Mercy came
back to stand beside him. "It's reading as some kind of poison.
I'm guessing her body is slowly working it out of her system.
Sascha or Tammy would probably be able to tell more."

Dorian forced himself to look at Mercy rather than giving in to the compulsion to touch Ashaya. *To make sure she was okay.* "What the hell was that—slipping up with Sascha's name?"

Mercy's cheeks heated. "She's not stupid, and neither of us is exactly low profile." Her tone was low, harsh. "For crissakes, you're the frickin' poster boy for DarkRiver with your 'Gee, shucks, I'm harmless' act."

Dorian was used to being ribbed about his looks. With his blond hair and blue eyes, he looked more like a surfer hanging out for the right wave than a blooded DarkRiver sentinel. "Look who's talking, Miss Bikini Babe 2067." Even as he teased Mercy, he found himself alert to the steady rhythm of Ashaya's breathing.

Mercy's face grew black with fury. "Never, ever mention that. You understand me?"

He smirked. "I especially liked you in the polka-dot— Jesus, that hurt." He rubbed the spot on his ribs where her elbow had hit home, grateful for the distraction provided by the stab of pain.

"It's just the start. I plan to kill you in your sleep," Mercy said conversationally. "And stuff that damn polka-dot biki—" She paused, glanced at the door. "Did you—?"

"I think it's Vaughn." He nodded at her to answer. "I'll cover the Psy."

Mercy gave him an odd look. "She has a name. You should know, given your teensy obsession."

"Preparation, not obsession." Dorian had made it his business to learn the name and address of every powerful Psy in the area. He'd torn Santano Enrique's heart out with his bare hands, but it hadn't been enough, not when he knew the evil that had spawned the Psy serial killer continued to exist and grow. He intended to chop off the head of the beast, and if it grew back, he'd damn well do it again. And again. *And again.* As many times as it took.

Perhaps then his sister's ghost would stop haunting him.

Kylie's blood had still been warm when he reached her. The cuts that Santano had made . . . they had destroyed her beauty, turned her from his mischievous, barely grown-up baby sister, to a piece of torn flesh and blood. No matter how many Psy he killed, he couldn't change that, couldn't bring Kylie back from the grave. But he could make damn sure no other brother lost what he had, no mother cried as his had, no father screamed.

His parents had coped by leaning on Pack . . . and going

roaming. Anytime the memories got too bad, they turned leopard and left. Dorian couldn't deny them their escape, but he couldn't follow either. Not only did he lack the ability to go leopard, he was a DarkRiver sentinel and they were at war, even if it was a quiet, stealthy one most people didn't know was happening. Lucas had allowed Dorian's parents their grief. He'd given Dorian his shoulder, but in the end, he expected Dorian to deal.

It was exactly what Dorian expected of himself—any special treatment would've been an insult. More, he needed that responsibility to Pack. Sometimes, it was all that kept him from picking up a rifle and going rogue.

That truth was at the forefront of his mind as he watched Mercy open the door with sentinel cautiousness. Vaughn raised an eyebrow at their guarded expressions. "What, do I smell like wolf now?" He sniffed at his arm. "Nope. I smell like my gorgeous Red." A slow smile as he mentioned his mate and walked in.

Dorian didn't shift from his position by the bed—he'd brook no interference in his dealings where Ashaya was concerned, regardless of how he felt toward her. If Vaughn was here to assume control, blood would spill. "If you'd smelled of wolf," he said, trying to sound as if bloody possessiveness didn't have a chokehold on him, "I'd have had to kill you."

Mercy closed the door and grinned. "It would've been a mercy killing."

"Reduced to making bad puns, *Mélisande*?"

Mercy's eyes narrowed. "Everyone's got a death wish today."

Ducking the punch Mercy threw at him, Vaughn leaned indolently on the wall beside the door. "What happened to her leg?"

Dorian let Mercy give Vaughn the lowdown, viscerally aware of how vulnerable Ashaya was right then. That didn't mean she wasn't a Council spy.

His hands fisted. "So," he said to Vaughn after Mercy finished, "why are we running a taxi service for lost Psy? Hell, how did she even get to the Grove?"

"Aleine's defected," Vaughn said.

The leopard wanted to purr. The man wasn't so easily convinced. "How sure are we?" What better way to infiltrate an enemy citadel than on the back of an innocent child? Everyone knew predatory changelings were savage about protecting cubs, no matter if they wore human or Psy skin. "She was in deep with the Council."

"Anthony confirmed she's got rebel sympathies." Vaughn didn't have to say any more. Not only was Anthony Kyriakus the father of Vaughn's mate, Faith, he was the leader of a quiet revolution against the vicious straitjacket of Silence. "He's the one who arranged the pickup, though Aleine doesn't know about his involvement, so keep it quiet. He's certain she isn't a spy, but the fewer people who know about his activities, the better."

Much as Dorian respected Vaughn, he had no intention of trusting Ashaya until she proved herself. *To him.* Because this was a personal war. "She hooked up to the Net?"

"Yeah." Vaughn straightened. "So treat her as a possible leak. I think Anthony's solid, but until we're absolutely sure about her, we don't take any chances."

Mercy nodded in agreement. "Even if she really has defected, as long as she's linked to the Net, they might be able to suck information out of her."

Dorian had never been able to think of the PsyNet as anything other than a hive mind, but now he wondered what it would be to know that the very thing you needed for life could also lead death straight to you. "Where are we going to put her?" It was a question he hadn't realized he was going to ask until it was out.

"Why do we have to put her anywhere?" Mercy said, displaying the ruthless practicality that made her a sentinel. "She could be more trouble than she's worth if the Council's after her. She saved Noor and Jon; we repaid the debt by saving her son and stitching her up. Anthony must have people who can take her in now."

Dorian found his beast's lethal attention focused on Mercy. The reaction came from the same place as his irrational possessiveness—the thinking part of him knew Mercy was simply doing her job and watching out for the pack's interests. It was exactly what he should've been doing—instead of standing guard over a woman who might yet stab the knife of treachery straight into DarkRiver's back.

And still he couldn't make himself move. *Fuck.*

Vaughn's voice broke into his razor-edged thoughts. "Anthony said she's been given details of a new identity, complete with bank accounts and a path to follow, so, could be, she wakes up and goes. If she doesn't, we might as well take advantage of what she knows—trade-off is we help her."

"True." Mercy frowned. "Plus we do have the woman's son. She won't leave without him, not after everything she risked to set him free."

"And he can't be disconnected from the Web," Vaughn reminded them. "We all know it doesn't hold any of us back from traveling, but I had a talk with Sascha and she's not sure what would happen to a Psy member who tried to go too far. Wouldn't want to test it on a kid."

Dorian glanced at Ashaya and wondered if Mercy was right. Had Ashaya fought for her son? Or had she simply removed him from the equation so she could focus on her own twisted goals? Cat and man both brooded over the answer, because one thing was certain—if she *was* a spy, she'd have to be broken.

Seated at a table in his home deep in another section of DarkRiver's territory, Clay Bennett stopped what he was doing to check a message that had set his phone to flashing. "It's from Teijan," he said to Tally, handing over some sticky tape at the same time.

Taking it, she blew him a kiss and continued to wrap Noor's birthday present. The little girl was so active during the day, it was hard to keep a secret. "What does he want?"

"I asked for some intel." He pressed in Teijan's code and waited.

The Rat alpha sounded surprised when he answered. "What are you doing awake at midnight?"

"None of your business." He smiled at Tally's admonishing frown. She kept trying to get him to be nice to people. "You got something for me?"

"Yes." Teijan paused. "Hold on, Aneca's sleeping."

Clay waited until Teijan had moved away from the girl. The six-year-old was the first changeling rat to be born in the city in the past decade. It was a measure of the growing trust between the Rats and DarkRiver that Teijan had shared that information. "What are you doing with her?" he asked.

"Babysitting. It's date night."

Clay grinned at the thought of the small, feral fighter of a rat playing babysitter. "Late date."

"They mentioned a hotel room. Bet they'll be back in a couple of hours, though." Laughter in his voice. "Can't stay away from her."

"Wait till you have a kid," Clay warned. "They get their tiny little claws into you when you're not looking, and that's it." Lips curving at the thought of how Noor had suckered him into reading her four bedtime stories tonight, he reached over to hold down an edge as Tally taped it. Her fingers brushed his in thanks and his gut clenched. "So, you hear anything?"

"About the scientist who escaped? Bits and pieces. What do you want to know?"

Clay had no idea how the Rats knew most of what they did. He was just damn glad they'd allied with DarkRiver and not the Psy. "Any word on pursuit?"

"Heard nothing that specific yet—only some whispers of a high-level escape. Did hear something else interesting, though."

"Yeah?"

"Word from Vegas and out Los Angeles way is that Jax junkies are disappearing off the streets."

Jax addicts were Psy as a rule. The drug mutated changeling bodies, a surefire way to keep any of them from trying it. It apparently didn't have much of an effect on humans at all, leaving it a strictly Psy scourge. "Council cleanup?"

"Hard to say. There's something weird about it—with the Council, one day there'd be ten, the next day zero. Right now, it's like they take one or two, come back later for another couple."

Clay didn't have a high opinion of junkies—of any race—but if this was another case of a Psy crazy loose on the streets, they needed to know so they could protect those under their care. "Call me if you hear anything concrete, or if there's any sign of humans or changelings being targeted." If it was contained to the Psy, the Council would take care of it. Say what you would about them, the Council was efficient at cleaning up its messes—except, of course, when it was one of its sanctioned killers that had escaped.

After hanging up, he told Tally what Teijan had shared. "Looks like Aleine is safe for now."

"I want to see her." Her lips set in a familiar line as she

repeated the demand she'd already made three times this past hour alone. "We might not have saved Jon and Noor without her. I need to say thank you, offer her my help."

God, she was stubborn, but he was a protective, possessive cat. "She's a threat right now." He growled when she began to argue. "When we're *sure* she's clean, then you can have a tea party with her for all I care. And you are helping her—through Pack."

"What about Keenan?"

"Kid's probably fast asleep."

"Not funny. I meant later."

"If Sascha okays a visit, fine. Happy?"

"No." She got up, came around the table, and slid into his lap. "You're such a bully."

He felt his lips twitch. "And you're still a brat."

Ashaya came to consciousness in a single heartbeat. Her telepathic senses flared out at the same instant, an automatic reaction honed from years of living a double life. Her Tp status was weak, but it was enough to tell her she wasn't alone.

"You're awake." A familiar masculine voice. "I can hear the change in your heartbeat."

She turned her head toward him. "You're lying."

A raised eyebrow from the lethally beautiful male who sat in a chair in front of the unlit fireplace, playing a pocketknife over and through his fingers. "Are you sure?"

No, she wasn't. Those eyes were piercing in their directness. She could well imagine his senses were acute enough to detect the spike in her heartbeat as she'd woken—a purely physiological reaction she couldn't control. Now, she focused on bringing it back down to a resting rate. "My leg feels much better." She tested it, stretching the muscle, but remaining on her stomach. "Mercy is a good medic."

Dorian spun the knife on the tip of his finger, a feat of balance and skill that held her absolute attention. One slip and that blade would go through flesh and bone both.

"Speaking of Mercy," she said, mesmerized by the incredible grace with which he handled the blade, "where is she?"

A hard glance out of those pure blue eyes. The knife disappeared so fast, she didn't even catch a glimpse of where it went. "You've been out for a couple of hours. Mercy had things to do."

"It's"—she glanced at the clock on the wall by the fireplace—"one a.m."

"That's when Psy like to attack us."

Muscles warming up, she turned to sit up. "I see."

"Your eyes are the wrong color."

"You saw me once in the dark."

"I have the vision of a cat."

Instead of responding, she swung her legs off the bed and, after resting a few seconds, tried to stand. Her muscles complained but held. Mercy was indeed good. She wouldn't be running or winning any endurance contests, but she was no longer dependent on others. Especially not on a leopard who watched over her, but with an edge in his gaze that told her he was barely leashed. "My son," she said, knowing she chanced giving herself away, but unable to stifle the need to know. "Is he truly alive?"

He threw her a small cell phone. "Click through to video."

She did. And found herself watching a minute-long recording of Keenan curled up in sleep, his breathing steady, his hand pressed to the pillow by his cheek. *Her baby boy was safe.* A rock lifted off her chest. Still, it took considerable force of will to turn off the recording even after the third repetition, and throw the phone back to Dorian. "Thank you."

He caught it with lightning-fast reflexes. "Do you want to see him?"

Ashaya felt a curious stillness in that newly awake section of her brain, the part where her bond with Keenan had lived in secret for so long. "No."

Dorian's lips thinned. "That's what I thought."

The door inside her mind, the one that had slammed open once and never quite closed again, pushed outward. It was only an inch, but it permitted something volatile to break free, something that ricocheted violently through her veins.

"He's not safe with me," she blurted out, knowing it for a mistake the instant the words were out. She could already feel

Amara's mind attempting to shove through what should've been the impenetrable ice of Silence, drawn by the pulse of her forbidden emotion for Keenan . . . drawn, too, by something new. Something dark and raw, and vicious—her reaction to Dorian.

CHAPTER 10

Why do you try to hide from me? You know I'll always find you. I live inside your mind now.

—Handwritten note left in Ashaya's hospital locker, circa 2068

Ashaya used every tool she knew to calm herself before her agitation caused enough damage to allow Amara to get a lock on her. When she glanced up, it was to see Dorian watching her with disturbing intensity.

"You saying you care about your son's safety?" A mocking question, but his eyes were those of a hunter. If she wasn't careful, this highly intelligent predator would discover her most deadly secrets.

It was better not to engage with him. No matter the depth of her curiosity.

As she looked away from Dorian and the danger he represented, her eye fell on her pack. She walked carefully to where it stood leaning against the wall by the door. It was torn in a couple of places and dirty, but otherwise fine. "Thank you for retrieving this."

"Don't thank me—Vaughn got it. I stayed to make sure you didn't pull any Psy tricks."

She laid the pack on the floor and opened it up, not bothering with secrecy—Dorian had had plenty of time to go through it if he'd wanted. "Then please pass on my thanks to Vaughn." She wondered if all male changelings were as hostile as Dorian, then squelched the thought when it threatened to feed her visceral awareness of him.

No sound of movement, but he was suddenly crouching beside her, close enough that the scent of him—wild, fresh, with bite—washed over her.

She immediately put more distance between them. "Why are you here?"

"You're pretty skittish for a Psy," was the cool response.

Deciding to ignore him—a difficult task—she began to go through the jumble he'd created while looking for the first aid kit. Her hand threatened to tremble as she touched the edge of a holoframe she'd asked Zie Zen to retrieve from its hiding place and keep safe for her. Dorian didn't notice her betraying gesture, distracted by something else, something she'd expected to have to buy on the outside—whoever had packed this bag had clearly realized how integral record keeping was to her work.

"Top-of-the-line organizer." Dorian picked up the device, currently encased in an air cushion. "Only available to CEOs of major Psy corporations." Whistling through his teeth, he pricked the air bubble with his knife. "Nice."

She resisted the urge to snatch back the object. Little breaks, little fractures. The door opened another inch. "Do you always touch others' belongings?"

One corner of his lips curved upward and she realized Dorian was quite capable of charm. "*Now* you sound Psy. All pissy and icy." Getting rid of the packaging, he turned on the organizer. "Password-protected."

She leaned in and stared at the screen for several seconds. "Give it to me."

He swiveled the device so it remained on the flat of his palm, but faced her. Too intrigued by the intellectual challenge, she didn't argue his interpretation of her order. "I wasn't given the code," she murmured, "so it has to be logical, something I alone would know."

"Keenan?" For once, he didn't sound like he was baiting her. The cat apparently liked gadgets. It was an unexpected discovery.

"No." She looked up, startled at his closeness. "That would be the first word Ming LeBon would use."

Narrowing his eyes, Dorian pulled the organizer out of reach.

"Now that's a question I want answered. Why exactly was the Council able to keep you leashed by holding Keenan?"

She could've lied, but the truth, she decided, would serve as well. It would reinforce his image of her as a cold monster without any maternal feelings. She needed him to continue to treat her with disgust—because even this tiny hint of a thaw in his attitude was threatening to erode the Silence that was her only protection against Amara. "I was already working for the Council in another capacity," she began, "when the Councilors asked for my cooperation with Protocol I. Since I disagree with the aims of the protocol, I refused. Keenan was an infant at the time and living with me."

The tiny hairs on the back of Dorian's neck rose in warning. Whatever was coming was going to be bad, very bad.

"One night," Ashaya continued tonelessly, "I went to sleep in my bed and woke up in a room at the Center. I was told that my fallopian tubes had been tied." Her expression didn't change but he saw her hands clench on the holoframe she'd been attempting to slide quietly out of sight before he'd put her on the spot.

The gesture set all his sense to humming. It was the first true indication she'd given that maybe, just maybe, she wasn't the perfect Psy everyone believed her to be—Psy fully enmeshed in Silence *never* made any physical movements without purpose. Either it was an act to put him off guard, or M-Psy Ashaya Aleine had more secrets than anyone knew. There was nothing Dorian's cat loved better than a mystery.

He turned his mind to what she'd said. "I don't get it. It's reversible, right?"

"The technique they chose, yes."

"Then?"

"The point wasn't to make me infertile," Ashaya said with frightening calm. "The point was to teach me that they had control over every aspect of my life, including my body itself. I was told that if I dared reverse the procedure and get pregnant, they'd make sure my child was aborted."

Fury boiled in his gut. He stared at her, somehow knowing that that wasn't the worst of it. "And if you continued to defy them, they'd do worse?" The torture of it, of never knowing when you'd be violated, it gave him one hell of an insight into this woman's internal strength.

"They said they would remove my uterus and cause enough scar tissue that even a cloned organ wouldn't heal me."

"Okay," he said, clamping down on the need to touch her, to give comfort in the affectionate changeling way, "that leaves Keenan as your only child. But there's no emotional connection, so why would the threat to him hold you?"

"Psy are quite fanatical about bloodlines. Did you know?"

He shook his head, intrigued by the changes in her scent as she spoke. Snaps of cold, flares of heat. As if she was fighting a silent battle to maintain her conditioning—and yet nothing showed on her face. She was a very good actress, something he'd do well to remember, he thought, even as he said, "Enlighten me."

She seemed to take his words at face value. "We're a race that leaves behind no art, no music, no literature. Our immortality lies in the genetic inheritance we pass on to our offspring. Without that, we're nothing once we cease to exist. Our psychologists believe it's a primitive need for continuity, as well, of course, for the perpetuation of the species, that makes us reproduce, though children suck up time and effort that could be better spent elsewhere."

Smart words, cold words, but her tone was just a fraction off. "So that was all they had on you—if you didn't cooperate, there goes your genetic legacy?" Perhaps the Council had believed her motivation, but Dorian had seen her bleeding and wounded . . . and the only thing she'd cared about was whether Keenan was safe.

"No, there goes my immortality." She refused to break their locked gazes and the leopard approved. "You have no hope of understanding," she added. "You're changeling."

He scowled. "We love children."

"Children are commodities," she corrected. "Keenan, by virtue of being the single child it appeared I would ever produce, gained a higher market value. He was worth enough to me that I agreed to the Council's demands." She could've been talking about stocks and bonds. "Now that I'm out of their reach, I'm free to bear other children. Keenan is no longer important."

"Callous," he said, but he was watching that betraying hand. Those clever scientist's fingers were wrapped around the edge of the holoframe so tightly that bone pushed white against the thin membrane of her smooth, coffee and cream skin. "Except for one thing—why did you go to so much trouble to get Keenan out if you don't care if he lives or dies?"

A minuscule pause. "Because I knew changelings would be more inclined to help me if I showed some kind of an attachment toward a child." She looked down and began to shift things in the pack, finally releasing the holoframe. "I knew I'd need changeling assistance in certain matters, and your race's attitude toward the young is well-known."

What a load of crock. Dorian smiled behind her back, and it was a smile that held a bite. He'd caught the first hint of the true scent of his prey. Now it was a case of hunting her down until he could work off the fire in his blood, the darkly sexual craving in his gut. Because if sex was the only way to fight this, he'd swallow his damn principles and take her. Once he'd indulged the need, it would most likely abate.

She blinked those big brown—*wrong color,* the cat growled— eyes. "May I attempt the password now?"

"By all means." He echoed her arch tone, but his mind was busy going over everything she'd said and done since that night two months ago. An intricate game of subterfuge? Or something more intriguing? "Here."

Put on guard by his easy cooperation, but wanting to check if she was right, Ashaya went with her first instinct and used the touch screen to input a single word: ILIANA. The screen cleared. "Not difficult after all."

"Who's Iliana?"

"An entomologist who specialized in the medicinal properties of insects—her philosophies had a big impact on my own work," she said, and it was *a* truth.

"Not exactly the hardest thing for anyone familiar with your work to figure out," he muttered. "And it's a single word—so easy to hack, my great-granny could do it." Turning the device toward himself again, he sat down cross-legged and brought up the menu. "Huh. Lots of applications but no files. No wonder they put in such a hopeless password."

"I've heard this new line of organizers requires a password before any usage."

Dorian nodded. "You're right—they must've put one in so they could add all these specialist medical programs."

As his fingers moved over the screen, she realized something. "You know more about the functions than I do."

"I bet you just know how to use one or two programs." His smile was bright, teasing, and so unexpected, it sneaked in through her defenses.

Amara's voice, through a rain of white noise. Unintelligible. But getting closer.

Shoving away the brilliant temptation of Dorian's smile, she brought up the familiar image of a sheet of ice crawling over her mind, Silencing everything in its path. "I know how to utilize the aspects of the device that relate to my work." She began to take out the other things in the pack, making an inventory as she progressed. It only took a couple of minutes. She was about to repack when Dorian said, "You forgot the holoframe." There was a very catlike glint in his eye.

Realizing there was no rational reason to continue hiding it, she pulled out the frame and pressed the On button. An instant later, an uncountable number of light particles came together to form a three-dimensional image of Keenan as a baby. The person holding him—a woman with pale blue gray eyes, curly dark brown, almost black hair, and mocha skin—looked straight at the camera. Her gaze spoke of the Arctic.

"Who the hell is that?" Dorian asked.

It was an unexpected question. "It's me, of course."

"Don't lie to me."

Dorian was uncomfortably close, his body a heated wall, but she couldn't move away. "It looks exactly like me."

He snorted. "And I'm the fucking tooth fairy."

She stared at the image, unable to escape the truth—her secrets were beginning to escape. And this particular secret would find her sooner or later . . . then one would die, and one would live. "This is Amara," she said. "My sister . . . my twin."

CHAPTER 11

Amara didn't know how Ashaya had done it, but her sister had literally died for a period of time. Amara wasn't pleased her twin had given her no warning of the plan—the psychic trauma from the disconnect had left her unconscious for hours. That was how Ming LeBon had managed to track and capture her without a fight.

Now, he stared at her from the other side of a glass wall. "Your sister is gone, dead."

Amara smiled, aware it irritated Ming to see her parroting human and changeling emotions. He knew nothing. Amara was connected to Ashaya on a level beyond the PsyNet. Nobody had ever discovered that link and as far as Amara was concerned, it wasn't something that could be permanently destroyed by anything other than death. *True death*.

"Good," she said. "I always hated the competition."

"Hate and love are emotions."

She shrugged. "Semantics." What she felt for her sister, it couldn't be defined, couldn't be put into one of the nice little boxes preferred by the Psy. "I am who I am."

"A failure."

"Ouch." She put her hand over her heart, pretending shock.

"You know, Ming," she said in a stage whisper, "you shouldn't throw stones—you're a cold-blooded murderer."

"You broke Silence. Your emotions control you."

Amara smiled again, slow and dark, well aware there was nothing but emptiness in her eyes. "Are you sure?" Ming was attempting to use psychological warfare on her, treating her as if she really was insane. Perhaps she was, but she was also highly intelligent and more than capable of seeing through his attempts to undermine her self-confidence. "What do you want, Councilor LeBon? What need is great enough that you've hunted down the rabid wolf you once called your pet?"

Ming's eyes faded to pure black, an eerie darkness that Amara was used to seeing in the mirror. "You're the only one capable of completing your sister's work. You must conclude what she began. Finalize the Implant Protocol."

"So little?" She smiled again, showing teeth. "Consider it done."

CHAPTER 12

I heard the sniper's voice against my ear when I woke today. He whispered sensual promises so savage, I can hardly believe these thoughts come from some corner of my own psyche. And yet they must. Because, at the end, he called me prey.

And told me to run.

—From the encrypted personal files of Ashaya Aleine

Half an hour after waking, Ashaya snapped on a pair of thin latex gloves included in her first aid kit before heading into Mercy's kitchen and beginning to open cupboards.

"That's not polite." The drawled warning made her glance over her shoulder.

Dorian had been fiddling with the organizer's security codes for the past thirty minutes, giving her time to clean up and consider her next move. She'd expected him to push for more information about Amara, but so far, he'd remained quiet. She wasn't fooled—leopards were masters at stalking prey. "I need some household chemicals."

He raised an eyebrow. "Try under the sink."

She did so and found most of what she needed. Aware of Dorian's interested gaze as he came to stand in the entrance to the kitchen, she found a bowl and began mixing the chemicals together. "Would you mind getting me the pale blue tube from my first aid kit?" She expected a refusal, but he left and came back with cat swiftness. "Here."

"Thank you." She emptied the pure alcohol into the mix.

Dorian stepped closer, until he was leaning against the side of the counter, his arm braced on the upper level, while she worked on the lower level. She couldn't help but note that despite his white-blond hair, his skin was golden, as if it tanned easily.

He peered at the mixture and sniffed. "Smells acrid, bitter."

At that moment, he appeared more feline than ever before. Once, she'd had a neighbor's domesticated cat sneak into the house she'd called home before the Council moved her to a lab—the creature had watched her experiments with the same fascinated expression.

Not sure how to take his continued lack of aggression, she fell back on Psy practicality. "You'd be surprised at how caustic household chemicals can be, especially when mixed with each other in a selective way." She shook the bowl gently and saw it was beginning to scar on the inside. "I'll pay Mercy for this."

"Don't worry," Dorian murmured. "It's not expensive—I can smell the strength of your brew. Whoa!" His exclamation had her looking down.

The mixture was bubbling.

"Excellent." Taking the bowl, she carried it carefully into the bathroom, put it in the sink, and pulled out the tissue-wrapped chip from her pocket. "May I borrow your timepiece?"

He snapped it off and handed it to her. An instant later, he gave a horrified shout as she opened the tissue and dropped the tiny piece of hardware hidden inside into the caustic mix. "Jesus, woman!" His hand clenched on her upper arm—the flesh bare since she'd showered and changed into a short-sleeved tee. "What the hell—?"

She forced herself to speak with Psy calm, even as her heart rate skyrocketed. "Twenty-four hours prior to my defection, I coated the chip with a protective layer so it would survive my stomach acids." She'd put the poison over it, and protected *that* with a weak substance that would be destroyed the minute the chip touched her mouth. "It made the chip nonfunctional. I need to clean off the coating to get to the data."

Dorian moved closer, his hand still on her arm, his thumb moving absently against her skin. She almost missed his next words, she was so focused on the stark intimacy of skin-to-skin contact. A normal human or changeling interaction. Except she wasn't human or changeling. She was Psy. She hadn't been touched that way . . . ever.

"How will you know when it's done?"

She picked up the tweezers she'd found in the small cosmetic set in her pack. "Release me." As soon as he did, she retrieved the chip and put it on a soft face towel.

"I used your watch to time it," she explained, returning the timepiece. "The final parts of the solution will evaporate within the next minute, ensuring no moisture damage."

Dorian left without a sound.

Putting the sudden move down to feline capriciousness, she focused on the chip. It contained data the Council would kill for. And not all of it had to do with the Implant Protocol. Now, she just had to survive long enough to— Her head jerked up as Dorian's wild energy washed over her, through her. Her eyes dropped to his hands. "Messing with someone else's property is rude in any culture," she commented, trying not to think about the implications of her extreme sensitivity to his presence.

"Oops." He smiled and there was something different about it, something . . . playful. "Here." He handed her the organizer he'd pretty much taken over.

"Charm is wasted on me." A lie. Charm, anger, or outright hostility, something about Dorian touched a part of her that hadn't seen daylight since those lost hours on the day of her seventeenth birthday.

His smile widened. "Come on, Ms. Aleine. I want to see if that chip still works. I'll even say please."

"You have a very catlike curiosity." She'd never spent much time around changelings, was unprepared for how unlike a human—in the broader sense—he acted. "Do you exhibit human characteristics in leopard form?"

The charm faded away to leave his face expressionless. "I wouldn't know. I can't shift."

She halted in the process of sliding off the back of the organizer. "That's not normal."

He blinked, then burst out laughing. Again, the reaction was not what she would've predicted, having realized too late that her bluntness would probably be taken as an insult.

"Yeah, that's me," Dorian said, the grin creasing his cheeks turning him from beautiful to devastating, "an abnormal freak."

He confused her. She knew how easy it would be to change that. All she had to do was unlock the emotional center of her brain, give up Silence, and accept emotion. Yes, there were pain controls built into the conditioning, but she had a passive ability and her scientific instincts told her that the more active the ability, the higher the pain. The Tk, aggressive Tp, and exceptionally rare X designations would probably suffer the most.

Of course, as far as she was concerned, the point was moot—for her, the pain would be negligible if perceptible at all . . . because the controls were already rotted away. One moment of decision was all it would take to break the shackles that remained. Then she could be a mother in more than name only. Then she could find a way to comprehend this leopard in front of her.

So easy.

And impossible.

She'd spent years determined to maintain total Silence for a reason, had succeeded so well that she'd fooled Ming LeBon himself. She'd even fooled herself, until—

A hand waved in front of her eyes. She blinked. "I apologize," she said, scrambling to rebuild the wall of lies that had kept her alive this long. "I occasionally become lost in thought."

Dorian watched her with disconcerting intensity. She wondered what he saw. But all he said was, "Switch the chips."

She did so, then slid the cover back on. Dorian held it for her while she stripped off her gloves. When she took it back, she found herself staring at the blank screen for several seconds. If she'd made a mistake, the game would be over before it began. Evidence was crucial. Otherwise the Council would squash her like a bug.

"Give it to me." Dorian took the device with impatient hands and put in the password.

Files began scrolling across the screen at an unreadable speed. Ashaya's legs threatened to turn to jelly.

"Hot damn." Dorian whistled. "Guess you know what you're doing after all. Brains *and* curves."

The admiring whistle snapped her upright. "I had the distinct impression you wanted to kill me, not appreciate my curves."

His teeth glinted as he gave her a grin that held a distinctly savage edge. "They're not mutually exclusive."

Flawless logic. Incomprehensible logic. She decided to return her attention to something she had a hope of understanding. "I need to get some of this information out into the media." It would break her promise to Zie Zen, but her loyalty to Keenan came first. To keep him safe, she'd lie, cheat, even kill.

Turning off the organizer, Dorian gave her a lazy kind of look that did nothing to dull the steel in his tone. "Well, now, according to the intel I got while you were napping, you're supposed to go under."

She maintained eye contact, reaching into the same icy reservoir of calm that had helped her fool Councilors. "I try not to make a habit of doing what others expect."

"So you want to put a bull's-eye on your back instead?" He gave her the organizer, lazy tone disappearing to expose the predator within. "You really don't give a shit about your son, do you?"

A sharp stroke of pain, deep, so deep within that secret part where Keenan had lived and where there was now a gaping wound. The brutal strength of it caught her unawares, annihilating her hard-won calm. "It's the only way I know to protect him." He was her baby, her precious little man.

Dorian's leopard pounced on the weakness in her armor. She'd made a mistake at fucking last. "You told me he didn't matter. That he was a commodity."

A slow blink and he could almost see her scrambling to regroup. "No," he said, gripping her forearms and forcing her to look up. "You don't get to do that." *Not with him.* If he was going to be held hostage to this unwanted compulsion, then she was damn well coming along for the ride. "You don't get to hide behind Silence."

"How do you plan to enforce that dictate?" she shot back, unflinching. "I've been threatened by Councilors. What do you think you can do to me that they couldn't? That they *didn't?*"

The verbal volley took him by surprise. "Don't you dare compare me to those murdering bastards!"

"There's violence in your eyes when you look at me," came the quiet but pitiless response. "Even when you turn on the charm, the violence remains, simmering beneath the surface. Something about me antagonizes you."

He gritted his teeth. "I had you in my sights two months ago. I could've shot you then. I didn't." And it *had* been a choice. The part of him that needed her to live had overruled the cold calculation of the sniper who saw her as a threat. "Unless and until you betray DarkRiver, I won't ever lay a hand on you in anger."

Her eyes went to the hands he had on her right then.

"Am I hurting you?" he asked when she stayed silent. "You brought it up, now answer the fucking question." Knowing he was crossing a line, but unable to pull back, he stepped so close that her breasts brushed against his chest with every indrawn breath. *"Am. I. Hurting. You?"*

"No." A toneless response. "But it wouldn't take much to push you into a killing rage."

He let go, so furious with her that his leopard tried to growl through his human vocal cords. It made his voice half-animal when he said, "One of your people, one of your *Councilors*, killed my baby sister. Santano Enrique was the perfect Psy, Silent to the max." A mocking laugh. "So yeah, your presence, your Silence—how did you put it?—*antagonizes* me."

She went preternaturally quiet, prey in the direct path of a predator.

That just enraged the leopard further. Shaking with the brutality of his emotions, he strode out of the bathroom and to the living room. He had to get away from her before he did something unforgivable. Because that woman in there, the one who for some uncomprehensible reason drew him like a moth to a flame, she didn't have the first clue about how to deal with the trapped leopard inside of him. Contact, be it good or bad, physical or emotional, was the lifeblood of changelings.

Dorian knew he needed such contact more than most. He'd healed from the torture of his sister's murder, but Kylie's death and the blood-soaked aftermath had forever changed him. There was a darkness inside him now, an angry, vicious thing that he kept under control only by sheer force of will.

Now that darkness had become tangled up in his savage hunger for Ashaya. And this desire—this violent hunger shot through with the rage he felt at being attracted to one of the enemy, to a woman who had worked for the very Council he'd vowed to destroy—was nothing he welcomed.

He'd never hurt a woman in a sexual way in his life, but there, in that bathroom, he'd come perilously close. He hated that he couldn't control his body around her, hated the man he became when with her, hated that her presence alone was enough to strip away the veneer of civilization that was all most people ever saw.

"Dorian."

Her voice was sandpaper over his skin. Keeping his back to her, he drew back from the blood-hazed darkness and tried to find some hint of the man he'd been before the night he'd first seen Ashaya Aleine. "I'll organize a meeting with our communications people. They'll set up a broadcast—hell, we live to irritate the Psy Council."

"Thank you."

Hidden behind the familiar chill of her voice, there was a whisper of fear, of terror. It threatened to push him back into the darkness, but he fought to remain human, remain civilized. "You're afraid," he said, turning around at last. "Terrified. Of me?" He waited to hear her lie to him, to pretend that she was a perfect inmate of Silence.

"No. I'm . . . afraid that I'll lose my grip on the conditioning," she said, holding his gaze, "that this outside world will make me slip, make me feel."

It was an answer he hadn't expected, one that poured the cold water of surprise over his anger. "You're an M-Psy. It's not like your abilities need to be contained. Unless you're hiding a nonpassive ability?"

"No."

"Then that leaves choice—you don't want to break Silence?"

"That's an illogical question." Her lips formed the rational words but the leopard sensed something else in the air, the finest of emotional tremors. "To admit to a need for change is to admit that I feel enough to know the difference between what I am and what I could be."

He crooked an eyebrow, calmed by the fact that she'd come to him, was now tangling with him, if only on an intellectual level. "Trying to snow me with words? Won't work. I'm a stubborn bastard, and you've already admitted fear. You feel." But how much? And would it ever be enough to placate the increasingly violent cravings of his leopard?

She stayed on the other side of the room, as if she knew how fine a line he walked. "You're very intelligent."

"Flattery will get you everywhere, except out of this conversation." He didn't like the distance, so he closed it, until he could've reached out and touched her if he wanted. "You know the difference between Silence and sensation, don't you, Ashaya? Not only that, but you want to step out of the cage."

If she walked away from Silence, perhaps his guilt would fade. Perhaps he'd be able to look at himself in the mirror again. "Do it," he whispered. "Break Silence. Love your son." It was a low blow and he saw the impact of it in her eyes.

"You're right," she said, voice husky. "I know the difference between what is and what could be. I also know that my conditioning is imperfect." A confession without lies or half-truths. "But none of that matters. Because even now, when I have a choice, I choose to embrace Silence . . . of my own free will."

CHAPTER 13

Councilor Henry Scott pulled up a computer screen and began to input data.

Names.

Entire families.

It was a list of flawed Psy, a list he'd been compiling for years. Several of the people on the list had already been rehabilitated, but far too many mistakes continued to slip through the cracks. Like this boy.

He read the report again—the eight-year-old was showing signs of increasing rebellion. In response, his trainer had put him on a harsher regimen. Henry believed the boy should have been eliminated at the first hint of trouble. There was no cogent reason to perpetuate the cultivation of defective genes.

But he didn't have carte blanche over such decisions—the other Councilors had vetoed his suggestions. Too many childhood rehabilitations, they'd said, and the populace would begin to grow uneasy.

"Another flaw," he noted, inputting more data. Silence should've made them impervious to such concerns. But too many of his brethren—no, not his brethren; they were nothing more than dull primates to his mind of absolute Silence—were still driven by the primitive instinct to protect the young, even when those young proved defective.

Entering two more names, he closed down the encrypted file and sent it to its hiding place deep within his computer archives. He didn't keep as much on the PsyNet as he once had. His wife, Shoshanna, had long overstepped her bounds, prying into things that were none of her concern.

But she didn't know everything.

His eyes slid to the left corner of his desk, to the heavy white envelope edged with gilt. A gaudy, flashy thing, stamped *Private and Confidential.* It was, he had to admit, the perfect disguise. Even his normally astute assistant had put it in the in-box reserved for human media invitations and the like.

Picking it up, he opened the flap and removed the card. It was heavy white board, the lettering dark gold.

It would be our honor to have you join us.
The password has been e-mailed to the Councilor's
private address.

PURE PSY

A numerical URL followed.

This was no petty group—only a few, very important people had his private e-mail address. Like most Psy, he rarely used that form of communication, but it did come in useful now and then. As it had today. The password had come in under the subject line "Purity."

Making a decision, he turned to his computer and accessed the Internet. The pathways of this network were extremely slow in comparison to the microsecond fluidity of the PsyNet, but that also meant it was disregarded by the majority of his race. The numerical URL would also assist in keeping this under the radar.

However, the biggest advantage of the Internet was that it was completely outside the purview of the NetMind, the neosentient entity that was both the librarian and the guardian of the PsyNet. Henry considered the NetMind nonpartisan, but as a cardinal Tk, Kaleb Krychek had considerable control over it, which meant his fellow Councilor was likely privy to information others would prefer stayed secret. Such as the existence of this group.

With a discreet beep, the browser deposited him at the site. The entire page was black, except for one line of text in white and an empty box.

ENTER PASSWORD

Henry didn't need to check his e-mail. The password was easy to remember.

F_GALTON1822

CHAPTER 14

The inevitable future is fast approaching, but there's time. Time enough to convince you of what you must do if they ever discover the truth. Run and hide. It's the only way to survive. But even as I try to convince you, I know I'll fail. She might appear stronger, but you've always been the brave one, with more courage than I could ever imagine. But courage won't stop a Council assassin. *Run.*

—*From a handwritten letter signed "Iliana" circa July 2069*

Things happened faster than Dorian had anticipated—he found himself playing bodyguard in the first subbasement of DarkRiver's San Francisco HQ at nine the next morning. While the pack held shares in CTX, a major communications company, this basement was set up for guerrilla broadcasts. Ashaya's segment would go out on the Internet and all of CTX's stations at the same time.

A makeup girl dared approach Ashaya, fluffy brush brandished like a peace offering. Dorian glared. The nineteen-year-old—a packmate like every other person in this room, bar one—swiveled on her heel, and went in the opposite direction.

"Very effective."

He turned to the woman who'd spoken. He was still pissed off with her.

I choose to embrace Silence of my own free will.

He wasn't stupid enough to believe that Silence could be easily shrugged off—it had taken Judd Lauren more than a year, and the catalyst had been finding his mate. But Ashaya had a child. A child she'd refused to see again this morning. Disbelieving, Dorian had left her with Mercy for a couple of hours while he went to speak to Keenan.

The boy had been quiet, but he'd allowed Dorian to hug him.

"He trusts you," Sascha had said, having spent the night at Tammy's.

"I promised him I'd be there for him." And he kept his promises. As Ashaya should have been keeping the promises she'd made simply by giving birth. He knew Keenan mattered to her—she'd given herself away there too many times—so what possible justification could she have for depriving her son of the love and affection he deserved? It was an abandonment neither man nor leopard could accept. "What?" It was a growl.

Her spine went rigid. "The way you got rid of the makeup artist. Efficient."

Instead of increasing as it had till this point, Dorian's temper receded at the ice in her voice, his instincts shifting in a different direction. *Challenge.* Let's see how long Ashaya Aleine could hold out against a cat determined to charm her out of the cold world she clung to. He wasn't some green juvenile. No matter how bad things got, he could control his cock. But he wouldn't have to if he could thaw her enough to shatter her Silence, get her into bed . . . and work this clawing sexual need out of his system.

His conscience gave a twinge at the ruthless way he was planning to pursue, then take her, but he figured Ashaya could look after herself. The woman was no pushover. She'd make him work for it, he thought, his aggression turning into a lethal kind of focus. "I got rid of her because you don't need makeup," he said after a long pause. With her hair pulled off her face in a tight bun that irritated him, and her eyes naturally wolf blue, she looked like a perfectly cut diamond.

"You're correct," she replied in that perfect diction of hers, devoid of any hint of personality. "While good grooming and makeup arc considered useful tools among the Psy, I need to appear professional to the utmost. A more ascetic approach is the better choice."

Dorian wondered if she really was as calm as she seemed. He couldn't scent deceit, but he was beginning to see that Ashaya was an expert at faking Silence. She was also good at stonewalling—he hadn't been able to get her to tell him why she was so intent on doing this broadcast. But he'd find out. "That's not what I meant." He kept his hands behind his back, though his fingers itched to trace the warm silk of her skin. Her voice might've been ice, but her skin . . . her skin called to him with a seductive whisper. Maybe he wasn't as in control of his cock as he'd thought.

"No?"

"No," he said. "Your skin is flawless." It was a deliberate attempt to make her uncomfortable, to push her into betraying the humanity he'd glimpsed mere hours ago. "If you lay naked under the sun, would you glow that same luscious shade all over?"

Her face remained expressionless, but he saw her hands curl. "That is an inappropriate question."

He smiled, and it was a smile designed to get under her skin. "Why? You're a woman of science—it's a simple biological query." Mocking her to see how she would react. Testing her. The leopard inside him wanted to gauge her strength, find out what its prey was made of. The man was testing her for other reasons—learning her beyond the savage, sexual instincts of the beast.

She tugged at the cuffs of her white shirt, aligning them to perfect straightness and breaking eye contact in the process. "You appear to enjoy playing psychological games with me."

He didn't respond, just waited. She was a scientist. He was a predator used to hunting with stealthy patience. He couldn't go leopard, but it was a wild, integral part of him, filled with the same hungers and needs as that of any other cat in DarkRiver. As a child, he'd sometimes thought he'd go mad with the craving to run, to hunt, to feel his teeth and claws sink into the living flesh of prey.

Then, one freezing winter's night, he'd gotten up and gone running in human form, breaking all his parents' rules. He'd stayed out the entire night. The soles of his feet had ended up shredded, but his soul had been at peace for the first time in his life. It was then that he'd decided he would never again consider himself crippled. He would simply become so tough that no one would dare question his changeling identity.

He had been six years old.

Perhaps that was why he'd connected so easily with Keenan Aleine. There was something about the boy that spoke to the child Dorian had once been. Though clearly of high intelligence and young enough that Silence hadn't yet got its hooks into him, there was a weight in Keenan's eyes, a knowledge that shouldn't have been there.

The same knowledge rested in Ashaya's eyes, magnified a thousand times over.

Ashaya had played mind games with Councilors. But she'd never felt as in danger as she did at this moment. Because while she looked into a face that held all the hallmarks of humanity, she knew the man she spoke to was something other, his leopard instincts evident in every facet of him. Even now, he stood so still, a cat waiting for his prey to make a mistake.

"Play your games," she said, refusing to back down, though he unknowingly held the advantage—he'd gone to see her baby today, was watching over Keenan like the protector he was, and for that, he owned an indelible piece of her loyalty. "But know that I grew up in the viper's nest of the PsyNet."

A slight curve to his lips. It was odd what made him react favorably. There was no logic to it. Last night, she'd retreated from a fight, and his anger had been a whip against her skin. Today, she spoke to him with the blue frost of Silence in every word, and he smiled.

"You calling me a lightweight again, Ashaya?" he said, his voice threaded through with amusement as well as a feline arrogance that said he knew he was the most dangerous creature in the room.

She got off the stool and made sure her severe black pants were sitting straight before picking up her suit jacket and slipping it on. "In this, yes. You're a physical creature—used to fighting with your body. I'm used to having only my mind as a defense."

"Then I guess you won't mind playing."

Having finished buttoning the jacket, she looked up. "On the contrary, I would prefer to live in a world where every word didn't have a double meaning." Where she wasn't constantly watching and waiting for a knife in the back. "It would considerably simplify my life."

She'd surprised him, she saw that at once. His eyes narrowed and he raised a hand ostensibly to straighten her lapel, the act holding a primitive edge that she "saw" with a rusty section of her brain this leopard alone seemed to awaken.

"That," he said, "would bore you, sugar. Straight and easy is not what you were born for."

He'd used an endearment, but his gaze was pure watchful cat. No, she didn't understand Dorian at all. "We'll have to agree to disagree on that point. It's time."

He dropped his hand from her lapel and she was discomfited to find she'd been clenching her stomach muscles so tightly they hurt. Another mistake. She attempted to relax—the producers of the show were heading her way. If the Psy Council didn't succeed in disrupting the feed, she'd soon be in living rooms and on billboards from here to Paris and beyond.

Though CTX, being a joint leopard-wolf communications company, was not the Psy media of choice, her broadcast would be picked up by enough rebellious Psy networks that the message would spread. After it was over, she knew full well she'd go to the top of the Council's hit list. But that was a future concern.

Right now, she had to lay the framework of a chaos that would disrupt everything in the Net, hiding the truth in the midst of lies—lies that would ensure Keenan's safety. That was the only thing that mattered.

She ignored the burst of activity in that now familiar primitive section of her brain. Dorian intrigued her to the depths of her being—she'd never met anyone so complex. He was light and shadow, savagery and charm, predatory fury and sniper calm. She found herself wondering what it would take for him to drop his guard, and allow a woman to see beyond the surface. Perhaps, in another life, she might've taken up the invitation to play his double-edged cat games, and discovered the answer. But in this life, she had no such choice.

"Ready, Ms. Aleine?" The producer had listening devices clipped to both his ears, but appeared to be focusing on her.

He was changeling, too, a leopard; handsome, she supposed, But he didn't awaken that primitive set of neurons the way Dorian did, didn't threaten to derail a plan she'd died to put into place. "Let's go." She began walking alongside him, very aware of Dorian's alert presence at her back. He didn't particularly like her, that much was obvious, but he wouldn't let her be assassinated. No, if this cat wanted to get rid of her, he'd do it himself.

Oddly reassured by the thought, she stepped in front of the camera, looked it straight in the eye, and waited for the signal to proceed.

"Three, two, one . . . we're live."

Dorian watched Ashaya's absolute stillness, her unfractured composure, and knew it for a lie.

It's the only way I know to protect him.

He'd been considering the implications of that unguarded statement ever since their arrival at the basement studio—it put her seemingly reckless broadcast in a whole new light. Somehow, some way, this was meant to help Keenan live a life free of fear.

Ashaya Aleine, he thought, was the most intricate of puzzles. The layers of deceit and truth only added to the challenge of her. It was tempting to push her until she surrendered, but sometimes in a hunt, you had to play nice. That thought in mind, he shifted so that he was in her line of sight. It was a silent promise of safety, of protection.

She understood, the knowledge betrayed by the barest flicker of an eyelash. And then she began to speak.

"My name is Ashaya Aleine. I'm a Gradient 9.9 M-Psy and the scientist formerly in charge of Protocol I, otherwise known as the Implant Protocol."

Her tone was cold enough to freeze summer rain. For the first time, he saw exactly how she'd survived detection in the PsyNet. It created an unexpected burst of pride in his gut—this woman was made of ice-fired steel. She might bend, but Ashaya Aleine would never, ever, break.

"The information I'm about to share is highly classified," she continued. "In doing so, I break my contract with the Council, but keep the one I made as a scientist—to pursue the truth."

In the PsyNet, *a red alert blasted into the mind of every Councilor.*

"While the theoretical research behind the Implant Protocol is common knowledge," Ashaya continued, "what is not widely known is that the Council is going ahead with the Protocol, in direct violation of its duty to consult the populace on matters of this scale.

"Silence itself took ten years of debate before it was implemented, and yet this implant, an implant that would enable the imposition of Silence on the biological level, turning many into one—in effect, creating a hive mind—is being railroaded through without even cursory consultation."

Across the country, *across the world, power started failing in a relentless cascade. Entire towns, then cities, were blacked out as the Council shut down every one of its power providers.*

"Not long ago, an attack on my lab put the development of the implant back to square one. But it can be rebuilt. I'm not the only scientist with the capacity to do the work."

Psy telekinetics were *dispatched to cause "accidental" breakdowns in media outlets not under the Council's direct control, including the usually ignored highways of the Internet. The blackout continued to explode across the world in a violent wave. Then the satellites started to blink.*

"This information is classified but has been the subject of widespread rumor." Ashaya paused. "But what I tell you next is known only to a select few. The Council-funded research on Protocol I speaks of absolute equality. That is a categorical lie. The implants were never intended to make us all the same. Their purpose is simple—to create a society of ciphers, slaves for whom obedience to the Council and its favored associates is a biological imperative."

Hackers—Psy, human, *and changeling—worked furiously to reboot systems. They failed. Humans swore, changelings* *threw things, Psy began a rapid-fire telepathic "tree" to link to anyone who had a signal and could feed them the broadcast.*

"However, while the implants remain a priority for the Council, after the rebels' successful attack on the original lab—when it became clear that they might possibly realize their aim of halting the Implant Protocol—the Council decided to widen the scope of my mandate."

Backup Internet servers *hidden all over the world came online with a hum, hand-crank radios were unearthed from attics and basements, and the telepathic "tree" grew until still-functioning feeds were found in rural Russia, in the deep-sea station, Alaris, and in several tiny towns in New Zealand.*

"The Omega Project existed before Protocol I, before most of us were born. It has always been a possible tool in the Council's arsenal. Three months ago, I was instructed to begin familiarizing myself with all data pertaining to Omega, as the dormant project would be reinitiated the instant the Protocol I was complete. The aim of the Omega Project—"

High above the *earth, three seemingly long-dead satellites came to life, controlled by changelings and humans at a facility buried within the Sierra Nevada mountain range. Their sudden reemergence took everyone by surprise.*

"—is to wipe out all spontaneous conception among the Psy."

CHAPTER 15

The hush that *fell across the world was audible.*

"The delivery system is meant to be a virus. The virus is intended to have a cure. That cure would be controlled by the Council. The result hardly needs to be stated—anyone who dared rebel would find their familial line discontinued."

Lights flickered around Ashaya, but she saw Dorian make a "keep going" gesture. It steadied her enough to continue. And why a cat who disliked her so openly should have that effect on her was not something she had the luxury to consider at this moment.

"As for my proof—in terms of the inequalities in Protocol I, that proof consists of thousands of bytes of data, including copies of orders bearing the Council seal. Some of that information is being streamed along with this feed—information that makes it clear the implants were to be made to different specifications. You, the masses, were destined to be nothing more than insects in a hive."

* * *

Those who still *had the ability attempted to grab the data packets.*

"As for the aims of the Omega Project, you have only my word, the word of a scientist with an unblemished record. If successfully manufactured, the virus would be a weapon, one intended to be used against us by our own Council. Now consider its potential as a weapon in the hands of those who hate the Psy."

She paused to let that sink in.

"Though Omega has never come close to completion, the scientists who worked on it over the years created a rich archive of data, data that may have included the genesis of a viral recipe. That data is now gone. I destroyed every byte of it in the weeks before I defected. The Omega Project is dead." Ashaya told the most dangerous lie of all with every ounce of cold conviction she could gather. "I don't ask that you believe every word I say. I don't even ask that you consider me anything but a traitor to our race. All I ask is that you think for yourself . . . and question your Council."

She stepped away from the microphone and toward the soft darkness that surrounded the cameras, and—even if she couldn't admit it anywhere but inside the walls of her mind—toward the dangerous safety of the man who stood there. Her bones felt oddly hollow, breakable. She wasn't certain she wouldn't fracture like so much glass.

Suddenly, there was an arm around her shoulders, leading her toward a door, almost carrying her up a flight of steps and out onto a tiny balcony hardly big enough for two people. The piercing brightness of daylight stabbed into her irises with the ferocity of a thousand sharp knives.

"That was one hell of a surprise." He pressed her face to his chest, rubbing her back with a firm hand.

She should have pulled away, but she didn't. She knew herself, knew her weaknesses, knew that at this moment, she was incapable of standing without assistance. She also knew that she *liked* Dorian's heat around her. "It had to be done." For her people, for her son . . . and, despite everything, for Amara.

Dorian pulled out his cell phone with his free hand. "Nothing. They must've done something to the cell transmitters."

"I apologize—I knew the backlash would be severe, but I didn't think they'd be able to move so fast." Breaking away from him, she leaned back, her hands closing around the cold iron of the railing. Over his shoulder, she could see only a thick wall of green foliage. To her left was a closed door that led down into a basement she didn't yet have the strength to reenter—it had taken all her willpower the first time around. "They shut down power?"

He nodded.

"Hospitals," she began.

"Generators," he told her. "I'm guessing most of the power and comm lines are going to be back up in the next few minutes anyway—Psy businesses would lose too much revenue otherwise, and without their support, the Council falls."

She nodded. "Do you think my broadcast got through to any appreciable extent?"

His nod was immediate. "We had backup satellites ready to go."

"Oh?"

"We like to be prepared." Raising his hand, he traced the curve of her cheekbone.

She stood absolutely motionless. Though she had trained herself to appear exactly like her brethren, she wasn't averse to touch. And out here, no one would punish her for taking strength from this most simple of human contact. What held her frozen was that she didn't know the rules of touch in changeling society. In her time with them so far, she'd seen them touch easily . . . but only each other.

Except Dorian's touch was hot against her, as if every stroke left a permanent imprint.

"Sascha and Faith say Psy like to mix it up genetically," he commented, his fingers sliding down and off.

She didn't say anything, waiting, expectant.

"I can see why." He leaned against the railing opposite her, his arms folded. "So what's next for the infamous Ashaya Aleine?"

She wanted to move but there was nowhere to go. A single step and they would touch again. She could still feel the heat of his skin against hers, an impossibility that was somehow real. "The first part of my plan is complete." What a joke. She had no plan beyond getting both herself and Keenan out from under twenty-four-hour Council surveillance.

All it would've taken was *one* slipup, and she'd never have seen her son again. The ironic thing was that by holding him hostage, the Council had unknowingly protected him from another danger. However, that protection had come at a cost. They'd kept her baby like a rat in a cage, until she could see his very soul beginning to shrivel.

Now, he was free . . . and vulnerable to the pitiless menace that had stalked him his entire life.

"Hopefully," she said, trying not to crumble under the wrenching force of the need to hold her son, "I'm now too famous to die a quiet death." More importantly, too famous for Keenan to be made a target without severe political repercussions.

"Phase two?"

She started to make something up, but knew it would be a waste. He'd see right through it. "I don't know." Logic, sense, reason, it all told her to run, to draw the danger away from Keenan, but rational thought collided with raw maternal need and came away the loser. She couldn't leave him behind.

"What about Keenan?" Dorian asked, almost as if he'd read her mind. "You planning on seeing him anytime soon?"

Her palms tingled with the memory of her son's soft skin, his fragile bones. He was so small, and so easily hurt. But this cat, there was such strength in him, such purpose—he'd stand by Keenan if she fell. She met those eyes of icy blue. "He's safe as long as the Council thinks I have no interest in him." Not a lie, but not the whole truth either. She knew this was the right choice, the only choice while she tried to find an answer that wouldn't leave her with her twin's blood on her hands. But her heart still twisted—Keenan would think she'd lied, that she'd abandoned him.

Too much emotion, she thought. Her Silent shields, crucial protections against Amara, were beginning to erode. But she couldn't rebuild her buffers. Not with Dorian so close, the wild fury of his emotions evident in every breath.

"That's your justification for ignoring him?" His eyes had gone flat, no hint remaining of the man who'd held her with gentle protectiveness. "But then again, I suppose a child is simply a collection of genes to you, not a flesh-and-blood creature of spirit and soul. Do you even know anything about him? Do you care that he's probably waiting for his mom to come hold him and tell him everything's gonna be okay?"

She let the whip of his words draw blood, but stood firm. "If I go to him, I'll put him in harm's way." For Keenan, Amara was the true nightmare. But she couldn't tell Dorian that. Because then he'd want to know why. And to share that deadly secret, she'd have to trust him more than she'd trusted anyone her entire life.

I found you!

Ashaya tried to slam the mental door shut but it stuck. Too late. It was too late.

Dorian snorted, shattering her focus and making her fingers slip off the doorway. "You shook off excess baggage." He straightened. "Well, that's just too bad, Ms. Aleine. You're going to be a mother to your son. That kid deserves for you to fucking give a damn."

"No," she began to say, shoving back against Amara's insidious presence even as the primal energy of the changeling in front of her threatened to overwhelm her defenses. "I can't—"

"I don't care what you can or can't do." Dorian crowded her against the railing, his hands on either side of her. Pure heat. Pure muscle.

Trapping her.

Caging her.

Claustrophobia rose. And the door shoved wide open.

Oh, Ashaya, you've been very, very, bad.

CHAPTER 16

Kaleb watched a replay of the Aleine broadcast and knew that Protocol I was dead. There was no way for the Council to recover from this. Despite her statement about others being able to continue her work, Ashaya had been the linchpin of the entire operation, her expertise unique, her focus unparalleled.

Protocol I was finished. But Omega . . . that was a discussion that couldn't wait.

Not bothering to unfold the sleeves of his shirt, he walked out of his study and through to the balcony behind his home on the outskirts of Moscow. Night lay thick across this part of the world but he didn't turn on any of the external lights. Instead, he leaned against the outside wall and opened his mind to the dark skies of the PsyNet.

There was nothing else like it—an endless field of black, littered with the pure white of stars representing the minds of each and every Psy in the world, but for the recent renegades. And the Forgotten, of course. But those few lost ones took nothing away from the PsyNet. It was the largest mental construct in the world, the biggest information archive. Its pathways flowed with more data per second than even the most efficient computer highway.

However, today, Kaleb had no interest in mining the PsyNet

for data—except for the one crucial piece of information that he searched for constantly, day and night, awake or asleep. That task hummed in the back of his head as usual, but his conscious mind was focused on reaching the dark core of the Net, home to the psychic vault of the Council chambers.

He was the first to arrive, followed by Shoshanna Scott, then Nikita Duncan. Ming LeBon and Anthony Kyriakus came together but from different directions. Henry Scott appeared an instant later. Tatiana Rika-Smythe was the last entry. The door to the vault slammed shut and the seven minds within it flared bright.

Nikita started the discussion. "I initiated emergency procedures since I was closest to the focal point. It worked as projected—we always knew there would be a high chance of failure in any worldwide shutdown. Aleine's message got through."

Tatiana spoke as soon as Nikita finished. "Then she's sunk the Implant Protocol."

"Isn't that a fatalistic approach?" Shoshanna queried. "We still have the relevant data—it was backed up in networks she couldn't access."

"Tatiana isn't talking about the technical aspects." Anthony's controlled mental voice. He was the newest member of the Council, but he'd ruled the influential NightStar clan for decades, was powerful enough that he'd defied the Council with impunity before his ascension. So when he spoke, everyone listened. Even Shoshanna.

Interesting.

"It's the political aspect," Anthony continued. "By associating Protocol I with Omega, and muddying the waters of what we have and have not told our allies, she's manufactured a political schism between the Council and the most powerful of those who support us."

"I don't agree," Shoshanna said. "We may not have stated it definitively, but our supporters have to know they would've been accorded preferential treatment under the Protocol."

"Yes," Anthony agreed. "But what use is having power over the masses if you have none over your own biology? Aleine has made it appear as if we were making fools of our allies, promising them supremacy, while planning to neuter them."

Kaleb made his move. "As to looking the fool, Anthony is

correct—I'd like an explanation as to why there was nothing about Omega in the data files I was given at my ascension." He wondered if Anthony had known about the project. Likely. The NightStar clan was famous for the number of F-Psy in its gene pool. And foreseers saw many things when they looked into the future. Perhaps they had seen a tomorrow without progeny.

"An oversight," Ming said, his tone dismissive. "The project has been stagnant for so many decades, it's in mothballs—Aleine was never told to oversee it."

"Neither did she receive instructions to reinitiate the process," Nikita added. "In fact, her only involvement with Omega stems from some general research she did several years ago, when she first began working for us."

"That wasn't what she stated," Anthony pointed out.

Ming was the one who answered. "She lied. Ashaya knows full well that Protocol I has gained some support in the Net. If she'd based her broadcast on that alone, she would've chanced being ignored by a large number of people. So she increased the stakes and used her basic knowledge of Omega to turn her broadcast into a virtual nail bomb."

"Omega has always been more concept than reality." Nikita, siding with Ming once again. "If we'd thought there was any chance that Aleine was close to a breakthrough, we would've had her focusing on the virus, not Protocol I."

Kaleb couldn't disagree with that logic. Had Protocol I succeeded, the implants would've required a far longer rollout period than an easily transmittable virus.

Nikita continued to speak. "We can't allow Aleine's use of Omega to distract us from the real issue. Though the data leak is a problem, especially given the Net's current instability, our priority has to be on stemming the ripples caused by her defection."

"How do we discredit her?" Shoshanna asked. "Not only is it clear that she's in full control of her faculties, it's well known that she worked for the Council."

"The easiest way would be for her to retract her statement," Nikita said. "Doesn't she have an identical twin? Would we be able to use her to complicate things?"

"That's . . . problematic," Ming said. "Though Amara Aleine's mind is brilliant in certain useful respects and she may, in fact, be able to complete her twin's work, it's doubtful she could appear enough like her sister, in terms of Ashaya's control, to pull off a broadcast. Even telepathic coercion may not work. If it doesn't—"

"—the attempt will do more harm than good," Nikita completed. "Ashaya Aleine's child?"

"Dead, but we haven't yet found a body."

"Convenient, but it matters little," Tatiana said. "The boy lost his value as a hostage the instant Ashaya escaped our control. Getting back to Amara Aleine, do we need her anymore? The inception of Protocol I is now highly unlikely."

"I predict that will change," Shoshanna said. "We need to be ready with a functioning implant when that happens."

Kaleb knew she was right. Tides changed swiftly in the rapidly flowing rivers of the PsyNet. A man who intended to hold the Net in the palm of his hand had to be careful which rapids he rode.

"The most efficient way to stop discontent would be to take Ashaya out of the equation," Henry said, breaking his silence.

Kaleb watched the other Councilor. Of course, the man's shields made it impossible for Kaleb to read his patterns, but the fact that Henry had put forth such a radical idea without input from Shoshanna was another piece of the puzzle he'd suddenly become.

"She's high-profile," Nikita pointed out. "It could backfire."

"But Henry is correct—dead women can't speak." Tatiana's practical mind. "It may take years to recover from the effect of Aleine's revelations, but the process will go much faster if she's not around to feed the populace on rebellion."

"I'd advise caution." Anthony's compelling voice. "Ashaya has influence in intellectual circles. If we attempt to assassinate her, we chance alienating the very scientists we'll need if she carries through her implied threat and releases a bioagent as a weapon."

"Surely you're reaching with that interpretation," Tatiana said. "This is a political issue. Ashaya won't take it to the level of war."

"We're the ones who've become too political, too worried about perception," Shoshanna said, pure ice in her tone. "There was a time when we would've had no hesitation in executing Ashaya, as well as any who dared stand with her."

Kaleb waited, expecting Nikita to speak. She did.

"Times have changed," she said. "We are—through our own mistakes—no longer the sole powers in the world. If we become too openly manipulative, the defectors may decide to look to the changelings for protection."

"They're not that much of a threat," Shoshanna retorted. "Perhaps in California, yes, but elsewhere? They're too caught up in their petty animal concerns."

"But are you willing to chance a war on US soil for the sake of a single scientist?" Kaleb asked, backing Nikita. "If we do come down hard and even a small percentage of the populace decides to turn to the changelings, we'll have the beginnings of an untenable rupture in the Net." He would not allow war to shatter that which would one day be his.

"Might I suggest a two-step approach," Anthony said into the silence. "As a first step, we attempt to recapture her, with the aim of forcing her to recant. We're all capable of overcoming her psychic defenses—she's an M-Psy, with no offensive abilities."

"An excellent point," Shoshanna accepted. "And step two?"

"We take her out of the equation."

"It's a sound plan," Tatiana said. "It won't only silence her, it'll have the dual effect of demoralizing the rebels—they'll see that even if they manage to get their voices heard, it means nothing."

"Agreed." It was a unanimous decision.

Kaleb was about to move back to his study when he caught the edge of a different newscast burning up the Net. He made immediate telepathic contact. *Ming, I assume you're behind this?*

It's a message. Ashaya Aleine is not a stupid woman. She'll understand.

CHAPTER 17

I've just seen a broadcast that could change everything. We
need to meet. 0800 hours. Tell the others.

—*Handwritten note slipped under an apartment door in the*
sunken city of Venice

Dorian had trapped her against the balcony railing and
Amara was trying to claw into her very psyche. Ashaya snapped,
and, mind screaming at the sense of entrapment, shoved at Dorian's chest. "Get away from me." She snatched back her hands
as the heat and power of him soaked through her palms.

He smiled and it wasn't pleasant. "Scared?"

"I'm Psy." Reminding herself of that helped block Amara.
She was safe. This time. "I feel nothing." It was the same lie she'd
told herself her entire adult life, only allowing the truth to surface
in the deepest depths of night, when she was sure Amara slept.
To leash her sister, and survive in the Net, she'd *become* the creature everyone expected her to be. The unrelenting charade had
taken a toll, but she refused to crack. Not yet. Not while Keenan
remained at risk.

"My conditioning may have malfunctioned once or twice,"
she said, since he'd caught her lapses, "but it's now repaired.
I'm fully enmeshed in Silence."

"Liar. You're hiding behind the conditioning like a scared
child."

She held her ground. "Believe that if you want. It doesn't
change the truth."

He snorted. "You know what, Ashaya, I thought you had a heart of fucking ice the first time I met you"—he leaned so close, his breath whispered across the curls that had escaped the knot at the back of her head—"but I never took you for a coward."

For a moment, claustrophobia retreated under the thundering force of a clean, bright wave that fired energy through her body. It undermined every one of her efforts to keep Amara at bay, but for that single instant, she didn't care. "What right do you have to call me anything? You, with your prejudice and your self-pity."

Golden skin pulled taut over his cheekbones. "Careful, sugar. I'm not real nice when I'm pissed."

"How would I know the difference? You've been unpleasant to me every chance you get. If that's the result of a lifetime of emotion," she said, deliberately coating each word with frost, "then I prefer Silence."

The door to the balcony swung open, hitting Dorian on the shoulder. He didn't turn, but Ashaya glanced over—to meet the vivid green eyes of a man with savage clawlike markings on one side of his face. He raised an eyebrow. "Takes most people a few days at least to get Dorian that close to a killing frame of mind. You have talent, Ms. Aleine."

Dorian growled low in his throat, warning Lucas to back off. This was between him and Ashaya. "What the hell are you doing here?" He took his hands off the railing on either side of Ashaya and shifted so the door could be pushed fully open.

His alpha leaned against the wall opposite the door, looking like a fucking CEO with his dark gray suit and crisp white shirt. And a tie. Jesus H. Christ. "I just had some information come through," Lucas said, "thought Ms. Aleine might be interested."

Dorian shifted to place himself between Lucas and Ashaya. He saw Luc note the move, and knew the other man understood the way of things when he kept his distance, though he spoke directly to Ashaya. "We need to get you to a safe house. That broadcast didn't declaw the beast."

Some of the anger riding Dorian shifted into steely focus. "You sound sure."

Lucas jerked his head in the direction of the subbasement. "Follow me."

Dorian moved to let Ashaya brush past him. When she

hesitated at going down the steps, he leaned in to whisper in her ear. "Want to stay up here with me, instead?"

"I'd rather eat dirt."

The cat liked that acerbic response. So did the man. Biting back a smile, he followed her down into the now empty studio. Only one of the control screens was on, the image paused. "This transmission came through in bits and pieces through various networks," Lucas said. "The fact it got through at all, given the current state of communications, speaks for itself." Without further explanation, he touched the screen and the recording began to play. Images of smoke and debris, the reporter shouting through a face mask.

". . . massive underground explosion in . . . ebraska. Possible covert . . . facility. Casualities . . ."—crackling white noise, but the last words were clear—"We're told there was no time to warn anyone of the malfunction. There were no survivors."

Dorian watched as Ashaya reached forward, rewound the broadcast, and watched it again. And again. He gripped her wrist when she would've done it a third time, aware it was her former lab that had been buried—he recognized the area from the mission to rescue Jon and Noor.

Her bones were fragile under his as she stood there unresisting, the complete opposite of the woman who'd shoved at him bare minutes ago.

"Ekaterina was in there." Her voice was as cool as always but he felt the finest of tremors beneath her skin. "You met her, interrogated her."

Dorian recalled the blonde at once. "Shit. She was one of yours."

"Most of them were mine. And that's why they died." She looked at the screen, eyes strangely flat. "I'm responsible for this. If I had run—"

"—they'd have hunted you down like a rabid dog." Of that, Dorian had no doubt. The Council maintained its power by cold-bloodedly wiping out any opposition. Except, most of the time, it was done in darkness and shadow, with assassins and poisons. "All you did was bring their bullying tactics out into the open."

Ashaya didn't answer him, her gaze locked on the screen.

* * *

Dorian closed the car door behind Ashaya's still figure and turned to Lucas. "If she wasn't Psy, I'd say she was in shock." Though the window was down, Ashaya gave no indication of having heard him.

Lucas narrowed his eyes. "Might help if she sees her son."

"Any change since this morning?" Protective instincts rose to the fore.

"I talked to Sascha before that transmission came through. She said he seems okay, but quiet. Even Tally couldn't get him to talk and she can get anyone to open up."

"Don't call her Tally in front of Clay," Dorian said, thinking of the small human female who loved Clay so desperately. "He's a little territorial."

Lucas's eyes flicked to Ashaya. "So are you."

Dorian wanted to bare his teeth, warn Lucas off against interfering. "Yeah, I am."

"I know better than to step in between," Lucas said, as they both moved far enough away that Ashaya couldn't hear them. "But you might be better off gaining some distance so you can think—right now, your aggression levels are through the roof."

"I can handle it."

"But does she want to be handled?" A question that cut out the bullshit. "Doesn't look like she's going to hop into bed with you anytime soon—and from what I saw on that balcony, that's what your cat wants. You're getting belligerent because you're frustrated." Blunt words from one man to another, a warning from an alpha to a sentinel. "I don't care if she is the enemy— you don't touch her unless she agrees."

Dorian felt his leopard thrust its claws out under his skin. "That's a fucking insult."

"Then tone it down." Lucas's markings stood out starkly against his skin. "Or I'm pulling you off protection detail."

"Try it." Dorian made his tone sniper flat.

"Damn it, Dorian, stop being so fucking pigheaded. We both know you're not rational where Psy are concerned."

"Yeah? I seem to get along fine with Sascha."

"She's Pack, and so is Faith. Judd's close to Pack." Lucas shook his head, "Any Psy outside the right circle of what you consider family is automatically an enemy in your eyes. That makes you the worst person to guard Ashaya."

Dorian fisted his hands. "Back off, Luc. I don't know what the fuck is going on with me and Ashaya, but I'll sort it out. Bloody hell, you know me better than to think I'd ever force a woman, no matter who she is."

Lucas stared at him for several minutes before giving a slow nod. "She might never be willing—the first time you met her, you told us she was so cold you got frostbite."

"I was wrong." He'd seen the desperate flashes of love in her eyes when she spoke of Keenan, felt her hand tremble as she realized her colleagues were dead. "She's not who I thought she was." He just had to coax the real Ashaya Aleine out of hiding.

"Doesn't matter." Lucas glanced at the car. "She doesn't seem to like you any."

"I've been less than charming." He gritted his teeth. "I'll work on that. She'll thaw out." She had to, because he sure as hell wasn't going to walk around with blue balls for the rest of his life. The sexual nature of the thought was a deliberate attempt to offset a more worrisome emotion—it disturbed him how protective he'd begun to feel toward her.

Lucas's eyes gleamed with feline humor. "Can you lay on the charm and protect her at the same time?"

"Keep insulting me, and I'll forget you're my alpha." It was said without heat, both their beasts having retreated from the razor-sharp edge of violence. "What's the security plan?"

"You're her shadow," Lucas said, humor replaced by the keen intelligence that made him an alpha who commanded respect as well as obedience. "Anthony doesn't want her dead and he's not an ally we can afford to lose."

"What about his own resources?"

"They're at our disposal, but things are a little hot for him right now—he doesn't want to tip his hand if we're willing to cover."

Dorian nodded. "Council needs at least one sane member."

"Yeah." A grim look. "Our job is to keep Ashaya alive. Nothing else. Anthony might be family through Faith, but I won't put my pack in the middle of an internal Psy war."

Dorian raised an eyebrow. "That's a load of shit. We've been involved from day one."

Lucas looked at the woman sitting in the car. "You're right.

But this particular storm is all about them. We facilitate the transmissions—"

"That's not involvement?"

"It's the scoop of the century." He shrugged. "It's business."

Dorian saw his point. "The fact that we get to irritate them is a nice bonus, but not one that'll put us on their shit list." Psy understood business.

"This time, they're looking at their own."

"She's not theirs anymore." The denial came out without thought, from the heart of the cat he was.

Lucas glanced at him. "Are you sure? From what I've seen, she's got the balls to pull off a double cross."

CHAPTER 18

Deep in the heart of the sunken city of Venice, six men and five women sat around a long, oval table. They were silent, their attention on a holographic recording playing in the center of the table. Patched together from a number of different sources, the recording was neither smooth nor continuous, but it provided the information they needed.

When it ended in a rush of white noise, the man at the head of the table switched it off, his cuff links glinting rose-gold in the artificial light. "I don't think I need to explain our interest in Ms. Aleine."

"She made a point of saying she destroyed the data."

"She's a scientist. They never destroy their work."

Silence as they considered their options.

"We don't need her, simply the data itself," one of the women said. "The Psy might consider themselves the best at research and development, but we have people fully capable of utilizing the information."

"Exactly my thoughts," the man at the head of the table said. "Then I assume there's no opposition to my motion—to send out a team to question Ms. Aleine?"

"She's being protected." A new female voice, liquid soft

vowels and drawn-out syllables. "No one knows by whom, but they've hidden her."

"The broadcast originated from a CTX transmitter in San Francisco." The man with the cuff links leaned back, his gaze on the water that lapped at the edges of the mostly undersea habitat. "Could be DarkRiver and SnowDancer gave her a platform because they like to get in the Council's face, or could be they're the ones protecting her. But if she's still in the city, we'll know within a few hours."

"What about her abilities? She may have aggressive ones."

"We've got that covered," the man next to her said. "It's time the Psy learned they aren't as all-powerful as they think."

CHAPTER 19

When the psychologist suggested I keep a journal of my nightmares in order to better find a way to negate their effect, he inadvertently gave me a priceless gift. As far as anyone knows, that journal was closed the day I was pronounced stable. The truth, of course, is that I never recovered from the trauma and the journal was never closed.

—From the encrypted personal files of Ashaya Aleine

Ashaya lay in the dark, exhausted but unable to sleep.

Ekaterina was dead.

So were the others. All because they'd thrown their loyalty behind Ashaya. She wanted to believe that some had escaped, but she knew Ming LeBon. He would've struck hard and without warning. The entire lab had always been rigged to blow from the inside—a supposed precaution against the spread of a lethal bioagent.

Now Ming had utilized that "safety feature" and unless he'd pulled Ekaterina out because he had some use for her, she was dead. Even if he *had* done that, the woman Ashaya had known was as good as dead. Ming would've used his abilities to turn her into a mindless automaton. Ashaya didn't want to think of Ekaterina being violated that way. Better that she'd died in a single instant.

Like the others. So many others.

Ashaya wanted to turn away from the brutal reality of all

those deaths, but she had no right. Because no matter what Dorian had said, this was on her. If she hadn't provoked the Council with that broadcast, Ekaterina would still be alive. What she couldn't understand was why Ming had done it, killed so indiscriminately. He knew Ashaya only as the most perfect of Psy, without an emotional flaw that would lead her to mourn her lost colleagues. Had he done it for no reason other than to send her a message? Was he that coldly practical?

Yes, she thought, remembering what he'd said to her once.

You are necessary. I would never simply kill you.

No, he'd torture her, break her, first. Even if that meant he had to kill everyone who might have stood with her.

No survivors.

Wrong, she thought fiercely. There were survivors—scientists on the outside who had sided with her over the implant issue. They were the ones who'd made sure her note about Keenan reached Talin McKade—she hadn't trusted Zie Zen not to stop her. As far as Ashaya was aware, she and Zie Zen alone knew the identities of those courageous men and women. Zie Zen would never be suspected of rebel activities. Which left Ashaya. She couldn't let Ming recapture her. Because if he tore open her mind, more people would die.

More blood would stain her hands.

Oh, Ashaya, you've been very, very bad.

You're going to be a mother to your son.

Ashaya curled into a fetal ball, telling herself she was merely thinking things over so she could plan her next step. But the lie was too big to swallow. The past was catching up with her, cracking the brittle wall of false Silence around her mind.

I thought you had a heart of fucking ice the first time I met you, but I never took you for a coward.

Dorian was right. She was a coward. Staying away from her son when all it would take to keep him safe from the worst monster of all was a single bullet. Keenan would never have to know the chilling truth once Amara was gone. All she had to do was look into eyes identical to her own, into a face she'd promised to protect, into a mind linked to hers since before birth, and pull the trigger.

Her stomach revolted.

Resisting the urge to throw up, she began to chart the cool certainty of DNA patterns inside her mind, giving herself a firm mental command for sleep. It didn't come. At least not then. She lay awake, perhaps for minutes, perhaps for hours, and when exhaustion did finally suck her under, it was only to return her to the one moment she most wanted to forget . . . but that she relived every night with clockwork precision.

She was in a hole, hard-packed soil all around her.

A grave, her mind whispered.

Like before.

No, she told herself, reaching for Silent calm. She was seventeen years old, had basically completed her progress through the Protocol and graduated with honors in her chosen specialty. The Council was planning to offer her a training position in one of its top labs. She was going to accept. *She couldn't be in a grave.* There was wood above her—planks, they were planks.

See, not a grave. But the air was growing heavy, dirty, harder to breathe.

"Amara," she said, asking for help, for an explanation.

Only the rumble of earth and rock greeted her. Dust whispered through the planks. One of the pieces of wood fell in, crushing her leg. She didn't notice, knowing only that her resting place had been covered with earth, that no one would hear her. She could've gone into the PsyNet, could've screamed for help that way.

But she couldn't. Because in that moment of understanding, of knowing that she'd been entombed again, something snapped inside of her. She lost her sense of humanity, of logic, and became a creature of pure primitive chaos. She screamed until her throat was raw, until her hands were bloodied and her cheeks wet with tears.

She screamed until Amara decided to dig her up again.

Ashaya came awake with sudden, *quiet* alertness. It could be no other way. If she'd woken up screaming in the lab, it would've alerted others to her aberrant mental state. And Ashaya had no wish to end up in the Center, her personality erased, her mind reduced to the level of a blithering idiot's.

Conscious that sleep would elude her now, she got up and walked out of the bedroom, judging her dark red pajama bottoms and black T-shirt reasonable enough should Dorian prove to be awake. Her hand stilled on the doorknob as she considered whether or not she wanted to venture out and chance speaking to him.

He would call it cowardice.

She called it self-preservation.

Because Dorian was creating giant chinks in her armor, making her question everything, even her decision to keep her distance from Keenan. Her hand tightened on the knob. He didn't understand. Everything she'd done, every single act in the years since his conception, had been to ensure Keenan's safety.

Choking dirt in her throat, grit in her teeth.

Shaking off the flashback, she opened the door. There was no one in the living area of the apartment—the safe house—but a wall sconce had been left burning. It gave her just enough illumination to make it to the kitchenette. Once there, she turned on the light using manual rather than voice activation and, since it was five a.m., began to prepare breakfast.

Psy lived on nutrition bars and she found them perfectly acceptable—they provided everything a body needed to survive. However, she was also fully capable of making do. That thought in mind, she found milk and a sealed container of some kind of wheat cereal, as well as a banana.

Food prepared, she stood at the counter and ate it in measured bites. Taste was nothing that could be bred out, but those of her race were conditioned to consider it a danger. To prefer one taste over another was a slippery slope, one that could easily lead to sensuality in other areas of life. Considering how precariously she was balanced on that slope, Ashaya ate with a deliberate lack of attention to the tastes.

Amara was asleep now; Ashaya could feel it. It gave her a chance to fix the fissures in her shields that had allowed her twin to slip through and find her. She filled her mind with the patterns she knew best—the twining strands of DNA, the proteins glittering like gemstones on a twisted wire of bronze. White noise. A shield.

Hiding from Amara.

Protecting Amara.

She finished the meal in five minutes, and only then realized that her injured leg hadn't so much as twinged. Excellent. Cleaning up after herself took only another three minutes. Rather than go back into the bedroom, she walked to the large French doors that led out to a small balcony overlooking the bay—the glass was clear, the balcony railing formed of iron bars that sliced the view into rectangular pieces. She took a cross-legged position on the soft carpet, her back straight, her eyes on the dark swell of water in the distance.

It was cool where she sat, as if the chill of the outside air had stained the warmth inside. She resisted the urge to touch the glass, and turned her senses inward, into her mind. It was where she felt the most free. She wasn't quite sure who or what she was in her body—it had never truly seemed to belong to her. The psychological separation wasn't healthy, she knew that. But it was a coping mechanism. After the horror of her seventeenth birthday, she'd needed some way to keep her psyche together.

Dorian threatened that separation. She didn't want to know what the result would be if she tried to reintegrate the pieces. Dangerous thoughts. Again, she pushed them away, concentrating on the white noise of DNA . . . and, behind that psychic wall, on the lethal chill of secrets she'd carried so long, they were burned into her very cells.

She'd told a number of lies during the broadcast.

But those lies hid a far more perilous truth, and it was a truth that Ashaya intended to protect to the death. Except Ming had upped the stakes and her original plan of publicity, misdirection, and distraction lay in shreds at her feet.

The entire plan had been stupidly simple—to make herself so visible that neither her nor her son's death or disappearance could be swept under the carpet. Zie Zen was a good man and his advice to run had been reasonable, but she knew exactly what happened to those who tried to outrun the Council—she had an eleven-year-old death certificate to prove it. Ming had been tracking and executing rebels for decades.

Since she had no chance of killing Ming, she'd weighed the variables and decided to take a stand. The bonus had been the destruction of Protocol I—she didn't want any child exposed to the horror of implantation. It had all been going as it should . . . until Ekaterina's murder.

Her mind filled with images of the destruction of the Implant lab, but this time, she maintained her calm. Ekaterina was dead, but Keenan, her little man, was alive.

She would let *no one* snuff out that life.

Dorian watched Ashaya from his bedroom doorway. He'd been sleeping the light sleep of a leopard on guard, but even so, he'd dreamed. Not of ice and death, but of a beautiful woman's cries of pleasure. In sleep, he'd run his tongue over that perfect silky skin, so rich, so tempting that he'd barely resisted the urge to bite, to *mark*.

Then she'd whispered, "Do it. Take me."

He'd woken hard as a rock, and very aware that Ashaya, too, was awake. He'd listened to her move around, figured out that she was grabbing some breakfast. Joining her had sounded like a good idea. But by the time he got his erection under control, she'd finished her cereal, and was taking a seat by the window.

Intensely curious about her, he simply watched as she brought her breathing and heartbeat under a level of control he'd never witnessed in any living creature. It was almost as if she'd willed herself out of existence.

He came closer on silent feet. It was as he crouched down beside her that he realized how fragile she really was. Intellectually, he'd always known that her bones were weaker than his, her physiology much more breakable. But when she was awake, he tended to forget. He saw only the cold steel of her spine, the chilly determination of her gaze. *Strength.* He saw a woman of incredible strength.

But now, as his eyes took in the naked skin of her nape, framed by two tight braids, he glimpsed the vulnerability of her. Her body was curvy, quintessentially female, but delicate, too. He had the certain awareness that he could close his hand over her shoulder and crush it.

His beast snarled at the idea.

Agreeing with the sentiment, he maintained his silence and continued to study her. As he'd witnessed a number of times now, she could put on the appearance of a perfect Psy on cue, but he knew in his gut that that was all it was—an appearance. No woman could have faked the reaction he'd scented in her on the balcony. Fury. Pure, pissed-off female fury.

But not only was her act damn good, the fact that she'd survived in the Council ranks for as long as she had meant she was also brilliant at the games of manipulation that were the Council's stock in trade. Yet she'd never played those games with him, choosing brutal honesty instead.

What right do you have to call me anything? You, with your prejudice and your self-pity.

It made him want to bare his teeth, but not in anger at her—he'd been acting like an ass and she'd called him on it. But there was one thing he couldn't understand—the way she wouldn't go to her son. He'd offered to take her again this afternoon. She'd refused.

Yet even that disquieting fact wasn't enough to temper his hunger where she was concerned. Lucas was right—he was snarling at her because he wanted her as he'd never before wanted a woman. His leopard was constantly fighting him for control, trying to overrule his humanity. It was strong. Getting stronger. So strong that Dorian had begun to wonder if a latent could go rogue in the true sense of the word, losing his humanity and surrendering completely to the savagery of the cat . . . becoming a leopard on two legs, a man who cared nothing for a woman's fragility, only for her submission.

Her eyes opened.

Locked with his.

"Why are you watching me?" Her eyes, he saw, were not blue, not truly. They were a vivid pale gray with blue shards coming in from the outer ring to hit the pure black of her pupils. Strange eyes. Wolf eyes.

"My leopard is fascinated by you." By her sensuous, flawless skin, her wild hair, her damn curves. He leaned in and blew a gentle breath that made a rebel tendril dance. "I dreamed of running my tongue across your skin." He spoke to release some of the tension, to leash the beast before it broke its bonds. "Of exploring you in long, slow licks."

She didn't break the deeply intimate visual connection. "You're crossing lines again."

Hell, yeah. It was either that or go insane. "And your heartbeat just got erratic." The cat smiled, pleased. Ashaya Aleine wasn't as immune to him as she liked to pretend. "What would happen if I tasted you? If I took a bite out of you?"

Another spike in her heartbeat, music to the leopard's ears. But when she spoke, it was to say, "Nothing."

He gave her a sleepy-eyed look that he knew screamed challenge. "Then come here."

"You're disturbing me."

"Good." He smiled, playful and wicked, realizing he had the advantage—Ms. Aleine wasn't used to playing with cats. "I don't like being ignored."

"Get used to it," she said, surprising him, delighting him. "I'm working."

"Oh?" He was genuinely interested. "I though M-Psy saw inside the body and diagnosed illnesses." His family had consulted several when his inability to shift had become apparent. All had been brilliant, but not one had *understood* what it meant to a changeling to be denied half of who he was.

Ashaya's gaze skimmed down his body. "Isn't that an uncomfortable position?"

He'd listened to her body, knew she was aware of him on a level she'd never admit. It soothed the cat, even as it ratcheted up his need. "I'm fine, sugar," he said, fighting the urge to sink his teeth into the delicate curve of her neck. He tended to like his sex slow and intense, but right now, with this woman, his body wanted hard, furious, a little rough. Reining in the leopard's territorial instincts made sweat bead along his spine. "M-Psy?"

She became very still, as if she'd sensed his tenuous control. But she didn't retreat. If she had . . .

"Like all Psy designations," she said, "medical, or M, is an umbrella term that covers a wide range of specializations. It includes those unusual few who can actually heal—"

"Anything?" He'd never heard of a Psy with that power.

She shook her head. "No, their scope is limited. Some can reset bones, while others can seal wounds—the types of things that might be needed in the field. The healing abilities apparently appeared in children born during the Territorial Wars, though there's no proof of that. As far as I know, no M-Psy can psychically cure diseases or reverse hereditary conditions. May I continue?" A scientist's cool question.

He wanted to bite her. "Go on."

"The scanning you mentioned is the most well-known and prevalent manifestation of the M designation. My ability is a subset of that—I can't see broken bones or diseased organs, but it's because my mind sees too deep."

"How deep?"

"To the DNA level."

His cat's attention was momentarily diverted from the seduction of her skin. "No one can do that. It would make you a walking DNA scanner."

"Yes," she said, not seeming to realize she'd maintained constant eye contact. "Only a very small percentage of the M designation possesses the ability. Even fewer master it to the level where we become more accurate than the machines." Her eyes traced his lips and his entire body grew taut with the caress—she might not call it that, but that's what it was. She was stroking him. Purring inwardly, he didn't move, didn't break the spell.

"Because of available equipment," she continued, "it's a fairly redundant ability in itself. You have to pair it with study—it was my knack for working with nanotech and implants that made me of interest to the Council. My ability gives me an edge with technology at that level of miniaturization."

He wondered what she'd do if he gave in to temptation and flicked his tongue along her full lower lip. "How does your gift work?" he asked, curling his hand into a tight fist. "You see me and know my genetic blueprint?"

She shook her head. "Not quite. Depending on what I'm searching for, it can take hours, days, weeks, sometimes months, to tease apart the DNA."

"Why tell me all this?" He was a leopard sentinel. Even half-insane with this unwanted craving, his brain cells were working just fine. And he knew there had to be a reason for her unusual openness. "What do you want?"

She bit her lower lip.

His blood rushed to his cock. The roaring in his ears was so loud, he almost missed her next words.

"I want your DNA."

CHAPTER 20

A kiss is a melding of mouths. I've considered every aspect of this form of affection since the last perplexing dream, but I still don't see the point of it.

—*From the encrypted personal files of Ashaya Aleine*

Surprise hit Dorian hard. "You obviously weren't this blunt with the Council."

"I can play political games if necessary." Cool voice, jittery heartbeat. "It's not who I am."

He believed her. "Are you planning to mutate my DNA?" he teased.

"Obviously not." She straightened out her legs, stretching until her toes touched the clear glass of the French doors.

He looked at her primly cut, unpainted nails and felt another urge to bite. Then she said, "If I planned to get rid of you, I'd do it silently and with such efficiency that everyone would think you'd died a natural death."

If any other woman had made the threat, he'd probably have grinned and said something about never making her mad. But this wasn't any other woman. Ashaya was a scientist who'd spent years in the arms of the Psy Council. She was also the only female to have ever threatened his control. "You could try." It was a soft, lethal threat.

Ashaya hadn't expected that response, though why, she couldn't say. It just seemed wrong on a fundamental level. "Would you kill me?"

"No. There are other ways to break a woman." An answer that told her nothing, but tore a ragged hole in that primitive core Dorian alone seemed to awaken. She staggered under the mental injury, scrambling to regather her defenses.

And in that instant, Amara found her again.

Naughty, naughty, Ashaya. Trying to hide.

Ashaya broke the connection with the frantic speed of experience, knowing she was only patching up the cracks, only delaying the inevitable . . . but she didn't want to kill her twin. Because no matter what else she'd done, Amara had upheld the bonds of sisterhood—she'd never revealed Ashaya's secrets.

Feeling psychically battered, she raised her head to find Dorian scowling at her. "Your eyes just bled to pure black," he said, looking at her with a quiet intensity that reminded her of the predator he was.

"I didn't expect you to threaten me," she said, but couldn't stifle the urge to ask, "Is Keenan still safe? You haven't had any reports of problems?" She didn't care what it betrayed, she had to know her baby was okay.

"He's fine—I checked. Cell phones are functioning again."

"Thank you." She wanted to beg for more information, but swallowed the need. To know too much would be the same as going to see him—she'd lead Amara right to his door.

Dorian continued to stare at her. "Were you playing with me?"

"What?"

"The crack about the natural death."

She didn't know how to answer him. So she told the truth. "You weren't being serious. Neither was I."

He blew out a breath. "I'm sorry I snarled." When she just stared at him, too surprised to respond, his expression turned into a scowl. "How much DNA do you need?"

She blinked, staring into the extraordinary blue of his eyes. He was so beautiful it seemed impossible that he should exist. "Aren't you curious as to why I want it?"

"To see my abnormal genetic structure."

Her guard immediately went up—he was being far too cooperative. "Yes," she said warily. "I want to see why you are as you are."

"Why not steal my DNA? Easy enough to come by."

"Because," she said, not trusting the strange light in his eyes, "as telepaths don't cross certain ethical boundaries, neither do I. And I just need a minute fraction. Give me a moment."

Making a quick trip to her room, she grabbed the small scientific kit she'd found hidden in a side pocket of her pack—Zie Zen knew her well—and returned to her previous position. "A slide," she explained to the cat who'd waited suspiciously patiently for her. "It's the only one in the kit, so I'll have to get it right first time. A drop of blood would probably work best—white blood cells 'show' better to my mental eye."

"I don't feel like cutting myself." That strange light glimmered brighter. "But I will . . . for a price."

Freezing, she returned the slide to the tool kit. "I'm not that curious."

"Yes, you are."

Yes, she was. It was why she was a scientist. "I have nothing to negotiate with."

"I told you, Shaya," he said, eyes grazing over her lips, causing an almost painful tightness in her stomach, "my cat wants to know what you taste like." A slow feline smile. "And since you're Psy, it's no skin off your back to give up a kiss. Just a primitive animal thing after all. Deal?"

"I knew your cooperation was too good to be true." And that apology was too confusing to even think about.

A grin that creased his cheeks with devastating charm. "I'm a cat, sugar. What did you expect?"

She decided she'd have to research leopards, learn more about their behavior. But one thing she knew—they were highly intelligent. "I want the blood first." She didn't allow herself to think about her end of the bargain.

"Don't trust me?"

"No."

Another sharp grin and then, to her shock, a knife was in his hand. He pricked a finger and held it over the slide she hurriedly readied. A single drop and she closed it. To take the mental snapshot, she'd have to focus on the drop for a long period of time, until her brain saw through the cell walls to the nuclei, to the strands of DNA twisting within.

Dorian let her put the slide back into the tool kit and close the lid before he said, "Now, pay up."

Her heart thudded, her shields began to unravel . . . and

Amara's presence pushed heavily against the psychic walls of her mind. But she didn't tell him to stop.

His lips pressed over hers.

And her rotting foundations collapsed around her feet. For a second, she thought Amara was in her mind again, but no, this chaos was acting as another kind of anchor, another kind of wall—her twin was being held back, shoved out. A flash fire second of thought and then even thought was lost.

His taste was inside her mouth, a dark and richly masculine thing at odds with the sheer beauty of him. Protected by the strange, twisting, chaotic shield that blocked Amara, she broke every rule and savored the experience. When his tongue swept against hers, she felt her throat lock. He did it again. Shuddering, she dared explore him in return. His growl poured into her mouth, making her nerve endings sizzle.

He was the one who broke the kiss. Blinking, she tried to steady her breathing. But his taste lingered on her lips and all she could think was that she wanted more.

"I can smell something." His face went quiet, hunting still. "An intruder."

Ashaya, what are you doing? Why can't I see it?

The words snapped her back to full awareness. The instant Dorian had stopped touching her, whatever it was that had protected her from Amara had disappeared. The shields against the PsyNet were holding—how or why, she didn't know—but she didn't have time to consider that miracle, because Amara had broken through again. Her twin fought to retain control, but, her recent slew of emotion-induced mistakes aside, Ashaya had been doing this for years. And now she had Keenan to protect.

No one would hurt her son.

Powered by that absolute vow, she got her sister out, though it left her mentally bloody.

Dorian's growl raised the hairs on her arms. "It's gone. What the fuck was in the room with us, Ashaya?"

This was one secret she couldn't share. "Nothing."

His nostrils flared. "That *nothing* came through you. Are you a spy, Ms. Aleine?" His eyes held a knife-edge gleam. "Your scent changed."

The accuracy of his changeling senses staggered her. "What kind of change?"

"A lot of Psy"—he sniffed at the curve of her shoulder in a way that was definitely not human—"have this ugly metallic edge to their scent changelings can't stand. You don't. But whatever it was, it was close."

Perhaps she should've been considering the ramifications of the scent and what it denoted about Amara's increasing strength, but she found herself stuck on the first part of his comment. "That's good, isn't it? That I don't stink." She stared out at the water as day grew lighter. "It would make it impossible for you to guard me otherwise."

Dorian didn't like the metallic taint he could still feel on his tongue. Reaching forward, he slanted his open mouth across Ashaya's, knowing he'd taken her by surprise. Heat and ice, honey and spice, the taste of her flooded his mouth. "That's better," he said, retreating before the urge to move his mouth to lower, hotter places became irresistible.

Ashaya stared at him, lips kiss-swollen. "That wasn't part of the deal."

"I decided to demand an interest payment." The trapped leopard inside him reached out with claws that could never become real. Instead, the echo of them scraped along the insides of his skin, finding grooves laid by a lifetime of futile stretching. The movements of his beast hurt, as if skin were being torn apart. It had always hurt. And Dorian had never told anyone that it did.

Pity was the one thing he'd never accept or allow.

Now, the changeling heart of him had him moving his hand to brush over the smooth curve of Ashaya's shoulder. Hot chocolate and cream, warm and vibrant, the feel of her soaked through his fingertips and into his blood. There was no fear or panic in the profile she showed him, but he felt the faintest of tremors deep within her skin. "How bad are the fractures in your conditioning, Shaya?"

For the longest time, she said nothing. He closed his hand over her arm, and slid it down, indulging himself in the feel of her even as he pushed her to react. That deep-seated tremor didn't ebb, and then he saw her swallow.

"Bad," she whispered. "The foundation was swept away a long time ago."

He hadn't expected the admission. "And you consider that a flaw."

"No," she said, surprising him a second time. "Psy were always meant to feel. Silence is the interloper. It cripples us even as it saves us."

He stopped his stroking of her arm. "Then why not break it fully? Why cling to it?"

"Because"—her eyes locked with his, eerie in their crystal clarity—"Silence keeps the monsters at bay."

"Are you one?" He found he'd moved closer, the exotic scent of her—thick honey and wild roses—seeping into his skin, curling around his senses.

"Yes." An absolute whisper. "I'm one of the worst."

The bleak darkness of her words should have cut through the strange intimacy growing between them but it didn't. Dorian raised his hand to cup her cheek, to make her turn and look at him. "What kind of a monster saves the life of not one child but three?" He needed the answer to that question, needed the absolution it would provide.

He heard his sister's screams in his dreams. He didn't want to hear her accusations of betrayal, too. His heart twisted as the leopard withdrew into a tight ball of pain and sorrow, but still he touched Ashaya. "What have you done?"

Her lashes lifted. "I've protected a sociopath for most of my life, someone exactly like Santano Enrique."

Fury rose in a blinding wave and his hand tightened on her skin. *One second's loss of control and he could break her jaw.* Swearing, he released her and got up, turning to press his palms flat against the French doors. But the coolness of the glass did nothing to chill the red-hot crash of his anger.

From the corner of his eye, he saw Ashaya get to her feet, begin to move away. *"Don't."*

She froze, as if hearing the lack of humanity in his tone. Perhaps it was because the beast had been trapped inside him for more than three decades. Perhaps it was because he'd done everything he could to turn himself leopard though he couldn't shift. Perhaps it was just Ashaya. But at that moment, he was an inch away from losing the human half of his soul and giving in completely to the blind rage of the beast.

"I—"

"Be quiet."

Dorian's words were so lethally controlled that Ashaya knew

he was fighting the finest edge of rage. She'd miscalculated badly. No, she thought, the truth was that she hadn't calculated at all. When she was with this changeling, all her abilities at subterfuge and self-preservation seemed to disappear. With him, she spoke only the truth. But, as she had learned in the twenty-six years of her life, truth was a tool. It should never simply be said. No, it had to be bent, twisted, colored, until it became a weapon.

Now, she looked at the tight plane of Dorian's bare back, all taut muscle and golden skin, and knew that self-preservation dictated she should obey him. She should stay silent, give him time to get his emotions under control. But Ashaya hadn't escaped one cage only to be forced into another. And she didn't like the idea of a cold, controlled Dorian. It was a dangerous confession, but one that gave her the courage to face down his leopard. "You ask me to tell the truth," she said, fighting the surely lethal temptation to touch him, stroke him. "And yet when I do, you order me to silence. Hypocrisy isn't limited to the Council, I see."

His head snapped in her direction, his eyes almost incandescent with rage. "Keep going."

She might've spent her life in a lab, but she wasn't stupid. She understood he wasn't giving her permission—he was throwing down the gauntlet. Going against every one of the rules that had kept her alive this long, she picked it up. "You're attracted to me." The lush hunger of his kiss had been a living brand, leaving her permanently marked.

The bunched muscles of his forearms turned to granite. "A Psy expert in emotion?" Mockery laced with the iron strength of an anger that stung at her with the force of a whip.

"You touched me," she said. "I don't have to be an expert to understand the reason behind that."

"Do you think that makes you safe?"

"No." She took a step forward. Stopped. Because she hadn't meant to do that. "I think it puts me in more danger. You don't want to be attracted to me and I unders—"

"Don't you dare tell me you understand." He pushed off the glass to stalk to her. At that moment, she saw not the man but the leopard within. And she realized the truth far too late—he wasn't human, wasn't Psy, was *changeling*. The leopard lived in every aspect of him, from his strength to his anger to his rage.

She tried to move back. Not fast enough. He gripped her chin, held her in place. "Do you know what I understand?" he whispered, crowding her. There was no wall at her back but she couldn't make herself move, unable to break the dark intimacy of his hold. "I understand that you come from the same psychopathic race that took my sister from me.

"I understand that you're one of the monsters who protects those murderers. I *understand* that, for some reason, you make my fucking cock twitch." Brutal words, delivered in a voice that was so soft, so exquisitely balanced, it cut. "I also understand that I'm not led around by the balls and that I'll kill you before I allow you to bring that sickness into my pack."

She believed him. "Just don't take that step because of your discomfort at being attracted to me." It was a compulsion to push him, to claw back. A strange thought, since she had no claws.

His fingers tightened fractionally and he swore, low and hard. "Oh, don't worry, Ms. Aleine. Now that you've shown your true colors, all I have to do anytime I'm tempted to make a pass at you is remember that you have a hard-on for sociopaths. Any attraction I feel will die one hell of a quick death." Turning away, he strode toward his bedroom. "Get dressed. We have an early meeting to get to."

She stood in place long after he'd disappeared, staring out through the glass, but seeing nothing. Her mouth pulsed with the faded imprint of Dorian's lips, hard yet soft, a strange dichotomy. His anger had flamed off him, hot enough to singe. But—her fingers lifted to her lips—he hadn't used his power to bruise her. Not even at the end.

She knew that didn't denote any care on his part. No, it was merely part of the code he lived by. Dorian would take her life without a blink if she proved a traitor or a threat, but until then, he wouldn't hurt her. Predatory changeling men were rumored to be protective as a rule. She didn't think Dorian was any different.

Why, then, did his reaction matter? Why then did she have to fight the urge to walk into his room and demand he stop yelling at her and listen? Why then did he make her so blindingly angry that it spilled out past the broken Silence she kept trying to fix, past her need to protect Keenan, past everything?

Why then . . . did Dorian make her feel?

CHAPTER 21

There's no more time. I'll be a fugitive by the time you wake and find this letter. I go knowing that you'll keep your promise, that you'll protect her.

—From a handwritten letter signed "Iliana," circa
September 2069

Dorian was pulling on a white T-shirt when his phone beeped. "Yeah?" he snarled.

"Make sure you get Ashaya out without anyone spotting her." Clay's voice. "Teijan says people have been sniffing around."

"Gee, that's a news flash. We know the Council is hunting her."

"Not Psy. Humans."

That gave him pause. "Shit. The Omega virus. Some lamebrain wants to use it as a bioweapon."

Clay grunted in agreement. "One way to take out the Psy."

Dorian thought of a world without Psy. His gut twisted at the wrongness of the idea. "Genocide isn't pretty, no matter the target."

"I'm not going to argue with you. Tally's three percent Psy—Damn it, she hit me."

Clay's joking comment caused something to click in Dorian's brain. "Don't these idiots realize the virus would jump the race barrier so fast it'd give us whiplash? Before Silence, Psy were having children with the rest of us—hell, half the planet probably has some Psy blood. Like you said, Tally's—"

"Did I say you could call her Tally, Boy Genius?"

"And didn't I tell you to stop using that nickname or I'd throw *Talin* in the nearest body of ice-cold water?" Dorian shot back, but some of his tension receded. He frowned. "Talin's Psy blood is negligible, but if Sascha and Lucas have a kid, or Faith and Vaughn . . ."

"Council had to know," Clay said. "Omega would keep their people in line. And as a bonus, it'd wipe out the humans and pesky little changelings." A pause. "Tally says they'd probably keep some humans around to clean, sweep, and bow to their greatness in the streets."

Dorian smiled. Tally had that effect on him. If he'd expected anything, he'd expected to fall for a woman like her. Hot-tempered, crazy possessive, and loyal as hell. Instead, he found himself drawn to a woman he— He blew out a breath, trying to get a handle on his reignited temper. "Council might know, but I bet you the people trying to get their hands on the data haven't thought this through. You can't contain a virus to one race, no matter how you engineer it."

"Yeah, well, the world is full of idiots. Just keep Aleine safe." Another pause. "Tally says be nice to her—she's the reason Jon and Noor are alive. If you hurt her, I've been ordered to kick your pretty ass."

"Tell Tally thanks for the compliment." He hung up to the sound of Clay's growl. The instant he stopped concentrating on something else, Ashaya's scent rushed back into him in a wave of intoxication. Wild honey and the lush, hot bite of woman. His body grew heavy. Hungry.

I've protected a sociopath for most of my life . . .

And still he wanted her.

He didn't know who he was more disgusted with—her or himself.

They were in the car, heading out of the city, when Ashaya finally asked Dorian where they were going.

"Someone's coming to see you."

She thought that over. The list of people who might know to contact DarkRiver to reach her was very, very short. "Where's this meeting going to take place?"

"A location that won't compromise the pack."

That told her less than nothing. But she was patient. Her ability required hours upon hours of pure thought. Falling back on that ability, she brought out the slide she'd put into the small knapsack at her feet and began to focus her psychic eye. It was the part of her mind that saw not a spot of blood but the clear shapes of cells, of chromosomes, of genes.

Of the three races, it was the changelings who'd proved the most difficult to fully fingerprint. Whatever it was that allowed them to shift, it had refused to give up its genetic secrets. Ashaya knew the likelihood of her finding an anomaly, where others had failed, was very low. But for that very reason, the task was intellectually stimulating, a puzzle she was confident would take her mind off the changeling sitting only a foot from her.

She was wrong.

It was as if there was a wash of psychic heat coming off Dorian. When she paused to push up the sleeves of her white shirt, it was to find the tiny hairs on her arms standing up. "Can you tone down your energy?"

"I'm not Psy."

She pushed her sleeves back down, covering up the evidence of her unruly physical response to his proximity. "You're not a restful individual to be around."

"And if that's a surprise, you really know shit-all about changeling males." He snorted, wondering what kind of men she was used to. Then he remembered. "Larsen." The other scientist had taken, experimented on, and killed children. "You're used to reptiles."

"Larsen," she said quietly, "was truly abnormal and I knew that from the instant I met him. That's why I refused to work with him."

He'd expected a political nonanswer and gotten a glimpse of the complex, fascinating woman within the Psy shell. In spite of the caustic mix of anger and sexual need that continued to simmer in his veins, he wanted to peel apart all those layers and find out who Ashaya Aleine really was. Protector of monsters or savior of innocents? "I thought he was running an independent project in your lab."

"Later, he was." Her voice chilled a few degrees. "An experiment I didn't authorize. However, prior to that, the Council presented him to me as an assistant."

"Did anyone ever figure out that you helped Noor and Jon escape Larsen's experiments?"

"I told them the children were dead. That's why I said both the boy and Noor had to disappear when they left the lab. I don't suppose it matters now."

It mattered, Dorian thought, though he didn't say it out loud. Both children had been given new lives, a new start. They'd never have had that chance if this enigma of a woman hadn't put her life on the line. "Why did you do it? Help the kids?"

"I told you that the first time you asked me—politics."

He'd been lying along the solid branch of a heavily leafed tree at the time, eye to the scope of his rifle. Ashaya's tangled sheets and blue ice of a voice had hit him so low and hard, he'd been ready to take her then and there. "It didn't mean anything that they were innocent children?"

A long silence. "It meant something." So quiet it was less than a whisper.

The possessive, protective nature of the cat uncurled in a lazy movement. It pushed at him to reach out, to show her she wasn't alone. But that was the way of Pack. And Ashaya was nowhere close to Pack. "Another fracture in Silence?"

Putting away the slide, she leaned her head against the window. "To kill your young is a sign of true evil." There was something in that tone, a hidden secret that set his senses searching. "I prefer not to think of my entire race as evil."

"Evil, an interesting concept for a Psy."

"Is it?" She looked at him. "It's an intellectual idea as much as an emotional one, the dividing line between being human and being monstrous."

He was about to answer when she snapped upright and grabbed his arm. "No! Take the next exit."

"This is our one."

"*No.*"

Given that she was Psy, he wondered if she'd picked up something. "We being trailed?" Even as he spoke, a strange sense of dread whispered into his mind.

"Please, just go that way."

He went with gut instinct and listened. "Where are we going?"

She didn't answer, but she was doing something very un-

Psy-like and leaning forward, her hands braced on the dash. He couldn't see her eyes but he had a feeling they'd gone the pure black of a Psy utilizing a lot of power. But Ashaya was an M-Psy and, as she'd told him herself, didn't have any powers that were useful outside the lab. So either she'd lied or something else was going on.

She didn't say anything for a very long time. He'd have worried that she'd gone into some kind of a trance except that he could feel her alertness, her absolute focus. "Ashaya, we keep going this way, we miss our meeting." His own urgent sense of something being seriously wrong kept him driving.

"Don't turn back." It was an order.

Leopards, as a rule, didn't listen to anyone outside their hierarchy. In Dorian's case, the list of men and women he'd obey was very, very short. Ashaya wasn't on it. "Give me a reason."

"Get off here." She was leaning so far forward, her head almost touched the sloped windshield of the bullet-shaped car. "Get off." The strain increased when he didn't change lanes.

Intrigued despite himself, he moved with cat-swiftness and took the exit. "Now wha—"

"Straight through the intersection."

The directions kept coming, though when he asked Ashaya where they were going, she remained silent. He might've kept questioning her except that fifteen minutes from their destination, he realized where it was that she was taking them. His mouth tightened, even as he wondered how she could've possibly found out.

Twisting the wheel, he pulled to a stop on one side of a wide street, shocking Ashaya into a cry as her body slammed back in the seat. "Why are you stopping?" Her eyes were liquid night when she looked at him, so black that he could see his reflection in the mirror smoothness of them.

He turned to brace one hand against her headrest. "The only way you could know is if someone's feeding you information via the PsyNet, or through telepathic contact."

"What?" She seemed to have to force herself to think. "No one's feeding me anything."

"Then how do you know?"

"Know what?!" Her voice rose. Again, it wasn't particularly Psy. "Drive, Dorian."

He thought he heard a plea in those words, told himself he was imagining it. This woman would never unbend enough to beg anyone for anything. "Not until you tell me why we're going where we are."

"I don't know where we're going," she said, eyes wild. "I'm just following his voice."

His cat stilled. "Whose?"

"Keenan's." Her own voice was a fierce whisper as she touched her fingertips to the windshield. "My son is screaming for me. If you won't drive me, I'll walk." Her hand went to the door.

He hit the child lock. "You aren't going anywhere in this condition." She wasn't acting like herself. The ice had well and truly cracked, but it hadn't cracked right. She was unbalanced, not thinking straight, not functioning on all levels.

She slammed a fist against the door without warning. "I have to get to him."

He scented blood and he realized she'd broken skin with that single hit. Swearing, he reached over and grabbed her hands. "I'll take you."

She stared, as if she didn't believe him. "Then drive." Another order.

Releasing her hands, he did as directed. He didn't need her to tell him where to go anymore but she did so anyway, as if she couldn't control herself. The second they pulled up in front of the ranch-style house, she began to try to open her door. He hit the unlock button and she was out a second later. Even with his changeling speed, she was on the porch by the time he caught up.

He wrapped an arm around her waist. "Wait."

She twisted. "I need to—"

"You go into a leopard home without invitation, be prepared to get your face torn off." He forced her to look at him. "There might be cubs in there—their mother will rip you to shreds first and ask questions later."

Something of his words seemed to get through. "I . . . see." A battle for rational thought that made her cheekbones cut sharply against her skin. "I need to get inside."

Continuing to hold her, he pushed open the door, knowing it wouldn't be locked. Tamsyn wasn't stupid, but she also knew this home was guarded around the clock by changeling soldiers. They hadn't challenged Ashaya, but only because he was with her.

The instant they stepped foot inside the house, she elbowed him in the ribs, brought a booted foot down on his own, and took off up the steps. Too late, he remembered that Ashaya Aleine was very good at faking calm.

"Son of a—" Growl building inside his chest, he went after her.

He caught her in his arms in front of an open upstairs bedroom. He could scent Pack, but he could also scent Keenan Aleine. When he glanced inside, it was to meet Tamsyn's surprised expression as she looked up from her kneeling position beside the boy's bed. The child was lying on his side in the fetal position, apparently asleep. Tammy's cubs were nowhere to be seen so they were probably still at their grandparents' but Kit, one of the older juveniles, knelt on the other side of the bed, a frown on his face.

"Dorian?" Tammy said, her eyes flicking to Ashaya.

The sound seemed to snap her out of her shock. "Let me go!" Another elbow jab but he was already releasing her. Because there was something seriously wrong with Keenan. Dorian could feel it in his chest, a dark knot of dread, a psychic cry for help his changeling brain hadn't been able to translate into words.

But Ashaya had known.

Now, she ignored everyone to crawl into the bed and take Keenan in her arms. As Dorian watched, stunned by her transformation from logical scientist to this . . . this leopardess with her cub, she gathered the boy into her lap and spoke. "Keenan, stop it." Her voice was an unsheathed blade, ruthless and cutting.

Tammy sucked in a breath, disapproval apparent in every line of her face. "He's a child. Tone it down."

Ashaya didn't seem to hear her. "Snap out of it right this second. Do it!" Another order, this one frosted over with Psy ice.

When it looked like Tammy was going to physically intervene, Dorian stepped between her and the pair on the bed. "No," he said, not sure why he was supporting Ashaya, not sure what the hell was happening. All he knew was that Keenan was in deep trouble. "Kit," he said, when the juvenile moved, "don't touch her." Kit froze, caught between a sentinel and a healer, in a situation where rank was unclear.

Aggression rose, filling the air with the promise of violence.

CHAPTER 22

Tammy glared at Dorian. "She's whipping the boy with that voice."

"What's wrong with him?" Dorian asked, his eyes on Ashaya as she rocked back and forth, her son held fiercely tight. "I thought Sascha was staying here."

"I don't know." Tammy shoved a hand through her hair. "Sascha was here—she just popped out to deal with another situation. I was about to call her back."

"I came by for breakfast a few minutes ago," Kit picked up. "And Tammy sent me up to wake this little guy. I found him like this—he's alive, but it's like he's in a coma."

"Keenan," Ashaya said again, in that same strict voice, "if you don't stop this, you'll die."

The words were grenades thrown into the hush of the room.

"What's she talking about?" Kit whispered.

Dorian had no answers for him, but he recognized the apparent heartlessness in Ashaya's voice for what it was—sheer, maternal terror. Whatever this was, it was deadly serious. He found himself moving to put his hand on the boy's soft hair. "Keenan, wake up." A command given in the tone he usually reserved for misbehaving juveniles.

Ashaya's head jerked up. Those eerie midnight eyes held a fear so deep, he wondered how he could've possibly not seen it at the very start. She looked back down an instant later. "Keenan," she said once more, but this time it was a whisper . . . a welcome.

The boy's lids lifted. "You came." It was that old-man tone in a child's voice.

He saw Ashaya's arms clench. "I told you to never do that. *Never*, Keenan. You promised me." Again, that barely concealed thread of terror. It was the voice of a mother who'd been to the edge of desperation and who still shook with it.

"I wanted you to come," Keenan said in response, staring up at his mother, but making no move to touch her.

Ashaya said nothing, but the way she looked at that boy's face . . . it wasn't anything Dorian could've imagined. "Go," he said to Kit. This was a private moment, a moment he had to protect for Ashaya because she was too shattered to do it herself.

The boy left without a word. Tamsyn shot him a worried glance, but followed Kit out. Closing the door behind them, Dorian walked to stand at the side of the bed.

The boy's eyes flicked to him, then away.

Dorian didn't know much about Psy children, but he'd seen that same expression on too many changeling kids to count. Relief sang through his veins—Keenan truly was okay. "He broke the rules, didn't he?" He folded his arms, trying to maintain a stern expression when all he wanted to do was pick the damn cub up and make sure he hadn't harmed himself doing whatever it was he'd done.

Ashaya looked up. "Yes. What he did, it's highly dangerous." Her tone was beginning to lose that edge of panic, but she continued to crush Keenan to her. "He promised me he'd never do it again."

Dorian met Keenan's eyes. "You make a promise, you don't break it."

Keenan was only four and a half. He swallowed under the force of Dorian's quiet disapproval. "I wanted her to come."

Dorian felt for the kid. But Keenan had put himself into lethal danger. "No excuses," Dorian said, enunciating a rule taught to all cubs in DarkRiver. "If you can't keep a promise, you don't make it."

Keenan struggled to sit up in his mother's arms. After a pause when Ashaya seemed unable to let him go, she allowed him to perch in her lap. But the boy's attention was on Dorian. "I'm sorry."

Dorian raised a brow. "Sorry doesn't wipe the slate clean. You can only do that by keeping your promise from now on." Perhaps he was being harsh but if this was life-and-death, Keenan needed to have that drummed into him. "Can you do that? Can we trust you?"

A quick nod. "Yes. I won't do it again."

"Promise," Ashaya demanded, her voice husky. "Promise me."

Keenan turned to her. "I promise." Then he laid his head against her shoulder and wrapped his arms around her neck. "I knew you'd come."

After a fragile, frozen moment, Ashaya seemed to crumble. Her hand rose trembling to his head, her body softening and curving in a protective curl. "Oh, Keenan." It was a whisper that held such abiding love that Dorian couldn't believe she'd managed to hide it for so long.

What had it cost her to bury that depth of emotion?

Ashaya knew she'd made what could be a fatal mistake, but she'd stopped thinking like a rational being the instant she'd felt Keenan's withdrawal. She hadn't cared that Amara could exploit the weakness of emotion to burrow into her mind. But now, the fear that Amara had done exactly that, and discovered the fact of Keenan's continued existence, had her checking desperately for any hint of a breach. What she found was something else altogether—a wall of powerful new shields between her and Amara, shields full of color . . . and chaos. Beautiful and *wild*, reminding her strangely of Dorian.

A movement in her arms, as Keenan wriggled to a sitting position.

A child, she thought, he was only a child. No one should have to carry the burden that Keenan carried, a burden she'd never been able to shield him from. Because he had to know why there were some secrets he could never whisper, some truths he could never tell.

"Can I go play?" he asked . . . but not of her.

"Go on." Dorian nodded, pushing back that silky hair of his when it slid onto his forehead. "But stay in the house for now."

"Okay." Scrambling off the bed, he scampered across the floor.

Dorian picked him up before he could reach the door. Keenan made a startled sound, but threw his arms around the changeling male and whispered something Ashaya couldn't catch. It didn't matter. The sharp grin that cut across Dorian's face said everything—her baby boy trusted him. She could almost see the bond between the lethal sniper and the tiny boy he held tight in his arms. It was as solid as rock.

"Try and be good the rest of the day, K-Man." Before putting him back down on his feet, Dorian kissed Keenan on the cheek with an open affection that made her wonder what it would be to have his trust.

"I will." Keenan nodded and headed for the door. But he stopped before opening it, looking over his shoulder at Ashaya. "Are you going?"

She knew she should leave, draw Amara away. But still she said, "No. I'll be here."

A shy little smile. Then, reaching up on tiptoe to twist the knob, he wandered out. Ashaya didn't move from the bed, intensely aware of being watched by Dorian, this male who made her react in ways wholly outside her experience.

The door closed again with a quiet snick. "Ignoring me won't make me go away." A low masculine statement devoid of the mockery she usually heard. Instead there was a dangerous kind of beauty in it—something deeper than charm.

Her instincts snapped awake in wary defense. "I was simply contemplating how to repair this break in my conditioning." She'd been hiding her true self for so long, it was an automatic response.

He sat down bare inches in front of her, a living wall of warm male flesh and intractable leopard will. "Admit it before I make you."

There was no way she could avoid meeting his gaze now. The intimacy of it threatened to steal her breath. "I can hardly deny the truth. My maternal instincts broke through the currently fractured walls of my silence."

"Bullshit." The harsh word cut through the air with the

efficiency of a knife. "Forget the crap about fractures and repairs. We both know you haven't been conditioned in a long time—if ever." He lay back down on his elbows, looking up at her. The pose was relaxed, his eyes anything but.

Ashaya had prepared for this contingency, for being found out so very completely. But her scenarios had all revolved around the Council. Around lies told with a face devoid of emotion. "I suffer from severe claustrophobia," she said, unable to lie to Dorian, but needing to distract him from the one secret no one could learn.

His eyes darkened to a deeper, almost midnight blue. "And the Council let that go?"

"It didn't affect my work," she said. "I was even able to survive in the underground lab—though it was becoming increasingly difficult. I lost sleep, began to be prone to erratic behavior." She was hoping he'd make his own conclusions, but Dorian was too intelligent to be that easily led.

"How long have you been claustrophobic?"

Dirt sliding through the cracks, the most vivid nightmare memory. But it hadn't begun then. "Since I was fourteen. Amara and I were both buried during an earthquake—we were living in Zambia at the time and the structure wasn't earthquake safe. The house literally collapsed on top of us." They'd been encased in a pitch-black nightmare of pain for close to forty-eight hours. Her twin had kept Ashaya sane. And that was both an irony . . . and the chain that tied her hands.

"That's when you first broke Silence?"

She nodded. "Though I hadn't finished my course through the Protocol. That happens unofficially at sixteen, and officially at eighteen."

"And Amara?"

"Her Silence didn't fracture." Not the truth. Not a lie either. She kept talking, hoping to distract him from the treacherous subject of her twin. "I was given intensive reconditioning, and everyone—including me—believed the damage done by my inadvertent burial had been corrected."

Dorian sat back up in a graceful move that made her stomach clench, and reached out to tip up her chin. "You were a child, injured and traumatized—that kind of thing doesn't go away."

She shook her head, undone by the gentleness of his touch . . . the tenderness of it. "It can. Psy trainers are very, very good at wiping away emotional wounds. I would've been . . . grateful had they wiped away mine."

He continued to touch her, the wild energy of him an electric pulse against her. "Pain is a sign of life," he argued.

"It can also cripple." She held his gaze, saw his understanding in the hard line of his jaw.

His fingers tightened, then dropped off. "We're talking about you. What happened after the reconditioning finished?"

"I thought I was coping, but it soon became apparent that the damage done during the quake was permanent. My conditioning kept splintering."

"You didn't tell anyone." He shifted closer, into the direct path of the sunlight coming in through the bedroom window. The golden beams skipped over his hair to graze the shadow of his stubble.

"No, I did." Her fingers curled into her palms as she fought the sudden, sharp urge to know what the roughness would feel like against her skin. "I told my mother."

"And?" His tone of voice said he knew about mothers in the PsyNet.

But she knew he didn't. "She told me to hide it." Ashaya had argued with her mother. She'd just wanted the nightmares to go away. "She was . . . different." A difference that had sealed her short, brilliant life. "She told me that Silence was the imposition, that I would be better, stronger, more human, without it. Then she told me to learn to hide the broken pieces, hide them so well that no one would ever question who I was."

Neither Ashaya nor her mother had ever stated the other thing that had become obvious in the preceding months, the thing that meant Ashaya's Silence would keep fragmenting, no matter how hard or well she tried to follow the rules. Her claustrophobia had simply given them a convenient target on which to place the blame.

"A wise woman. Her name was Iliana, wasn't it?" Dorian's fingers trailed over her cheek. It was a featherlight brush, gone within an instant, but her stomach tightened, growing hot with a new kind of terror.

He could break her, she thought, this leopard with his blue eyes and his deep-rooted rage. "Yes. She's dead. The Council killed her."

Dorian found that he'd moved so close, his lips were now bare centimeters from hers, the scent of her an intoxicating brew that almost made him forget why he'd been so angry with her. "You sound very sure."

"She worked for the Council's pharmaceutical arm." The buried anger in her words scraped a claw over his skin. "She was also a rebel. When they found out, she tried to run. They tracked and bagged her like you would an animal."

Another piece of the puzzle that was Ashaya Aleine snapped into place. "I'm sorry."

"Why?" A cool question, yet it held an almost childish lack of understanding. "Why does my attachment to Iliana matter to you? You had no connection to her."

"Because she mattered to you."

"You have no connection to me, either." Wary eyes.

He'd been a fucking stupid bastard, he thought with cold fury. Ashaya might not be Sascha, with her open warmth, but she was no calculating monster, either. She'd not only cared for her mother, she loved her son. And that excused a multitude of sins.

I've protected a sociopath for most of my life.

They'd get to that, too, he thought with grim purpose. He was through being blinded by the bloody darkness of the past. "Don't I?" Moving with the whiplash speed that was natural to his kind, he changed position to kneel on the bed. She remained absolutely still as he began to undo the tight braids she always wore. A couple of minutes later, her hair tumbled around her in crackling waves. It was just past shoulder length, but so curly, so wildly beautiful that the animal in him was entranced by it.

He thrust his hands into it and tipped up her head, looking down into the crystal clarity of her eyes. "Don't I?" he said again and this time it was a demand. "Answer me." The cat was possessive by nature. So was the man. And both had marked Ashaya.

"What answer do you want to hear?" It was a dare to his feline soul.

He growled low in his throat and the sound translated through his human vocal cords. "The truth."

She stared at him for several more seconds. "You're something I've never experienced. I'm fascinated by you and I know that's a weakness you'll exploit."

"That much honesty can be dangerous." He dipped his head

while tugging hers farther back, the electric wildness of her hair moving over his hands like fire. That stuff, God, he knew he was going to be having all sorts of erotic dreams about Ashaya's hair.

"But," he whispered against her mouth, "it can also reap rewards." Knowing he'd never be able to stop if he started kissing her, he brushed his lips over the taut cords of her neck. She sucked in a breath. Unable to resist, he grazed her with his teeth. Her start was slight but he felt it. He nuzzled at her. "I won't hurt you."

Her hand crept up to his shoulder. "You yelled at me. You said I had a hard-on for sociopaths."

He didn't want to think about that right now, didn't want to consider the irrevocable lines he was crossing . . . the betrayals he was committing. Against Kylie's memory, against his own vows—to annihilate the Psy, to keep his distance from this woman who might yet prove to be an enemy.

For this one instant, he was just a man and she was a beautiful woman who was his own personal aphrodisiac. "Doesn't mean I can't take a bite out of you." He closed his teeth playfully over her pulse for a second.

She shuddered. "I don't understand you."

"Your body does." He tasted the ragged beat beneath his lips. "Does it feel bad?"

The unambiguous question seemed to be what she needed. "No. The sensations are . . . pleasurable. But it's dangerous—I'm in the PsyNet."

Frowning, he raised his head. "And no one's unmasked you?" There was something very wrong about that.

Before she could answer, a noise intruded.

The leopard went hunting quiet.

CHAPTER 23

I've met him—the sniper . . . Dorian. He confuses me on the
most fundamental level. I have the irrational fear that if I'm
not careful, he'll take me over. Yet part of me wants to take
the chance. Part of me hungers to tangle with this leopard
barely clothed in human skin.

—From the encrypted personal files of Ashaya Aleine

Dorian relaxed as he recognized the approaching tread.
"Kit's coming."

"Let go." Ashaya tried to pull away the hands still fisted in her
hair.

He liked the feel of her touching him, soft feminine heat and
frustration. "Kit," he called out, not releasing her, "we'll be down
in a sec."

The juvenile stopped, his hearing good enough to have
caught Dorian's words despite the distance and the closed door.
"Oooookay."

Ashaya tugged at his wrists again. "I need to go check on
Keenan."

He freed her—the terror she'd felt for Keenan continued to
echo in her eyes. "What did he do?" he asked as he got off the
bed. "What freaked you out so badly?"

She stood up and began to twist her hair into a single braid.
"Keenan is highly intelligent. His IQ has been tested in the genius
range." Finishing her braid, she turned back to the bedspread to
search for the hair ties.

He leaned against the door and watched her. It was a nice view. "And?"

"And"—she found the hair ties and secured her braid before turning to face him—"it means he likes playing inside his mind. That's fine, but because of his telepathic gifts, he possesses the ability to go so deep that his brain 'forgets' about his physical body. Things stop working—I'm afraid one day, he'll compromise a critical organ."

Dorian scowled. "No fail-safes?" Most living organisms had some natural fight reaction.

"No," she said and glanced away. "No, he wasn't born with those."

He tasted the lie, but couldn't figure out what she could possibly have to hide on the point. "His stay with the Council had to have exacerbated the tendency." Violence stirred within him at the memory of how he'd found Keenan—the blindfold, the earplugs.

"Yes." A flat statement that may as well have been a blade, it held such deadly intent. "But we practised building a manual fail-safe each time he came to visit—doing it until it was almost instinctive—and he kept his promise."

Stubborn kid, Dorian thought, pleased. "Can we trust him to keep his word after this lapse?"

"I think so." A pause. "I believe he only broke it today because he was scared of being in an unfamiliar environment."

Dorian gave a short nod, and pulled open the door. Ashaya's face was perfect in its expressionlessness as she walked through, but he wasn't going to be fooled again. He could scent the confusion in her—and, hidden in that confusion—a distinct thread of feminine arousal. His leopard clawed at him, desperate to get to her. It felt like knives gouging at him from the inside out. "Let's get downstairs," he said, knowing his tone was on the wrong side of feral.

Ashaya began to follow him down. "You're prone to mood swings."

Mood swings? He stopped halfway down the steps. "Women have mood swings. Not men." It was a growl.

"That's untrue." She kept walking, completely unaware of the danger of having a pissed-off leopard at her back. "But it's a misapprehension many people share," she threw back over her shoulder as she reached the ground floor. "Men are as prone to the chemical imbalances that cause shifts in mood."

Dorian caught up to her in seconds, but didn't have time to correct her own "misapprehension" before they reached the kitchen. Tammy and Kit were both sipping coffee inside, and he could hear the sound of cartoons from the living room off to the right. "Twins still at your folks'?"

"Yes." Putting down her coffee, Tammy shot Ashaya a considering glance. "I apologize if this offends you but we weren't sure about Keenan. I sent my children to stay with my parents until we could figure out if he was safe to have around the cubs."

Ashaya didn't look away from Tammy's direct gaze. "He's only dangerous to himself. His telepathy is strong, but nowhere near strong enough to break changeling shields."

Tammy nodded. "Fine. But I'm going to wait for someone I trust to confirm that. Right now, he hasn't interacted enough with Sascha for her to make the call."

"Of course." Ashaya sounded so cool and collected that if Dorian hadn't seen her curled around Keenan today, he'd have believed she didn't care a whit. And he wouldn't have heard the fury buried beneath the politeness.

Ashaya *did not* like her son being treated as if he might be a danger to others. Dorian couldn't blame her. Neither, he knew, would Tammy. Protectiveness in a mother was expected. They'd just never thought to see it in one of the Psy. Not after the way Sascha's mother, Councilor Nikita Duncan, had cut her off.

"Kit"—Dorian jerked his head toward the lounge—"go make sure Keenan's okay."

"He's fine." Kit watched Ashaya with barely hidden fascination—he'd clearly picked up too much in that short visit upstairs. Dorian wasn't surprised. Not only did Kit carry the scent of a future alpha, he was very close to having his rank shift officially from juvenile to adult. "I checked on him a minute ago."

Dorian didn't say a word.

"Shit," the tall, auburn-haired male said and walked out, mumbling "I never get to hear anything interesting" under his breath.

Tammy's lips curved slightly after he was gone. "He's turning into a wonderful young man, but sometimes the child shows through."

"At least he has the excuse of being in his teens," Ashaya said so primly that it took Dorian a few seconds to realize she was referring to him and his "mood swings."

His eyes narrowed, but the cat was delighted at what it considered "play." "Tammy needs to know what you told me about Keenan."

For a moment, it looked as if she'd refuse. But then she nodded and complied. "If this ever happens again, and I'm out of contact, get one of the Psy in your pack to do a telepathic blast. It's a very loud noise on the psychic plane. Or"—she paused, glanced at Dorian—"you could shake him awake via whatever network it is that he's linked into."

Dorian shrugged. "I have no idea what you're talking about."

"Keenan is no longer in the PsyNet," she said. "Psy need biofeedback to survive. Which means—since he's alive and well—that you've found an alternate way to feed his mind, just as your pack feeds Sascha's and Faith's minds." Her words were staccato, perfectly enunciated. "You're lying to me."

Dorian stepped closer, until they were toe to toe. "So?"

She blinked, as if caught by surprise. "So don't treat me like an imbecile."

"Then don't ask questions to which you haven't earned an answer." Ashaya might love her son, but too many questions remained. It was one thing for him to kiss her, quite another to trust her with information that could be used to hurt the pack. Especially when she kept her secrets. "You haven't exactly been forthcoming, Ms. Aleine."

"Why would I want to share anything with a man who yells at me twenty-three hours of every day, then kisses me?"

A pointed cough had him snapping his head toward Tamsyn. The DarkRiver healer's face held open interest. He felt his jaw set. "Leave it," he said, turning on his heel and pulling out his cell phone at the same time. "I'll call and reschedule Ashaya's meeting." He pushed through the back door, heading out into the yard.

Leave it, he'd said to Tammy. But he knew she wouldn't. Pack was family. But it was also a pain in the ass sometimes. Hell, he didn't know what the fuck was happening with him and

Ashaya. He didn't need anyone else pointing that out. Nor did he need their censure.

Not when Kylie's ghost berated him with every breath he took.

I've protected a sociopath for most of my life.

Yeah, he knew exactly how big a mess this was.

Ashaya looked across the counter to the tall brunette who'd been taking care of her son. "Thank you for what you've done for Keenan."

"He's a child," came the response. "There was no other choice."

"Even when he might be a child who could hurt your own?"

The woman named Tamsyn walked to the eco-cooler and pulled out a gallon of milk. "I don't think Keenan would do anything on purpose. Like my cubs would never seek to use their claws and teeth to maul a human playmate. That doesn't change the fact that they *do* have those claws and teeth." Putting the milk on the counter, she went to grab containers of cereal as well as a loaf of bread.

"He has control," Ashaya argued. "My son has more control than any child his age should have."

"I'm beginning to see that." Tamsyn put several bowls and spoons on the counter. "Could you set the table?"

Ashaya did as asked.

"Does he need to have that control?" Tamsyn asked, betraying a knowledge of Silence that didn't surprise Ashaya, not when DarkRiver was home to two incredibly powerful Psy. Sascha Duncan was rumored to possess an ability that wasn't in any of the classification charts, while Faith NightStar saw the future itself.

"Not in the sense that his abilities are dangerous," she said.

"But?" The other woman's eyes were dark, intent.

"But he needs the control right now." Ashaya decided to stick to the bare facts. "There are those who would track him." If Amara got her hands on Keenan— She cut off that line of thought before it could attract the very person she wanted to avoid. "I'm working to ensure his safety, but until then, he has to be very careful how much of himself he reveals on a telepathic level." Technically, Amara's telepathy was as weak as Ashaya's, but Ashaya had learned to never underestimate her twin.

Tamsyn folded her arms. "I accept that. But let me tell you something, Ashaya—I love kids. I won't stand for his being in pain."

"Good."

"You know," the other woman said, breaking into a sudden smile, "I think you and Tally will get on very, very well."

Right then, Dorian walked back in. "I've rescheduled—had to move the meeting to a central location to accommodate your guest. We have to get going."

"Give me a minute." Making her way to the living room, she found Keenan seated quietly in front of Kit, absorbed by the fluid movement of Kit's hands.

A coin trick, she saw a moment later.

Keenan's fascination was no surprise—her baby had always been attracted to shiny things. A small flaw, negligible in a child. Only Ashaya had wondered if the predilection arose from the secret he carried within. The shiny things would reflect attention off him, making him invisible. Or perhaps, she thought as she knelt beside him, she was seeing too much into a child's simple pleasures.

"You're going," he guessed, lips trembling for an instant before he bit down, reining in his emotions.

Her heart hurt. One day, she promised silently, one day, he wouldn't have to hide anything. "But I'll be back." It was out before she could censor herself. So she didn't even try. Raising her hand, she cupped his cheek as she hadn't dared to do for so many years. "Be good, little man. I return tonight."

Thin arms wrapped around her neck with surprising strength. "I'll wait for you . . . Mommy."

They were in the car before Ashaya allowed the impact of those words to filter through her. How would it affect Keenan if she didn't return as she'd promised—tonight or any other night? "Will you look after my son if I don't make it?"

Dorian's jaw firmed to a tight line. "The fact you need to ask that tells me how little you know about DarkRiver. And no one's touching you while I'm around."

She didn't know where her next words came from. "You're the only one allowed to execute me if I prove a traitor?"

His lips twitched. "Yes. So you be good, too."

Feeling the quicksand shifting under her feet, she took a step back. "You didn't tell me who this meeting was with."

He made a sound of disappointment at her retreat. "Kiss me and I'll talk."

She knew he was trying to annoy her on purpose. "Do cats take pleasure in being inscrutable?"

"Maybe. How's the DNA voodoo going?" Amusement, not mockery.

She didn't blame him for his disbelief—to him, her avowed ability had to stretch the bounds of impossibility. But to her, it made perfect sense, being the extreme end of the M-Psy spectrum. "It's a slow process. Do you think I could get a control sample from one of your packmates for comparison?"

"Sure." He shrugged. "It's not like the Psy haven't got our DNA already."

"I was never in that field of research."

"Field?"

"Biological weapons designed specifically to target your populations."

Dorian's hands clenched on the manual controls. "We guessed, but no one's ever been able to confirm."

"That outbreak of virulent flu in Nova Scotia three years ago? It was meant to be limited to the changelings in the area." She finally felt as if she was giving DarkRiver something of value in return for the priceless gift they'd given her in protecting Keenan.

Dorian whistled. "It spread—to humans and then the Psy. Damn, I was right."

"About what?"

"You first."

Curious, she decided to cooperate. "What the scientists working on these projects don't seem to accept—and I don't know if it's willful blindness, or an inability to see the obvious because of bias—is that despite our racial differences, we are one species. It's why we can interbreed. Our genes are simply expressed in different forms."

"You can't engineer a virus to affect one without affecting the others?"

"Yes."

"That's what I thought about Omega," Dorian said. "It was never about controlling the Psy, but the world." He glanced at her, smiling in a way that made her stomach feel all tight and hot. "Bet you didn't think us nonscientist types could figure that out."

Again, the words came out without thought, born in that cluster of neurons that sparked for him alone. "Bet you didn't know anything about Omega before my broadcast."

"You win . . . this time." He smiled, but his next question was serious. "Is there any chance that you're wrong and a completed virus exists?"

Ashaya lied without a pause. "No." On this one subject, he'd have to earn her utter, unflinching loyalty before she trusted him. And it wasn't exactly a lie. Because there *was* no Omega virus. There was something worse.

Dorian didn't say anything for several minutes. "You're lying, Shaya."

Her palms dampened. "Excuse me?"

"Stop freaking out." Reaching over, he slid his hand behind her nape, tugged her to him, and nipped at her lower lip, startling her into a gasp. "I've decided not to kill you, whatever happens." He released her. "I'll just keep you in my personal dungeon instead."

Ashaya swallowed, her wires completely scrambled by the raw hunger of that kiss—and the teasing amusement in his voice.

"Whatever it is you're hiding," he said, turning into a busy street in Chinatown, "I'll figure it out."

The warning was enough to snap her brain back into action. "There's nothing to figure out." People crossed in front of them, paying no heed to the traffic signals. "This area of the city is notoriously chaotic. Why here for the meeting?"

"Because"—he beeped the horn and the wave of humanity parted—"Psy don't like chaos." He rolled down the window as they passed and called out a greeting in what she thought might be Cantonese.

It felt like several thousand people responded. But only one lanky boy ran up to them. "Hey, Dorian." The youngster's face was bright with mischief, his eyes sparkling obsidian in a face that spoke of eastern shores and California sun all in one fine-boned package. "We had some folk"—his eyes flicked to Ashaya—"come around asking about her. They showed her picture around."

CHAPTER 24

We wait. We can't yet afford to openly challenge the Psy Council. But be ready to take advantage of any mistakes. As for the changelings, they're focused on the Council. They won't expect us. We're no threat, after all.

—Encrypted e-mail sent from the sunken city of Venice to unknown number of recipients in San Francisco

"Human?" Dorian asked, recalling the Rats' tip about humans asking after Ashaya.

"No. Like her."

"They get anything?"

The boy looked insulted. "Hell, no."

"Watch the language, Jimmy. I know your mother."

The teenager rolled his eyes. "They asked about your sexy girlfriend"—a mischievous grin—"but it's *amazing* how many people are shortsighted around here. Man, it's like an epidemic or something."

"Maybe we should hire an optometrist," Dorian said dryly.

"If you do, tell the doc the shortsightedness comes on without warning, and seems to affect dozens of people at a time." Grinning, Jimmy glanced down the street. "Some traffic coming up. Anyway, we'll let you know if they come back." He slipped away, merging expertly into the energetic bustle of Chinatown.

Dorian rolled up his window and continued through the intersection. "No surprise they're hunting you."

"No." She wrapped her arms around herself. A betraying gesture if he hadn't already known her Silence for a sham. "You didn't pay the boy for his information," she said. "Isn't that how it works?"

"Not here." He turned down a narrow street lined with tea merchants on either side. "We're part of Chinatown. We take care of them, they take of us."

"They can't be bought?"

"The relationship's had over a decade to mature—the people round here know they can count on us when the shit hits the fan. We've busted heads for them, tracked down missing children, dragged others back to face judgment." He shrugged. "So no, they can't be bought. We're family."

"But only Pack is family for you."

He reached over and ran his knuckles down the curve of her neck. A fleeting touch, but it took the edge off the escalating depth of his need. "Pack is family," he said, knowing it was no longer a question of *if*, but *when* he'd have Ashaya in his bed. "But we can widen the net if we choose. And we stand by those who stand by us.

"Plus, some of them *are* Pack." Dorian had first met Ria on these streets. Fully human, the vivacious brunette was now Lucas's personal assistant and mated to a DarkRiver leopard. But the night Dorian had first seen her, she'd been crawling backward on her hands and feet in a dark alleyway, face bloodied and shirt ripped.

Her parents had fallen foul of some would-be shakedown artist and he'd decided to use her to teach them a lesson. A few years older at the time than Kit was now, Dorian had taken one look, picked the creep up, and thrown him against the nearest wall. It happened to be old-fashioned brick. The bastard had had twenty broken bones when they peeled him off the ground. "Who do you stand by, Shaya?"

The answer was unexpected. "Keenan, Amara, and a handful of others."

"Good answer," he said, conscious of the leopard padding restlessly around the cage of his body. The hunger to shift, to release the other half of his soul, was a familiar ache—the leopard had never truly understood that it couldn't get out.

Thankfully, Ashaya spoke then. "Was it a test?" The blue ice and wild honey of her voice wrapped around the cat, soothing it into settling down.

"Don't worry. You passed." He shot her a grim look. "The Council didn't have to resort to medical torture to hold you—you would've done it for the love of Keenan."

"Yes. But they don't comprehend love."

He turned the car into the wide-open goods entrance of an empty warehouse. Behind them, the door rolled down. He knew that within two minutes, the street outside would be covered with market stalls selling anything from fresh produce to touristy shtick.

One time Aaron had lost his mind and put up a stall selling those yapping dog robots that drove Dorian insane. The younger male hadn't made that mistake again. And he'd become damn smooth at his job. No one saw a twenty-one-year-old DarkRiver soldier when they saw Aaron. They saw a slender Asian teenager with a bright smile who drove a hard bargain. That reminded Dorian—he needed to talk to Lucas about Aaron. It was time to move him up the security hierarchy.

"Zie Zen," Ashaya said, staring through the windshield to the man who sat in a chair in the middle of the warehouse, his hand on a cane.

There were several DarkRiver men and women in the warehouse, but no one disturbed his solitude. Zie Zen's face was sharp, lined with age but not fragile. Instead, there was a honed strength in it. Dorian found himself judging the other man and finding him a worthy opponent. But he was far too old. "You chose him as the father of your child? Why?"

Ashaya stopped with her hand on the door handle. "It's not sexual in the way of changelings. Zie Zen had the best genes."

"Wait," he said when she would've exited. "According to our sources, he's a powerful man—why did he let them take Keenan?"

Her hand tightened on the handle. "Zie Zen has other biological children—going up against a Council order mandating 'specialized instruction' for a single child, a child without any exceptional psychic abilities, and one for whom he isn't the custodial parent, would've rung serious alarm bells."

"Let me guess—a true Psy would simply write that child off as a bad investment?"

A nod. "However, his position meant the Councilors treaded softly—they didn't want to make an enemy out of him when they could keep things trouble-free by allowing him his rights under the co-parenting agreement, and acceding to his request that I continue to train Keenan."

"But if he'd pushed for much more," Dorian said, seeing the tightrope they'd walked, "the Council might've become suspicious enough to investigate, and discovered his rebel activities." Leaving Keenan utterly vulnerable.

"Yes." With that Ashaya got out and began to walk toward the man who, in changeling society, would have been her mate.

Dorian didn't like it. Gritting his teeth, he slid his own door up and reached her just as she got to the rigid figure of Zie Zen.

"What are you doing here?" Ashaya asked, not touching him, not making any contact at all.

Zie Zen put weight on his cane and stood. "I have information for you." He glanced at Dorian. "Confidential information."

"Wait." Dorian called out to the others, clearing the warehouse. When he turned back, Zie Zen looked at him questioningly. "I stay."

The Psy male held his gaze for several long moments, then nodded. "Your shields are very strong."

Dorian wondered if the old man was trying to make him angry by implying that he'd attempted some form of mental persuasion. Psy were more than adept at exploiting the "weakness" of emotion against the other races. Instead of getting angry, Dorian folded his arms and shrugged. "Lucky for me. Now talk. We don't have much time. This place is clear for the moment, but that won't last." Chinatown was a safer meeting spot than pretty much any other part of town, but, as the SnowDancers had recently discovered, spies were everywhere, even where you least expected.

Ashaya shot him a quelling glance. "Treat Zie Zen with respect. He is as much a warrior for my people as you are for yours."

It was a slap down—delivered in a very prissy ladylike voice—but a slap down nonetheless. Dorian's cat liked the show of feminine strength. "Respect is earned." But he toned down his aggressiveness.

The old man looked from him to Ashaya, appearing to see

more than he should. But when he spoke, it was all business. "You've made yourself the number one priority for the Council. They'll attempt to capture you first. If that fails, the death squads will be set loose."

Dorian felt his leopard flex its claws. "How good's your information?"

Zie Zen looked to him. "I was told we have a mutual acquaintance. He can't risk contact with DarkRiver at present, even that which appears for business alone."

Anthony Kyriakus.

"Then your information is good." He was aware of Ashaya looking from him to Zie Zen, and, though her expression didn't change, he could tell she was irritated. Ms. Aleine, he thought with an inward grin, didn't like being left out of the loop.

"Ashaya." Zie Zen's attention shifted. "We had a plan in place to extract Keenan."

"Not fast enough." Ashaya's jaw set. "Any more waiting and he would've been permanently damaged by the circumstances of his confinement. They were *hurting* him."

"I'm not going to argue with you about Keenan's welfare, but you took another step we weren't prepared for." Censure, delivered in cool Psy tones, but Dorian recognized an elder's criticism when he heard it.

Funny, he was no longer thinking of Zie Zen as Ashaya's husband of sorts. The relationship was clearly something quite different. He got more proof of that when Ashaya looked down at her feet.

Well, hell. Dorian's eyes narrowed—*he'd* never been able to make her back down. But, he thought, even he—tough-shit sentinel that he was—bowed his head in front of his mother. He'd bet on Zie Zen not being Keenan's father, even in the cold, scientific way of the Psy.

"It was the only way," she said at last. "I had to make sure Omega would never be completed."

"We both know that Omega is not, and has never been, an active project. You also know that we were working to remove even the idea of it from the arsenal."

This time, Ashaya's spine went stiff and she looked up. "Too slow."

Zie Zen held her gaze. "You lied in order to gain publicity.

What we can't understand is why, not when you've never before shown any political aspirations." When Ashaya remained mute, he said, "Amara has been co-opted by the Council."

Ashaya's defiance seemed to disappear. "No. She's too smart to get caught."

"Something tripped her up." Zie Zen reached into his pocket.

Dorian didn't make any aggressive moves—he worked with weapons almost every day; he knew the older man had plain paper in his pocket.

"Here." The Psy male passed an envelope to Ashaya. "It's a message from her."

Ashaya stared at the envelope as if it was a live snake. "I don't want it."

"That's irrational behavior. She's the only one capable of reinitiating the Implant Protocol and undoing everything you've achieved."

When Ashaya still refused to accept the letter, Dorian reached out and took it from the other man. "I'll make sure she reads it."

Zie Zen gave a slow nod. "Make certain she also gets her shields back in place. She's breaking."

"No." Dorian would not put Ashaya back behind that wall of ice. "She's becoming who she was always meant to be."

Zie Zen's eyes flickered, before snapping to Ashaya. "You haven't told him."

Dorian felt a prickle at the back of his neck, the honed instincts of a hundred predators before him. "Ashaya?"

She gave him a look that could've cut glass. "This is not your business."

And that was when Dorian crossed over a very defined line in his head. "Yes," he said. "It is."

Zie Zen glanced at his sleek silver timepiece. "I must go."

"Your pickup about to arrive?"

Zie Zen nodded. A second later, a Psy male in a black uniform blinked into place. Ashaya glanced at the Tk-Psy but didn't say anything as the man nodded once at Dorian, then teleported both himself and Zie Zen out of the warehouse.

"Don't you care that they know about your pack's part in this?"

"They have no real information to use against us." Dorian shrugged. "And the Council knows we hate their guts."

Ashaya refused to look at him as he moved ever closer. The heat of him seeped through her back and into her bones as he stopped behind her. She waited for him to speak but he said nothing. She'd noticed that about him. Dorian always waited. Knowing the tactic didn't make it any less disconcerting.

A breath whispered past her ear and she knew he was bending down. His lips touched the sensitive skin of her nape. Light, so light, they could've been butterfly wings. But she felt them. They burned. And still she didn't move.

"You lied about Omega being an active project."

Relieved at the topic, she said, "So?"

The next question wasn't so easy. "What was Zie Zen talking about? What haven't you told me?"

She kept her silence even as she felt her body begin to burn from the inside out.

His fingers brushed over her. Gentle, teasing touches along her neck. Invitations to surrender . . . to sin. "Stop," she whispered.

"Why?"

"Because I can't break open. Not fully." Every time her internal shields dropped, Amara whispered to her. Ashaya was in no doubt that her sister already had a lock on her physical position.

Heat, sweet, teasing heat against the lobe of her ear. The brush of lips that looked so hard when he was angry, but felt velvety soft. It made her shiver. "Dorian, you have to stop. I told you, I can't simply forget Sile—"

"Why?"

He was so close, the lean hardness of him pressed against her like living fire.

She swallowed. "I *can't.*"

"Why?" Insistent. Adamant.

"Because if I do," she said, shattering a silence she'd kept for more years than she could count, "then Amara will find me." She hoped he hadn't noticed her minute hesitation. Because it wasn't for herself that she feared—she would live if Amara found her.

Keenan wouldn't.

And even that wasn't the true horror of it.

Dorian pulled back. "Explain."

Ashaya wondered where to start. She'd just opened her mouth when Dorian's cell phone began beeping. He kept one hand on her hip as he checked the readout. "It's Jimmy." A pause, followed by a rapid-fire conversation. "Yeah? When? Okay, get the hell away from them. No, that's all I need." Hanging up, he filled her in. "More Psy on the streets—they obviously know you're here but not where."

"Amara." She knew in her gut that the information had come from Amara, but her sister wouldn't have given them the exact location. That wasn't how the game was played. "She—"

Dorian cut her off. "You can explain later. Right now, we need to get you out of the hot zone."

"Why can't we stay here?"

He squeezed her hip and the sensation was an electric current crackling over her body. "Telepathic scans might be illegal, but these aren't boy scouts we're dealing with. All it'll take is for them to scan one person who saw you in the car. Come on." He grabbed her hand.

To her surprise, he didn't lead her toward the parked car. They headed to the back of the structure instead. He pushed open a small door and pulled her through to the bright sunshine of the early summer's day. She was still trying to acclimatize her eyes to the light when they went through the back door of another building and then downstairs.

"Where are we going?" she gasped as they jogged down the narrow corridor and to the door at the end.

"Wait and see." Giving her a sharp grin, he twisted open the lock on the door and began to pull her through.

She had just enough time to see the exposed earth walls, the wooden beams holding up the ceiling, the darkness, before her mind revolted. "No! Dorian, no! *Please!*" She dragged her feet, but he was too strong and his momentum threatened to carry them through the door and into the pitch-black of the tunnel.

CHAPTER 25

The second he heard Ashaya scream, Dorian came to a complete stop. She slammed into his chest as he turned instinctively to catch her. The air punched out of him but he was more worried about the damage to her. Psy bones were far weaker than changeling or even human. It was the trade-off nature had apparently made for their powerful minds.

He held her to him as he ran his hands over her back, silently calling himself every name in the book. "Jesus, I'm sorry." He couldn't get the absolute terror in that begging *"please"* out of his mind. He'd made this proud, strong woman beg, and he hated himself for it. "Are you all right?"

He thought she might've nodded against his chest but didn't take any chances, running his hands down her arms to check for injury. "Shaya?"

"I'm fine." She pushed away from him and though she tried to appear unfazed, there was a broken wildness in her eyes that he couldn't bear to see.

"Hold on." He grabbed her hand again, felt her stiffen. And realized he'd lost her nascent trust through his own idiocy. "I'm taking you back upstairs," he said, tugging her up the same flight he'd pulled her down only seconds ago.

Neither of them spoke until they arrived back in the gloomy belly of the warehouse. It was piled up with boxes, but light came in through several narrow windows near the roof. He heard Ashaya release her breath in a rush. "Thank you."

The sincerity of it made his gut clench. "Don't thank me." He reached for his cell phone. "I almost made your mind snap."

Ashaya pulled at his hand. Tightening his hold on her, he turned. "Yes?"

"I'm not that brittle." Her face was smooth, showing no sign of her earlier panic. "I had to learn how to keep it together. I was underground in that lab for a long time."

He felt a layer of deepest respect coat his understanding of this woman who'd gotten to him from day one. "How did you do it?"

"When something has to be borne, there's no choice." She looked to him. "You know that better than anyone."

He gave a slight nod. His latency—what it had cost him, what it demanded from him—was something he rarely discussed. He was who he was and people had learned to accept that. But Ashaya had a right to an answer after he'd scared her that badly. "And you had a son to protect."

Her face softened in a way that was everything female, speaking to a part of him that had nothing to do with lust and everything to do with tenderness. "Yes. The worst mistake the Council made was taking him from me." She held out her free hand. "Give me the letter."

He handed it over, amazed but unsurprised by her strength. "What does it say?"

" 'Hide and seek, hide and seek. Boo! I seeked you!' " Ashaya glanced up. "It's what I thought—she has a lock on me, but she hasn't told the searchers the precise location."

Nodding, Dorian punched in a familiar code on his cell. "I need an extraction. Quiet." He gave the details of their location.

"The Rats' tunnel—" Clay began.

"Not an option."

The other sentinel didn't argue. "I'm sending one of the vans to pick you up. It'll be"—a pause—"an old ice-cream one."

"Thanks."

"You can swap to a normal vehicle once you're out of the immediate danger zone—it's the Council's spies, isn't it?"

"Yeah. You heard anything?"

"They're sniffing, but they don't have the scent. We know where they are and we're letting them know that, too. Five minutes." Clay hung up.

Dorian told Ashaya what was happening, then picked up the thread of their earlier conversation. "Now, tell me about your sister and why she can track you when the others can't."

"It's complicated." She pulled at her hand. "Please, let go. The more physical contact I have with you, the harder it becomes to maintain what shields I have left. One slip and the Council won't have any need to physically hunt me—they'll find and cage my mind."

Releasing her hurt. The leopard clawed at the inside of his skin, until Dorian could almost feel skin break and muscle tear. "Start."

She looked at him with cool brilliance. "You have a habit of doing that—treating me like someone subservient. I'm not."

"I'm used to dominance. It's part of what makes me a sentinel." Only the strongest of the pack became sentinels. They had to be the alpha's protectors, his enforcers if need be.

"Then become unused to it in my presence," was the immediate response. "I'm not part of your pack and even if I were, I would hold equal rank."

He felt his lips curve upward. "That certain of your strength, Shaya?"

"I saw the respect you showed Tamsyn. Yet she's nowhere near as physically strong. Therefore, your pack gives women high rank. Given my abilities and focus, yes, I'm certain."

He bowed his head in a slight nod. "Point taken. But I still want to know about your sister and you still have to tell me. Right now you're a refugee seeking sanctuary. DarkRiver's giving it to you for a number of reasons, but we won't do it blindly—protecting our young comes first. *Choose.*" He held back the other truth—that she was going nowhere without him. The leopard wanted to keep her. And that, Dorian knew, spelled a very special kind of trouble.

"What about Keenan?" she asked, eyes locked with his. "If I don't tell you what you want to know, will you withdraw protection from him, too?"

He heard the smooth engine of an arriving van. "I think the

real question is—will you keep hiding what we need to protect him effectively?"

She sucked in a breath just as he jerked his head toward the door. "Transport's here. Come on."

He was aware of her jogging behind him as he ran to the door and pushed it up. The van had been backed up right against it. "In," he ordered, pulling open the vehicle's back doors. As she scrambled inside the seatless interior, he closed up the warehouse and followed, pulling the van doors shut behind him. They were moving an instant later.

"Where are we heading?" he asked, recognizing the driver's scent as that of Rina, Kit's sister and one of the younger DarkRiver soldiers.

"Out to the Presidio. Jamie's gonna meet us there with a car for you. Okay?"

"Works." He propped his back against the side wall of the van, aware of Ashaya attempting to do the same across from him. Stretching out his legs, he braced his feet on either side of her. She didn't hesitate to put her hands on him. "You couldn't find something with better suspension?" Not that he minded Shaya's touch, but his teeth were about to rattle out of his head.

"Oh, hold on." A few mechanical groans, the slight jolt of wheels retracting, and then the ride smoothed out. "I turned on the hover-drive. Barker told me this vehicle's not really meant to be run on wheels. Sorry, forgot." A sheepish sound.

"You're doing fine." Rina was under his direct command, and now that she'd figured out he was immune to her sensual nature, she was turning into a good protector for the pack. If the girl learned to control her quick-fire temper, she'd become one of the best. He switched his attention to Ashaya, keeping his legs where they were. "Better?"

She nodded, looked toward the front, then shook her head. Strangely, he understood. She would tell him her secrets but not with a witness. He'd accept that. But he'd keep nothing from his packmates that they needed to know—Ashaya was smart enough to have figured that out.

"Did you troll the message boards like I asked?" he said to Rina, keeping his tone low because changeling hearing was acute in close quarters.

"Yeah. Hold on." Rina made a sharp turn. "Found out something you might be interested in—you know how we thought there had to be backup root servers since the Internet was only down for thirty seconds?"

"Yeah?"

"Word is there's a network of paranoid computer hackers who've made it their business to set up secret fallback servers all around the world."

Dorian considered that. "Paranoia isn't always a bad thing."

"So says a computer geek," Rina teased. "Anyway, Ashaya's broadcast is doing the rounds—we uploaded a perfect version to make sure. Council seems to have given up trying to keep it under wraps."

"Then I was a success," Ashaya said.

Rina made a noise in the front. "I dunno. A lot of the posters are questioning whether you're for real or just a publicity hound. Then there are the ones who accuse you of being a vindictive bitch because you were taken off a multimillion-dollar research project in favor of another scientist."

"So"—Ashaya's eyes filled with a quiet intensity—"since they weren't able to stop the broadcast, they're going to try to discredit me."

"You knew that would happen." Dorian watched her, examined her, knowing he'd never have a better opportunity. She was beautiful, something her intense intelligence had a tendency to overshadow. And beautiful in a very feminine way. Yet there was something missing—the spark that turned beauty into the truly extraordinary.

He knew what that spark was, of course, knew it was missing because he'd seen it light her up from within bare minutes ago.

Emotion.

Heart.

Soul.

Ashaya had retreated, rebuilding her shields as she went. She'd said it was necessary but he wasn't convinced. He didn't *want* to be convinced. Because the woman who'd told him to get unused to ordering her around, hell, she was just about perfect.

"You ask me, you have to do another broadcast pretty soon," Rina said, breaking into his thoughts. "Right now it looks like you've cut and run, and that's not exactly good for your image."

"I'm not particularly concerned about my image."

Dorian shook his head. "You might not be, but it's what's going to keep you alive."

"My becoming infamous hasn't kept them from hunting me."

"It's given them pause." He considered what Zie Zen had said. "It's probably why you're not on the kill-on-sight list right now."

"Possible. But more likely, they want access to the data I have. Ming is perfectly capable of siphoning it out of my mind and leaving me an empty husk."

Dorian looked at her face, her slender shoulders, and knew she had the strength to carry this burden. "You'll beat him. You made a stand when it would've been easier to run. That takes guts."

"You know why I didn't run." Iliana had run. She'd returned home in a body bag.

"That doesn't mean it took any less courage to go out there and fight for your son's right to live, your people's right to have a choice in whether or not they become nothing more than insects in a hive." He quoted her with unerring accuracy.

Ashaya broke eye contact. Dorian saw too much with that vivid blue gaze. "I'm not that noble. I did what I did out of selfishness—to save Keenan."

He shrugged. "I fight monsters to protect Pack. They aren't any less dead because I do what I do out of a selfish need to save those I love."

"People who stick up their heads have a way of getting those heads blown off," she said, clenching her hands on the denim that coated the muscled length of his legs.

"I've got your back." There was a promise in those words that whispered down her spine with the exquisite heat of a leopard's touch. "You want us to set up another broadcast?"

She swallowed, but nodded.

"We're here." The driver brought the vehicle to a smooth stop.

Dorian was already moving. She'd come to expect that from him. He could wait with a predator's silent grace, but in life he was full of movement. Now she watched as he pushed open the back doors and jumped down. When he raised a hand to help her out, she shook her head and gestured for him to go on ahead to speak with his packmates. Her shields were already paper-thin. Much more and they'd be nonexistent. And to think how arrogant she'd once been, considering her defense of faux Silence unbreakable.

What a joke.

Of course it had been unbreakable in the Net. There was no one there who lived emotion every moment of every day, no one who challenged her as this wild changeling did. Other than her indefinable relationship with Amara, only Keenan had been a point of emotional weakness, and Ming had cut her off from him for months at a time.

Her lips pressed tight as her feet hit the ground and she knew that, no matter what, she would never again let anyone keep her son from her. It had almost broken her when the connection between them had been sheared off. She wasn't strong enough to bear the loss a second time.

The connection.

In the chaos of everything that had taken place, she hadn't even thought about how she'd known to go to Keenan this morning. The link had shattered—she'd never forget the tearing pain of it—when he'd dropped from the PsyNet. And since that link should never have existed in the first place, she had no way to search for it. Yet she knew it had re-formed—the knowledge had nothing to do with logic, and everything to do with love.

A hand on her lower back. Dorian's voice in her ear. "Get in the car. It's around the front."

They pulled away less than a minute later. "This is a longer route to Tammy's," Dorian said. "I want to make sure we don't have a tail."

Heading into the shadows created by the tall stands of trees that covered the Presidio, he put the car on automatic. While most forested regions weren't embedded for automatic navigation, this area was close enough to the city that it was a wild playground of sorts, hence the embedding, at least along the main route through it.

"Now," he said, sliding away the manual controls and turning to face her, his arm braced on the seat behind her, "tell me about your twin."

CHAPTER 26

•

Amara's lips curled upward when Ming LeBon's face appeared on the large communications panel at the other end of the lab, a lab located somewhere in Death Valley—they'd moved her there after she'd told them she could find Ashaya, but only if she was in the same state. It was a lie, of course. One that got her closer to her twin. "Councilor. I trust your hunt was successful."

Ming looked at her with those too black eyes of his. Conversely, one side of his face was covered in a bright red birthmark. Some problem with pigmentation, Amara thought, unconcerned. Very few things concerned Amara.

"No," Ming finally replied. "Your coordinates were incorrect."

"Truly?" Amara played innocent. "She was there."

"There were indications she might've been in the area. But the net was too wide."

"Ah." She smiled and spread her arms open, palms upturned. "I'll try to do better next time."

"I would rather you tell me how you're able to track her in the first place."

Raising a finger, she waved it in a chiding manner. "No, no, no. That would break the rules."

"Rules?"

"Oh, no, Councilor." Amara laughed, and it was a premeditated act. "We both know I'm not quite right in the head." She took a cold delight in being deliberately offensive to his calculating Psy mind. "But it doesn't affect my intelligence so don't treat me like I have the IQ of one of the rehabilitated."

"My apologies."

She knew the words were meaningless. He was humoring her because he thought she could hand him the implant that would allow him to control the entire Psy race. Perhaps he would share it with the other Councilors. Perhaps he wouldn't. It made no difference to Amara. "As to how I track Ashaya, I—" She broke off with a theatrical gasp. "Oops, I almost let the cat out of the bag. Naughty me."

Ming stared at her and she wondered if he expected her to break. However, when he spoke, it was nothing expected. "You and Ashaya are identical genetic specimens. You gestated in the same womb, were brought up in the same environment."

"Until you made me run away." She pouted. "Why did you have to go put a rehab order on me?"

"And yet," he continued, as if she hadn't spoken, "you are fundamentally flawed, while Ashaya—despite her unfortunate political bent—has always been the perfect Psy."

Amara wondered if Ming really was as blind as he appeared. Or had her twin managed to perfect her mask to that high a degree? Well, now, if that was true, then the game was going to be very, very interesting. Goody. "We are an enigma. Perhaps you'd care to study us before you eliminate us?"

"You speak of your death with ease."

"I'm no fool, Ming. The second I hand you the implant, I'm dead and so is Ashaya."

"Which gives you good reason to delay."

"True," she agreed with a careless shrug. "However, I find the thought of immortality quite . . . enticing. The implant will live on long after we're both wiped from existence."

"Then you're certain you can deliver?"

She raised an eyebrow, giggling inwardly at the secret only she and Ashaya knew. Ming would forget all about the implant if he realized there was something far better already in existence.

But that was their secret. Hers, Ashaya's . . . and Keenan's.

CHAPTER 27

When he smiles, he could demand anything from me and I
would give it to him. I've never felt more vulnerable in my
life. This man, this leopard, he could break me.

—*From the encrypted personal files of Ashaya Aleine*

Ashaya took a deep breath. "My sister." She stared out at the
eucalyptus trees that had been brought into the region in an eco-
logically ill-informed decision, and survived all attempts at erad-
ication. When fire struck, they burned up in a blaze of sublime
fury. "My sister is like these trees. Perfect to look at, brilliant in
her design—her brain is flawless, her intellect staggering—but
all it takes to crumble that perfection is a single match."

Dorian brushed her shoulder with his fingertips, and she
found herself leaning toward him. Right then, she needed his
strength, needed to know she wasn't alone. "She's not insane,"
Ashaya said. "On the surface, she appears to understand the difference between right and wrong. But . . . she doesn't, not really.
She does things without thinking through the consequences,
things an ordinary person would consider cruel."

Dorian's eyes turned flint hard without warning, his fingers
stilling in their stroking reassurance. "*She's* the sociopath
you've been protecting."

"Yes," she admitted, refusing to look away, refusing to apologize. "She's my twin." And the giver of the greatest gift in
Ashaya's life. "It was the only possible decision."

"Not for a true Psy."

"I suppose both of us were born flawed, just in different ways." She waited to see what he would do, this predator who hated the Silent chill of her race with a blind rage that cut.

"The rest, Ashaya, tell me the rest."

It was a relief to talk about Amara without having to obfuscate the truth. "We have an unbreakable twin bond—it's why she can always find me unless I'm shielding to the best of my ability." She kept her gaze on the distinctive red girders of the bridge rising up ahead, not wanting to face Dorian's anger.

Then his hand closed over the back of her neck and her stomach unclenched. She'd become strangely addicted to his brand of touch. Returning her gaze to him, she found his eyes heavy-lidded as he focused on tracing the line of her collarbone. Somehow, that made it easier to carry on. "The bond's been there since birth and it's not something anyone else has ever been able to detect. I don't know how much you know about psychic networks . . ."

"Some." He glanced up and the stroke of his eyes was a caress she could almost feel.

She barely stopped herself from reaching out to outline the perfection of his lips. "From what I've been able to discover, in the past, most emotional connections were visible in the PsyNet. Today, those links have been obliterated." No more bonds of love. Or even of hate. Just emptiness. "Each mind is now a separate entity."

"Yeah? Then how the hell does Keenan know you love him?"

"He doesn't." And that destroyed her. In protecting his life, she'd hurt his child's heart so much.

"Hell he doesn't." Dorian snorted. "That's why he pulled that stunt—he knew his mom would drop everything and run to him."

Ashaya felt something in the region of her chest bleed at that statement and the shock of it was so powerful, she almost surrendered everything. "There *is* a link with Keenan—but it's not visible, either." Her voice broke. "I think my attempt at maintaining Silence is what makes it invisible—I've stifled my own son's efforts to reach me."

"Stop." He squeezed her nape in a gesture that was as dominant as it was . . . tender.

It awakened even more of those conflicting emotions inside of her, the very things she needed to keep contained. Because when Amara started playing . . . "My twin will never kill me or put me in lethal danger, however harsh the game. In her own way, I think she loves me—I'm her only playmate, her only friend. But she might kill Keenan."

"Why? He's a child, more importantly, her sister's child."

Her heart rippled again and this time it was a different emotion, a wild, raw thing armed with claws and teeth. "Amara," she said, trying to ride the violent power of this new feeling, "doesn't see it that way. She thinks of me as belonging to her and of Keenan as an interloper." And that was a bizarre twist in an already twisted tale.

"Are you saying she's the real danger?"

"I'm saying that even if I somehow manage to hold off the Council, Amara will never stop hunting me. It doesn't matter where I go, she'll find me and she'll start to play her games, start to try and push me to the edge of sanity." She took a deep breath. "The most horrible thing is, when *I* feel, *she* becomes worse. It's as if my emotions feed her madness. I'm afraid she'll push me too far one day, make me hurt Keenan."

Dorian tilted her face toward him when she would've looked away. "What did she do to you, Shaya?"

"You keep dropping the *A* off my name."

"Do I?"

Another game. But this one held no intent to harm. "Dorian, your touch unbalances me, and that doesn't just make Amara worse, it strengthens our twin bond. If she gets inside me, she can see what I see, hear what I hear. I don't want her in this car with us." *I don't want to share you.*

Dorian couldn't ignore her plea—even if it provoked the leopard to vicious frustration. Shifting back to his side of the car, he took the chance to check they were on track to Tammy's house. "So, to chain Amara, you'll go through life half-alive?"

"If it will keep Keenan safe, then yes." A calm answer but her lips trembled before she pressed them into a firm line.

"She's a danger to a son you love more than life, and yet you protect her." Dorian couldn't understand that.

Then Ashaya said, "She's my baby sister, born a minute after me. I've been looking after her my whole life."

His heart just about broke. Because he knew about baby

sisters. He knew about the kind of love that bond engendered, how it was set in stone, how the thought of harming that precious life was anathema. You forgave little sisters for things you wouldn't even consider forgiving others. But . . . "If she came after Keenan," he asked, "what would you do?"

"You know." A shattered whisper. "I would kill her. And it would destroy me."

That's the real reason why she ran, he thought, not because she was scared of Amara, but because she was afraid her sister would back her into a corner from where the only escape would be over her sibling's dead body. One hell of a mess. "How, Shaya?" he found himself asking. "How is that you're you and she's—"

"—a monster?" Ashaya completed. "I don't know. Don't humans believe in a thing called the soul? Maybe that element comes hardwired. Maybe we were just born with different kinds of souls."

Hearing the shredded heart she was trying so desperately to hide, Dorian wished he could reassure her that it wouldn't come down to sister against sister. But he'd lost his illusions a long time ago. Sometimes evil did win. Sometimes, baby sisters did die.

The image of Kylie's brutalized body was so fresh in his mind that when the dying woman staggered onto the road in front of him, he thought he was seeing a ghost. "Jesus!" He and Ashaya were both slammed forward against their restraints then hauled back as the car's sensors picked up the obstruction and brought the vehicle to a shuddering halt.

Dorian recovered in less than a second, pushing up his door and running out to catch the woman as she collapsed. Her eyes were already filming over with the haze of oncoming death, her plain white shift so bloody it stuck to her slender frame. Flashes of ravaged flesh showed where the fabric had been torn by whatever it was that had cut through her body with such lethal ferocity.

"Hold on," he said, bending to gather her into his arms so he could drive her to the nearest hospital.

"I can't get her to respond to telepathic messages." Ashaya's shock was vivid enough to escape even her incredible control.

"Keep trying." He picked up the woman, even though he could hear her heart beginning to stutter. She stared up at him but he knew she didn't see him. "Who did this to you?"

The answer came out strangely clearly. "My father."

She had soft brown hair, gilded skin. And the pitch-black eyes of a Psy in the death throes. Then those eyes faded to gray, her body going limp against him. He felt his arms clench, his heart twist. But the memories evoked by the sight of this girl's body could wait. Leopard and man both had only one priority right now—to protect the woman who stood beside him, one hand clasped around the lost girl's. "Leave," he said.

Ashaya looked up at him. "Dor—"

"She's dead. A Psy team will be sent out to investigate within the hour." Sascha had taught him that—death alone was an acceptable excuse for leaving the PsyNet. All Psy who dropped from the Net without explanation were searched for, a search that didn't stop until a body was found, or death confirmed. "It might be sooner if she got out a telepathic mayday. You can't be here when they arrive."

Ashaya didn't release the girl's hand. "What about you?"

He met her eyes. "I won't leave her alone in the dark."

"A silly emotional choice," Ashaya said, but her voice shook. "One I find myself wishing I had the freedom to make."

He shook his head, his leopard clawing at him in angry panic. "Go, Shaya. I keyed the car to you and the route's pre-programmed. Set it to automatic and get the hell out."

She withdrew her hand slowly from around the girl's. "This was a frenzied attack. She was cut so badly that she can't have come far."

"Go!"

His snapped command made her give a stiff nod and run back to the car. A minute later, she drove past him as he carried the girl off the road and through the stand of manicured trees that lined the road. The line of greenery acted as a fence for the complex of homes behind it. Small, contained buildings no predator would live in, but that suited the Psy. It was obvious the girl had come from the nearest house.

The door stood open and even from the bottom of the drive-way, he could see the bloody handprint on the door. It was stretched, as if she'd slipped. More blood lay drying on the steps leading down from the entrance hallway, on the white cobble-stones of the drive, on the ground inches from his feet.

Carefully skirting the last of her lifeblood, he carried the girl's body back up to what had once been her safe haven. *Like the site of Kylie's murder.* The scent of an abattoir hit him as he neared. There was a sick miasma to the smell that he knew he'd never be able to explain to anyone who didn't possess the same acute sense of smell. Something had gone terribly, violently wrong in that small white house.

Then he was on the doorstep and what he saw made him wish, for one selfish instant, that he'd driven by a minute earlier, that he'd missed seeing the carnage. Now these images were imprinted on his retinas, to be filed away beside the ones that tormented him night after night. Holding the girl tighter, he stepped inside the house.

A single delicate hand was all that showed of what had to be another female body in the room to the left. He glanced inside, saw that she couldn't have been more than thirteen. She'd been stabbed only once but the weapon had hit her heart. The acetic furniture preferred by the Psy lay overturned, as if she'd made a desperate bid to escape. She hadn't even reached the doorway.

Not moving from his position in the center of the hallway, he looked to the right. Another room. Another body. This one was a male. Slender, perhaps in his early twenties. He'd fought hard—his hands were bloody and broken as they lay upturned on the pale carpet, his chest a veritable mass of stab wounds. The room paid silent testament to his struggle to survive, the hard-wearing plastic of the chairs cracked and splashed with the rust red of drying blood.

He looked down at the carpet. Following the trail of lost life, he found himself in what had to be the bedroom area. In the first room, he discovered a lone middle-aged male. The man lay on his back, dead from what appeared to be a self-inflicted stab wound to the heart. One of his hands was still wrapped around the blade. There was no peace in his face, none of that icy Psy calm either. No, this man looked tormented. As if he'd seen a glimpse of hell itself.

A flicker of movement behind him. Dorian turned slowly.

The Psy who'd teleported in was dressed in the head to toe black of elite Psy guards. His uniform bore the now familiar image of two golden snakes twined in combat—Ming's emblem.

Their eyes met. Cool Psy gray. Bright changeling blue.

Dorian recognized him in a single instant. Ming's emblem but Anthony's man. Zie Zen's pickup.

The Tk-Psy's attention went to the girl's body. "You need to leave." He raised his arms.

Dorian held her tighter. "What will you do to her?"

"Erase her," was the pitiless answer. "Erase all of them."

Dorian's jaw set. "No. Give me her name."

The Psy male held his gaze for almost a minute, then blinked very deliberately. A thin piece of plaspaper appeared in his hand. "Her birth ID."

"Aren't you afraid I'll talk about this and blow your cover?"

"No. In an hour, this place will be clean, so clean that not even changeling noses will be able to sniff out the blood." As if to prove that, he looked at the carpet and Dorian saw the blood drops literally detach from the fibers and rise to hover an inch above.

Dorian's leopard growled low in his throat. "Where's your team?"

"They're coming by car." The man raised his arms again. "You need to give her to me and disappear. I can't hide your presence if you're still here when the cleanup crew arrives."

"Why do this if you don't believe in your Council?"

"Every freedom has a price." His eyes shifted from gray to crawling black. Dorian saw more and more blood begin to rise out of the carpet and off the walls. "You need to leave. The PsyNet isn't ready to know this yet. But it will be one day."

Dorian walked across the now clean stretch of carpet and faced the Psy, the girl's body between them. "My memories will be your proof?" A Justice Psy could pick out those memories if he cooperated, and broadcast them to the court. "What about yours?"

The Psy took the murdered girl with the same care that Dorian handed her over. "I'm tired." A calm statement. "I can't continue to erase lives as if they were nothing more than marks on a page. I'll make a mistake. Then I'll die."

Dorian's ears picked up the sounds of steps on the cobblestones. "You don't have the right to be tired." He took the girl's birth ID, which was hovering in the air between them. "When you can write her name on a memorial, when you can honor her blood, then you'll have earned the right." He didn't give the Psy man a chance to answer, turning to make his way out the back door as the other members of the cleanup team came in through the front. As he moved, he could feel a screen of blood rising behind him.

Another image to add to the gallery of nightmare.

CHAPTER 28

Obsession comes easily to Dorian. It worries me. If he walks back into the abyss, if he chooses the darkness, I'm not sure we'll be able to pull him out.

—*E-mail from Sascha Duncan to Tamsyn Ryder*

Ashaya had disobeyed Dorian's direct order. She knew she was taking what could amount to a stupid risk, but had found that it wasn't in her to leave him behind. She'd driven a mile down the road, raised every one of her shields to conceal her presence in case of telepathic scans, and pulled off into the shade of a large tree. The vehicle remained visible from the road but there was nothing she could do about that.

She'd wait another fifteen minutes, she rationalized. If he wasn't back by then—

The driver's-side door wrenched upward.

"Slide into the passenger seat." Dorian's tone was clipped, his clothing streaked with blood.

She moved swiftly and they were on their way seconds later. "What did you find?"

"An entire family, dead. Murder-suicide."

She swallowed. "Someone breached Silence," she guessed, "and didn't come out sane on the other side. There were vague rumors that that was happening—"

"I told you to get the hell out of here." Dorian turned in to a side road with a jarring movement. "What the fuck did you think you were doing?"

She'd been fooled into dropping her guard by his apparent calm. Her head jerked up. "I thought you might need hel—"

"I'm a sentinel," he interrupted, his tone cutting. "That means I can take care of myself. Contrary to what you think, I'm not a cripple."

"I never—"

"Yeah, you never thought," he said and it felt as if he'd scraped a razor blade over her skin, his rage was so sharp. "Did you even consider how it would've hit Keenan if you'd been captured or killed?"

Guilt grew a taut knot inside of her. "No."

"Christ."

She felt her desperate grip on her emotions begin to unravel. She tried to rewind the unraveled thread. Failed. Her hands curled. "Don't make judgments about my feelings toward my son." Keenan was her weakness. They both knew that.

"What feelings?"

It was a direct hit, but she stood firm. She knew she was right—and she wasn't going to let him intimidate her into silence. "I was concerned for you. Your emotional reaction to the girl was so strong, I thought you might not make it out before the Psy team arrived." All his rage, his need for vengeance, it had been in that final chrome-blue glance.

Dorian shot her a furious look. "You're so brainwashed you can't even accept your own emotions and you're judging mine? That's fucking rich." He shook his head, the blond silk of his hair shifting with ease.

She wanted to do violence. "Next time," she said, gritting her teeth, "I'll leave you to your self-destructive urges. It would make my life considerably simpler."

Dorian was still fuming more than an hour later. He'd showered at Tammy's and changed into the spare clothes he always kept there. With Tammy being their healer, they often came to her bleeding or worse. Now he stood with his body braced against the frame of the back door, staring out at Ashaya and Keenan as they sat politely across from each other at the picnic table in the yard.

"You want to talk about it?" A warm female voice.

He glanced at Tamsyn. "No. I told Sascha the same thing before she left."

She wrapped an arm around his waist, leaning against him until he put an arm over her shoulders. "Always were stubborn." A smile. "Sascha figured we'd tag-team you. She was round one. I'm the closer."

"Damn Pack," he muttered. "No one's heard of fucking privacy."

Tamsyn chuckled. "So? Ashaya hides it well, but that much ice in a woman's eyes when she looks at a man spells trouble. What did you do?"

"She disobeyed a direct order, put herself in harm's way." He watched as Keenan took something out of his pocket and put it on the table. Ashaya took the object at once, enclosing it tightly in her fist.

"Are you sure you're really angry at her, and not at what you saw inside that house?"

He thought of the wall of blood droplets, the metallic bite of iron in the air. "What I saw inside that house was a nightmare," he admitted. "But I'm very definitely furious with her." The cat nodded in agreement inside him.

"Why?" Tamsyn insisted. "She only did what any other woman would've done for a man she cared for, in the same situation."

Ashaya looked up at that second and even from this far away, he saw the primal awareness in her eyes. She looked away an instant later, but the damage had been done. His body tightened, the anger transforming into something else. "It was easier to keep her at a distance when she didn't act so human."

Tammy hugged him, her warmth soaking into his bones. "I don't think your cat wants to keep her at a distance."

"That's the problem." He broke their embrace. "I want her so badly I'm burning up from the inside out, and I can't justify it." He'd hungered for her from the start. But now that hunger was clawing into his heart.

"Just because she's Psy—"

He cut her off with a sharp slice of his hand. "It's not that. She worked for the Council, Tammy. How do I face Kylie's memory if I feel this way about a woman who was part of the machinery that led to her death?"

"Ashaya had nothing to do with Enrique."

His cat hissed at the sound of that name. "She kept the Council's secrets, worked for Ming himself."

"You're not making any sense." Frowning, Tammy folded her arms. "Sascha was a Councilor's daughter and, granted, you wanted to rip her throat out once, but you adore her now. Faith did predictions for the Council and you never reacted to her like this. What is it about Ashaya that makes her worse?"

Dorian couldn't betray Ashaya's secret, her love for a sister who was more than broken, more than damaged. "Just leave it."

Tammy's eyes widened. "Oh, my God, Dorian, it's not only lust, is it? You're starting to fall for her. She matters."

Tammy was wrong, Dorian thought, looking out and into the yard again.

The truth was, he'd already fallen for her.

Did you even *consider how it would've hit Keenan if you'd been captured or killed?*

The truth was, Ashaya hadn't thought at all. She'd acted . . . on instinct. The need to protect Dorian had slammed into her without warning, broadsiding her with its sheer strength.

It wasn't as if she was a stranger to irrational behavior. She was used to acting that way where Keenan and Amara were concerned. They were both blood of her blood, flesh of her flesh, linked to her with invisible psychic threads. It made a certain kind of sense that she wouldn't be entirely logical where they were concerned.

But today, she'd acted against all reason and sense for a man who was wholly unconnected to her. She'd disregarded her own safety—the first priority for most Psy—disregarded common sense, disregarded her other obligations, everything but her driving need to ensure Dorian made it out alive.

Now she sat across from her son, and instead of the guilt that had first hit her, she felt a kind of peace. Because in doing what she'd done, she'd taken an irrevocable step. A step out of even the pretence of Silence. On the PsyNet she continued to protect her mind, but within, the last vestiges of her conditioning had ceased to exist.

Come on, Amara, she whispered. *Let's end this.* Because Dorian was right, she couldn't keep living this half life.

"Mommy?" Keenan's solemn little face, looking at her quizzically. "Where are you?"

"Right here." Standing, she walked around the table and picked him up in her arms, hiding nothing of what she felt. "I love you, my baby. I love you."

He gave her the sweetest smile. "I know that, Mommy."

Even as her heart broke under the lash of that confident voice, she looked up to see Dorian stalking toward her. Her body tightened, her heart thudded, and her mind grew frantic with a need so primitive and sensual, it threatened to make a slave out of her.

Dorian spoke to Keenan first. "Tammy made cookies."

Keenan immediately wiggled to be put down. "I like cookies!"

Ashaya set him on the ground and watched him run to the house. "Has there been a decision on her cubs?"

"They'll be back tonight. Sascha's confident he won't hurt them, but when you're not with him, she and Faith are going to take turns at keeping an eye on things."

Ashaya nodded, understanding the caution. Keenan was a strong telepath, and conversely, the cubs did have claws and teeth. "I want him to have friends." To have a life.

Dorian stepped closer, backing her against the picnic table. "What did he give you?"

"None of your business," she snapped, not having forgotten his earlier temper—nor the way he'd deliberately put her on the defensive so she'd back down. It had taken her too long to recognize that bit of feline trickery, but now that she had, it made her wonder what secrets *he* was keeping. Not that he would tell her. That thought gave her voice added force when she said, "Go away."

Instead of complying, he put his hands on either side of the table, trapping her. "They can see us from the kitchen, so play nice." His eyes gleamed in a way that turned the word "play" into something sinfully sensuous.

Ashaya felt her cheeks heat up in a feminine response she hadn't known she had the capacity to experience. Dorian, she realized, was a very dangerous male when *he* decided to play nice. "You were yelling at me not so long ago. Why the charm?"

"I want you." A blunt statement. "I decided I could continue to stave off the need by remaining angry with you, or—" He paused, his eyes turning to blue fire in front of her.

"Or?" she prompted, knowing she shouldn't, but unable to resist.

"Or I could feed the hunger."

She swallowed.

"Guess which option I chose?" A silken whisper that made her nerve endings skitter in warning.

"Number one?" Her voice came out oddly husky.

He pressed into her, his thighs hard and powerful against her own. "Wrong." His gaze drifted to her lips. "No bonus points for you. But that's okay—I'll go easy . . . the first time."

CHAPTER 29

Somewhere in the murky depths of the Tenderloin, a place some still called the dark heart of San Francisco, an exchange took place.

"Careful," came the hissed command as a box nearly hit the alleyway floor. "We've only got two boxes of this stuff."

"More than enough," another person scoffed. "All it takes is one hit, right?"

"Not with your shooting," the first voice said. "Now concentrate."

Silence reigned for the next ten minutes, until everything was stored in its proper place. "Word from Venice is that this operation is a go, *if* we can do it without attracting the wrong kind of attention—our top priority is to remain under the radar." The speaker waited to make sure that was understood before moving on to more practical matters. "Some of us will be shooting with modified tranquilizer guns, so I want everyone to start practicing. If we get a chance to take Aleine, we need to be ready. Because we'll only get one shot."

"Then let's make sure we hit the bull's-eye first time out."

CHAPTER 30

Dorian wasn't wearing a shirt when he gave me his DNA. It made it difficult to concentrate. Even if I didn't know his changeling affiliation, I'd guess him for a hunting cat. The way he moves, it's an erotic dance . . . or perhaps that's only the effect he has on me. If I dared throw caution to the winds and stroked the cat within, would he bite off my hand, or would he purr?

—*From the encrypted personal files of Ashaya Aleine*

Dorian took Ashaya back to the apartment later that afternoon, after she'd read Keenan a story and assured him she would return in time for dinner. Satisfied, the boy promised to behave for the couple of hours they'd be gone.

"It's important that I be with him tonight," Ashaya said as they grabbed a quick bite before leaving. "He needs to know I'll be there when he needs me."

Dorian didn't argue with her decision—kids were the most precious aspect of Pack. But that didn't mean he was going to forget the teasing threat he'd made outside. The guilt, the anger, none of it was enough to stop him—Ashaya Aleine was going to be his. "I can pack up your stuff, bring it to you." He could play very nice when he was in the mood.

She gave him a suspicious look. "No. It's better if Keenan doesn't come to expect me here all the time. Just in case—"

He kissed her without warning, taking his time with those full, *bitable* lips that drove him crazy. "You'd better start trusting me to keep you safe," he said against her kiss-wet mouth, "or I don't know what my bruised ego will make me do." It came out not as a warning, but as a promise.

He intended to further her education in the care and feeding of the male ego at the apartment, but when they arrived, it was to find Faith waiting at the top of the stairs, fingers plucking at the ends of the green silk scarf she'd used to pull back her hair. Vaughn lounged by the doorway, back against the wall.

Dorian moved smoothly in front of Ashaya. "What are you two doing here?" While Vaughn was a good friend, Dorian's relationship with Faith was a little more problematic.

"I wanted to talk to you," the cardinal Psy said, biting her lower lip. "And Ashaya."

Protectiveness gripped his throat. "This is meant to be a safe location. You could've led someone here."

"Don't insult me," Vaughn said, not changing his relaxed stance despite the aggression Dorian knew he was giving off. "We weren't followed. Even if I had gone senile and lost the ability to spot a tail, I have a mate who's real good at seeing threats in our future."

Dorian's eyes flicked to Faith and he caught the gentle plea in her distinctive night-sky gaze. He and Faith had a silent understanding. F-Psy had stopped forecasting anything but money and economics over a hundred years ago. Perhaps if they hadn't, Kylie would still be alive. But Faith was doing what her brethren wouldn't, opening her mind to a future as filled with nightmares as happiness. For that, she'd earned his respect.

He moved up the steps, but continued to keep Ashaya behind him, very aware of her unusual quietness. Vaughn tended to have that effect on those who didn't know him. The jaguar couldn't pull off harmless, not like Dorian. Vaughn looked lethal even when he was playing with strands of Faith's dark red hair, his lips curved in possessive satisfaction.

"I thought the flirting happened before the mating," Dorian said as he unlocked the door and pushed it open. He nudged Ashaya through.

"Then I pity your mate," Vaughn let Faith's hair slide out of his hands, but tangled his fingers with hers. "I can give you lessons in romance if you'd like."

Dorian snorted at the same time that Faith gave a disbelieving laugh. "And where have you been learning these lessons?" she asked in an arch tone at odds with her smile.

"From you, Red, who else?" Teasing grin slashing across his face, Vaughn followed Dorian and Faith into the apartment, kicking the door shut behind himself.

Ashaya was already in the kitchenette, heating water. "Coffee would probably be a good idea," she said, looking not at him but at Faith.

The F-Psy let go of her mate's hands, stared back. "You know."

"No." A quick shake of her head. "But when an F-Psy comes calling, it's better to be prepared. You're Faith NightStar, aren't you?"

As Faith nodded and introduced Vaughn, Dorian wondered if the other couple heard what he did in Ashaya's voice—a fine thread of suffocating panic. Closing the distance between them, he put a hand on her lower back. "Want some help?" Protective instincts clawed through his veins. It should've been an unwelcome shock. It wasn't. It felt right.

"No." A stubborn answer, but when she looked up, he saw the truth. She was terrified.

He caught Vaughn's eye. There was no way to have a private conversation with the other sentinel in the room—his hearing was too acute.

"Mind if we go out onto the balcony?" Vaughn was already opening the French doors that led out to the tiny outdoor area.

Dorian threw him a grateful look, knowing that once the doors were shut, the noise from the streets below would drown out his and Ashaya's voices. The instant the other couple stepped out, he forced Ashaya to look at him. "Now talk or I'll have to get mean."

"You're always mean." Despite the words, she came into his arms without any hesitation, displaying a trust that tamed the leopard.

"Hey." He found he'd curved his body over hers, his lips brushing her temple. "Knowing the future means you can change it."

"I've never feared emotion for its own sake," she whispered, "only for what it would mean—Amara's deviance being set completely free, perhaps leading to both our deaths. But today, I'm afraid and I wish I could erase that feeling from my mind."

He thought of the carnage he'd seen in a small white house, the body he'd held in his arms. "I know." Because he'd had those same thoughts. "After Kylie was murdered," he said, tearing open a piece of his heart that he'd protected with feral viciousness, "I was so angry the rage ate me up from the inside out." His recollection of those days was a foul pit filled with hatred and violence. "But I never wanted to be without emotion. Do you know why?"

"No."

"Because if I wiped out emotion, I wiped out Kylie." His arms clenched around her, the embers of his deep-seated anger stirring anew. He'd torn out Santano Enrique's heart with his bare hands, but his leopard wasn't satisfied. So long as even one of those who had allowed Enrique to roam free remained alive, he would hunt. "Our emotions color our memories. Without them, one day would be the same as another . . . and my sister would've faded long ago."

Finally relaxing her hold, Ashaya backed up a little, those amazing eyes holding him in thrall. "You should hear your voice when you speak of her. It hurts my heart and I know that's not possible."

"Yes, it is. You know love when you hear it." He'd adored Kylie, had no problem admitting that. "And she lives right here." He thumped a fist over the pulse of his heartbeat.

"Dorian." Her hand lifted as if she'd touch him, but then she shook her head and turned. "I need to prepare the coffee."

He should've kept his hands to himself. He wasn't much good at doing what he should. And he needed a little joy to alleviate the chaos of emotion that always came with thoughts of his murdered sister—maybe someday he'd stop blaming himself for not saving her, but that day wasn't today.

Putting his hands on Ashaya's hips, he pulled her back against his chest.

"Dor—"

He kissed the curve of her neck. "Just want to give you a friendly warning." She tasted so good, he licked at her with quick catlike flicks that made her pulse turn to thunder. When she couldn't seem to gasp in enough breath to ask him about the warning, he smiled. "I wasn't kidding about having you in my bed. Get ready to dance with me." Pressing another kiss to the soft warmth of her, he drew back to his previous position.

It took her a minute to stop staring at his mouth after she turned to face him again. "You're used to getting your own way."

"So?"

"So now you look like you want to take a bite out of me."

He let his eyes close to half-mast, his lips curving into a slow smile. "That's because I do." Delighted by the flush that brushed over her cheeks, he decided to indulge himself a little more. "I want to have you flat on your back in my bed. Then I want to spread your thighs, and—"

"Coffee!" She gripped the edge of the counter. "It'll be ready soon."

"Oh?" Disappointed, he leaned forward and nipped lightly at her ear. "I'll tell you where I intend to take that bite out of some other time then." Leaving her flustered but definitely not scared any longer, he walked to the balcony doors and gave Vaughn the signal to return. There was a momentary rush of noise from outside as the mated pair entered.

A few minutes later, Ashaya put the coffee on the low table in the center of the room and took a seat on the sofa that faced the balcony, while he leaned on its back. Faith took a seat on the opposite sofa, with Vaughn sprawled beside her.

"Aren't you going to have some?" Faith asked when Ashaya didn't pour herself any coffee.

Ashaya shook her head. "I'm not used to it and it tends to have a strong effect."

"I understand." Faith took two cups, passing one to her mate. "I've become addicted to the stuff but it's far more potent than I initially realized." Her words were friendly, but there was a jerkiness to her movements that gave away her unease.

"Whatever it is you've seen," Ashaya said, her tone a fraction too calm, as if she was barely keeping herself together, "just tell me. I'd rather know than imagine."

Faith's hands shook as she put her near-full cup on the table. Vaughn, holding his in his left hand, curved his right arm around her waist. "I had a vision," she began, "but it was one of those where it's impossible to tell when the event might take place . . . or whether it might already have done so."

"Backsight," Ashaya said. "Someone in my extended family tree was born with a low-Gradient ability in that specialty."

Dorian stared at the back of her neck, itching to touch her

again, finish what he'd started in the kitchen. It went against every one of his instincts to fight the urge, but he knew she wouldn't appreciate it. Not when she was trying to present such an unruffled facade. She was so damn good at it, it annoyed the leopard. The trapped creature inside of him didn't like being ignored.

That was when Ashaya turned to meet his gaze. "Did you say something?"

Well, now, that was interesting. "No."

Giving him a skeptical look, she returned her attention to Faith. "What did you see in this vision, or flash of backsight?"

"Ashaya, I'm going to be honest with you," Faith said, and there was a steel to her tone that Dorian knew often surprised people. "From what you've done, what you've said, you appear to be a rebel. But people lie."

"True." Ashaya nodded. "I'm also still linked to the PsyNet. You shouldn't tell me anything you wouldn't want the Council to know."

"Pretty certain they'll get you." Vaughn took a sip of coffee.

Ashaya shifted the tiniest fraction of an inch toward Dorian. "I'm an M-Psy," she said. "No matter my classification on the Gradient, it's primarily a nonaggressive ability."

"Yes," Faith agreed, then paused for several seconds. "As for secrets, someone on the Council most probably already knows, so even if anything leaks out . . ." An eloquent shrug. "How much do you know about the NetMind?"

"It keeps order in the Net," Ashaya answered. "Makes it less chaotic, organizes things. Some people say it spies for the Council, while others think that's anthropomorphizing. Everyone agrees it's neosentient at best, and its age is a complete mystery."

"It's not alone," Faith told Ashaya. "When Silence took root, it split the NetMind into two. One part is good, able to act with sentience. The other part, the entity I call the DarkMind, is made up of all the emotions the Silent have rejected, particularly the violent ones."

"Because," Ashaya murmured, "the violent, angry emotions are ones we're conditioned most strongly against."

Faith nodded. "When I defected, I was hunting a killer. He was tainted with a malignant darkness. That darkness is a marker of the DarkMind's psychic control—it uses these already mentally unstable individuals to give itself a voice. It's not only feeding off their evil, it's effectively nurturing the worst serial killers on the planet."

Ashaya didn't seem shocked by Faith's revelation. "Silence cuts us off from a fundamental aspect of our psyche. It makes complete sense that that would be echoed on the psychic plane." Her back suddenly went ramrod straight. "My twin," she said to Faith. "You saw the darkness wrapped around my twin."

"I don't know how I knew it wasn't you," Faith said, "but it's like that sometimes in a vision—I just know things. And this time, I knew that the woman I was watching wasn't Ashaya Aleine." A pause. "She was doing terrible things . . . killing, torture, blood."

Vaughn put down his coffee and moved to press a kiss to Faith's temple. The F-Psy leaned into his hold but her eyes stayed on Ashaya. "Was it backsight?"

Ashaya didn't hesitate. "No. She's never murdered, never spilled blood."

"Are you certain?" Vaughn's question was a challenge.

Dorian didn't tell the other sentinel to back off. He didn't need to. The cat growled in silent pride as Ashaya met Vaughn's eyes. "Yes," she said, "I'm sure. I'm connected to my twin on a level beyond the PsyNet. The second, the *instant*, Amara became a killer, the knowledge would bleed into my mind. She hasn't crossed that line."

"I believe you," Faith said softly. "But she will if you don't change the future."

"Perhaps my defection is the thing that pushes her over the edge." Ashaya's shoulders slumped. "I've always known that the more unstable my own emotional state, the worse her episodes."

Dorian wanted to haul her to him and order her to stop hurting. Gritting his teeth, he glanced at Vaughn. "That it?"

"Yeah." The other sentinel put down his coffee and stood, tugging Faith up with him.

"Wait," Faith said, eyes locked with Ashaya's. "Was I right about your sister? Is she . . . ?"

"Disturbed?" Ashaya supplied. "Yes. Smarter than most people on the planet, but broken in some fundamental way."

"I understand." Faith's eyes held the knowledge that, in the PsyNet, all F-Psy eventually ended up clinically insane. "There was something else—there's no way to prove this, but maybe your twinship is the *reason* you and your sister are so different."

Dorian understood before Ashaya. "A direct reflection of the twinning in the PsyNet, one good, one bad?"

"No," Ashaya whispered. "It's not that clean-cut, not yet. I have fragments of badness and she has some goodness."

Nobody said anything to dispute that, but they all knew that even if she was right, Faith was an F-Psy who never saw an untrue future. If steps weren't taken to prevent it, her vision would one day come true.

And Amara Aleine would bathe in the blood of innocents.

Five minutes later, Faith stared at the dull green of the paint on the landing as she and Vaughn made their way out of the building. She found herself torn over whether or not to share a different vision with Vaughn. Usually, it wasn't even a question, but this one was so riddled with emotional land mines, she wasn't sure she wanted the weight of it on his shoulders . . .

Then he made up her mind for her. "Spill it, Red," he drawled as they emerged onto a street drenched with the smell of the salt water coming off the bay. "I can hear you thinking."

"I saw something about Dorian a while back," she admitted, "around the time we mated." She'd glimpsed him as a leopard, a creature with eyes more green than blue and dark facial markings. "I never told him because it was a distant knowing. Years, I thought . . . and the future can change."

"You going to tell me the details of the vision?"

Having come this far, she couldn't retreat. She told him. "I didn't want to give him false hope—what if it never came true?"

"Hell of a thing," he whispered, shaking his head. "You really think he might be able to shift one day?"

"I used to." She blew out a shuddering breath. "That vision is gone, Vaughn. Something's changed."

"What do you see now?"

"Nothing." She gripped his hand. "I see nothing at all around Dorian now. I don't know if it's because his future is in flux—"

"—or because he has no future." Vaughn's jaw was a brutal line. "Aleine might get him killed."

"He's made his choice," Faith said, though her heart was a

rock in her throat. Sometimes she hated the price her gift demanded. "Like we made ours."

"That was different."

It made her smile. "The Council tried to kill you, too." The memory still made her entire body burn with a violent mix of rage and fear. "We made it. I have faith Dorian will, too." Even if his future was a formless darkness filled with complete and utter emptiness.

CHAPTER 31

Amara couldn't see him, but she knew he was there. Ashaya had never managed to keep her out for this long, not when Amara really wanted to get in. But *he* was doing something, making Ashaya turn her back on her sister.

That wasn't allowed.

As she tried again and again to break Ashaya's shields, her eye fell on a small pressure injector filled with a lethal dose of narcotic.

"So easy," she whispered. A simple, permanent solution.

CHAPTER 32

The temptation is a physical ache. Now that I've seen him, met him, *kissed* him, my mind won't stop bombarding me with images of my body intertwined with his, his golden hair brilliant against my skin, his hands powerful against my breasts, his tongue flicking over the damp heat of me. My hands tremble as I write this. I can't sleep. I can't think.

What is happening to me?

—*From the encrypted personal files of Ashaya Aleine*

Dorian walked around to sit beside Ashaya. When she made no move to acknowledge him, he growled low in his throat and tugged back her head using her braid.

"Dorian!" she snapped, her shell cracking. "Faith's information means I have to maintain—"

"Shut up, Shaya." He wrapped her braid around one hand, gripping her jaw with the fingers of the other. "Yeah, your sister sounds like a serious problem, but fuck it, she's going to come after you sooner or later. Let it be sooner because I refuse to let you bury yourself for her. We stand and we fight."

Ashaya didn't reply, didn't say a word. If he hadn't already begun to sense her with a part of him he'd never thought would awaken for a Psy, he wouldn't have picked up the distress behind her implacable mask. "What is it?"

She pressed her lips together. Damn, stubborn woman. Eyes narrowed, he thought over what he'd said, coupled it with her vulnerabilities. *I refuse to let you bury yourself for her.*

"You were buried in a quake." Close, he thought when her lashes fluttered down for an instant before rising resolutely. "But you dealt with that. Hell, you worked in an underground lab for months. So it's not the idea of burial that scares you . . . it's the idea of being buried by Amara."

"Stop it." A harsh whisper. "Let me go and stop it."

"Oh, no, Shaya." He released her chin but maintained his hold on her braid. He was careful of his strength, but implacable. He knew she'd refuse to talk unless he made her. "This is how it's going to work," he said. "You tell me what the hell your crazy sister did to you, or every time you try to flick me off—or tell a lie—I'm going to kiss you."

Her eyes widened, then grew hot with the blinding fury of a temper she'd never before shown. "Dorian, despite what the Psy Council likes to release via its propaganda machine, you're not an animal. You're a civilized being who understands the rule of law."

He'd already given her a warning. So now he just kissed her. Her mouth was open and he was oh-so-tempted to sweep his tongue inside, to savor what he craved with every hard inch of him. But, though he might not believe it, he was trying to be good. She had no idea how good he was being.

The second their lips parted, she took a deep, shuddering breath that did all sorts of interesting things to her breasts. He looked down and realized he had plans for those breasts, such sinful plans. "Talk," he ordered.

"Even the Councilors couldn't make me talk," she taunted. "What makes you think you can break me?"

He smiled, slow, sensual, pleased. *Finally*, she was playing with him. "I don't want to break you, sugar." Giving a chuckle, he dipped his head and licked at the jumping beat of her pulse. "Hurting women isn't my style. But I do want to handle you"—free hand smoothing down her arm—"pet you"—the slightest brush of his knuckles against her generous breasts—"devour you." He closed his teeth over the fullness of her lower lip and nearly forgot about his good intentions.

Color rode high on her cheekbones when he released her after a stolen kiss, but she met him eye to eye. "You pointed a gun at me. You told me you'd kill me if necessary."

"You weren't a woman then, you were a Psy scientist." A feline answer, full of a cunning Ashaya realized could get her into very hot water very fast if she wasn't careful.

She could feel her breath coming quicker as he began to place suckling kisses along the bared line of her neck. "That's against your own rules." She didn't know why she'd said that. It was blatant encouragement, no two ways about it.

His teeth grazed her pulse as he spoke against her neck. "I said I would kiss you. I never said *where* I would kiss you."

Of course Ashaya knew about the mechanics of sex, though it was an act the Psy had phased out as soon as technology allowed. But, she now realized, there was a giant hole in her knowledge—practical application. "A kiss between two people is, by definition, on the lips," she argued.

He chuckled and she swore she could feel the sound across her skin. "But this isn't about two people kissing. It's me kissing *you*." He opened his mouth on her neck and sucked. Hard.

Heat exploded from that point outward, devastating her defenses even as that strange layer of chaos went up between her and her twin, shutting Amara out of this intimacy. "Dorian, please." An ambiguous plea.

He released her heated flesh, but only after a final, warning bite. "Talk."

Bright blue eyes clashed into hers, demanding a form of surrender she didn't know how to give—she'd spent her entire life protecting herself from someone who should've been her one point of safety. Trust didn't come easily. "What if Amara—"

"Let her try to hurt Keenan." Another kiss, this one pressed to her parted lips. The dark taste of male fury entered her mouth. "Let her fucking try."

"You're so arrogant you don't even realize she could kill you," she snapped. "She might be an M-Psy, she might be my twin, but she's got the calculating mind of a sociopath. She won't worry about honor or courage. She'll stab you in the back, shoot you with a gun, poison you, whatever it takes!"

"I know *exactly* what Psy killers are capable of." He tugged her head farther back.

"She's not a killer!"

"Fine." He didn't know whether to be infuriated or impressed by her loyalty. "I know how sociopaths think."

When he ran his knuckles over her arched neck, she reached

up with both hands and gripped his wrist. "You think of her as a woman, like me. She's not."

"So tell me what she is like." A face that was a warrior's, ruthless, without mercy. "Or would you like me to kiss you . . . elsewhere?"

She could almost see flames lick their way across the extraordinary color of his eyes. Then he whispered, "Lie to me, Shaya."

Her thighs pressed together without conscious thought and she found herself fighting the desire to give him exactly what he wanted. That much sensation might finally shatter her PsyNet shields, exposing her to the hunters. Which left her with only one choice. "On my seventeenth birthday, Amara put something in my water glass."

Dorian didn't release her hair, but he relaxed his hold enough that she could straighten up. Then he listened with the quiet, lethal focus of the leopard within.

"After I lost consciousness, she dragged me into a hole she'd dug under the house—it was an old building, raised up off the flood-prone ground. We'd been moved to it after we completed our run through the Protocol at sixteen." Ashaya felt her skin begin to crawl with the sensory memory of insects scurrying across the exposed skin of her face. "The hole was shallow, but it was . . . enough." For sheer, unrelenting terror.

Dorian didn't say a word, but he released her . . . only to pull her down against his chest as he sprawled lengthwise on the sofa. Her head, he held pressed to his chest, his free hand stroking up and down her arm. She should've fought him, but she had a feeling this was a battle she'd lost the day she'd first spoken to the sniper in the trees.

"Go on," he said when she went silent. "I've got you."

She took a deep breath, drawing the scent of him into her lungs. "Amara had made a lid for the hole. Nothing complicated—just slats of wood nailed to each other—but she'd weighed it down so it couldn't be pushed up. When I woke, I could see the light shining down from the torch she'd left hanging over an exposed beam. I tried to sit up, hit my head, panicked." Her hands had been bloody by the time she realized she couldn't get out, her vocal cords able to utter nothing but paralyzed whimpers. And her Silence had broken so suddenly and irrevocably that only memories of the pain controls remained—because what her trainers had never considered was that there could be worse terror, worse pain, than the backlash of Silence.

Her brain had come through the break unscathed, perhaps because of the adrenaline, perhaps because Amara had never let her be truly conditioned in the first place. But her mind . . . "She was there the whole time, listening to me. She knew no one would come—she'd drugged our guardian's drink, too."

Oddly, Dorian's bitten-off curse made her feel safer. Amara couldn't get to her here, she dared to think for the first time. "After the blind panic passed and I was able to comprehend where I was, she started to talk to me."

How does it feel?

Has your conditioning fragmented, or are you holding on to some of it?

Come on, Ashaya, don't be a spoilsport.

"I begged her to let me out. But she said the experiment wasn't over yet. I don't know how long we stayed like that—perhaps an hour, more likely two. Then . . ." Her throat dried up. She found she was digging her fingernails into Dorian's chest, gritting her teeth so hard her jaw hurt. "I'm sorry." She tried to release her fingers, couldn't make herself let go.

"I'm tough." His voice was sandpaper over rock. "You hold on however hard you damn well want."

She took him at his word. "Amara began to bury me. Some of the dirt fell through the cracks where the light had been coming through, and crumbled over my face, my body. Then one of the planks broke over my leg . . . and I shattered."

The past and the present had melded, until she was sure the earth was closing around her, smothering her in a wave of violent tremors. "I screamed, begged, promised to do anything she wanted if she'd only let me out." Her entire body shook with the memories and she felt the constant cord of her connection to Amara begin to gain in strength. But still, her sister continued to be blocked out.

By chaos touched with feral protectiveness.

She was a psychic being—she knew that that strange shield was connected to Dorian, to what he made her feel. She tried to follow the thought, but terror sucked her under. "I shredded my hands, ripped off my nails trying to get out. My own blood dripped onto my face until the iron of it was all I could smell."

Dorian's hand tightened on her nape. "Listen to my heart-beat, Shaya. Focus."

Trapped as she was in the madness of that grave, his words made no sense, but because he'd said them in such a command-ing tone, she obeyed. The beat was hard, steady, certain. A life-line. "She left me in there for . . . a long time." Her voice broke. "I was conscious the entire time."

"Jesus, baby, why didn't you ask for help—you're Psy. You could've telepathed someone."

"I was so phobic, Dorian. It was literally my worst nightmare come true. At first, I simply wasn't rational enough to telepath." She'd become a primal being, terror her lifeblood. "And later . . . she's smart, Amara. She locked me inside her own shields while I was unconscious. I could've smashed my way out, but by the time I realized what she'd done, I was also thinking logically enough to know that I *couldn't* ask anyone."

Dorian muttered a few choice words. "Because if you'd asked for help, they'd have punished you, too. For breaking Silence."

"Yes." She pressed herself deeper into the living warmth of him, so strong, so safe. "At that age, we were valued but not in-valuable. They would've rehabilitated us in a second, wiping our minds until we were little more than walking vegetables. I knew to survive, I had to wait Amara out. And . . . I knew some of it was my fault."

A growl that sounded very, very real.

"Listen." She fisted her hand against him. "She was always a little different, but most geniuses are—even in the Net. Things really only began to deteriorate after my claustrophobia devel-oped. My emotional control or lack of it feeds her instability. That's part of why I became so good at hiding my emotions. Even inside my own mind, I had to believe the lie—anytime I slipped, Amara degenerated."

Both Dorian's arms came around her, unbreakable steel bands. "If she's that smart, she has to know the triggers, too. But she's let you be the one to carry the weight. Enough, Shaya." The leopard was still in his voice, rough and protective. "You're not to blame."

Shuddering, she buried her face against him. "I have to stop." The memories were sucking her under, taking her back to that grave. "I'm not strong enough to do this."

"You stood up to a sniper—most people start running when they see me." Hard words, but his fingertips were tracing the shell of her ear with utter gentleness.

She'd never expected tenderness from her sniper. It kept startling her. "Probably because tales of your meanness precede you."

"That's my girl." Pride overlaid with a raw kind of possessiveness. "You've kept it inside you long enough." Lips brushing over her hair, a firm hand stroking down her back. "It's time to let it go."

She wondered what it would be like to have that extraordinary strength of will always by her side. Dorian would never surrender, no matter what.

"Why did you stay conscious?" he asked. "How?"

"She was in my head the entire time." The memory of violation caused bile to rise in her throat. "She'd been doing that since childhood. That's why my shields are pretty much impenetrable under normal circumstances"—*when she wasn't drowning in emotion*—"sheer self-defense."

"And the intrusions weren't picked up when you were younger?"

It was a good question. "Most telepathic children slip in and out of younger siblings' minds until around the age of two. With twins that goes both ways. It's an accepted part of a Psy child's development—it teaches us shielding, and most kids stop spontaneously when the time comes."

"They learn it's not an acceptable thing to do," Dorian said. "Like cubs learning it's not okay to bite or claw."

Ashaya nodded. "Amara never made that cognitive leap—to her, we're not two people at all."

"Obviously, you learned to block her, or you wouldn't have developed a personality."

"You're extremely intelligent." Not many non-Psy would've understood the consequences of such long-term telepathic interference.

"No way. I'm here for the beer and the babes." The tone was pure California surfer "Now, stop stalling." And the lethal Dark-River sentinel was back.

Anyone who fell for that harmless act, she thought, deserved what they got. "You're right. If a child is psychically directed from an early age, that child becomes nothing more than a shadow, a living echo of the controlling personality. I was lucky because Amara never *did* anything when we were young. She just liked being with me all the time."

"You're the stronger personality," he said quietly. "You could've controlled her."

"I never wanted to." Even the idea nauseated her. "Eventually, I got very good at blocking her. But in that grave, I fractured . . . and she slipped in. She spied on my emotions, prodded me when I threatened to lose consciousness, made sure I lived every moment."

Wakey, wakey, big sister. Tell me some more, show me.

"She knew how afraid I was of being in a small, dark place. She was curious about where that fear came from, since she'd been buried right beside me in the earthquake when we were fourteen and had had no adverse reaction. That was her justification for what she did." Ashaya felt a cool trail down her cheek, and didn't know what it was until the salt of it touched her lips.

Tears.

She was crying. She hadn't shed a single tear since those mindless hours trapped in a pitch-black grave. "But still, I protected her. Because she was—is—broken, and I couldn't let them destroy her, and because—" Her breathing caught, becoming so ragged, she could barely form words. But she had to finish, had to make Dorian see. "She was the single person in the whole world whom I was certain would never betray me to others, not for money, or status, not even to save her own life."

Dorian understood the ties of family, of Pack, and today, he began to understand what drove Ashaya to protect Amara. "She didn't care that you weren't the perfect Psy."

"Back then, she was the more outwardly Silent of the two of us. She would've been believed, but she never threatened to tell on me. Never. Not once." Ashaya's voice hitched as she tried to speak through her tears. "Whatever happened, whatever she did or I did, it was only ever between the two of us. I've never betrayed her and she won't ever betray me." A sob that made her entire body tremble. "But I'm tired, Dorian. I'm so tired. I don't want to be stuck in this twisted bond forever, but I can't see a way out."

Dorian could, but the catch was, not everyone would come out of it alive. Leopard and man both agreed—Ashaya and Keenan were his to protect. Amara Aleine was a threat. A simple equation. And one that, if it came down to the killing fields, might just shatter Ashaya's mind. To lose a twin . . .

"Make me forget." A whisper, a plea.

Not giving her what she wanted wasn't even an option. He switched their positions so she was under him. "Aren't you afraid I'll take advantage?"

She wiped away her tears. "Please do."

"Ask nice."

"Why don't I make you angry instead? That gets me kissed a lot."

He smiled and began to place kisses along the rim of her lips. He had no intention of abusing her trust by taking her while she was so distraught. But, he thought, sliding his lips over hers, changelings understood all there was to know about healing through touch. If Shaya needed a little stroking, he was more than happy to do the job. "Open your mouth."

She did.

And his erection threatened to poke a fucking hole in his jeans.

Ashaya shifted instinctively beneath him, cradling him right where he wanted to be. Groaning into the kiss, he tried to stop himself from thrusting. Then she arched up, rubbing her body against his.

He tore his lips away. "Shaya, baby, I'm not that good."

"I called you 'the sniper' in my journal. I know exactly how bad you are." Her hands slid under his T-shirt to lie flat against his back.

Sizzle. "Harder," he told her when her nails dug into him.

"Like this?"

"Mmm." Dropping his head, even as he smoothed his hand down her back to tilt her heat tight against him, he began to kiss the sensitive line of her neck. Ashaya needed release. He'd damn well give her release. And he'd keep his promise to never hurt her. Even if she was driving him insane with those urgent little movements of her body. "That's it, baby. Let me take you over." He ground himself against her, startling a sharp little cry from her throat. "Shh, darling. Hold on to me."

The scent of her was hot, wild, arousing as hell.

At the edge of his control, he took her mouth in an open-mouthed kiss, insinuating his hand between their bodies at the same time, and using the heel of his hand to give her the sexual friction she needed. He couldn't handle any more. "Come on, sweet darling. Come for me."

"Dorian." It was a gasp as her eyes went pure black and her body arched like a bow, her breasts crushed against him.

"Good girl," he whispered. "Good girl. I should get sainthood for this."

She didn't hear him, and that was fine. He liked seeing her like this, all loose and relaxed . . . and his.

CHAPTER 33

I'm latent. That used to make me angry. But that was before I decided I was going to become a sentinel. My mother thinks I'm pigheaded. I think I know what I want. And no one is going to stop me. No one had better even try.

From an essay titled "What I Want to Be When I Grow Up" by Dorian Christensen, age 8 (Graded A+)

They made it back to Tammy and Nate's house around six thirty.

Something struck him as they entered. "Your PsyNet shields?"

"I'm safe." She gave him a puzzled look. "I shouldn't be. Dorian, what we did—"

"Don't look a gift horse in the mouth." His guess was that Amara was protecting Ashaya. But he didn't want to bring up her twin again so soon. "Keep your head down and don't get lazy with the shields."

She nodded. "Sound advice."

It made him smile to hear her being scientist-like after she'd just exploded in his arms. "I forgot to tell you—Rina's set up another broadcast for tomorrow."

Her eyes met his. "Maybe we can discuss it after dinner." An invitation, a gesture of trust.

"It's a date." He let the memory of their earlier pleasure color the air.

"*Dorian.*"

Grinning, he nudged her upstairs. "Go on—Keenan's probably wondering what's keeping you. I'll come up after I talk to Nate."

When he finally did get upstairs, it was to find both mother and child asleep despite the early hour—Keenan lay tucked against Ashaya, her arms holding him tight.

The sight was a violent kick to his heart.

And he knew.

No more dancing around the truth. No more suspicions. *He knew.*

Chest brutally tight, he walked out into the hall, leaving the door ajar. The staggering weight of the realization had him shaking. Ashaya was his mate. That was why his leopard had gone so crazy around her from the start. It had known. But the man had been too angry to listen. So the cat had shoved all that need, all that hunger, into the most vicious sexual need. "Christ, I'm blind." And he knew the blindness had been at least partly willful. He hadn't wanted to feel such excruciating tenderness for the enemy.

It was so much easier to hate.

Ten minutes later, when he could breathe again, he walked back into the room and closed the door behind himself. As he slid down the back of it to sit on the floor, his eyes on the bed, he saw that his hands were shaking.

The tenderness was there deep inside, mingled with a feral protectiveness. But it was need that had him in its claws. Raw, visceral, painful. Their play this afternoon had already ratcheted up the level of his hunger, and now that he consciously knew the truth of what she was to him, the drive to possess her was close to crushing.

But he wasn't an animal, so he wrenched the hunger back under control and kept watch as they slept. That sleep was of the truly exhausted—deep and intense—as if they finally felt safe. Realizing that calmed the leopard enough that he could think—given the current hour and the fact they were missing a meal, chances were high that his mate and child would wake during the night. He had to be alert when they did.

Whispering the situation to Tammy when she came upstairs to grab them for dinner, he ignored the red gold glow of evening sunlight and forced himself into the light doze all soldiers used when necessary. The scream had him jackknifing to a standing position what felt like an instant later—however, one glance at his watch told him it was ten after nine. The house was quiet, peaceful. But for the rapid breathing of a frightened child, and a woman's soothing murmurs.

"Nightmare?" he asked, after running an automatic security sweep—and letting Nate know things were under control when the other sentinel ran in. As Nate left, Dorian turned back to the room. "Shaya?"

"Yes, a nightmare." She looked to him with a quiet need in her eyes. He could no more have stopped himself from walking across the room to sink down on the bed beside her than he could've stopped breathing. "You want to talk about the dream, K-Man?"

Keenan cuddled deeper into his mom, but nodded. "She's looking for me."

"Who?" Dorian asked, though he already knew the answer.

"My mother."

Dorian saw Ashaya go pale under her dark honey and sunlight skin. "Your mother's right here."

"No." Scowling, the kid shook his head. "My mommy's right here, but my *mother* is looking for me." He emphasized the word very carefully. "She's doesn't like me, not like Mommy."

Dorian figured the boy had confused Amara and Ashaya in his mind, but that didn't explain the terror emanating from Ashaya. "How do you know she's looking for you?"

"I can feel her poking at my head." He frowned. "She can't come inside me because I'm in your net. But I think she's seen Mommy." A jaw-cracking yawn.

"Sleep, baby," Ashaya whispered. "We'll keep you safe." The promise was fierce.

"I know." A childish smile, but the eyes remained those of an old man. "Dorian?"

"Yeah, kiddo?" He took the hand Keenan held out. It was warm, fragile, a precious indication of trust.

The boy fought the wings of sleep to say, "Don't let her hurt my mommy."

"I won't." His heart a knot in his throat, he held that tiny hand as Ashaya stroked Keenan back into an easy sleep. "So what aren't you telling me?" he said when he was certain Keenan was well and truly out for the count. Her fear had been too piercing for this to have been a mere dream.

Ashaya's face was stark with dread when she looked up. "He called her his mother, Dorian."

"You're identical twins and he's not even five."

"He shouldn't know that she's his mother." Ashaya's breath grew choppy. "I've raised him from the day, the *hour*, he was born. Me, always me."

She might as well have slammed a brick into his chest. He couldn't speak.

"That means she isn't just poking at his mind, Dorian. It means she's *talking* to him." Her voice rose. "Who knows how long it's been going on? She could've been telling him anything, influencing him—"

Having regained control, he pressed a finger to her lips. "Shh, don't wake him." He saw her struggle to master her panic as he dropped his hand. "I think you've been keeping more secrets." He was furious, but attempting to come across as calm. "But we'll talk about that later. Right now, you need to tell me if we should move Keenan."

"I don't want to be separated from him." Her voice trembled. "But you're right, we can't be together, not until Amara's been . . . contained. Even if she has a lock on him, she'll come to me first—the farther away he is from me, the safer he'll be."

Dorian had figured as much. "I'll have—"

"Don't tell me where he'll be." A tight order. "I could still be compromised."

"You can leave the Net." She damn well was going to leave it, even if he had to drag her out kicking and screaming. "There's a way."

Her eyes locked into his. "No, there isn't. I need to stay." A resolute answer, but the need in her eyes was a wild, angry thing. "Amara will spin completely out of control if I don't."

His eyes narrowed, but her stubbornness wasn't something they could deal with right then. He spent the next few minutes with Nate and Tammy, making arrangements for Keenan to be taken up to the SnowDancer den, the most logical hiding place. Not only was it almost impossible to find if you didn't already know where it was, but Judd and his brother, Walker, would be able to keep a psychic eye on Keenan. "I'll drive him up—" he began, knowing Ashaya would be safe under Nate's watch. And since the other man was already mated, Dorian's leopard didn't snarl at the idea.

"No," Tammy interrupted. "Sascha needs to go up with Keenan. I've already called her and Lucas—we need to monitor if the Web is elastic enough to cover him at that distance, despite the fact that he's connected directly to you."

"I promised him I'd take care of him." And Dorian kept his promises.

Nate scowled. "He's Pack now. You don't think we have rights over him?"

Man and leopard both calmed at the mention of the solid strength of Pack. "Yeah, you do." He thrust a hand through his hair. "Kid's got a grip on my heart, Nate."

"They have a way of doing that." The other sentinel slapped him on the back. "You'll get over it sometime in the next hundred years or so."

Strangely, that made him feel better. Because there was no way he was letting his mate, and the boy he already considered his own, go.

Lucas and Sascha arrived less than an hour later, and Dorian ran upstairs to fetch Keenan—he'd reawakened on his own twenty minutes earlier, stomach rumbling. It had given Dorian the opportunity to make sure Ashaya ate as well before she headed up to prepare Keenan for the change in location.

"Keep your mind quiet," she was saying now as she zipped up Keenan's insulated jacket. "Don't listen to her."

"I won't." Keenan shifted from foot to foot. "It's getting fuzzy anyway. Her voice."

"That's good. Don't be scared, baby. This is only for a little while."

Keenan threw his arms around Ashaya. "I'm not scared, Mommy. I can feel you inside my head. If I need you, I'll call. I know you'll come."

Ashaya's face was a study in wonder as she hugged her son. "Yes, I will."

Walking over, Dorian picked up the little knapsack she'd packed for Keenan. "We'll keep him safe, Shaya. I give you my word."

She glanced up, a silent trust in her eyes that the leopard accepted as its due. Nodding, she kissed Keenan and rose. "Come on, little man. You're going for a ride."

Instead of following her, Keenan turned and pulled on Dorian's pant leg with a confidence that clearly startled Ashaya. What appeared to startle her even more was that Dorian simply bent down and picked the boy up. "Go on, Shaya. I need to chat with Keenan."

Her forehead wrinkled. "He's—"

Dorian shook his head slightly, gratified when she left the room. "You have to trust me with your mom," he said to the boy in his arms.

"*She's* mean." A ferocious protectiveness filled that small face. "She wants to hurt my mommy."

"I know. But I'm pretty mean myself." He let Keenan see the lethal edge in his eyes, something most children wouldn't have understood. But Keenan Aleine was no more a child than Dorian had been at his age. "No one will get close to her."

A small nod. "Dorian?"

"Yeah?"

"I want my mommy in our web."

Dorian's heart kicked in his chest. "She will be." It was the one thing he wouldn't compromise on. And if that made him animal in his possessiveness, so be it.

After Keenan left, Ashaya went back upstairs and began to pack her stuff. "I have to move as well. Nate and Tammy's cubs returned tonight, didn't they?"

"Yeah." He'd already made the same decision, but the leopard was proud of her instinctive need to protect the pack's young. "We definitely need to get out of here if Amara's hunting."

Ashaya halted in the act of closing up her bag. "You're angry."

Angry didn't even come close. "Tell me about Amara being Keenan's mother."

"I don't know if I want to with you growling at me."

His hands clenched. "Sugar, I'm *this* close to tearing off your clothes and teaching you exactly how badly I take you keeping secrets from me. Your choice. Talk or get naked."

Ashaya felt her throat dry up. "You won't hurt me."

"No. But I bet I can make you whimper."

Her thighs pressed together and she knew he was right. Part of her, the part that had been fascinated with Dorian since the moment she first heard his voice, was tempted to taunt him until he made good on his promise. However, right now she needed to keep her wits about her. "Amara is Keenan's biological mother. Both the level of his intelligence and his lack of a fail-safe switch come from her. But *I'm* his mother in every way that counts."

"I'm not arguing." His tone had smoothed out a little, but the growl was still there, under the surface. "What I don't get is— you were both in the Council substructure. How could anyone not know which one of you was pregnant?"

"We're so identical that people—and even Psy are prone to this failing—often mixed us up. Not only that, but we worked in the same lab, on the same projects. We made the decision early, and it wasn't hard to imitate one another once the pregnancy began showing. Those months, I allowed Amara to shadow my mind and vice versa." It had been worth every painful second. "We did get lucky once—when they tied my tubes. Since physical injury wasn't the point, the medics used noninvasive keyhole surgery." If they had opened Ashaya up, there was a good chance her body would've given her away.

Dorian grabbed the bag as she closed the last flap. "Come on—you can tell me the rest on the way." He headed downstairs and out to the car.

Nate and Tammy watched them drive off, the senior sentinel standing with his mate in the circle of his arms. *I want that,* Dorian thought. A family. His mate safe with him. His child sleeping within hearing distance.

But at this precise second, he was well beyond annoyed with said mate. "What was the trigger for the swap?" he said as he pulled out onto the main road.

"Don't. Growl. At. Me."

He hadn't even realized he was making the angry sound. *"Talk."*

Her back stiffened but she answered, speaking so fast he could barely separate out the words. "Amara used her own eggs and donor sperm to create an embryo, which she then infected with a disease. She intended to kill the fetus when it was born and dissect sections of its brain to study the progress of that infection."

The horror of it stunned Dorian. It took him several minutes to fight past the clawing protectiveness of the cat. "She intended to kill her own child?" *Kill Keenan.*

"I told you," Ashaya said, voice trembling with a mix of anger and anguish, "Amara doesn't really see people as people. The only person she's ever seen as human is me—and until Keenan, I was able to keep her from crossing the line into murder."

He tried to wrap his mind around the sheer weight of that responsibility and couldn't. How the hell had Ashaya survived? "Can't have been easy."

"Actually, it was," she said to his surprise. "She's a sociopath, but she has no desire to kill for the sake of it. She is, in fact, the perfect scientist in her capacity to be completely impartial, and science is her life. All I had to do was keep an eye out to make sure she was being given work that challenged her." A shaky breath. "But this time, the science was going to lead to death. I knew I'd kill her before I allowed her to harm the baby. Except . . ."

He shook his head. "I understand that it must be hell to even consider killing your twin, but women have a way of being feral about their cubs. You're no different. Why is Amara still alive?"

"Don't you see, Dorian?" A shattered whisper. "For better or worse, she *is* his biological mother." The words were like hidden grenades, blowing up in his face. "She's the reason he exists— how could I steal her child and then get rid of her? How could I go to my son with his mother's blood on my hands?"

The emotional knives kept twisting deeper, harder. "So you somehow convinced her to give up maternal rights? How?"

"I had to speak to her on her level." An unflinching answer, a leopardess fighting for her cub. "I had to pretend I understood and accepted what she'd done. I talked her into making it a long-term experiment. She said it would be far too much work, but I said I'd take care of the long-term part."

"The infection—oh, Jesus. Omega?" It was such a vile thought the cat refused to believe it could be the truth.

"In a sense." A calm tone, but her hands were trembling so hard he saw her grab hold of one with the other to immobilize it.

Dorian let out a slow breath. "Does the Council know?"

"They didn't when I left and I highly doubt they do now. Only Amara and I know everything. Keenan knows a little—just what he needs to protect himself. I *hate* that he has to know anything."

"Keenan's a smart kid," Dorian muttered, pride thickening his voice, "and Amara will never betray you." Yet she was a monster who'd planned to kill her own child. The discordance between the two was harsh, allowing for no easy answer. "Zie Zen?"

"A former associate of our mother's. I asked him to tell this one lie without asking me why, and he did." She met his eyes. "Do you understand now why I will get very angry with you if you treat him with anything less than respect?"

He bowed his head. Sometimes, even a leopard had to admit being in the wrong.

Apparently satisfied, she continued. "Technically, Keenan has no biological father—Amara spliced together genetic material from an incredible number of donors, most likely so no one else would have a claim on the embryo. I used that. I told everyone his DNA scan didn't line up with Zie Zen's because we experimented on it in vitro. They believed us—after all, we are the DNA specialists.

"That understanding both increased Keenan's value as a hostage *and* kept him safe from discovery—while the Council was certain he was important to me because I was using him as an experiment, they didn't think to go beyond the DNA."

For the first time in hours, Ashaya felt a hard push at her mind. It was a surprise, but she held Amara back, the task far easier than it should've been. Something had changed in her. She checked her PsyNet shields again, relaxing only when she saw that she continued to remain anonymous. "We all knew about the idea of Omega," she continued, "but Amara became obsessed with it. Except, she didn't see the point in making everyone infertile. It would still leave the insurgents alive and able to agitate."

Dorian blew out a disbelieving breath. "Why worry about procreation when you could have control over life and death itself?"

"Yes. She decided to create a lethal and easily transmissible bioagent."

The coldness of the equation chilled Dorian's beast. At the same time, he was struck by Amara's almost childlike lack of concern for others. It made a twisted kind of sense if the Dark-Mind was involved—the twin of the NetMind *was* a child in many ways, a stunted creature with no real sense of the world outside its cage. "What did she base her virus on?"

"It wasn't actually a virus. Do you know anything about prions?"

"I've heard that somewhere." He frowned, thinking. "Mad cow disease?"

"Bovine spongiform encephalopathy," Ashaya said. "Prions are responsible for that as well as transmissible spongiform encephalopathies in humans. They're the most deadly infectious agents in the world because no cure has ever been discovered. The only reason TSEs haven't wiped us out is that they're extremely hard to catch."

"Hell." But he could see the logic of it, as Amara must've seen it. "Aren't prions proteins?" At her nod, he blew out a breath. "Easy stuff for her to work with." Ashaya and Amara could both see proteins without the need for a microscope.

"By the time I found out what she was doing," Ashaya said, her crisp scientist's voice beginning to grow ragged at the edges, "she simply wouldn't be stopped. The science, you see—it was brilliant, cutting-edge science." She seemed to be waiting for a response.

He shot her a dark look. "I'm not going to blame you for what she did. Go on."

"I heard Tammy say you could be charming. I haven't seen any proof yet."

Oh, his cat liked that. "I thought I was very charming when I petted you into orgasm." He shot her a look filled with sexual heat. "I plan to do more of that—right after I teach you about keeping secrets."

Her eyes narrowed, and color rode high on her cheeks, but the byplay seemed to have given her the will to go on. "I switched to damage control when I couldn't stop her—I pointed out that by killing everyone, she'd negate the reason for Omega in the first place. That's when she realized she'd need to work out a way to ensure the disease lay dormant until necessary. Once activated, there would have to be a means to either reverse it or slow it down. I was happy for her to work on that—to have a cure for prion diseases would be a good thing, but it's also such a difficult task that the answer's eluded scientists for over a century."

"You thought it would keep her occupied."

"Yes. But"—her next words were shredded with a violent mix of rage and pain—"I didn't know enough about prions then. They're notoriously difficult to culture."

Dorian didn't need her to explain the rest. "So she created a living petri dish." He imagined that was how Amara must've thought of it. To use a child in that way—it was a concept utterly abhorrent to his nature. And yet Amara *was* Keenan's mother. That was something that couldn't be ignored in any decision they made. Neither could his duty to DarkRiver. "Is he infectious?"

CHAPTER 34

Amara threw the glass beaker against the wall and watched the liquid dribble down the white surface without seeing anything.

"Sir?"

She glanced at Keishon Talbot, her assistant, and probable spy for Ming LeBon. "Get out before I kill you."

The other woman left without a word.

Amara threw another beaker, her mind chaotic. Ashaya had done something. The link between them, the one that nothing could break, it was getting weaker. It had always shifted in strength—from background noise to a pure telepathic bond when they both focused. But it was always *there*, easy to pick up from either end.

Not now.

Something was interfering with the transmission—Amara didn't know how that was even possible. She considered all the parameters and came to the logical conclusion: *he* was the cause. The intruder. He had to be destroyed.

Calm descended with the decision.

She stepped over the broken glass on the floor and headed outside—though the psychic link between her and Ashaya was erratic, it was enough to lead Amara to her twin. The guards would try to stop her, of course. But they thought of her as a polite, controlled M-Psy, like Ashaya. Of course, Ashaya had never *actually* been controlled, either, but that was their secret.

She picked up several loaded pressure injectors as she walked.

CHAPTER 35

Clay lets you get away with far too much, Ms. Smart-Ass.
My mate is going to adore me so much, she'll do everything I
say.

—Dorian Christensen in a text message to
Talin McKade, six weeks ago

Is he infectious?

"I won't let anyone touch him," Dorian promised Ashaya,
"and the pack will stand by you." As he'd stood by their mates
and children. "But we need to know."

"To catch it from him," Ashaya said, her voice thick, "you'd
have to cut him open and ingest sections of his brain tissue.
Amara got that idea from an obscure New Guinean prion disease called *kuru*. She tinkered with the protein until ingestion
was the *only* method of transmission—she didn't want anyone
to be able to steal her research."

Unable to put the car on automatic, he reached out and tangled the fingers of one hand with hers. "Is he terminal?"

"No." To his amazement, her face lit up. "Keenan is absolutely, utterly healthy and he'll stay that way. I don't know what
Amara did to him in the test tube, but Dorian, he's a miracle . . .
he has antibodies in his blood."

He wasn't a scientist. It took him a second. "He holds the answer to a cure for all prion diseases." Hard on the heels of that
joyful realization came another, darker one. "He's also the key

the Council needs to unleash Omega." It was a truth they could *never* be allowed to discover.

Ashaya nodded. "Amara has no idea about the antibodies—I sabotaged her tests. But no matter what, I knew it would come down to her or him." Her eyes met his and in them he saw a heartbreaking decision, the bloody protectiveness of a mother winning out over the ties of a bond formed before birth. "Age five was the point at which she planned to dissect his brain."

Jesus. "You were racing a deadline from day one."

"Yes, at first. Then two and a half years ago, when Ming began to pay her too much attention and she went underground, I thought he was safe."

"But she didn't forget him," he guessed.

A jerky shake of the head. "She considers him the first step in her most important piece of work."

Her fingers were clenching around his hard enough to bruise. She was, he realized, barely keeping it together. "You want to talk about something else for a while?" He wasn't up to subtlety at the moment, but he needed to take care of her.

She grabbed on to the offered escape with desperate quickness. "Yes."

"How about my abnormal DNA?" he teased, though the cat was still snarling in protective fury. "Have you fixed me?"

"I'm working on it." Her fingers relaxed as she found her footing in science.

His leopard growled in pleased approval. Ashaya's internal strength was a thing of beauty. Yet she'd let him soothe her. It was as much a caress to his predator's soul as if she'd curled those long, talented fingers around him.

That was all it took.

Sexual heat was suddenly a talon inside him, his beast one step closer to animal savagery. "Tell me." Letting her go, he squeezed both hands around the steering wheel in a vain effort to stop the primitive fury of his reaction. He'd waited too long, and now his cat was no longer giving him a choice. Either he coaxed Ashaya into melting for him in every way . . . or he got the hell away from her. And right now, there was no damn way he was going to leave her unprotected.

"It's a puzzle," she said, unknowingly stoking his hunger

with the primness of her voice. Especially now that he knew how uninhibited she was in bed. He could still hear her gasping little cries from this afternoon, all hot and demanding.

If he didn't have her naked and under him soon, he'd go fucking insane.

"Your DNA is identical to normal changeling DNA in every respect that I can see, but—"

"Where did you get the control sample?" A flash of dark heat raced through him and he knew himself well enough to identify it as a dose of pure jealousy.

"From Tamsyn." A pause, as if she was debating whether to continue. "I knew you'd react negatively if I approached a male. You're . . . possessive."

"Sugar, I'm way past possessive." His voice was no longer fully human.

"Dorian?"

The sound of her voice, thick velvet and honey, wrapped around him like a silken fist. "Be quiet." He focused his attention on getting them where they needed to go.

"I won't take being talked to in that tone."

She was worried about his tone? If she didn't stop inciting the beast, she'd be hot and tight around his cock before they even got off this bloody highway. He growled low in his throat, releasing the leopard the only way he could. "Be. *Quiet.*"

Ashaya seemed shocked into silence. It lasted about six minutes. "Predatory changeling men are meant to be protective toward women."

He kept his eyes on the road.

"Their women, in any case," she said after another pause.

Fifteen more minutes and he'd show her exactly how protective he was.

"I suppose technically I'm one of the enemy, so the protective element of your nature wouldn't apply."

Where the hell was the turnoff? There! He swept the vehicle into a narrow dirt track, taking Ashaya deep into an isolated section of the sprawling Yosemite forest. While most of it was a national park, habitation was allowed under certain restricted rules.

"Dorian?"

Ten more minutes, he told himself.

"I'm right, aren't I? You consider me an ene—"

"Shaya," he gritted out, "you're babbling."

That made her snap her mouth shut for several more minutes. "A nervous reaction. I should be able to handle it using the same tools I used when sitting face-to-face with Councilor Ming LeBon."

The dirt track became nothing more than the most primitive of paths a hundred meters ahead. Switching to the hover-drive, he took them into the shadow of the majestic guardians of the forest—the giant sequoias.

"However, none of my tools seem to be working."

He slammed the car into low gear, maneuvering them over a small outcropping of rock. Even using the hover-drive, he could cause damage, but he knew the forest well enough to avoid going near anything that wouldn't regenerate quickly. Right now, he was more worried about his cock regenerating. It was going to end up cut in half if he didn't lower the zipper soon.

"I can't stop talking," she said, her shock open. "Why? My stomach is full of butterflies, my heart is thundering, and my palms are damp." A small pause, followed by a relieved sigh. "Must be fear. You've got a very threatening look on your face."

That did it. He brought the car to a halt in front of a cabin so well hidden by greenery, not even cats would find it if they weren't actively looking. He wondered what Ashaya would think of it. But first things first. "You," he said, turning to glare at her, "are never to be threatened by me. Understood?"

She blinked. "Actually, right now you're—"

"Tell me you understand." He leaned closer, eyes narrowed. "But—"

"No buts, no nothing. You have the ability to piss me off without even trying, but I'll fucking take a gun to my head before I lay a hand on you. You clear on that?"

She was crushed against the door now, his hand palm down beside her head. But her face was one of rebellion. "No. Not while you're being so aggressive."

"Go on, baby, push me a little more." He smiled.

Ashaya had a very bad feeling about that smile—but it was the kind of bad that had her body melting from the inside out. "Dorian, maybe we should go inside the house . . . I assume there *is* a house close by?"

He smiled widened. "Sure."

Wary of his agreement, she waited until he moved back and then quickly got out. He followed a few seconds later, stopping to get her pack out of the back. "This way." He jerked his head toward a heavy mass of foliage.

Her eyes widened as he nudged aside a sweep of trailing vines dotted with tiny white flowers and put his hand on a high-tech scanner, unlocking the door. She entered to find that the entire place was—but for a corridor that she assumed led to the bathroom facilities—a single large room shaded with the green dark of the forest.

"Lights," he said a second later, and cunningly placed fixtures bathed the cabin in what felt like sunshine.

"It's all glass," she breathed, taking in the way he'd brought the forest inside. The leaves and flowers felt so close, she was tempted to reach out and touch. While the greenery was all shadowed curves outside, clean lines dominated inside. The bed took up the left section, but with plenty of room to move around it. To her right was a comfortable seating area, and beyond it, a small kitchen.

Suddenly, and though she'd heard no voice command, the lights all dimmed, except for the one that lit up the sleeping area. Turning, she opened her mouth to ask him—"Oh."

Dorian was unbuttoning his shirt.

Her throat dried up as inch after inch of golden male flesh was revealed. A strange heat washed through her body, a turbulent internal storm. This afternoon, she'd held on to him because she needed to forget. Tonight, she knew she'd remember every touch, every caress . . . every hard male demand.

He shrugged off the shirt, and she saw it glide to the floor in a motion that seemed ridiculously slow to her heightened senses. In front of her, he was all sleek muscle and heat, a leopard contained in a body blessed with quicksilver grace. Whenever Dorian moved, she felt compelled to watch, it was such a beautiful thing.

Now, with his shirt off and an intrinsically male look on his face, his grace turned into the stalking prowl of a big hunting cat. And she knew very well she was the prey. Still, she stayed in place as he circled around her without speaking before stopping at her back. Tugs on her braid, her hair being released into a wildly curly mass. Then strong male hands stroked over her, sliding her cardigan down her arms.

She should've resisted . . . except she could find no reason to do so. What he'd done to her on the sofa—it had been beyond pleasure. She wanted more—to touch him as he'd touched her, to explore, to taste. And, given that her PsyNet shields were miraculously solid, she had no cause to fear. As for the rest . . . she didn't know how the chaos of what she felt for Dorian kept Amara at bay, but it did. For these stolen moments, she was free. To live. To touch. And be touched.

The cardigan made a soft shush as it hit the floor.

"I'm going to take that as a yes," Dorian said, his fingers resting on her hips, at the very edge of her waistband. "If you want to say no, do it now." Taut strain in every syllable.

The practical question should've broken the sensual spell, but all it did was unlock her tongue. "You're distracting me from my work on your DNA," she said, trying to tease him. It came out wrong—she wasn't used to this kind of play. And her mind wasn't quite functioning, her body having taken complete control.

"I'm latent, not broken."

Something stilled inside her, the primal heart of her—a heart that had come to screaming life entombed below the earth—understanding that his words weren't a statement at all. "You're a lethal, dangerously skilled sniper," she said, speaking the absolute truth because she seemed unable to lie to him. "In many ways you're tougher than those who know they can fall back on the strength of their beast."

Clever fingers slid up and under her T-shirt, stroking skin that quivered at the first touch. "So why bother?"

She drew in a shuddering breath, put her hands on his wrists. "Slower."

His fingers played over her ribs. "I told you the time for saying no was over."

Despite the harsh words, she knew he'd never hurt her. She *knew* in a way that she'd never before known anything. As if the truth was carved deep inside her soul. "I'm not going to say no." Against her skin, his fingertips were slightly rough, quintessentially male in a way she couldn't define. She just knew that the feel of it was an erotic sensation she'd never have expected.

"But sensuality is a drug I need to get used to in small doses." She thought she might've surprised him when his fingers paused.

An instant later, they began moving again, stoking the fire within her with dark precision. "I'm patient."

"I know." He was also incredibly focused—he'd become a powerful and respected member of his pack despite being born with what many would've considered a handicap. But . . . "You hurt, Dorian." A whisper that froze him. "I might be Psy, but I can *feel* your hurt at being unable to shift." The knowing bewildered her, but that made it no less true.

Dorian felt as if she'd knocked him flat with that single quiet statement. He'd done such a damn good job of moving past his genetic flaw that he'd convinced everyone—even himself—that it didn't matter. And on one level, it didn't. He was proud of what he'd become, a changeling fully capable of defending his pack, his family. But . . . *"I couldn't save her."* A gut-wrenching confession.

Ashaya's hands slid under the tee to clench on his. "From all I know, Santano Enrique was a monster in every way. Don't allow the echo of his evil to taint your memories of your sister."

"I swore to destroy the Psy Council." Sascha's empathic gift had saved him from becoming a beast ravaged by vengeance alone, but he was a predatory changeling male. He couldn't forget. "They nurtured Enrique, protected him. I want their blood to flow in the streets."

"Hate will destroy you," she whispered. "It'll destroy . . . us."

He shuddered, burying his face in the curve of her neck. The electric curls of her hair cushioned him with a soft warmth that was so intrinsically female, he couldn't hope to explain it. Wrapping his arms around her waist, he simply held her, allowed himself to hold her, to accept that she was his mate. And that she came from the very race he'd made the target of all his rage, all his pain . . . so that he wouldn't have to face his own guilt.

A scientist's practical hand rose to press against his cheek as Ashaya tilted her head in a sweet gesture of acceptance. "People always say it's changelings who most crave touch, but that's not the truth. A long time ago, long before Silence, Psy craved it more than any other."

He let her words wash over him like affectionate rain. His

mate, his *mate*, was trying to temper his grief, trying to tell him they weren't so very different after all.

"We were becoming so mentally inclined, living so much on the psychic plane that it scared us. We sought out physical sensation to anchor us, to bring us back to reality."

"Did it work?"

Her hand rubbed gently and he felt the cat in him shudder in surrender. "Yes," she said. "It turned the course of our history so powerfully that even Silence couldn't derail it. Not even the strongest among us retreat wholly from their physical bodies. Touch saved us."

"Then save me, Shaya." He laid his heart bare, invited her to savage it.

Dropping her hand, she turned in his arms. Then, rising up on tiptoe, she cupped his face in her palms and drew him down. Her kiss was innocent, vulnerable, a caress so gentle that it made him her slave between one breath and the next.

"Dorian," she said and it was another caress. One hand fluttered to rest on his shoulder, the fingers of the other tracing a line across his cheekbone, along his jaw and down until she splayed her hand flat against his heartbeat.

Whether she understood or not, he knew he was being marked in a very feminine way. "More," he demanded, greedy, starving, ready to take.

CHAPTER 36

She curled her fingers into his chest instead of complying. "You're an incredibly handsome male," she said. "Perfect bone structure, pure blond hair, eyes so blue they should be impossible. Your only 'flaw' is this tattoo." She traced the three jagged lines on his right biceps. "It's an echo of the markings on your alpha's face."

He gave a short nod.

"A symbol of absolute loyalty." Her lips parted. "Knowing that just makes you even more dangerously beautiful."

He felt a blush heat up his cheeks. His looks were simply another hurdle he'd had to overcome as far as he was concerned. "Took a long time for people to take me seriously."

"Yes, but you see, Dorian," Ashaya said, stroking her hands down his chest and back up, "you intimidate me."

"You didn't seem intimidated on the couch in the apartment." He raised a hand, fisting it in her hair. It fascinated him, it was so wild, filled with what felt like a thousand colors from pure black to a golden brown. He wanted to know what it would feel like brushing over him. It also made him wonder about the colors in other, lower places. His fingers curled in anticipation.

"That was an aberration. I know you did what you did to

help me." She pressed a kiss to his chest and glanced up through her lashes. "Tonight, I find myself asking how I could possibly measure up to a man so beautiful."

Dorian wondered if women were born with the ability to cut their men off at the knees. "Shaya, I look at you and I think sex."

Her fingernails dug into his chest, making his cock jump.

"Then I think about all the ways in which I'd like to *have* sex with you. All of them involve licking my way across every inch of you." Bending his head, he flicked out his tongue and tasted her just above the ragged pulse in her neck. "God, I love your skin."

"My skin?" She glanced uncomprehendingly at her own arm when he rose from nibbling at her. "It's brown."

"It's melted chocolate and coffee with cream, exotic as the fucking desert, and so damn erotic, I have wet dreams about you naked on my sheets, your skin smooth and hot from the sun's rays."

She swallowed, chest heaving. "You make me sound edible."

He purred. "You are." He wanted to strip her bit by slow bit—the cat was desperate to know if her skin was the same luscious shade all over. "If it isn't," he whispered, taking her mouth in a ravaging kiss, "I'll happily rub every inch of you with sweet, lickable oil and stroke you until the sun has its way with you."

She seemed to be having trouble breathing. "Dorian, that made no sense."

"Didn't it?" He bit her lower lip and saw her pupils dilate as her hands moved down to grip at his waist. "I have this fantasy."

"Oh." She rose up on tiptoe, unconsciously following his mouth.

He rewarded her enthusiasm with another kiss. "Of sliding my hand from your nape, down the sweep of your back and over the sweet, sweet curves below."

She blew out a shuddering breath when he cupped her bottom with one hand. "I said, slow."

"We're just talking."

Her next look was an accusation. "You know perfectly well what you're doing."

He smiled, feeling the cat purr again. He did know what he was doing. Ashaya was a creature of the intellect. She was so damn smart it turned him on like nobody's business. He knew instinctively that to truly reach her, to awaken her sensuality on the level he needed, he'd have to tempt her mind as well as her body.

With the smile continuing to flirt over his lips, he released her and moved his hands to his belt. Ashaya watched with unhidden feminine intent as he undid the buckle and pulled the belt slowly through the hoops. When the metal buckle clunked to the floor, she gave a little jump, but her eyes didn't move from the denim-covered erection he made no effort to hide.

"I want you so bad," he said, "one touch and I'll come."

Her chest moved up and down in a ragged rhythm.

He flicked open the top button, went to the fly, pulled it down a little. "Damn," he said, holding her eyes. "I forgot the boots." Grabbing one of the two chairs in the room, he sat down, legs sprawled. As he bent to undo the laces of his combat boots, he flicked his eyes behind Ashaya. Even this deep into sex, his protectiveness wouldn't allow her to be vulnerable. Only when he was sure the security panel was still flashing "Safe" did he pull off the first boot and drop it.

Ashaya remained in place as he did the same to the second. Neither did she move when he got rid of his socks and sat back up. She was rubbing her hands down the front of her soft khaki cargos, the dark blue of her T-shirt molding to the generous curves of her breasts. Damp, he thought, nostrils flaring at the scent, her skin was damp. That made him think of other, wetter, slicker parts of her.

Groaning, he sprawled back in the chair. "My cock hurts, sugar."

"What do you want me to do?" A husky offer couched as a question.

He waved a finger at her T-shirt. "Off. Please." He put every ounce of charm he had into his smile.

She didn't smile in return, but her eyes filled with something hot . . . exquisitely possessive. Putting her hands on the bottom edge of the tee, she pulled it over her head in a single efficient move. He about swallowed his tongue when she did the same with the black sports bra she had on underneath.

"Shit." He pulled down the damn zipper of his jeans, releasing the pounding length of his erection.

Her eyes went to him. She licked her lips. And he had to squeeze himself hard at the base to keep from coming right then and there. "You're not shy." His voice croaked, he was so damn hot for her.

She walked closer, pure, welcoming female. "You told me you look at me and think of sex. I assumed that meant you liked my body. Don't you?" Hands on hips, head tilted in a way that was woman personified. She was so confident looking, he almost missed the hint of uncertainty in her eyes. Then she spoke, and he remembered that his mate was very good at hiding her fears, her hurts. "Dorian?"

"Shh, I'm looking." He traced the lush weight of her breasts with his gaze, angled down the curve of her waist to hips that seemed made for a man's hands. Lower. God, he wanted to bite down on her flesh, mark her in the most primitive of ways.

The cat spread inside him in a languorous wave of sexual need. *Now,* it said, *she's ready.* Her arousal was a drug soaking into his very pores, threatening to make his earlier teasing come true—he might lose it simply by looking at her. In desperation, he squeezed himself tighter. "Baby, if I liked your body any more, I'd turn myself into a eunuch trying not to come." She was even more sexily built than he'd imagined, a curvy goddess straight out of his hottest dreams.

She looked down at his erection, fascination in her gaze. "Why"—her eyes traced the length of him, her teeth sinking into her lower lip—"do I find the sight of you holding yourself so arousing?"

"The same reason I'd love to see you pleasuring yourself." Oh, hell, he hadn't just said that and put the image in his mind! "Fuck." Squeezing his eyes shut, he tried to think of baseball, trees, anything but the vision of Ashaya with her hand buried between her legs, head thrown back in sweet release.

It didn't work.

His eyes snapped open just as Ashaya leaned closer and ran a single wondering finger down his aching cock. He came.

Ashaya had never considered pleasure before meeting Dorian. Even then, she'd considered it as something predictable in a general sense. When he touched her, she felt pleasure. That was the equation. Contact=pleasure. She'd never once thought that watching him lose control would birth a pleasure so deep and rich, it would eclipse everything that had come before.

His eyes opened after several long seconds. "That wasn't exactly what I had in mind."

She was startled to see a hint of embarrassment in the vibrant blue. "Dorian," she said, not bothering to hide the depth of *want* clawing at her, "that was the most erotic experience of my entire life."

Sensual charm curved his lips, wicked and teasing. "Give me a few minutes and I'll give you something to compare it to. You're so damn pretty, Shaya."

"A few minutes?" Feeling suddenly shy, she crossed her arms over her chest. The smile on his face widened, becoming touched with the feral wildness of the cat. It made thinking difficult. "I believed males needed a longer recovery time to mate."

"Not this kitty cat." Rising to his feet, he said, "Get ready to play."

She found her body straining after him as he disappeared down the corridor she assumed led to the bathroom. When he returned, he was completely naked. She heard a sound of incredible yearning fill the air, and was shocked to find it had come from her. Dorian's body went utterly motionless. A second later, he moved with such speed that she gasped to find him in front of her, pulling her arms apart.

"Let me see," he said, exerting gentle pressure.

She didn't fight him. "There's a hunger," she whispered, scared at the depth of that need, at what it demanded from her. "It's almost painful."

He didn't tell her to stop analyzing their interaction, didn't accuse her of not acting like a normal woman, both fears she'd harbored. Instead, he smiled and said, "Show me where."

When he let go of her arms, she spread the palm of her right hand over her navel, partly touching skin, partly the material of her cargos.

"There?" Brushing aside her hand, he replaced it with his own. She looked down, mesmerized at the erotic contrast. His hand was thickly masculine in comparison to her own, the hairs on the backs of his arms shimmering with light, his fingers marked with faded scars. He was beautiful to her. But when he looked at her, she saw a startling truth—she was beautiful to him, too.

"Yes," she whispered, and it was a permission not an answer.

He took her at her word, this man with a wounded soul and the heart of a leopard, a man so complex that she knew he'd be a puzzle she could explore the rest of her life, if she only had the chance. She sucked in a breath as he changed the direction of his hand, arrowing his fingers down under her waistband and inside her panties in a firm move.

Sensation exploded behind her eyelids. She felt her knees collapse, her body begin to quake with pleasure so extreme, it caused blackness to slide over her eyes. She should've been terrified. Except it felt too good to fight. So she surrendered.

There was no time for worry. Or fear. Only pleasure.

When the darkness receded, she found herself lying on the bed, still half-dressed . . . and being watched by human eyes that held a very feline satisfaction. "I said slow."

He smiled. "Oops."

Charm.

This leopard lying next to her had a whole arsenal of it. According to what she'd been taught during her passage through the Silence Protocol, charm had both negative and positive aspects. Some used it as a weapon, others as a tool. But, she realized as she lay there limp from pleasure, all that changed if trust was involved. Then, it became a caress, a stroke, a kiss. "When we first met, I would've never predicted you could be this way."

He circled her belly button with a finger. "When we first met, I was a mean bastard."

"I don't think that's changed."

He paused his playful touching. "Oh?"

"I've just earned a free pass through the meanness."

That made him relax, a husky chuckle her answer as he shifted position to brace himself over her. His kiss was deceptively lazy this time, a slow tasting that made her sigh. When he kissed his way down her neck and to the valley between her breasts, she thrust her hands into his hair and held on.

The scrape of his shadowed jaw was rough against the tender skin of her breast. She sucked in a breath. He murmured an apology, licking his tongue over the sensual hurt until she could barely bear it. There was so much more to this sexual dance than she'd ever imagined. So much more to the man she'd called the sniper.

"Thinking again?" he murmured, pressing his lips to her navel.

She looked down to meet his heavy-lidded gaze. "About you." In her hands, his hair was soft, sleek. "I know my Silence was broken, but I was brought up in an environment where control was everything. I thought it would be harder to give in this much." To trust this much—until both body and mind were so in sync, she couldn't imagine being any other way.

"Come on then, sugar. Give in to me some more." His lashes swept over her skin as he laid his forehead against her and pressed another kiss to her navel. When he rose, it was to his knees. Unsnapping the tab, he gripped the zipper of her cargos. "Down." He suited word to action.

It felt as if he was touching each newly exposed inch of flesh, his eyes were so intent. She discovered that she was holding her breath, released it in a slow exhalation as he got the pants off and threw them over the side of the bed, leaving her dressed in one last piece of clothing. Her panties were plain black, certainly nothing like the delicate, lacy garments she'd seen displayed in the windows of human and changeling boutiques.

But Dorian didn't seem to mind. "You're damp." He ran a finger over that dampness, making her bite back a cry. Then he did it again. And again. It sent twisting tendrils of sensation straight through her. But . . . it wasn't enough.

"I feel . . . alone." She needed something, something important. It felt as if she should be able to see it on the psychic plane, but the ephemeral something kept slipping out of her grasp. "Dorian?" It was almost a sob.

"I've got you." One smooth movement and the panties were gone. "Christ, you're beautiful." A harsh male exclamation and then he was spreading her thighs, whispering for her to wrap them around him. She did, able to feel him nudging at her, hot, hard, rawly male.

She cried out into his kiss as he began to enter her, stretching muscles that had never known such use. There was no pain, only the most exquisite kind of ache, as if her body had been made for this man, for this moment. The emptiness faded from inside her, overwhelmed by the amount of sheer sensation her mind was attempting to process. A part of her, a tiny hidden part, knew that something remained missing, but then Dorian bit her lightly on the shoulder and the thought fragmented.

"Biting is okay?" she gasped, adjusting to the blazing heat of him inside her.

He kissed his way up her neck, over her cheek, back to her lips. "Hell, yeah." One male hand slid under her to cup her bottom, angling her for a deeper penetration.

Arching upward, she dared to use her teeth on the powerful cords of his neck. He hissed out a breath, squeezing her bottom. "More."

No longer capable of rational thought, she dug her nails into his back and scratched hard. It made him growl and tug her head back for a firestorm of a kiss.

"Open."

She bit his lower lip instead.

Snarling, he held her in place as he tangled his tongue with hers. She wrapped her body around him, giving back as good as she got.

Then Dorian began to move.

Slow.

"Faster," she said, tearing her lips away from the seduction of his mouth.

Male heat in those bright blue eyes. "No." He drew out inch by torturous inch . . . then pushed back in the same way. It was like the first time all over again, her muscles stretching, her body quivering with a thousand tiny quakes.

"Dorian."

Teeth nipping over her lips, releasing. "You wanted slow."

Her hands slipped over his sweat-slick body as she tried to urge him to increase the pace. It was impossible. He was pure lithe muscle to her soft female form. "Now I want fast."

"No." Another smile, another slow withdrawal and reentry. "I want to play."

CHAPTER 37

Play.

Yes, she thought through the erotic haze of sexual need, a cat would want to play. "What game?"

"I'll go faster if you can talk me into it."

She wasn't even sure she could put together a coherent sentence at this stage. In desperation, she squeezed her internal muscles. It made him shudder and drop his head. "Do that again." A demand that held hints of the predator he was, the dominant sentinel used to command.

"Go faster first." Ashaya scratched him again, having realized his skin could take it, and not only that, that he liked it.

A low growl that shouldn't have been able to come from a human throat. He tore her hands off his body, pinning them on either side of her head. "Messing with a leopard, sugar? Not smart."

She tightened her muscles again, and saw his face suffuse with pleasure. It made her stomach clench, along with other, lower things. Her curiosity, always her biggest asset in the lab, was now fixed on Dorian. She wanted to explore his body in every way she could. Then she wanted to do it again in a thousand different positions. She wanted to make this cat purr.

"I can read your thoughts," he said, eyes gleaming.

"Can you?" She moaned as he continued those oh-so-slow movements of his.

He bit her shoulder again, harder this time. She felt her body coat his with another layer of hot dampness even as lights started sparking behind her eyes. "Let go," he said in a voice touched with a rough tenderness that undid her. "I'll hold you safe."

Yes, he would, she thought. So she rode the wave of pleasure, let him ride her through it, and when the next wave crested, she buried her face in his neck, licking at the salt of his skin.

Something very close to a purr rumbled through his chest. And at last, he began to move faster, the hard heat of him a pounding beat inside of her. She held on, was held safe . . . even as she held him safe.

Dorian was feeling very much the cat when he blinked open his eyes—after his heartbeat finally calmed. His first instinct was to check the security panel. Still okay. Good. 'Cause he had no intention of moving—his body was loose, his limbs relaxed, and his leopard curled up in a sexually satisfied ball, complete with smug feline smile. Not to mention, he had a damn sexy woman half-comatose next to him. He grinned at her complaining moan when he ran his fingers over her abdomen.

Ticklish, he thought, delighted. She was ticklish.

Flattening his palm on her, he rolled the good feeling through his mind, wrapping it around himself like a cloak. The guilt he'd deal with later, he thought, caging it when it began to rise. But it wasn't so easy. The thoughts ate away at him. His sister's death. His parents' pain. His own violent rage. And now his pleasure.

But though the realization hurt like hell, he couldn't regret it. Not this. Not his mate.

Ashaya turned her head, looking at him with those perceptive eyes. "Emotion is a complex system, isn't it?"

He traced her profile with his fingertip. "One way to put it."

"A plus B doesn't always equal C." Her tone was contemplative, her luscious skin warm and a little damp under his palm.

"No." Yawning, he glanced at the bedside clock. "It's almost one in the morning."

"Hmm." She gave a delicate yawn in response to his own.

"That's called the pandiculation reflex, you know—the urge to yawn when you see someone else do it."

"Now that's what I call pillow talk." He yawned again and had the surprise of seeing a tiny smile light up her face.

When sleep came, it was in a soft whisper. He slept curved around her, his senses alert for any hint of an intruder. But when he awoke no more than ninety minutes later, it was to the awareness of Ashaya watching him. "You look like you've never seen a cat in your bed before."

Color brushed across her cheekbones. "You know I haven't."

He was about to tease her some more when he caught the edge of a scent that didn't belong. Even as he moved to grab his jeans from where he'd left them, the security panel pinged to warn him of a breach in the outer perimeter. "Get dressed." Smile wiped off, he zipped up the jeans and headed to the door. "Be alert, but don't come outside."

He stepped out without waiting for a response. A minute later, another man appeared from the silky dark of the trees. Andrew had clearly been in his animal form, because he was naked now—and at ease with that fact, as was the way of changelings. Though Dorian was leopard to Andrew's wolf, they understood each other. The SnowDancer male's sister had also been taken by Santano Enrique. Unlike Kylie, Brenna had survived, but only after going through the worst kind of torture.

However, Dorian's acceptance of Andrew only went so far. And it was nowhere near enough to allow him this close to Ashaya. "What are you doing here?" Though SnowDancer and DarkRiver had free range over each other's territory, the wolves preferred to stick to the higher elevations.

Andrew's eyes shifted over Dorian's shoulder. "I can smell her."

"Don't."

The younger male grinned. "She's all over you, too. Is she as sexy as she smells?"

Dorian knew Andrew was deliberately jerking his chain. "Why don't you come closer and find out?"

"Do I look stupid?"

"You look like a wolf."

Andrew bared his teeth. "I thought we were friends."

"And I thought you got posted back to San Diego."

The other man shrugged. "I came back to visit my baby sister, check up on that mate of hers."

"She's fine," Dorian said, relaxing a little at Andrew's deliberately nonaggressive stance. "I've been keeping an eye on her."

"Yeah, I know. She's always muttering about how she has *three* overprotective morons for brothers now." Andrew snorted. "Wait till she has a baby girl. I can't exactly see Judd being any less feral."

Dorian grinned in agreement. Judd was his sparring partner and one cold son of a bitch. Except when it came to Brenna. "Cut the shit, Drew. You didn't come here wanting to shoot the breeze."

"To tell the truth, I wasn't planning to talk to anyone at all." Andrew rotated his shoulders, as if resettling his bones, before leaning up against a slender fir. "I was out for a good, hard run. Decided to come down here for a change of scenery."

Dorian nodded. "But?"

"But I saw something, thought it might be important. Then I caught your scent and voilà." A sly glance behind Dorian. "I caught another scent, too. A much more delectable one."

"You know, Drew," he said conversationally, "Judd's right—you have a fucking death wish."

"What the—!" Andrew stared at the quivering handle of the knife blade stuck into the tree trunk he'd been leaning against. "Where the hell did that come from?"

Dorian was about to answer when he heard something behind him. His senses sharpened—he hoped to hell that Ashaya wasn't about to do something stupid and walk out. The second she did, this would escalate. Because no matter how much he liked Andrew, Dorian wasn't ready to allow *any* unmated male near her. Not yet, not when the mating dance remained incomplete.

But the next sound he caught turned his cold fury into a smirk. "She has a gun pointed at you."

Andrew's eyes shot toward the cabin. "Should've known you'd hook up with some chick as crazy as you are." Light words but his eyes were already serious. "I saw Psy guards. Fully armed, black uniforms, right on the edge of your territory."

"Shit." He stuck his hand into a pocket and found the phone he hadn't bothered to take out when stripping earlier that night.

"Wait." Andrew thrust a hand through his hair. "It didn't seem like they were looking to mess with us or you. Far as I could tell, they were taking every care *not* to step over the boundary lines."

That made Dorian pause. "We've had no problems with the Council since we fucked with their computer systems." The sabotage had been in retaliation for an attack on a defenseless changeling group under DarkRiver's protection. "You sure they're not out to attack?"

"Seemed more like they were searching for someone."

Dorian's neck prickled. "Coordinates."

The SnowDancer male rattled them off. At the same time, Dorian's phone came to life in his hand. When he answered, it was to hear Lucas say, "Got reports of Psy activity on the borders."

"Hold on." He nodded his thanks to Andrew as the other man made good-bye motions. An instant later, the SnowDancer shifted in a shower of multicolored sparks and then a sleek silver wolf was shooting away in the opposite direction. "Luc, I think they're tracking Ashaya, probably through her twin." He'd already given his alpha a quick rundown on Amara's psychic bond with Ashaya when Lucas had arrived with Sascha to drive Keenan up to the SnowDancer den.

Lucas swore softly. "What else have you got?"

Retrieving his knife from the tree trunk, he slid it back into a pocket while telling Lucas about Andrew's inadvertent discovery. "If they have tracked Shaya here, might be they're trying to cut off her escape routes, set it up so they can grab her outside our territory." Not that it would work. Dorian would hunt down anyone who dared take his mate from him.

"Won't happen. I'm on my way to have a chat with them."

Dorian's instincts, the instincts of a sentinel sworn to protect his alpha pair, awoke with a vengeance. "Who's with you?"

"Mercy and Clay will have my back. Sascha's going to stay out of sight and keep an eye out for any attempts at psychic interference."

"Sascha's a cardinal but she's not trained in—"

"Did I tell you my mate's been hanging around with the bloody assassin?" A growl.

Dorian calmed. "Judd's been teaching her to scan for interference? Good." He switched gears. "When did you get back from the SnowDancer den?"

"Half an hour ago. Sascha decided Keenan would take it better if we all treated his being in the den as a normal visit. Both Hawke and Judd have their eye on him, but the kid settled down easy as pie after he met Walker," he said, referring to Judd's older brother.

"None of us up there?" Dorian was sure the SnowDancers would look out for Keenan, but he didn't want the boy to feel completely lost among strangers.

"Hawke thinks I have issues with trust, but I had Rina and Kit follow us up. Keenan knows Kit and it's good training for both of them to spend some time with our main allies," he said. "Look, I'm almost there. I'll give you a call afterward."

Dorian put the phone in his pocket and turned to find Ashaya in the open doorway. "I thought I told you to stay inside."

"The other man left." She held up the rifle he'd had stashed in his closet. "And I don't have to be a good shot to hit a man from this distance."

"Yeah?" He watched as she tried to tuck her hair behind her ears. The unruly stuff refused to stay in place, dancing gleefully in the quiet air currents rushing through the trees.

"I heard some of what you said—have they tracked me this far?"

He couldn't lie to her. "Amara must've told them."

"No." A stubborn shake of her head. "She would never betray me."

"Shaya—"

"No, Dorian." Her hand clenched on the rifle and she frowned. "Even if they broke her mind, she'd find some way to misdirect them. This is too close—there's too much of a chance they'll actually locate me. Not like in the chaos of Chinatown."

He was swayed by the sheer belief in her tone. "That leaves only one other option."

She gave him a questioning glance as he got rid of some of the vegetation from his front wall to expose a window. "They're not tracking you," he said. "They're tracking Amara."

The rifle trembled in her hand. "I guess I knew that."

"She in your head?" Walking up, he took the rifle and nudged her back inside.

"No." She thrust both hands through her hair. "The psychic

'door' on my end of the bond is closed. I don't know when or how that happened, but it doesn't matter. We're still aware of each other—she's following that awareness."

"Like a homing beacon."

"Yes."

Door closed, Dorian tapped in the security code and reinitiated the perimeter alarms. "Can you do it in reverse? Track her?"

"Yes, but I don't want to." Her cheekbones stood out sharply against her skin. "It's dangerous. If I focus on her, I might open my end of the link. There's no telling what she might attempt to send through or do. I can't risk it when I don't know how I blocked the link in the first place."

"Fine. Andrew didn't mention seeing her, so she can't be too close. We have time." He checked the rifle, then began to go through his other weapons, pausing only long enough to send Luc a quick message about the possibility of it being Amara the Council soldiers were tracking. "If you want to shower, do it now."

She hesitated. "What if it's a red herring and she's going after Keenan?"

Instinct had him shaking his head. "Amara's out for you." And the boy was as safe as they could make him, protected by a pack that took threats against children very seriously.

Ashaya nodded. "I'll be quick." Her voice shook a little, but she was as good as her word, returning in seven minutes.

Dorian decided to take the chance to shower, too—Amara might not be changeling, but it'd be plain lazy not to worry about a scent trail. "Use the window to keep an eye out." He put the rifle in her hands, kissed her because he missed having the taste of her in his mouth, and ducked into the shower.

Three minutes later, he was out and rubbing himself dry. "Shaya?"

"Nothing." She poked her head around the door to give him a troubled look. "How can I still want you even when things are so out of control?"

Throwing the towel over a railing, he began to pull on his clothes. "I once heard Faith say that some things are set in stone." Pants on, he tugged her to him with one hand behind the damp weight of her hair and took her mouth in a hotly protective caress. "We're one of those things."

She stayed in his arms for a few more seconds before pulling away. "You're saying we were inevitable."

"No." He shook his head, shoving wet strands of hair off his face. "We made choices, you and I. But the time for choices is over."

CHAPTER 38

How dare she?

In any other being, it might've been called anger, but what possessed Amara Aleine was a stunned kind of incomprehension. She literally couldn't understand why Ashaya had made the choice she had. Ashaya was Amara's. That was how it was. How it should be.

As she slogged her way painstakingly through the thick dark of the early morning forest—having been forced to abandon her stolen vehicle when the vegetation became too dense—she tried to order her thoughts, to find sense in the chaos. It was difficult. She wasn't accustomed to being outside the lab, had never once in her life been in a place so very *quiet*. And yet it was a quiet filled with things that scurried and whispered, eyes glinting out from behind the massive bulk of the trees in her path.

The ground tried to trip her up every second step, and her hands were bruised from having caught several falls. If she hadn't had Ashaya's mind to guide her, she'd have been lost two minutes after she entered this place.

But even now, Ashaya was refusing to answer her calls, blocking her end of their bond. Her twin had been doing that sporadically for years, but today, Amara could feel an increase in intent. More than that, she could feel the other connection, the one that threatened to dilute Ashaya's link to Amara until it faded entirely. And that was what Amara couldn't comprehend.

She knew that Ashaya had always had a weakness for emotion. That was a given, part of her sister's psyche. It interested Amara as everything about Ashaya interested her. But now Ashaya was doing things that defied the understanding between them. The worst thing was, she'd brought someone else into their game.

That was against the rules.

Amara tripped, fell heavily on one knee, and sat there until the physical pain became manageable. As she started walking again, the initially stiff joint loosened up. The second it did so, her attention shifted back to the real problem.

The third player in the triangle. The *threat*.

She patted the small lump in her pocket, checking to ensure the very special pressure injector, the one loaded with double the dose she'd used on the guards, hadn't fallen out. One shot was all it would take to kill him. And then things would return to the way they had been. She wouldn't be alone anymore, wouldn't be trapped in the endless darkness, her voice Silenced, her other half sliced away with clean precision.

Being alone frightened her. It made her angry, too. Until she had to scream. And when she screamed, the crimson lash of blood stained the world.

Had Amara been rational enough to think, she would've questioned the eerie nature of her thoughts—she'd never felt emotion. Fear was as alien to her as anger. Yet both rode her now. However, Amara was no longer capable of seeing the disconnect. She'd stopped being rational a long time ago . . . since the day the DarkMind first whispered in her ear.

CHAPTER 39

I feel tears in my heart. Such a strange thing. I know it's being fueled by Dorian's withheld rage. I might be Psy, but I can see that that rage is eating at him from the inside out. I'm afraid he'll let it destroy this beauty between us, this precious thing I never even dared to dream.

—*From the encrypted personal files of Ashaya Aleine*

Despite the Psy soldiers' night-vision equipment, Lucas had the clear advantage. This was his territory and he knew every inch of it. "Why shouldn't we kill you?" he asked the black-garbed male who came forward to meet him.

"We have no quarrel with you." The man's eyes were flat, his voice toneless. "We ask permission to enter your territory to hunt a Psy fugitive."

"Permission denied." Lucas folded his arms. "I don't make a habit of allowing enemies into my territory."

"This fugitive may be dangerous to you and your people."

Lucas smiled and it was nothing friendly. "Then the fugitive will die."

"We would prefer to capture this one alive."

"Didn't your mother ever tell you—you don't always get what you want?" He sensed Mercy moving around to flank the soldiers on one side, while Clay took the other. Desiree had proved available at the last minute and was holding a watch position high in the trees to Lucas's back. She was a good shot—not sniper good like Dorian, but good enough to blow out Psy brains all over the forest floor.

"Cooperation will be noted by the Council," the Psy male said.

Lucas felt a chill spread out from his heart. He let it feed into his eyes, into his voice. "Tell your Council that we never forget our dead. And we never forgive. Enrique might be gone, but the rest of them are still fair game."

A silence and he knew the Psy man was telepathing. "Is that a threat?"

Lucas knew without a doubt that someone else was now looking out from behind those dark eyes. "No, simple fact. If your men aren't out of here within the next ten minutes, blood will spill."

"Your people will die, too."

Lucas lifted an eyebrow. "It's going to be night-dark for another hour at least, the forest is thick with trees, and we're leopards in familiar territory. You want to take us on, go ahead."

"This fugitive is extremely dangerous. If we leave, the responsibility for any deaths or injuries resulting from her being at large is yours."

"Noted." He paused. "But if you want her alive, give us an indication of how long since you lost her. Betters our chance of running her down—we've got no problem handing your mess back to you."

A pause that spoke of decisions being made. "We believe she's been in the forest for an hour maximum. She's armed." With that, the Psy soldiers left in military lines. Lucas scented Clay and Mercy escorting them out. "Dezi," he said, after the echoes of their departure had faded from the earth beneath his feet.

Soft whispers of sound only an alpha would hear and then the vibration of Desiree's feet hitting the earth. She walked around to stand beside him, long and lean, with bronze skin brushed with gold and waist-length hair braided into what looked like a thousand sleek plaits. Her rifle, she'd slung across her back. "I saw nothing suspicious." She wrinkled her nose, green eyes so dark, they looked black in this light. "They smell like shit but that's no news flash."

Lucas nodded. These Psy had given off the cold metallic smell that made changeling stomachs turn. Vaughn's theory was that it denoted Psy who were so deeply enmeshed in Silence, they'd never find a way out. "They weren't lying about the fugitive. Think you might be able to pick up a trail?"

"Possible, but this group of lunkheads messed up the scent markers. If I go deeper, past their blanket of crap . . . maybe."

Lucas pulled out his own cell. "I'm going to call Jamie and get more people out here," he said, referring to Dezi's training partner. "You start on the trail." His grim mood turned to amusement as she shifted uncomfortably from foot to foot. "I'll call your mom, too, let her know you extended your shift."

"Damn it." She kicked at the blanket of pine needles on the forest floor. "I forgot my cell and she gets worried if I don't check in after a night shift. I keep telling her it's bad for my tough-ass image, but . . ."

"Meenakshi hasn't quite gotten used to her delicate angel turning into a soldier." In human form, Dezi's mother was a petite powerhouse with Dezi's skin and those startling green eyes she'd brought with her from a region in Kashmir. A star in the world of classical Indian dance, she loved both her mate and her daughter to pieces, but was still stunned her baby had grown up into such a lethal young woman. Not that Dezi couldn't dance. "You were cute in a tutu."

Desiree scowled. "Why don't you ever forget shit?" She turned on her heel without waiting for an answer. "Should've been an elephant instead of a leopard."

Smile widening, Lucas watched her disappear into the trees as he coded in a call to Dorian, very aware of the other woman who'd just moved into his line of sight. Sascha leaned patiently against a slender pine, so gut-wrenchingly beautiful that he was tempted to haul her to him for a long, hungry kiss. But he was an alpha and Dorian was a sentinel who'd bled for him more than once—that loyalty went both ways. "No confirmation that it's Amara," he said when the other man answered, "but at this point, they want her alive enough that they gave us the time when she went in."

"How long before she reaches my cabin?"

"She's not used to the terrain so I'd say it'll be daybreak by then—if she doesn't fall and break her leg, or run into some of the more unfriendly wildlife."

"Could be a ruse."

"Yeah. Dezi's backtracking and I'm going to join her. What I want to know is why they haven't grabbed her on the PsyNet."

Dorian blew out a breath. "One option is that they're using her to get to Ashaya. But . . . Faith saw the DarkMind around Amara. Maybe it's hiding her."

"Hell." Lucas had deep respect for the DarkMind. He knew exactly how dangerous the entity could be. He also knew there was little chance of Amara Aleine coming out of this alive—neither he nor Dorian would allow the DarkMind's insidious brand of evil to taint the pack. "What happens if we find her?" he asked, since Dorian was the one with the most information on this.

A pause and he heard the edges of a soft-voiced conversation before Dorian came back on the line. "Bring her here. This has to end."

"That's what I thought." Finishing the call, he made the promised check-in with Meena, then coded in Jamie's number. The soldier picked up on the first ring. Lucas gave him the location of Dorian's cabin. "Might be guard duty, might be more." Usually, he would've called one of his remaining sentinels, but since Jamie and Dezi were both being considered for that status in the future, he needed to see what they were made of.

Jamie made a sound of agreement. "I'll probably make it just after daybreak."

"Should be fine." Done, Lucas put away the phone and walked over to satiate his hunger for his mate. The kiss was slow, passionate, perfect. "I'm going tracking."

Sascha nodded. "Want me to wait?"

"Do I want my mate to wait in a deserted forest while a dangerous Psy fugitive remains on the loose? Wait, let me think."

"Sarcasm does not suit you." She kissed him again, laughter in her eyes. "No overt attempts at psychic interference that I could determine."

"Good. Go home and rest." Neither of them had slept much, but he knew it would hit her harder—she was physically weaker than he was. Simple fact. And something his protective instincts wouldn't let him ignore. "If this is Amara, I have a feeling we'll be needing your gift."

Sascha's face grew solemn. "To have a broken twin . . . That's got to be a powerful bond—even in the PsyNet, twins aren't separated. I can't imagine how this could possibly end happily." Her hand curled around his. "Dorian's emotionally involved."

"Yeah."

"If he loses another woman he considers his . . ." She shook her head. "He'll give in to the darkness. Nobody will be able to stop him."

Lucas didn't argue. He knew full well that if Ashaya died, Dorian would pick up a gun and go hunting. Only death would halt his quest for vengeance this time.

Ashaya met Dorian's eyes. "I want to stay on watch with you."

He scowled. "You have to go on camera again tomorrow—no, today. Catch some z's."

She sat on the edge of the bed, braiding her hair. "Yes," she said. "I have to make sure people understand that the Council murdered Ekaterina and the others."

He heard the anger and the leopard understood. For some crimes, there could be no forgiveness. "There's one other thing you need to take care of—we've had indications that some human group wants to use Omega to hit the Psy."

She blew out a breath. "I can't retract my statement. That'll undo everything we've achieved." A pause. "I'll make it clear the virus knows no racial boundaries."

"Should work."

"I never thought about that aspect of things," she murmured. "I used Omega because it was the biggest Council secret I knew—I wanted something that would cause so many ripples that they'd forget about looking for one small lost boy."

"You used the very thing that could've led to his death, to protect him."

"Ironic, isn't it?"

"Smart," he said, flicking his eyes toward her. She looked so solemn and neat with those tight braids on either side of her head that he had the wicked impulse to mess her up again.

She met his gaze. "You have the cat in your eyes."

In truth, the leopard was stretched out inside him, tense with worry. But it was also . . . happy. Because she was here. And both man and leopard would do everything and anything to keep her safe. "Whatever happens, you do the broadcast today. We need to make you so hot that your death would cause more problems than it would solve." For one, they'd have a sniper on their trail. It was an icy calm thought.

"The Council wouldn't have cared once," Ashaya said. "They'd have silenced me *and* any critics. I guess things are changing, but the pace is so slow."

"Silence has had over a century to take root," he reminded her. "It can't be ended overnight."

"I don't care so much about Silence."

He shot her a look of utter disbelief. "What?"

"I think most Psy would break Silence if given a choice, but others would choose to hold on to it. That should be an option."

He returned his attention to the window. "If you say so."

"It's not black and white." He could feel her glaring at his back. "Shades of gray dominate."

"Uh-huh."

Something hit his back. "Hey!" When he turned around, Ashaya gave him a prim look. "You weren't paying attention."

"I just don't get it—why the hell would anyone choose to remain an emotionless robot?" He lobbed the pillow back to her.

Grabbing it, she hugged it to her stomach. "Because there are some Psy gifts so dangerous that even we fear them on the deepest, most primal level. Silence is sometimes the only thing holding these powerful Psy back from the edge of the abyss."

Dorian folded his arms and leaned his shoulder against the wall next to the window, from where he could continue to keep watch while facing Ashaya. "No, Shaya, that's the one thing I won't accept. Silence spawned the fucking bastard who took my sister's life. I want it destroyed." Fury uncurled deep inside him, threading through his veins with savage intensity.

"And what about the innocent people who'll lose their minds to the blinding fire of their gifts?" Getting up, she walked over to touch his arm. "You saw the end result of that kind of degradation in the violence of that murder-suicide."

A sheet of red rising at his back, a broken woman in an assassin's arms. "Not my problem." He cupped her cheek. "You're mine. You matter. Pack matters. Everyone else can take their chances."

Ashaya shook her head. "You don't mean that."

"I mean every word. I'll do everything I can to bring Silence down." Because as far as he was concerned, the madness, the *evil*, it all stemmed from the imposition of a protocol that had eliminated emotion from the Psy.

"No, Dorian." She tugged at his wrist, but he broke contact and turned back to the window. "It's the Council that's the true enemy. Once they're gone, once we have a leadership that cares—"

He snorted. "Psy who lead tend to be power hungry."

"Not all." Pushing into his space, Ashaya gripped his arm, feeling herself teetering on the edge of some crucial understanding. Then he shot her a hard look and she knew. "You're not this bitter, hateful man who refuses to see the truth. You're better than this."

This time his glance was filled with cold rage. "My sister was butchered, Shaya. *Butchered.* One of the Silenced tortured her, cut her, broke her. Then he brought her home and killed her in her safe place." His hands clenched so tight she was afraid he'd shatter his own bones. "Her skin was still warm when I reached her. I heard the echo of her scream as I ran up the stairwell and some nights, that scream haunts me until it's all I can hear."

She couldn't imagine the depth of his horror, but that nameless knowing inside her, a knowing attuned only to this leopard in human skin, comprehended that his grief could also turn into a kind of poison. The wonder of it was that it hadn't already.

His pack, she thought, recalling the look in Lucas Hunter's eyes that day on the CTX balcony. Dorian's packmates hadn't just looked out for him, they'd refused to allow him to drown under the crushing weight of his tormented anguish. "You were getting better," she said, shoulders tight with sudden realization. "Before I came into your life, you were getting past the loss."

"You're mine." A flat declaration that was no answer.

"It was me," she said, hand dropping off his arm. "I pushed you back into the poison of rage."

"Ashaya." A warning.

"No," she said, raising her voice to be heard above the roaring silence of his anger. "I'm Psy and you swore to destroy the

Psy. This . . . connection we have, it's not something you were ready for, not something you're comfortable with—"

"I'm more than fucking comfortable with you." The words were bullets. "You don't get to walk away from this using some self-serving psychological bullshit."

"I don't want to walk away!" He was inside her, this cat. And his hurt pulsed in her own heart. "I just want you to face up to the truth."

He snarled at her, a sound that raised every hair on her body. "What the fuck do you want me to say, Shaya? That I never expected to fall for a Psy? That it kills a part of me that keeping you safe is now more important to me than destroying the Council? That the guilt of the pleasure you give me is a dead weight in my chest? Is that what you want?" A vicious question. "There, I've said it. But you know what?" He backed her to the window, closing his hand around the side of her neck. "It doesn't matter shit. The leopard recognizes you, knows you were meant to be mine."

"What about the man?" she asked, refusing to let him silence her with the sheer force of his anger. "What does the man think?"

CHAPTER 40

"The man wishes this was easy." His finger rubbed at the ragged beat of her pulse. "He wishes you were changeling or human so he wouldn't have to question his need to hate the Psy, so he wouldn't have to look into his sister's accusing face every time he closes his eyes, so he damn well wouldn't have to feel a traitor to his own vows."

Pain, such pain tearing through her. "I'm sorry."

"No, Shaya, don't be sorry. Because even while the man is wishing that, he knows that he wouldn't trade you in for anything . . . even if that trade would bring his sister back from the grave." The incredible depth of his guilt was a shadow that turned the blue of his eyes to midnight. "I'll stand watch outside." He left her without another word.

Ashaya stared at the closed door, her heart filled with a turbulence of emotion she was far too inexperienced to fully comprehend. All she knew was that Dorian was hurting. Hurting so badly that it threatened to break his heart. She raised a hand, rubbing it unconsciously over her own chest. She was an

M-Psy—she had no capacity to heal emotional hurts. She didn't even know how to begin.

The only thing she could do for Dorian, the only gift she could give him, was to enable his body to shift. That's what she would work on, she thought, clinging to the familiar, the easily understood. It was a good solution, a solution that utilized her skills . . . and yet she knew it was wrong. She couldn't sit here, willfully ignoring the truth—*she had shoved Dorian to the edge of the abyss.*

The only question was, was she ready to walk over the edge with him?

Ashaya had never considered herself a coward—she'd survived the Council with her mind intact, had put her life on the line to help others escape certain death. But tonight, this choice, it was the hardest of her life. She knew that if she went after Dorian, if she accepted his pain as her own, it would be an irrevocable step.

Keenan, she thought, her mother's heart clenching—he was already at home with these cats. This choice would take nothing away from him. But Amara . . . she didn't know what would happen to Amara. Her twin had been with her since birth, since before birth, their minds linked, their souls connected. A single tear streaked down her face as she cried for the loss of a relationship that had never stood a chance, but that held her prisoner.

Then she stood, wiped away the tear . . . and walked outside.

Dorian was standing with his back to the hidden wall of glass, his eyes focused on the shadowy bulk of the trees that faced his home. He didn't say anything when she opened the door and came out, as unmoving and unwelcoming as stone. But when she made a small movement toward him, he lifted his arm and dragged her close. "Don't cry." It was an order couched in a voice that still trembled with anger. But beneath the anger was a powerful, blinding emotion that threatened to wrench her from everything she'd ever known and throw her into the spinning darkness.

Burying her face in his chest, she wrapped her arms around him. "Then don't hurt." She felt something tug at her soul, inciting an odd kind of breathlessness.

Dorian went very quiet around her.

She fought the pull, knowing it would tear her from Amara. And while Amara was her jailer, Ashaya was also her keeper. Without Ashaya, Amara would kill, would murder, would become the very monster Ashaya had spent her life trying to prevent her from becoming. "I was born first," she whispered. "She's my responsibility."

Dorian's body stiffened for a moment. Then he shifted to drop a kiss on top of her head. "So was I."

"Will you tell me about her?"

He pulled her tighter against his warmth. "She was laughter," he said, a painful roughness in his tone. "Nothing seemed to make her sad. The only time I ever saw Kylie cry as a child was after someone taunted me for not being able to shift." His voice caught. "She was so mad. She said it didn't matter to her, that I was the brother she would've chosen if she'd been given the choice. God, she was a fighter."

Unbidden, an image formed in Ashaya's head, of a girl with Dorian's charm and mischief in her eyes. "Did she look like you?"

"Same hair, same eyes. But her smile—a knockout. She could talk anyone into anything." A husky laugh. "Even when she pissed me off, she could make me smile. She'd tell me stupid 'knock, knock' jokes until I broke. Then she'd hug me, call me her favorite brother, and smile because she knew she was forgiven."

Squeezing her eyes shut, Ashaya swallowed the knot in her throat. "She was precious to you."

"A piece of my heart died with her. I don't know if it will ever grow back."

"That's okay," she managed to whisper. "That piece was hers to take."

"I miss her." He buried his face in the curve of her neck as she rose on tiptoe to wrap her arms around him. "I miss her calling me up to pick her up from some club at one in the morning. I miss her telling me those stupid jokes. I miss her laugh. I miss her every damn minute of every day!" His body shuddered and damp heat bloomed against her neck.

Blinded by her own tears, she held this powerful leopard, this sentinel.

She held him as he cried . . . as he stole the last remaining pieces of her own heart.

Forty-five minutes later, Dorian watched dawn begin its stealthy creep across the sky and felt an odd kind of peace take hold in his heart. Perhaps it would last only a moment, perhaps longer. What mattered was that he knew the peace was a gift from the woman who moved so softly inside his home while he stood watch outside.

He'd tried to tell her to go back to sleep, but she'd shaken her head. Twice now, she'd come to tell him she could feel Amara getting closer. Once she'd worried that her twin was lost in the dark, a catch in her voice. When he heard her footsteps getting closer again, he expected another update.

But she exited with a cup of coffee in hand. "Here."

"Thanks." He looked intently at her, knowing he'd have to be careful with his mate—force of habit might make her hide what he needed to see. As he'd expected, her face bore no visible remnants of her sleepless night or the words spoken between them . . . until he looked into her eyes.

Those eyes, so fucking beautiful. Like one of the lakes up in the Sierra, before the snows. Silver-blue and so clear you could see the detail of every reflected leaf. "We'll do everything we can to take her alive."

A coolly Psy nod, but her hands had curled into fists.

"Lucas has her trail." His alpha had called ten minutes ago to confirm the sighting. "I asked him to let her reach us."

Her breath came out in a soft hush of sound. "Thank you."

"Luc and Dezi are hanging back. They don't want to chance being picked up by a telepathic scan."

"That's smart, but"—she shook her head—"I think she's so focused on me at this point, she's blind to anything else."

"Yeah, that's what Luc said." He took a sip of his coffee, letting his gaze linger on her. She was beautiful in the muted hues between dark and dawn, would be glorious when the sun's rays hit. "Apparently, she's not making even an amateurish attempt to hide her trail. From what he saw while tracking her, it looks like she lost her way a couple of times, but then that internal compass between the two of you seems to have put her back on the right path."

"I'm glad she's not lost." She took a hesitant step toward him. Exultation racing through his bloodstream, he shifted his coffee to his left hand and raised his right arm in welcome. It was another small surrender when she tucked her body against him.

But it wasn't enough. Neither was the physical surrender she'd given him in bed. His beast growled, wanting more, wanting everything.

I was born first. She's my responsibility.

The hell of it was that he understood. The leopard wasn't so civilized. "Can you feel this thing between us?"

A quiet nod. "What is it?"

"You know."

"I can't belong to you," she whispered. "I can't cut Amara free. Without me . . . she *will* become the creature Faith foresaw."

"You already belong to me." He wasn't human, wasn't Psy. And he wasn't particularly worried about the niceties of acceptable behavior. "At some point, the leopard is going to take over and I'll start hunting you."

Her hand clenched on his chest. "I'm a psychic being. I can block you for as long as it takes."

That was the real problem. The mating bond wasn't an automatic thing. For it to come into full effect, both halves of the pair had to accept it. That acceptance could happen a thousand different ways, but he knew that with Sascha and Lucas, it had required a conscious choice on Sascha's part. She'd had to decide to cut the life-giving PsyNet link and drop into Lucas's arms.

Dorian knew in his gut that Ashaya needed to take that same leap of faith, of trust. "You can try, Shaya." He shrugged. "But the mating bond's already there, pulling at you. The more we touch, the more we share our secrets, the stronger it becomes. At some point, blocking it will become impossible."

She turned slightly. "I can feel it *here*"—a fist pressed over her heart—"but I can't see it on the psychic plane. I can sense it pulling at me harder and harder and yet there's no possible way it could exist. You're not in the Net. You're not even a psychic being."

He wondered which one of them she was trying to convince.

"It exists the same way your bond with Keenan exists." But the mating bond was a far harsher thing, a thing of claws and teeth, created with the raw fury of changeling possession, and the endless devotion of changeling heart. "Leopards don't play nice when it comes to their mates. Wait too long and you'll become prey."

Ashaya felt the warning to the core of her being. Dorian was a sniper. He wouldn't run her to ground. No, he'd wait, he'd stalk, and then he'd take. "We'll see," she said. The leopard was attempting to bring her to heel. But even in the PsyNet, she'd never been very good at obeying.

Dorian's chuckle rolled like down her spine like a thousand tiny pinpricks. "You really like living dangerously, don't you, gorgeous?"

It made her remember what he'd said in bed, about messing with a leopard. Her heartbeat jumped. "It does make for an exciting life."

His hand moved to the back of her neck, tilting up her face. "And here I thought you were all about the science." The kiss was slow, intimate, rich with the taste of coffee and Dorian.

She had no will to resist, didn't know why she'd possibly want to. Such pleasure in her bones, in her blood, in the dip of her navel. Against her, he was all hard muscle and coiled power. If she had her way, she thought suddenly, she'd keep Dorian naked so she could indulge her hunger to simply watch that magnificent body flex and move.

There was an odd look in his eye when he raised his head. "I just had the strangest thought pop into my head."

"Oh?" She found she was reaching for him, wanting another taste.

He continued to hold his coffee with one hand, but dipped his head to satisfy her, nipping at her lower lip as the kiss ended. "Yeah. I was thinking of walking around butt naked. Weird. I'm more interested in getting you—"

Ashaya knew she'd somehow given herself away when he stopped midsentence and whistled softly. "I wasn't thinking that, was I?" His lips curved, a look that couldn't be described as anything other than wicked coming into his eyes.

"I have no idea what you're talking about."

He smiled and it was so slow, so very male, that she thought her knees would buckle from the power of it. "Oh, but I do." Nips at her lower lip, a catlike lick along the top one. "The mating bond's starting to fight you."

She found that she was stroking the skin of his neck, having learned he liked being touched that way. "Why would you assume that?"

"I ain't no Psy, Ms. Aleine, but even us dumb animals know when two people start exchanging thoughts, something's going on."

She narrowed her eyes at his smug tone. "It was a coincidence."

"Baby, when I think about my body, I don't focus on my cock."

Only years of controlling her reactions kept her from betraying the tight fist of need that formed in her stomach. "You think the bond's functioning on some level."

Another wicked, wicked smile. "Yeah. And I also think you're hot for me." He drew in a deep breath. "Fucking ambrosia."

She'd forgotten about his sensory abilities. It made her cheeks heat in an unfamiliar physical reaction. But, it also made her . . . happy. An odd thought, a strange sense of warmth in her body. But true. She was happy because he was happy. Neither of them had spoken again about what had taken place in the dark hour before dawn. There was no need for it. They understood that he'd trusted her more than he'd ever trusted anyone . . . and that she'd die before she betrayed that trust.

Because, no matter the ties that kept her bound to the PsyNet, he was hers. And she was his.

No! The vicious telepathic blow almost knocked her to the ground.

She clutched at Dorian, sensing his instant alertness. "She's close enough for telepathy." Close enough that though she couldn't get into Ashaya's mind, Amara could feel the weakening of the twin bond, the strengthening of something else. "Give me a second." Blinking past the lights flickering in front of her eyes, she tried to quiet the adrenaline-spiked beat of her heart. "She wants you dead." Ashaya's soul screamed in repudiation.

"I can take care of myself." Dorian urged her toward the door, handing her his cup. "Lock yourself in and—"

"No. I need to face her." She put the cup just inside the doorway.

"You can do that after I have her contained." Dorian was scanning the forest as he spoke, his nostrils flaring as he used every one of his superior senses. "I can't be distracted worrying about keeping you safe."

That made her mad. "I'm not useless, Dorian," she said. "If you recall, I got out of the lab without your help."

He shot her an irritated look. "You're going to do the pissy woman routine *now*?"

"You're hiding away the one individual who might be able to control Amara." She stood toe-to-toe with him when he shifted to face her fully. "You're being blinded by your protective instincts."

"So?"

The lack of denial threw her. But only momentarily. "That's stupid. I might be able to calm her before she incites a violent response in you."

Dorian's eyes glittered. "Shaya, she tortured you as a fucking experiment. I don't want you anywhere near her."

Get away from him!

CHAPTER 41

I know what I asked was unfair, yet I also know your shoulders are strong enough for the task. Ashaya—my stubborn one, my brave one. But she's mine, too. Ours. Broken, but still my daughter, still your sister. She's still a mind more beautiful than either of us has ever seen.

—Handwritten letter signed "Iliana" circa October 2069

On guard against her twin this time, Ashaya rebuffed the telepathic blow. But Dorian's eyes narrowed. "She's hitting you hard."

She stared out at the shadowed spaces dawn had yet to caress. "She sees you as competition." Reaching out with her telepathic abilities, she tried to calm her twin's erratic mind.

Stop! Stop! Stop!

The mental cadence was off, the sound wrong. Amara was beyond listening. Ashaya looked at Dorian. "She won't allow herself to be captured if she arrives to see you beside me. Take her in an ambush, bring her here. Don't hurt her." She walked out into the murky daylight of a forest morning.

After a few stiff curses, Dorian jogged past her—stopping only to press a possessive kiss to her lips—and disappeared into the trees. She knew he'd never let her out of his sight, but for an instant, she felt incredibly alone.

Keenan was linked to her. So was Amara.

But something was missing.

—the sensation of leaves brushing her hair and bark under her palms. A thousand scents in her nose and—

A shutterblink and it was gone.

"Dorian," she whispered, imagining their fledgling bond as a holovision set with bad reception. Or perhaps bootlegged cable was the better analogy. But who was the hacker? Thinking of the bond in such technical terms helped her get her mind around the shimmering wonder of something so outside her realm of experience, she barely dared imagine she might have a right to it.

She stepped over a fallen log and paused, listening with an inner ear that had nothing to do with being Psy, before turning left. The earth was softer the deeper she went, the trees closer together. But there were still large patches of open land covered with the debris of the forest—leaves and branches, rocks and moss. She had no difficulty skirting the obstacles—light had infiltrated but it was a subdued, heavy kind of light. A waiting light.

She paused again and listened, this time with her human ear. Silence. Dorian was good, very, very good.

—earth and the sharp bite of pine, concentration. The sight of a beautiful woman walking along the forest floo—

She glanced behind her, searching. But the man who thought she was beautiful was nowhere to be seen. Yet she could feel him inside her, though she was in the PsyNet and he was outside. How had he broken— "Of course," she whispered, coming to a standstill. Dorian *hadn't* broken in. No, she had invited him in.

The mating bond was piggybacking on the powerful emotional attraction she felt for him. Full of color and chaos, this emotion tied her to him far more powerfully than any psychic bond.

It didn't matter that she refused to accept the bond. She'd already accepted Dorian into her heart.

Amara walked out from behind a copse of tall firs at that instant, her face ravaged by scratches, dirt, and a mental disturbance that had given itself physical form. "No," she said, voice husky and lips parched. "He can't have you."

Seeing the loaded pressure injector in her sister's hand, Ashaya felt a wave of wild protectiveness sweep over her. "I won't let you touch him."

"You'd never harm me." Confident, brazen.

But she was wrong. Not giving herself time to think, Ashaya walked forward and kicked out her leg, hitting her twin's knee side-on. Amara cried out and collapsed into a whimpering pile on the forest floor. Ashaya could feel her sister's mind scrabbling at the surface of her own as she leaned down, took the injector, and stowed it away in a pocket.

"Your hurt me." An uncomprehending statement.

Heart torn and bloodied, Ashaya knelt down beside Amara and put her hand on her cheek. "To save you." She didn't glance up when Dorian dropped soundlessly behind Amara's fallen body. Her sister found her hands tied behind her back, her ankles roped together before she could struggle away. Betrayal turned her eyes indigo.

Ashaya felt the painful shove of her twin shutting her out completely on the psychic plane. "You need help, Amara."

Nothing from Amara's mind as Dorian swung her up over his shoulder. "I'll carry her the rest of the way."

Ashaya nodded and began to walk beside him. She kept trying to catch Amara's gaze, but her sister stared fixedly down at the forest floor. "Did I hurt your knee badly?" she asked.

Nothing.

She looked at Dorian, feeling helpless and in the wrong, though she knew she'd done the right thing. This way, Amara stayed alive. If she'd attacked Dorian, she'd probably have ended up de—

A telepathic strike that drove her to her knees, every ounce of Amara's meager Tp abilities focused over a very short distance and shoved like an ice pick into Ashaya's brain. Ashaya gripped her head, unable to see through the brutal ferocity of the pain.

Dorian saw Ashaya go down and made his decision in the flicker between one instant and the next. "Fuck this." He dropped Amara lightly to the ground. Then he coldcocked her.

She went out like a light.

But he wasn't looking at her anymore. He was cradling Ashaya in his lap, stroking his hand over her hair, dropping kisses along her temple, and wiping away her tears. She whimpered as if it still hurt. It was such a helpless sound to come from this woman who never let anything bring her down. The rage inside him was a powerful beating thing, but it had nowhere to go—because killing Amara would kill a part of Ashaya, too.

So he just held her until she raised her head. Her gaze went to her sister's unconscious body. "You hit her."

"Only way I could think of to cut off whatever it was she was doing to you." He figured she'd be shocked, maybe a hell of a lot more than shocked. He didn't care. Not when it came to protecting her.

But she didn't berate him. Instead, she nodded, a bruised kind of resignation in her eyes. "I'd almost convinced myself it would all work out, that she'd listen." She shook her head. "There's going to be no easy answer, is there, Dorian?"

He couldn't lie to her. "No, Shaya." This would make them all bleed before it was over.

CHAPTER 42

Kaleb watched the late afternoon foot traffic in the square outside his Moscow office and considered what Henry had shared at the Council meeting an hour ago. This group—Pure Psy—posed a potential problem. Vigilantes of any type had a way of turning against the very power structure they initially supported. "Silver," he said into the intercom.

His aide walked in from the outer office. "Sir?"

"I want you to find out everything you can about a group called Pure Psy."

Silver made a note on her organizer before looking up. "Sir, my family has been approached with an invitation to join Pure Psy."

Given the Mercant family's ruthless penchant for following power, Silver's willingness to share this information was an interesting comment on his own perceived status. "What can you tell me about them?"

"Not much at this stage. The group won't discuss the exact nature of its activities with nonmembers. My family is being cautious about getting involved—we don't want to do anything to jeopardize our standing with the Council."

It was a veiled offer to feed him information. Kaleb knew

Silver's family would cut his throat without a thought if he lost his power, but for now, he had the Mercant resources at his disposal. He'd have been concerned that Silver would betray him with the same glibness, but that wasn't the Mercant way. The family had a history of unswerving loyalty unless and until the object of that loyalty proved weak. "Thank you, Silver," he said. "I'd appreciate being kept updated on Pure Psy's activities."

"Yes, sir. Was that all?"

"Yes."

After his aide left, Kaleb took a small platinum charm from his pocket.

A single star. A marker.

The NetMind and DarkMind had both defied him in his search for the owner of the charm, but he *would* succeed. Failure simply wasn't an option.

CHAPTER 43

Iliana Aleine was interned at the Center as per Council order 507179, and given intensive rehabilitation. She did not wake from the final procedure. The death arose from complications due to her diseased mind and has been ruled natural.

—Death notice received by Ashaya and Amara Aleine,
December 2069

"**I asked Lucas** to get Sascha," Dorian told Ashaya after closing his phone and slinging Amara back over his shoulder. "Her gift might help with your sister."

Ashaya nodded, hovering as they returned to the cabin and he put his burden in a chair inside.

"We have to be safe," he told her as he immobilized Amara with ropes.

"I know." But she watched her twin with need in her eyes that Dorian knew would never be fulfilled. Amara was incapable of love as most people understood it—he'd got that with only a glancing acquaintance. But, he thought, tying the final knot, there was something there. It had driven Amara this far into dangerous territory. "Is she really out?" Going to Ashaya, he took her in his arms.

"Not as deep as before. She'll probably wake within the next few minutes. You should change. The broadcast." The plan was for her to make the morning news.

"I don't know if I can do it." She put her ear over his heartbeat.

Man and leopard were both pleased she saw safety in him. "Yes, you can. Don't give up."

"I can't leave her alone." She looked more lost than he'd ever seen her.

"We won't." He rubbed his thumb over her lower lip in a predator's soothing caress. "Dezi's already out there and more packmates are heading over. But," he added, "I'm not going to push you. I've been thinking about how far the Council seems ready to go—they came close to violating our implied truce today." It displayed an arrogant determination that had him questioning his earlier belief that a high profile would ensure his mate's safety. "We'll find another way to—"

Ashaya was already shaking her head. "No." A husky voice, crushed velvet and feminine will. "I need to do this, for Ekaterina. For my mother. They killed her for daring to speak out, then told us she'd died a 'natural' death." She took a deep breath. "I need to show everyone the Council hasn't intimidated me into silence."

His protective instincts collided with a raw sense of pride. "Once more," he said, voice husky. "After that, we renegotiate."

"One more broadcast might be all that's needed." She took a deep breath. "I'll go change."

Dorian nodded, but kept his senses focused on Amara. "Can she attack you from a distance?"

"No, not telepathically," Ashaya said from the bathroom. "She's not strong enough." The sound of crisp cotton sliding over warm skin. It made his body tighten, but he stayed put, his eyes on a woman who should've been identical to his mate but wasn't.

"What about through the PsyNet?" he asked.

A pause. "Possible. She's the only one who can find me there. If she does, it'll blow my cover . . . even though I'm starting to panic about exactly *how* that cover is staying in place. I'm feeling too much—my shields should've been compromised days ago."

Dorian ignored her final murmurs. "Would she do that, put you at risk?"

Ashaya walked back out, fingers busy with the buttons on the cuffs of her ice-blue shirt. "I broke the rules—I brought someone else into our game. I don't know what she'll do in retaliation."

About to answer, he heard Amara take a deeper, more conscious breath. "She's waking up."

Ashaya gave him a startled look. "How can you tell? She's shut me out, I can't feel her anymore."

"Good." Amara's head rose from her chest to pin Ashaya to the spot, but when she spoke again, it was to Dorian. "Wonder what the Council will say about changelings interfering in their business again."

"Don't know where you've been," Dorian replied conversationally, "but we don't give a shit about your Council."

Amara continued to stare.

He smiled. "Trying to crack my shields? You're not strong enough to do it."

Amara's head swung toward Ashaya. "You've been telling secrets. Ming won't like that. Should I contact him?"

"Are you sure he'll help you?" Dorian raised an eyebrow. "He left you for us to deal with."

Amara didn't blink. "I suppose I should've expected that—I put six of his guards in a narcotic coma."

"Will they live?" Ashaya asked.

"Should." A shrug. "*He* won't." A flat glance at Dorian. "I'm going to kill you."

"No, you won't," Ashaya said. "You're not a murderer."

"I know. I wouldn't kill you."

"Amara, you can't kill anyone."

Dorian's phone beeped in the ensuing silence. He glanced at the readout. "We'd better get going."

Ashaya looked at Amara. "You need to have a shower."

"I'll make sure she gets the chance," Dorian told her, knowing Sascha would ensure Amara didn't pull any psychic tricks. He would've preferred to have Judd come down, but didn't want to take the other man away from Keenan. Then there was the fact that like Ashaya, Amara was still in the Net. And according to the Net, Judd Lauren was dead.

Amara was now staring at her twin. "I saw your broadcast. You lied."

"What did you expect me to do? Let them continue to torture my son?" Ashaya's voice rose for the first time. "Or should I have handed him over to your tender mercies?"

Dorian found it interesting that Amara didn't challenge Ashaya's claim to Keenan. "What will you lie about this time?" she asked instead.

"I'm going to reiterate the message, make it clear I'm not out for political gain."

"It's obvious you feel things." Amara stared, unblinking. "Your eyes give you away."

Very perceptive, Dorian thought—Amara Aleine was a sociopath, but she was in no way stupid. "So what?" Dorian said. "It's the message that's important."

"The second my twin acknowledges a breach in her conditioning," Amara said, eyes never moving off Ashaya, "she loses all credibility. The Council won't have to *do* anything to rebut her accusations."

Dorian had an uneasy feeling her point might be valid. He met Ashaya's gaze. "She right?"

Her nod was reluctant. "Silence is being challenged on a number of levels. People know it's failing for some—there are whispers of violence, of madness, but for the vast majority, it's an indelible truth, something they'll fight to maintain."

"Because," Amara said with the absolute detachment Dorian was coming to expect from her, "at the heart of it, they're afraid."

"Psy don't feel." Dorian leaned back against the wall.

Amara turned to him, black pupils stark against the paleness of her irises. "It's the great irony of our race. Psy cling so hard to Silence because at the bottom of it all, they're terrified, afraid that if they let go, the monsters inside their heads will start crawling out, reducing them to the level of you animals once again."

Dorian understood when he was being played. Instead of letting her get to him, he raised an eyebrow. "But you don't think that. You feel."

She gave him a disappointed look. "No, I don't. I'm a pure sociopath. I can pretend, but I can't actually feel."

He was fascinated by the clinical way she described herself. "How do you know if you've never felt?"

She slanted a sly glance her sibling's way. "Ashaya's mind has all sorts of interesting nooks and crannies, doesn't it, big sister?"

"I told you she spied," Ashaya said, and there was pain in it. "Before I learned to block her, she used to shadow my mind every minute of every day. She's the reason Silence never stood a chance of gaining a foothold in my psyche." Her next words were directed at Amara. "You were never under, were you, Amara?"

Amara shrugged. "It's impossible to condition someone like me. Not when Silence is based on the theory that we all feel something to start with." She looked to Dorian again. "They tie the pain controls—the feedback loop that punishes us for 'bad' behavior—into emotion. Since I don't have any, the conditioning made no impact."

"And you made sure it didn't take with me, either," Ashaya said.

"Your mind was more interesting with emotion."

Ashaya's hand fisted. Pushing off the wall, Dorian began playing with his pocketknife, drawing Amara's attention. "Have you ever killed?" she asked him.

"Yes." In defense of those he loved, in protection. And once, in vengeance.

"What does it feel like?" Cold, scientific curiosity.

He balanced the tip of the knife on his finger. "Why? Don't you know?"

A shrug. "It's never interested me for its own sake."

He believed her. Ashaya's sister was a monster, but a monster of a different breed. Left alone, she wouldn't rampage through the streets spilling innocent blood. Nor would she abduct and torture for the sake of it. But, he realized, she would do any cruelty in the name of science, in the name of knowledge. And the true horror of it was that she might actually find answers to questions humanity had been asking for decades. A genius untrammeled by conscience or ethics. With no vulnerability . . . save one.

"Would you let the Council kill Ashaya?" he asked.

Something primal awakened in the depths of those blue gray eyes. "Ashaya is mine." Like a child staking a claim. "She's always been mine."

"No," he said, folding the knife closed and sliding it back into his pocket. "You can't get into her mind anymore."

For the first time, Amara struggled against her bonds. "I can feel her."

"I know." But he also knew something else. "There's a

stronger bond there now and it's so powerful, it strangles your connection to a trickle."

Amara hissed. "The boy?" A disdainful sniff. "I considered him a threat once, but he comes from me, therefore he is me. Her bond to him is mine."

He saw Ashaya sag in relief. He felt like doing the same. He had complete faith in DarkRiver's ability to protect Keenan, but—and so long as they ensured she could never get physically close to the kid—it looked like they wouldn't have to worry about Amara's particular brand of evil. But this wasn't about Keenan. It had never been.

"You can sense it," he said to her, holding a gaze that should've been familiar but wasn't. She even did her hair in the same braids as Ashaya, had the same distinctive skin tone. Yet he knew he'd never mistake one for the other. There was an emptiness in Amara, a strange hollowness that sucked in everything around her. "You know exactly what I'm talking about."

A mute pause, then a slow, malicious smile. "It's not complete. She chooses me."

"Do you think so?" He raised his head as he caught the scent of Pack. Moving off the wall, he strode to Ashaya, closing his hand gently around hers. "Let's go, beautiful."

She glanced at Amara. "Dorian, I—"

"Shh." Raising their linked hands, he brushed his lips over her knuckles. "You don't have to worry." He didn't have a clue in hell as to what they were going to do with Amara, but no one would hurt her while Ashaya was gone.

Amara laughed and it was hollow, too. "Letting a man control you, big sister? My, we have come down in the world." Cool acid in every word.

But the taunt had the opposite affect from the one Dorian was sure had been intended. All hesitation left Ashaya's face, and she met her twin's eyes with steely determination. "Should I let you manipulate me instead?" A soft question weighted with fury such as he'd never heard. "Should I let you bury my spirit as well?" Pulling open the door, she walked out.

Dorian was the only one who saw Amara's expression—pure, lost confusion. As if she couldn't believe that Ashaya would choose anything or anyone over her. But Amara wasn't the one on Dorian's mind right then. Striding out after Ashaya, he saw her standing several meters away, the pine needles a natural carpet around her.

Keeping her in his line of sight, he glanced at Clay, one of the two extra packmates he'd scented in the area. While Clay had come here after escorting the Psy guards out of their territory, Mercy had called to say she was heading to the station to prepare for Ashaya's next broadcast. "Amara," he said to Clay, "is narcissistic, completely without conscience. Single person she cares about is Ashaya. Watch your back."

The other sentinel simply folded his arms. "Exactly like the Councilors then."

Dorian grinned despite himself. "Yeah. Where's my Psy consult?"

"About ten minutes behind us. Jamie's here, too." Clay jerked his head toward the man who'd just walked out from around the side of the house, having apparently done a security sweep. The skilled soldier had a habit of dyeing his hair in incomprehensible combinations of color—today it was a deep indigo streaked with either black or green. He gave a short wave in response to Dorian's nod, but didn't walk over to join them, his eyes scanning the area with predatory watchfulness.

"That's pretty sedate for Jamie," Dorian commented.

"He said it's his camouflage look." Clay shook his head. "Getting back to Sascha—what the hell do you expect her to do?"

Dorian's gaze drifted out to the wolf-eyed woman who stood so alone against those trees. "I need to know if Amara Aleine can be allowed to live."

Leaving Clay, he walked out after his mate. Ashaya had moved deeper into the shadows but he could track her through anything. Reaching her, he put his hand on the back of her head, and urged her gently toward his chest. She came after a short hesitation, but there was nothing broken in her. Instead, she seemed to vibrate with a vivid rage he could feel in his gut. The leopard gave a growl of respect deep within him. This woman's anger was not something to be ignored.

"Ready to go?" It wasn't what he wanted to say, wasn't the question he wanted to ask, but she'd been pushed incredibly far today. And it would get worse still.

In his arms, she gave a short nod. "Let's get it over with."

As they parted and began to walk back to the car, he could almost see her changing, almost see her wrapping the layers of emotionless control around herself. By the time they drove out, she sat straight-backed and alien next to him. It infuriated the leopard.

CHAPTER 44

Ashaya Aleine is a threat to the Net. Given that the other Councilors seem more worried about their political positions than maintaining the purity of Silence, it appears I shall have to be the one to punish Aleine for her treasonous actions. And there has only ever been one sentence for such a crime: death.

—From the encrypted personal files of Councilor Henry Scott

Sascha arrived minutes after Dorian and Ashaya left. "I don't want to go inside." She hesitated in front of the greenery-cloaked door.

Lucas's arm came around her waist in a familiar embrace. "Talk to me."

"The badness coming off her . . . it's painful." She rubbed at her chest, trying to soothe the ache. "And yet at the same time, there's such need in it."

"Missing her twin?"

"Maybe." She bit her lip. "Since defecting from the Net, I've learned that not everything is black and white. There are shades of gray. But, Lucas, I don't know if I can accept this much gray." Her breath grew short, tight in her chest.

"Come on." He turned her toward the trees. "We'll go for a walk. Clay and Jamie have her covered." His hand slid down to tangle with hers as they walked a ways into the muted light of the forest. "This'll do." He moved to stand in front of her as she leaned back against the solid support of a tree trunk, his hands palms down on the trunk on either side of her head.

"Kitten," he said, his lashes sinfully rich against the deep green of his eyes. "Sascha, I can tell when you're not paying attention."

It made her smile despite her unease. "I was thinking you have pretty eyelashes."

"And I think you're trying to avoid the problem." The tough words of an alpha, but his lips had curved upward.

Sighing, she reached out to hook her fingers in the waistband of his jeans "I've felt evil—Santano Enrique was the most horrible thing I've ever touched. I've felt badness, too—what happened with the SnowDancer traitor. He wasn't evil, just rotten to the core." She felt her forehead wrinkle as she tried to find a way to explain. "And growing up with Nikita for a mother, I'm used to the peculiar coldness of Psy who are Silenced, but aren't sociopathic."

"Amara Aleine is different?" He braced his forearms alongside her head, enclosing her in a protective cocoon.

Sascha soaked it in, knowing it had been an instinctive act. Lucas was protective to his innermost core and she knew she'd always have to fight that part of him to exercise her freedom, but at times like this, it felt so perfect, she would give him anything. "Yes," she said, moving her fingers up under the fine linen of his shirt. "I'm messing up your shirt."

"Are you?" A kiss, a teasing flick of tongue along the seam of her lips. "Do it some more so I can be sure."

She laughed. "Cat." But he was her cat. "Amara," she said, taking strength from the incredible beauty of the mating bond that tied them together, "is oddly empty.

"Everyone has a . . . a taste, an emotional flavor," she explained. "Even newborns straight after birth—remember, I was with Anu when she delivered?" The memory made her heart swell with wonder. She'd been terrified at being requested to attend, but the joy had been incandescent. "But Amara, she's . . . a clean slate, but not. How do I explain?"

Then Lucas put into words what she couldn't. "There's no badness in her, no evil, but there's no goodness or hope of goodness either."

Sometimes, she thought, her panther understood her better than she did. "Yes, that's it. Now, I have to go in there and see whether we can guide her toward a more acceptable path." For Dorian. And for Ashaya. Not only because she was Dorian's, or because she'd helped save three innocent children, but because she'd renewed Sascha's faith in mothers in the Net—Ashaya loved her son, would never repudiate him as Nikita had repudiated Sascha. That knowledge healed a little of the scar Nikita had left in Sascha's heart. "If the DarkMind has Amara," she told Lucas, "change might not be possible. Even if it is, she won't ever be anything . . . good."

"At least she won't be monstrous." Worry grooved deep lines around Lucas's mouth. "If I could've picked a woman for Dorian, it wouldn't have been someone with this kind of baggage. He's been through enough."

Her own concern was a knot in her gut, but she shook her head. "Faith says some things are set in stone."

Lucas's green eyes darkened and then he kissed her. "Yeah, some things are."

Dorian had kept his mouth shut the entire drive. It was either that or yell at Ashaya for something he knew she had to do—it wasn't her fault other Psy would dismiss her if she didn't appear a fucking icy robot. Just as it wasn't the leopard's fault that in her retreat, it saw rejection.

Parking the car in the underground garage of the small, isolated station they'd decided to use this time around, he waited for her to join him. She did . . . and shot his good intentions to hell.

"I can sense it, you know," she said, her cool tone abrasive against his already ragged control. "Your anger."

"And that's a surprise?" he ground out. It didn't matter that he knew she was only going cold for the broadcast. The longer she blocked their mating, the more irrational he was going to get. Because he wasn't human. He was changeling. And the animal's heart wasn't always rational.

"The mating bond," she said instead of answering, "it's pulling at me, trying to tear me from the PsyNet. I should be afraid. But I want to go."

His mind blanked for a second. "Come, then," he said at last. "I'll catch you."

Ashaya's fingers on his face, delicate, impossible touches as fleeting as the brush of a butterfly's wings. "You can't imagine how much I want to follow that pull. I would give my life for it. But . . ."

He cupped her cheek, bending down to press his forehead against hers. "But what, Shaya? I get that you love Amara, but to allow her to imprison you?"

"For better or worse, I was born her keeper, Dorian. Sometimes"—a little of her shell cracked, exposing the raw center—"sometimes, the choking suffocation of that responsibility makes me want to scream and run. But I know if I let go, if I leave her completely on her own, I'm signing her death warrant."

"Because she'll attempt to kill me?" he guessed, his attention momentarily diverted to an opaque-windowed vehicle in the back of the lot. It wasn't a Pack car.

Ashaya's next words had him forgetting all about the suspect vehicle. "We both know who would win." Whispers against his lips, the ice melting moment by moment.

"Oh, hell, Shaya. Don't you dare tell me you're fighting the mating to protect me!"

A stubborn silence.

"Shit." The animal in him was *not* pleased. "I'm a DarkRiver sentinel, sugar. We're so fucking mean even the Council takes us seriously. I can take on Amara."

Stroking her fingers along his shadowed jaw, she shook her head in a gentle reprimand. "And what will it do to you to kill a sister?"

He couldn't breathe for a single, frozen instant.

"Oh, Christ." He trembled, physically nauseated by the thought. As long as he hadn't allowed himself to think of it that way, he'd been able to ignore the white elephant standing right in front of him. "Fuck."

Sascha sat across from Amara. The other woman had been given a chance to shower and now sat unrestrained. Lucas was outside by the front door, Jamie by the back, while Clay and Dezi ran perimeter watch. Sascha herself was in no way helpless. She had low-level telekinetic and telepathic abilities that she'd learned to use aggressively; *and* she'd spent many a sweaty afternoon with Lucas over the past year—getting yelled at and learning self-defense. She'd done some yelling of her own, too, she admitted. The outcome of it all was that even if Amara attacked, she wouldn't get very far.

Right this second, Ashaya's twin gave every indication of utter contentment. "One of the mysterious E-Psy," she murmured with perfect sincerity. "You look like any other person."

"Did you expect different?"

"I expected a corpse. No one survives outside the PsyNet."

Sascha gave a tight smile. "How did you know my designation?"

"Whispers in the PsyNet. It's not like you tried to hide it."

"No." She knew there was something very wrong with Amara, but it was eerie how very sane she seemed on the surface. "Why did you come after Ashaya?"

"She's mine." Flat, implacable.

Sascha saw a chink. "You'd never hurt her."

Silence, as if the question was too stupid to answer.

"She's yours, so if you hurt her," Sascha said, "it'll hurt you."

A glimmer of interest. "You're quite smart."

And Amara was a complete narcissist. "Dorian is Ashaya's," she said. "If you hurt him, it'll hurt her."

A blank stare. "She's mine."

Sascha had been straining to sense even a hint of emotion from Amara, but all she got were faint echoes whenever Ashaya was mentioned. She didn't know how to deal with this woman. Her gift lay in emotion—how was she supposed to reach someone who had none? She'd had a short conversation on the topic with Judd before heading over here.

"Maybe you should talk to her," she'd suggested to the face on the communications screen. "You're better with the darker aspects of our abilities."

"Sascha, I can break open her mind and I can kill her." Judd had shrugged. "Pick."

"Can't you talk to her some way? Understand her?"

Judd's lips had curved. "I'm a bad son of a bitch, but I have emotions despite all indications to the contrary. So we're not going to be able to swap sociopathic bullshit."

Sascha had found herself blushing. "Sorry. I know that. Your love for Brenna . . . it's so beautiful, I wish you could see it as I do."

"I do see it." His eyes had lit from within. "But I can only go so far with someone outside my circle. You want my professional opinion—Amara Aleine needs to die. It's blind luck she was born with a passive ability. If she'd been a powerful telepath or telekinetic, she'd be another Enrique." A pause. "Knowing that's got to be hell on Dorian."

Which was the reason why Sascha sat here, facing this woman who repelled her with her emptiness. "What's your plan?" she asked. "What do you intend to do if you succeed in killing Dorian?"

"I'll go back to my experiments and Ashaya will return to hers."

Sascha glimpsed the flickers of intelligence and knew Amara was seeing the flaws in her own answer. Good. "That's an impossible goal. Ashaya can't return to her previous life now that she's defied the Council so openly."

"Not if she retracts her statements."

"Do you really believe that?" A sense of quiet menace crawled over Sascha's skin as she spoke, and she wondered why she was so afraid. This woman hadn't yet killed anyone, nor was she violent in general. Perhaps, she thought, it was a simple case of her gift reacting negatively to someone who was so much the antithesis of everything she was.

"We both know," she said when Amara remained mute, "that she's made herself too public a figure. The Council would rehabilitate her in a heartbeat. Otherwise, she'd become a magnet for rebel activity."

"Then we'll go rogue." A shrug. "We can still do our work."

"True," she agreed. "Do you think that will be enough for Ashaya? Is she a creature of solitude?"

Amara's eyes stared into Sascha's, as if she was searching for something. "You're like me."

"I'm nothing like you." Sascha couldn't withhold her shock.

"You steal other people's emotions like some vulture or vampire, and then you use them up. It's what makes you so good at pretending. Inside, you're like me."

Sascha had faced down a Psy butcher who'd killed without

remorse, but she couldn't continue speaking to Amara Aleine, couldn't stand to listen to her sly whispers. Getting up, she walked out. Lucas came after her as she strode toward the woods. "I am not an emotional vampire!"

Her mate didn't miss a beat. "No, you're not. And she's a sociopath who you really shouldn't be listening to."

"I don't pretend!" She turned, pushed at his chest. "I love you so goddamn much it tears me to pieces. Why the hell would I feel that if I was pretending?"

"Again," Lucas said, holding her to him with his arms around her waist, "consider the source."

She muttered and yelled some more, releasing the anger, before collapsing against his chest. "She got to me."

"It happens to the best of us."

"Yeah? Who gets to you?" He was so strong that sometimes she worried. Everyone needed to bend a little, even a panther responsible for the lives of his entire pack.

"That damn wolf. He sent you a present last week."

Sascha smiled at the thought of Hawke's flirting. The Snow-Dancer alpha did it only to jerk Lucas's chain. "I never saw any present. What was it?"

"How the hell should I know? I stomped on it and threw it into the deepest crevice I could find." He smirked. "Then I called him to ask how Sienna was doing."

She burst out laughing. "Wicked, wicked man." Everyone knew Sienna Lauren was the short fuse on Hawke's temper. The Psy teenager appeared to have made it her mission in life to get on his last nerve. "What did he say?"

"That she's planning a party for her eighteenth birthday." The laughter in Lucas's tone told her exactly what Hawke had sounded like as he shared that tidbit.

"But doesn't she still have half a year to go?" She figured out her mistake before Lucas could answer. "Of course. She was sixteen when they defected, but that was months before we first met her." Her eyes went wide. "That means we've been mated close to a year and a half."

"Yeah." He stroked her back slow and sure, the caress of a panther being gentle with his mate. "And I've almost killed Hawke a hundred times since then. I swear to God, he calls you 'darling' one more time, I'm going to put him on his wolf ass."

She laughed, but he'd proven his point. Everyone had their tipping point. Hers happened to be Amara Aleine. But she wasn't the important one here. "I need to do something—this is bad, really bad, for Dorian. He was just starting to come back to us. When I saw how he was with Tally, I thought things could only get better." The sentinel seemed to adore Clay's mate, flirted with her on a regular basis. "Now this."

"Do I need to get rid of Amara?" The hard edge of an alpha in his tone.

Sascha had been part of DarkRiver long enough to understand the ties of loyalty, of Pack. But the harshness of it still startled sometimes. "You'd spill blood for him?"

"That's not even a question, kitten."

No, she thought, it wasn't. "It's too complicated, Lucas. Even in the PsyNet, twins tend to stick together. Most die within days of each other."

"Ashaya is Dorian's mate. I can feel it." Lucas's face was a study in shadow and light, pure strength and protectiveness combined. "She'll survive no matter what happens—he won't let her go."

"But she might be permanently damaged by such a traumatic loss." She shook her head. "We have to figure another way out."

Lucas didn't say anything, but she knew what he was thinking—there wasn't any way out that would leave all parties without scars.

CHAPTER 45

Dorian is in my blood, in my very veins. Never in all my lectures on "sexual biology" and "animal behavior" did anyone tell me of this incandescent joy. When I lie with him, there's pleasure, incredible pleasure—my cat knows how to drive a woman to insanity. But there's more, this indefinable, near-painful happiness. I don't know what to call it, how to describe it. I just know that I would die for him.

—From the encrypted personal files of Ashaya Aleine

Psy Councilor Anthony Kyriakus had been part of the rebellion for longer than most people had known it even existed. But now Ashaya Aleine had taken it public.

He could understand her actions—a life in hiding was nothing he'd choose for his own child either. He glanced reflexively at the holo-image he kept in a highly secure file in his computer: Faith, laughing. He could almost hear the sound. His daughter had grown into a beautiful, gifted woman. Anthony, too, had broken rules for his child. He'd let Faith know that she mattered. As her sister had mattered. As her brother mattered.

However, the goalposts had shifted again. He was a Councilor now, under intense scrutiny from every quarter. His contact with Faith wouldn't have to cease, but he'd have to be very, very careful. As he would have to be with this new contact. He touched the screen, pulling up the untraceable e-mail that had come in a week ago.

It was signed by the Ghost, the most notorious rebel in the Net.

Anthony wanted very much to know how and where the Ghost got his information. Only a select few knew Anthony's true loyalties. And no one in his tight circle would've betrayed him. Zie Zen had never even told Ashaya.

But the Ghost had a way of unearthing secrets—in this, the other rebel could prove an invaluable asset. Anthony didn't agree with everything the Ghost had done, but their basic vision aligned. Still, he hadn't risen to the Council by being stupid. This would be a very slow and careful process.

As he closed the message, he recalled the conversation he'd had with Zie Zen yesterday—they'd agreed that Ashaya needed to make a follow-up broadcast. Otherwise, she'd lose all the support she'd gained to date. And, since the Council had decided to focus on damage control rather than disruption, her message would get out far easier this time.

But, he thought, snapping upright, it would also leave Council resources free to trace any broadcast back to the originating location. When added to the fact that all his fellow Councilors knew Ashaya was in the greater San Francisco area . . . "It could be done." He picked up the secure line immediately and put through a call to his daughter. "Faith, you have to warn Ashaya," he said as soon as she answered. "Ming will be waiting to trace back any new broadcast signal. He could recapture—"

"It's too late," Faith whispered, her voice echoing the way it sometimes did in the midst of a vision. "There's blood, so much blood. Oh, my God, Dorian! *Dorian!*"

Dorian knew he'd made a fatal mistake the second he saw Ashaya walk out in front of the camera and begin to speak. She was bathed in light, the area around her in shadow. *The perfect target.*

Perhaps it was simply a leopard sentinel's honed instincts that had him moving before anyone else even realized what was happening . . . or perhaps he'd received a message he couldn't consciously hear, a scream from a cardinal F-Psy connected to him through the Web of Stars. It didn't matter why he did what he did. It just mattered that when the Tk-Psy blinked into place before Ashaya and fired the gun, it was Dorian who took the hit . . . straight through his carotid artery.

Ashaya screamed as she slammed to the ground, carried there by Dorian's momentum as he pushed her out of the way. But it wasn't physical hurt that had her screaming. She could feel Dorian's life slipping away, the fledgling bond that tied her to him retreating at the speed of light. "No, no, no."

Twisting out from under his unconscious body and into a sitting position, she cradled his head in her lap and tore off her jacket, using it in a futile attempt to stanch the bleeding. Blood soaked through the wadded material to drench her fingers. She knew what that meant—the wound was fatal. "No." A steely denial that hid her shattered heart. Forgetting about shields, about protection, she opened her psychic eye and searched for the bond she could feel sliding out into nowhere.

He was hers. He couldn't leave her.

But she couldn't find the bond, couldn't use it to hold him to her. It was still invisible, still piggybacking on her emotions for this man who lay dying in her lap. She felt hands on her shoulders, a familiar female voice telling her the paramedics were on their way. *Shut up*, she thought, *just shut up*.

In the chaos, a moment of silence inside her mind, of clarity. *She couldn't see the bond because she was locked into the PsyNet.*

She didn't know how to cut that link, but she continued to feel the pull of the mating bond. So she gave in to it. A choice made in an instant. A choice she'd made the first time she'd heard his voice.

The bond spiraled through her like wild lightning, ripping her from the PsyNet with such fury that she felt fine blood vessels burst behind her eyelids. As her mind screamed, she was aware of Amara screaming with her, struggling to follow. Ashaya held out a psychic hand.

She had been born first. Amara was her responsibility.

Amara grabbed that hand and left the Net with the same violence, falling into unconsciousness an instant later. Ashaya refused to go into the void with her sister. Shoving away her own pain as unimportant, she searched for and found the new bond that had snapped into place with such raw force. It was dying, fading in front of her.

She gripped it with psychic hands, holding on with every ounce of strength in her. *You can't leave me!*

Under her physical hands, his blood continued to gush with every beat of his heart, dripping past her fingers and onto the floor. Forcing herself to think past the terror, she scrambled for some way to fix this. But she was an M-Psy who worked on the level of DNA. She had no ability to heal the artery, close the wound.

The bond wavered, began to flicker.

She was going to lose him. "No!" It was an instinctive act to reach out with her soul, to pour her life energy into the bond, and force him to stay alive.

It worked.

For a single, shining second, the bond grew stronger. Then blood spurted harder from his neck and it flickered again.

Ashaya was a scientist. She understood cause and effect. And in that instant, she understood that she could hold Dorian here—hold him here long enough that maybe the paramedics could transfuse enough fluids into him to keep him alive, until a surgeon could fix the wound. She could hold him here as long as her life existed. And then she would go with him.

Keenan, my baby.

Her heart cried and broke in two. It wasn't a fair choice, she thought deep in her very soul. How could she possibly let her mate die? How could she leave her son? Perhaps if she'd had longer, the choice would've tormented her into madness, but she had only the barest fraction of an instant.

And Dorian's blood pulsed over her fingers like an endless river.

Don't leave me, please, Dorian.

Keenan would be safe, she thought, tears blinding her. He would be loved. She'd caught a fleeting glimpse of the small web she now inhabited. Her little man was linked to Dorian, but already, other minds were reaching out, preparing to hold him in the web if Dorian died. Because he was a child and these leopards didn't kill children.

Her sister would die with her, of that she had no doubt. It would end. She could accept her death, accept Amara's death, but she *would not* accept Dorian's.

So she poured her life energy down the bond, knowing it

would only last minutes at most—the psychic transfusion was directly related to how fast he was bleeding out. But it would double his chances of surviving till help came. Her hands were so wet, the jacket so heavy that she couldn't hold it in place any longer.

Then slender fingers were closing over her own, helping her apply the pressure. Somebody was at her back, holding her upright because she was losing the strength to do that herself. And suddenly, someone was shoving psychic energy at her in desperation.

You can't die. Please, Ashaya. Don't die.

Ashaya didn't have the strength to answer her twin. Her eyes fluttered shut, but on the psychic plane, she held on to the mating bond with gritted teeth, held Dorian to the world. As things started to go gray at the edges, she thought it was strange, but it felt as if Dorian was sending energy back to her. Odd.

Then it ended.

Mercy was crying and trying not to fucking break apart when two men appeared on Dorian's other side. She had her gun out and pointed at them in the blink of an eye. It flew out of her hand in a telekinetic blast.

One of them knelt, saying a single word, "Foreseer."

She stared at him, dull with sorrow but with a second weapon already in hand. However, neither he nor the Tk who'd brought him here had any visible weapons. The one on the ground pushed aside her bloody hand and Ashaya's limp one. Dorian's blood had slowed to a trickle.

"His heart's still beating," the stranger said.

She didn't know why she let him put his hands on her best friend's neck, didn't know why she didn't put the gun to his temple and pull the trigger. "Too slow."

"Enough. It's enough." He placed his fingers over the wound.

She could see nothing, but heat radiated out from that spot to where her bloody fingers lay against her knee. It made her glance up at Ashaya in hope. The M-Psy remained slumped against the cameraman, Eamon, her normally glowing skin lifeless and dull.

Eamon was crying, too. So was the director. The slender woman—Yelena—stood there shaking, her cell phone in hand.

She'd screamed at the paramedics, told them to hurry, all of them knowing it wouldn't be in time. The fucking Psy Council had got this one right. They'd timed it, used a gun instead of relying on a psychic strike that might've been deflected by tough mental shields, done everything with clockwork precision.

And now two people lay dying. Mercy reached out and gripped Ashaya's hand. "You hold on." To think she'd once wondered if the other woman felt anything for Dorian, she always looked so damn unaffected. *"Hold on."* Her other hand she closed around Dorian's. Linking them both. "Don't you dare die on me, either of you. I plan to be godmother to your goddamn brats."

The stranger kept touching Dorian. Heat kept radiating. When Mercy's cell phone rang, she ignored it. Then Eamon's rang. Then Yelena's. The other woman stared at it as if it was a snake.

"Answer it," Mercy said, starting to come out of the shock. The man working on Dorian, he reminded her a little of Judd. Not in looks. No, this guy's ancestors had come straight from some part of the Chinese subcontinent. He was all sharp bones, olive skin, and slanted eyes lashed with ridiculously long lashes. His hair was cut short but it was oil-slick black, straight as a ruler. No, he looked nothing like Judd. But there was an air about him, the air of an assassin.

The one standing looked even more the type. His eyes were gray, his hair black, but he was the same. And Faith had sent them to Dorian. No, Mercy thought, not Faith. Of course not Faith. She swallowed, looked down. "He's still bleeding."

"Patience. I'm a surgeon, not a miracle worker." Quiet, clipped words.

Strangely, they soothed her. Surgeons were always up themselves. And if this one saved Dorian's—and by association, Ashaya's—life, then he had a right to the arrogance. The man reached into his back pocket with one hand and brought out a flat box filled with lots of small tubes. Lifting his hand off Dorian's skin for only the instant it took to angle himself so he could get a better look at the wound, he flipped open a tube and began to pour white gunk on Dorian's bloody skin.

"It should work," he muttered. "I've repaired the artery temporarily."

Dorian's neck was still seeping blood. "Why can't you finish it?" She lifted her backup gun and, holding it deathly tight, pressed it to his temple. "Do it."

He looked at her without any hint of fear. "I'm a field surgeon, an M-Psy with the capacity to seal certain injuries, hold others until the microsurgeons get there. In this case, the sealant will do a better job than I can."

She pressed the barrel harder into him. "You're a hack?"

"I'm the man who just saved your packmate's life. Look."

She glanced down and the Tk used the chance to try to shove her gun out of her hand. Her arm flew back but the gun remained in her grip. She didn't care. Because the M-Psy had been telling the truth. Dorian wasn't bleeding anymore. But that didn't mean he was out of harm's way. Ashaya's heartbeat was as sluggish as Dorian's. Mercy knew if one died, so would the other.

"He's lost too much blood," the surgeon said, his kit disappearing back into a pocket. "He needs his fluids replaced fast. I don't know what's wrong with the woman. I do physical injuries and she's undamaged."

"Can you do anything about the blood?" Mercy asked.

"Possibly." He looked over his shoulder. "Emergency saline kit. Storage unit 1B, left-hand side. Telepathing the image."

The supplies appeared in the Tk's hand almost before the M-Psy finished speaking. He handed them over. "We have thirty seconds before our absence is noted."

The M-Psy worked in furious silence. "This is field surgery at its roughest. The paramedics shouldn't be long." He shoved a strange-looking needle into Dorian's vein with dexterity that spoke of experience, then pulled it out, leaving behind some kind of a small port. Attaching the saline line directly to that port, he told Mercy to hold up the bag of liquid, twisted a valve to release it, and said, "Go."

Both men blinked out, taking their tools with them. Mercy looked down and saw the rough IV was functioning exactly as it should. "Thank God for arrogant surgeons." She knew it was still touch-and-go, but at least now these two had a shot. God, please, they had to have a shot. "Don't you fucking die on me, Blondie."

"Mercy." It was Yelena, her voice wobbly. "The call, it was

Faith. She said she asked for help, wanted to tell me to tell you not to shoot them."

Mercy looked at the gun in her hand, then up at Yelena. "Our little secret?"

Giving a tearful laugh, Yelena went to take the saline bag. "I've got it."

"No." A gentle hand on her arm. "You have to stay on guard . . . in case they come back."

But, as things fell out, the enemy didn't come back. The next to arrive were the paramedics, followed by a swarm of Dark-River men and women led by a cold-eyed jaguar who rode guard on the two critically injured, then proceeded to lock down security in an entire wing of the hospital.

Vaughn bit out order after order until no one but Pack could get in. An oddly groggy Faith—her vision the reason Vaughn had arrived on the scene so quickly—took a seat in the corridor and told them she was scanning for psychic threats. Clay arrived over an hour later, having had to make the drive from Dorian's cabin. He brought a comatose Amara Aleine with him. "I left Jamie and Desiree in charge of the perimeter," he said, as he put Amara on a gurney and shoved a hand through his hair. "Sascha and Luc are on their way up. Sascha looks like hell." He frowned, eyes on Faith. "Like you."

Faith rubbed at her temples. "When Sascha realized what was happening, she shoved energy down Lucas's blood bond to Dorian. She took it from herself, Lucas, and me. Lucas probably doesn't look as bad because he's alpha—he's just stronger."

"Why not use the rest of us, too?" Mercy scowled.

"She had to take it from the people she knew would lower their shields in an instant. Even with her ability to get through changeling shields, it would've taken too long otherwise."

"Faith's right." Sascha's tired voice, as she came through the doors with Lucas's arm around her waist. "It only worked with Dorian because he was desperate to save Ashaya. When I shoved at his shields, he didn't hesitate to let me in."

Faith got up. "You saved their lives."

Sascha shook her head as they walked into the room where all three—Dorian, Ashaya, and Amara—lay. "It would've been too little too late if Ashaya hadn't held on for those first critical moments." She broke away to go to Dorian's side. Her fingers trembled as she brushed his hair off his forehead. "He came within a second of dying."

CHAPTER 46

She's injured, extremely vulnerable, but we can't reach her. I'd suggest waiting—if the Council backs off, the changelings will drop their guard. We can take her then. If she dies, we move on. We still have the drug.

—E-mail from Internet café in San Francisco to server in Venice

"She wouldn't have let him," Lucas said, touching Ashaya's face with his palm. It was a gesture of acceptance, as well as an alpha's offer of protection. "Dorian's mate is a strong woman."

Sascha nodded but her heartbeat was ragged. Because lying there, Ashaya looked very small, her color faded, her body almost lifeless. "Tammy?" The changeling healer could do more than any medical doctor—for Dorian at least. But Ashaya was connected to him, so if he improved, so would she.

"Should be here soon," Vaughn answered from the doorway, having come in to hug Faith. "She and Nate were on their way to drop the cubs at playgroup when I called."

After Vaughn left to take up his watch again, Faith sat down on a chair beside Ashaya's bed. "When I saw the shooting, it was strange—one of those new visions."

Sascha perched on Dorian's bed, holding his hand. Faith had curled her own hand around Ashaya's. Letting them know they weren't alone. It mattered, Pack mattered. "One of the ones that's not clear cut?"

Faith nodded, but waited as Lucas made a motion to head

out the door. "I'm going to check the body." His mouth was a flat line.

"Mercy tore out the assassin's throat," Faith murmured.

"Saves me having to do the job." With that, Lucas was gone.

"She took her cue from Dorian," Faith explained to Sascha, having heard this from Mercy when the sentinel first arrived at the hospital, "began running as soon as he did. She was right behind the shooter, managed to use her claws to bring him down."

Sascha was an E-Psy, but she couldn't find any pity in her heart for the shooter. Because that man had hurt her family, her pack. "Good." A pause to get her anger under control. "Tell me about the vision."

"I saw the shooting," Faith said with the quiet strength of an F-Psy who saw more than most people could imagine. "Then there was a sort of grayness that came down across it all, a kind of misty fog. I could hear garbled voices, glimpse bits and pieces of movement, but nothing concrete."

"Things in flux." Sascha looked from the fallen sentinel to his mate. Then her eyes drifted beyond. Releasing Dorian's hand, she walked over to Amara Aleine's bed. "Ashaya had to choose, that's why. If she hadn't accepted the bond, we'd have lost him."

She forced herself to take Amara's hand. Whatever she was, she was also a sentient being. And, "She made a choice, too," she said, trying to order the fragments of memory. It had been chaos in the Web of Stars as the mating bond snapped into place, then dragged Amara in with it. "She tried to save Ashaya." Amara had been ready to sacrifice her own life for her twin's.

A broken kind of love, but love nonetheless.

"Forecasting stock reports was never this heartbreaking." Faith rubbed at her temples again. "I almost forgot—in the last vision I had, before the grayness came down, I saw Amara, too. The darkness around her—the taint of the DarkMind—it was gone."

Sascha closed her eyes. "I can see her in the Net, and you're right—there's nothing sticking to her."

They both considered that. Faith blew out a breath. "The other man I saw. He was always a killer—the DarkMind only made him worse."

"Amara's never killed," Sascha murmured.

"So now, is she—"

"Good?" Sascha shook her head. "No, there's still an emptiness in her, still the presence of the seed the DarkMind used to get into her psyche. But . . . let's just wait and see."

Faith nodded. "Why do you think the DarkMind couldn't follow her into our web? The NetMind can." Sascha saw Faith realize the answer even as she spoke. "Because it's caged. The Psy do everything to contain their darker emotions, and so the DarkMind is trapped."

"Yes." Something else clicked in Sascha's brain. "I wondered how Ashaya managed to remain undiscovered in the Net, especially after she met Dorian. The mating dance simply doesn't *allow* for emotional distance."

"So why wasn't the force of it leaking out into the Net and giving her away?" Faith's eyes shifted from night-sky to obsidian. "Of course. If some sets of twins are becoming direct reflections of the twinning in the Net, and the DarkMind is attached to Amara—"

"—then the NetMind is attached to Ashaya. It's probably protected her for a long time. It's why no one ever saw her as a rebel threat." Sascha looked at the two women lying in adjoining beds. Identical and yet not. Twin expressions of the split in the PsyNet. It made her wonder if reconciliation was even possible. Or had the Net been irrevocably damaged?

Dorian came awake to the awareness that he was surrounded by Pack. They were everywhere in the air around him. But cutting through that familiar warmth was a shining presence that sang to his soul. His leopard uncurled and he turned his head. "Shaya." There she was, so beautiful.

Her color vibrant, she lay curled up on her side, head pillowed on one hand. Sleeping. Safe. His remembered terror at seeing the gunman inches from her face made him want to bare his teeth and growl. Unable to lie still, he struggled to sit up. He was mildly surprised when no one jumped out to stop him. Taking advantage of his good fortune, he swung his legs over the side of the bed.

His legs held after a couple of shaky seconds. He found himself wearing a pair of dark sweatpants, nothing on top. There was a bandage on his neck, but he could tell the wound was almost gone. Medical magic, he guessed.

When he reached Ashaya, he saw she'd been clothed in soft blue flannel pajamas. He just wanted to get in that bed and hold her. Then his senses alerted him to the woman who slept on the third bed in the room. She was dressed in pale yellow and lay on her back. Part of him he hadn't even known was wound up, relaxed.

Ashaya would've been devastated if she'd lost her twin.

Aching with the need to touch her, he was about to hop into Ashaya's bed when his luck ran out. A tall redhead with worry carved into her skin walked into the room, took one look at him, and yelled, "What the hell do you think you're doing?" Then she ran up, wrapped her arms around him, and kissed him full on the lips.

"God damn it," she whispered as she drew back. "You fucking took ten years off my life."

"Sorry, Merce." He tugged at one of her loose curls. "Did you kill him?"

"Of course I did. Ripped out his throat." She brushed at her eyes with the backs of her hands. "Son of a bitch was dead before he hit the ground."

"And Keenan?"

"No problems. Sascha said Ashaya protected him instinctively—he didn't feel a thing. Now that he can see his mom in the Web, he's as happy as a clam up there with the wolves." A sniff, another rub of her eyes. "We haven't been able to contact your folks."

Relief whispered through him. "Good. They'll take it better if I'm healthy when I tell them."

"That's what I thought." She tapped her finger on Ashaya's mattress. "So you got mated to a Psy."

Mate, he thought and there she was, a link tied straight to his heart. "Yeah."

"Surprise."

Something in her tone made him tear his eyes away from Ashaya's sleeping face. "Merce?" His stomach tightened. "You're not—I mean—" He was suddenly tongue-tied. Mercy had been his best friend forever. Shit, she'd helped him pull more pranks than he could name. "Does it bother you that I'm mated?"

She rolled her eyes and punched him on the shoulder, then steadied him when he swayed. "No, you buffoon. If I'd wanted you, I'd have made my move years ago."

"Hey. I'm injured." Leaning against Ashaya's bed, he pretended to rub his shoulder. "But thank the sweet Lord. I'd hate to think of you carrying around a torch for me. Sorry, Carrot, but I don't see you as a woman."

"Yeah, that's the problem." She snorted. "If you promise not to move after you get in bed with her, I'll leave you to make cow eyes at your mate." It was said with affectionate humor.

He wanted to do exactly that, but Ashaya was still asleep and he'd known Mercy since before they were both out of diapers. "You might as well tell me what's bugging you, or I won't make you godmother to our kids."

"You heard that?" Her eyes widened and she swallowed. "Shit, Dorian, don't ever do that again. You bled all over my best pair of pants."

He had no memory of hearing her words, not consciously. "Stop stalling."

"Oh, Jesus, fine." She rolled her eyes, cheeks a little pink. "It's weirding me out because now that you're mated, it takes care of the last male in the pack with the same or stronger dominance as me. I don't want *you*. But it was nice knowing that at least one strong male was unmated." Mercy had honestly never had the hots for Dorian. He was undeniably pretty, but he was her friend and colleague. End of story.

Now he blinked those surfer blue eyes. "Huh. Yeah, guess I never thought about that. I don't suppose you like BDSM?"

"What?"

"You know, you could crack the whip—" He didn't even try to avoid her second careful punch on his shoulder, he was laughing so hard. When he finally caught his breath, he grabbed her hand and tugged her close. "There are other packs, you know. You could ask Luc to arrange a short transfer."

Mercy had considered that. While predatory packs were very territorial, the sort of transfer Dorian was talking about did happen now and then. "I can't. Not now. The situation with the Psy is too unstable."

Dorian grunted in agreement. "I'll buy you a blow-up doll. I'm sure my mate won't mind when I explain how hard up you are."

She didn't bother to punch him this time, just glared with promise of future retaliation. "Very funny. You wouldn't be laughing if you knew how sexually frustrated I am right now." Changelings needed touch on a fundamental level. The problem was, Mercy didn't particularly enjoy sex with men who weren't equal to or stronger than her in the ways that mattered to changelings. "The last time was when that SilverBlade sentinel was in town for a communications meeting."

All amusement left Dorian's face. "You serious? That was months ago." A very long time to go without intimate touch. "Merce, that could get dangerous."

"I know. Do you think I don't know?" She thrust her hands through her hair. "Damn it, Dorian! It's getting to the point where I'm starting to wonder if some of the wolves would be good in bed." That was a lie—her recent slew of incredibly erotic fantasies hadn't focused on SnowDancer males in general, but on one very specific wolf. Not that she would admit that. To anyone.

"Cat and wolf isn't a . . . um . . . normal combination."

"And Psy and cat is?" She made a face at him. "Yeah, yeah, I know. Cat and wolf is strange." But the SnowDancer dominants were tough sons of bitches, part of a very small pool of men who might take her on and survive. And the one she was thinking about . . . No. Absolutely not. Never. *Ever.*

"How about one of the Rats?" Dorian's eyes gleamed.

She narrowed her own. "Cat and rat. Har-dee-har-har."

"It would definitely give a whole new meaning to the term 'black widow.'" He hugged her before she could kick him, his body shaking with laughter.

She hugged him back, so damn glad he was alive to tease her. "I'll get you back for that later, being that you're an invalid right now." Pulling back after another few moments, she nudged him toward Ashaya and walked out, closing the door behind herself.

She just missed seeing Ashaya open her eyes.

Ashaya had woken to the sound of Dorian's laughter and a woman's voice. She found herself tensing up, though she didn't know why. The words came into focus slowly, but by the time

Dorian mentioned rats, she was fully conscious and aware that everyone who belonged to her was safe. Mate. Child. Twin.

Dorian's laughter wrapped around her as she looked into her mind and found Keenan. His star shone bright in this strange, wonderful web that was her new home. When she contacted him through it, he said, "Sascha said you were sleeping." It was a whisper. "You slept a lot. Days and days. But I could see you in the Web, so I wasn't scared."

"I'm awake now, baby." She let all her love for him color her voice. "I'll come see you soon."

"I've got lots and lots and *lots* to tell you." He sounded excited. "I have friends. Ben's a wolf and Tally brought Noor to play, too. I'm going to marry Noor one day. And Ben's gonna mate with Marlee even if she is bigger than he is."

Ashaya's heart smiled to hear her son sound like a child. Behind her, Amara lay sleeping but uninjured. And Dorian . . . Dorian was alive.

She opened her eyes.

Her gaze met his. His smile slipped away, to be replaced by a look of such intense emotion that she felt it as a touch. Impossible . . . except that he was in her heart now, the bond between them a brilliant, golden beacon.

It scared her a little, the depth of this fury.

"It would've been easier," she whispered.

"What would?" He stayed beside the bed, as if he was content to simply watch her.

She felt embraced by his eyes, stroked by his soul. "If you'd fallen in love with Mercy."

A slow smile. "She's too mean."

It made her smile, too. "I'm going to tell her you said that."

"Aw, come on." That smile softened, his eyes filling with the chaos in her own heart. "You almost died for me."

She saw the frown lines forming, cut him off. "No, Dorian. You don't get to be angry at me."

"Why the hell not?"

She spread the palm of one hand against the sheet. "Your blood gushed over my hand, like a river." She shook her head as her heart stuttered in memory. "Why did you take the bullet? I wouldn't have survived if you'd died."

"Move over." Slipping into her bed, he cradled her against his chest. "You're wrong. You would've pulled yourself together for Keenan, for Amara. That's who you are."

He didn't understand, she thought. "But I wouldn't have survived." She put her hand on his chest, wanting to feel the pulse of his life. "Pieces of my heart, Dorian. You're in so many pieces of my heart."

He sucked in a breath at her use of those words, tightening his embrace. "Shh, now, sugar. I'm a tough bastard . . . though you'll have to explain how I survived a shot to the carotid."

The practical question anchored her, and she guessed he'd known it would. "I have no idea. I was unconscious."

Dorian began to say something, but right then, the door opened and Tamsyn walked in with several others. Ashaya found both herself and Dorian being bullied into a battery of medical tests. She told them she was fine, but no one listened. Tammy's eyes actually went leopard on her when she dared protest. Ashaya shut up.

"Let them fuss," Dorian whispered as they were being taken down for yet another scan. "They had a shock, too, need to convince themselves we're okay."

She could understand that. "Amara?"

"She's being watched. I talked to Sascha while you were having the bloodwork done. She thinks we woke quicker because we bolster each other's energy."

Ashaya didn't know enough about this new web to answer. Instead, she kept a psychic eye on her twin as they completed the scan. When it was time to return, she put her foot down and was allowed to walk—as Dorian had been doing all along. She was a little shaky, but no invalid to be pushed around.

Mercy was standing outside their room, waiting. "Hey, glad to see you're feeling better." Her smile was genuine. "If Blondie gives you any trouble, call me. I know all sorts of stuff you can use to blackmail him into good behavior."

Ashaya had the most startling thought—she liked Mercy. Mercy could become a friend. "Can I borrow your gun for a minute?"

CHAPTER 47

Mercy gave her a wary look. "Um, what did he do?"

Dorian put his hand on Ashaya's back. "What is it?"

Ignoring the sharp protectiveness lacing his tone, Ashaya held out a hand. "Please, trust me."

"You're Dorian's mate," Mercy said, as if that was an answer. "Here." Metal warm from Mercy's body touched her palm. "You know how to use it?"

"The basics, yes." Tucking the gun to her side, she went to the door.

Dorian slammed out his arm to block her but she ducked under and slid it open, knowing him well enough by now to have predicted the move. She swiveled to find Amara standing with her back against the wall by the door, a broken water glass in hand. Her twin froze at seeing Ashaya instead of Dorian.

"I won't let you hurt him." Aware of both Mercy and Dorian standing in the doorway ready to attack, Ashaya raised the gun.

Baring her teeth, Amara threw the makeshift weapon at the opposing wall. "You win today but what about other days? How will you protect him then?"

"Dorian can protect himself." Her hand began to shake. "Let it go, Amara. Just let it go."

"No. I'm a monster," Amara said with cool indifference. "I'll remain a monster. Kill me or you'll spend a lifetime waiting for me to strike."

Ashaya's hand wavered. "I can't." Because no matter what, Amara was her sister. "God help me, but I can't." Not like this, not in cold blood.

"Then we're at a stalemate." Amara looked at Dorian, then back at Ashaya. "You can't kill me, and I won't kill you. Nor am I unselfish enough to kill myself. Yet we both know I can't be allowed to live."

Ashaya envied her sister her emotionless calm. "You care nothing for your life?"

"My life . . ." A pause at last. "Have you seen the new network we're linked into?"

Ashaya gave a shaky nod. The Web of Stars, Dorian had called it. A minuscule network in comparison to the PsyNet, but instead of isolated white stars on black, this network, this web, was filled with connections. Golden threads that tied each star to another, sometimes to more than one. And in between streamed ribbons of color, streamers of joy and light, hope and forgiveness.

"Those pieces of color, they keep getting inside me and now I have these thoughts." Shoving both hands into her hair, Amara held her head. "I see with a clarity that wasn't a part of me before. I see that some lives should never come into being. The cost-benefit ratio is too unbalanced."

"You're brilliant."Ashaya dropped the weapon to her side. "Why can't you use that power to help our people?"

"Because my neural pathways have been permanently compromised. Perhaps I was born that way." Amara lowered her hands. "Or perhaps I became that way as a result of Silence. The point is moot. I have marked sociopathic tendencies. Those can't be remedied."

"What about Keenan? Is he going to remain safe from you?"

Shadows in blue. "These new thoughts . . . I find myself hesitant to kill a child born of my body." She shook her head. "But don't trust me. That decision may one day change."

"I have the same DNA," Ashaya persisted, realizing that Amara had set herself up to be killed. "We had the same upbringing."

"I can't become *good*, big sister. This is the only gesture I might ever be capable of making." Amara didn't say any more. She didn't need to. Facts were facts. If Amara lived, she would do evil. But to kill her? Ashaya turned to Dorian, lost. "What do I do?"

Dorian had once thought nothing could penetrate the scientific shell around Ashaya. Now he knew different in so many ways—but this link with Amara, it had the potential to destroy her. "Can you control her?"

Ashaya shook her head. "No."

"Incorrect, Ashaya." Amara raised an eyebrow. "If I allow you to embed a control link inside me, you can."

"Is she right, Shaya?"

Ashaya's fingers brushed his as she shifted to stand beside him. "Yes. Not mind control but—"

"—a leash," Amara completed. "Long enough to let me pretend I'm free but short enough to keep me from indulging in things my twin would deem unconscionable."

"Will it hurt you?" he asked Ashaya, ignoring Amara.

"No." Her fingers closed around his. "Our twin bond exists whether we like it or not. If Amara lets me in that deep, then I'd become the one in control. She'd lose the ability to enter my mind, but I'd be able to monitor her at will."

"You'd be her keeper your entire lifetime."

Ashaya looked at him. "I have help now. I have you."

The leopard inside him growled in a rush of possessive pleasure. "Glad you're finally beginning to understand that."

"Amara's in our web," Lucas said to Sascha as they stood outside the hospital. "What does that mean?"

Sascha leaned against the wall that faced the manicured front lawn. "It means there's darkness in the Web now."

"How do we fight it?"

"We don't." She thought back to when Faith had joined them, to the revelation about the DarkMind. "Amara is fundamentally flawed, but she exists. She's part of the world. We watch her, we manage her, but we don't imprison her on the psychic level. The instant we do, we sow the seeds of a split inside our own web."

"I don't like it." Lucas's tone was alpha-hard. "With her link to Ashaya, she could come through, influence you, Faith—hell, any of us."

"No," Sascha said, having spent hours looking at the situation from every angle. She and Faith both agreed on this. "Her link doesn't allow that."

"If she's in the Web, how can it not?"

"Think of it like a math problem." Grabbing her organizer from the pocket of her light summer coat, she slid out the attached laser pen. "First we have the large value—our web." She drew a circle and filled it with the members: Lucas in the center, herself enclosed within him, the spikes leading out to the sentinels, and then the connections to their mates.

"The mating bond links Ashaya into the Web." She connected the M-Psy to Dorian. "But our web is different from the PsyNet. It's a network you can only join via two methods that we know of—mating or a blood bond."

"Keenan," Lucas said, frowning. "Dorian said he had an open cut on his hand, and the skin on the kid's wrists was broken. The boy's need probably short-circuited the process I'd normally go through to blood-bond someone into the Web. The problem is, it takes control out of my hands."

"No, it doesn't," she said. "If asked, would you have denied sanctuary to a child dying of psychic starvation?"

He gave her a speaking look. "What do you think?"

"I think the Web knew you'd have said yes." She smiled at his expression. "It may be changeling, but it's still a psychic construct—it has the capacity to learn." Kissing his cheek when he blew out a breath, she returned to her diagram. "Because of the way he was brought in, Keenan is linked straight to Dorian, though he also has a very strong and visible attachment to his mother.

"The Web seems to have decided to treat him as their cub, giving him full access." She drew a triangle around the new family. "Amara, on the other hand, is connected through the twin bond." She drew a small circle that cut very slightly into the Web of Stars.

"I initially expected Amara to be connected to Ashaya, and otherwise isolated, but the Web's allowed her to be a peripheral part of it. I think it's because it understands that she's a psychic being, that she needs to know the Web is there. However, she can't actively surf or influence it. I'd worry about that limitation since she *is* caged in a way, but I think Ashaya is the sole person Amara truly cares about. As long as she can talk to her twin on the Web, she's not bothered."

Lucas continued to stare at the diagram. "If Ashaya dies, so will Amara. But not vice versa."

"Yes." Sascha put away the pen and organizer. "I don't think it could be any other way. Ashaya is a complete sentient being, but Amara . . ." She put her head against Lucas's chest, finding comfort in the feel of his arms coming around her. "She's only complete if Ashaya exists."

A pause and she knew he was thinking things through. "I guess we can find her a position at Sierra Tech," he said at last, referring to the research and development company in which DarkRiver held a major stake. "We'll give her a chance to prove herself."

"Who knows," Sascha commented, recalling Amara's piercing intelligence, "she might end up being an asset."

Lucas didn't look convinced but he nodded. "Do we need to tell Dorian all this?"

"I'll keep an eye on things, let him know if there's a problem."

"I guess I'll have to trust you." A teasing statement but one that held a question.

Of course he'd sensed her disquiet, she thought. He knew her to the depths of her very soul. "I need to tell you something."

He rubbed his hand along the sweep of her back. "Good. My patience was about to run out—you've been sleeping badly ever since you visited Amara." A lethal edge had entered his voice.

"It's nothing she did." Sascha said. "It's something she said."

"Sascha, we've had this conversation. The woman is a—"

She put a hand over his mouth. "Listen to me instead of acting all alpha."

He licked her palm. She dropped it and scowled at him. "Behave."

"Talk."

"Amara's words triggered some kind of switch in my mind, clarified something I've been getting hints of over the past few months." She took a deep breath, exhaled. "My powers . . . they're changing."

"How?" His expression grew solemn. "Is it something that's going to hurt you?"

"No, nothing like that. It's this . . . *sense* that they're spreading out, developing. I just have no idea what they're developing into." That scared her. Her mother was the best viral transmitter in the Net. She could kill with a single thought. "What if I turn into Nikita?"

"Not a chance." He ran the knuckles of one hand over her face. "Think of it as an adventure. We'll learn about it together." A pulse of love came down the mating bond, a pulse of devotion.

She felt her heart become his all over again. "I'm so glad you're my mate, Lucas." Whatever it was she was becoming, it was no longer so scary, not when she had a panther by her side.

On the other side of the car park, a dark-haired male lowered a pair of binoculars and coded in a call on his cell. "Definite no go," he said to the person on the other end. "The hospital's swarming with DarkRiver leopards."

"Options?"

"We wait until she's released. Quick, clean extraction. They won't be expecting us."

A small pause. "They never do, do they? After all, we're no threat."

"They'll learn different."

"When we're ready," came the order. "Keep watching. They'll drop their guard sooner or later."

"We should've taken her in the parking garage," the watcher said, referring to the location of Ashaya's final broadcast. "I was less than twenty feet from her and the cat."

"Too big a risk of being caught on surveillance. Surprise is our biggest weapon."

Because not even a leopard could hunt a phantom.

CHAPTER 48

Dorian isn't sleeping well anymore. I can feel the leopard's frustrated anger building once more. The intensity in him, the same intensity that drives his will to succeed, and powers his incredible loyalty, also lends itself easily to obsession. I will not let him go down that dark path. Not again.

—*From the encrypted personal files of Ashaya Aleine*

Dorian met with Lucas and the other sentinels a few days later, his body fully healed. "They tried to kill my mate. They broke the rules." A quiet statement made in the sniper's lethal tone.

His mate was Psy. The boy he already considered his own was Psy. It made it impossible for him to hate the other race as he once had. But there were some Psy he would never, ever forgive. The Council had taken his sister. Then they'd tried to take his mate. The monsters were all fucking dead.

"I know you want blood, Dorian," Lucas said. "But there's a problem."

Dorian respected the hell out of Lucas but the leopard wasn't just going to let this go. Neither was the man. "What?"

"We don't know who ordered the hit." Lucas held up a hand before anyone could interrupt. "Vaughn, you take it."

"I spoke to Anthony," the jaguar said. "He says there's dissension in the Council ranks. Ashaya was only supposed to be killed if all attempts to recapture her failed."

Dorian swore, low and hard. "It had to have been a Councilor. No one else would've had access to a Tk who could teleport."

"Anthony agrees, but he can't pin it down." Vaughn's face was full of the same cold rage as Dorian's. "Some of the Councilors are suggesting it was actually a vigilante pro-Silence group. They call themselves Pure Psy."

"Convenient."

"Yeah." Vaughn folded his arms. "But it leaves us with no clear target."

Breathing past the black chill of the sniper's fury, Dorian forced himself to think. "What's to stop them from trying again?" His need to protect Ashaya was a craving that ate away at him night and day. "She's so high profile, she's an easy target."

"Eamon got you being shot on tape," Clay said into the quiet. "He didn't drop the camera until after the blood started spraying."

"Gee, thanks for the reminder." Dorian scowled at the other man.

Mercy threw a cushion at him. "You're an idiot, Blondie. Clay's saying maybe the Council shot itself in the foot this time."

"No, they shot me," Dorian said, but he was thinking. "How much did Eamon get?"

"Full back view of the shooter, you taking the hit for Ashaya. It was a live feed—it's already out there." Clay shrugged. "You could stalk them, and maybe get yourself killed in the process, or you could sit back and let them implode."

"You're asking me to be fucking rational," Dorian muttered. "I haven't been rational in a long time."

Cool blue ice over his soul, passion and heart, gentle hands and sweet lips.

Shaya.

His mate. Safe and sound. And rational enough to anchor his more volatile personality. "Fine, push the feed again and again," he said. "Let's see how the bastards spin this." Psy were emotionless but they weren't stupid. "Get enough copies out there and someone will upload it to the PsyNet."

"Probably already done," Nate said from his position on the

door. "We'll have to wait and see which tack the Council decides to take. Could be it finally makes Ashaya too hot to hit, or . . ."

"Or could be they try to destroy the root of the problem."

"In which case," Lucas said quietly, "we'll all go hunting with you."

Dorian looked at his alpha and felt his leopard settle a fraction. He knew the promise would be kept. "Any other business?" he said, telling them the vicious edge of blood hunger had passed. Whether the calm would last was another question. He'd never been particularly good at letting things go.

"The humans," Clay said. "The ones that were sniffing around after Ashaya? The Rats thought they might have a base in the Tenderloin, but there's been no movement for days."

"Probably scared off by the shooting," Nate said. "Humans don't like to get in the middle of Psy-Changeling turf wars."

Dorian agreed. "We'll need to stay on alert, but there's very little chance of a human getting close enough to Shaya to do any damage. They don't have the physical senses to beat us on our own territory." Unaware of air currents and scents, humans gave themselves away the same as Psy.

"I'm going to tell Tally you said that." Clay smirked. "Your ass is toast."

"Nah." Dorian grinned. "Shaya will protect me."

Everyone laughed and the discussion turned to other matters.

"Aaron," Lucas said to Dorian. "I'm taking your advice, shifting him out of Chinatown. We need a replacement."

"Mia." Vaughn suggested. "She can fit in anywhere, and she looks about as threatening as a gnat."

"Fine," Lucas agreed. "Mercy—how's Cory?"

"Good. I think it's time he and Kit both got bumped up officially out of juvenile status."

"Nico, too," Clay said. "The other kids still have some work to do."

Several minutes of discussion followed as they considered the pros and cons. With changelings, adulthood wasn't a right. It was a privilege earned through hard work and maturity. With Kit carrying the scent of a future alpha, they had to be even more careful—young alphas could easily go off the rails.

But this time, they were all in agreement. Kit, Cory, and Nico had grown up a lot in the past year. All three would now carry the rank of novice soldier. Being a soldier wasn't about war. It was about protecting the pack. And about standing by your own.

In blood . . . and in joy.

CHAPTER 49

Shoshanna stared at her husband, Henry, across the width of her desk. "Why did you do it? We decided to go with the majority."

"She was a threat."

"How?" She glanced at the clip playing on her computer screen. "It's true Aleine's actions will equal the probable end of Protocol I, but her death would've only made matters worse." Shoshanna didn't like being thwarted, but she was also a creature of cold intellect. "You almost turned her into a martyr." Better that she was alive and digging her own grave. "It's obvious from this clip that Aleine has broken Silence. Any threat of her becoming a rebel leader has decreased to negligible levels."

Henry remained unmoved. "I was unaware of that fact at the time."

"Even so," she continued, "the assassination attempt has created a massive political quagmire." She turned the computer screen toward him. "Bloody violence. And at the hands of a Psy who is obviously one of our elite operatives." The Council's rule was built on Silence. And that Silence was supposed to have ended violence among their race. "You've undermined—"

"It was the correct choice at the time," Henry interrupted. "We can't keep allowing the changelings to get the better of us."

Normally, Shoshanna would have agreed. "Don't you comprehend what you've done? We *can't* kill her now. The instant anything happens to Aleine, it will confirm every one of her allegations and give the rebels all the ammunition they need."

"An unfortunate consequence." Rising, he walked to the window. "However, she's no longer on my list of priorities."

She didn't understand his behavior. Henry measured as a powerful 9.5 on the Gradient, but he'd always been the beta partner in their relationship. She was the one who'd made all the critical decisions—such as having them both implanted with stolen copies of the prototype Aleine had developed in the course of her work on Protocol I. Until the implants had had to be removed, she and Henry had been one mind, and even there, she had ruled. "Explain your reasoning to me," she persisted.

He turned to meet her eyes. "Why?"

"We're a team, Henry."

"When it suits you, my dear wife." A mockery of an endearment, completely devoid of emotion.

Shoshanna stared at him, belatedly realizing that he hadn't been acting like himself recently. "Your behavior isn't conforming to your known psychological profile."

"Perhaps I'm exercising a previously dormant aspect of my personality."

She listened to the cadence of his voice, measuring the physical distribution of his weight at the same time. "You're favoring your left side." It was such a slight flaw that it would be unnoticeable to anyone who hadn't known him as long as she had.

"Are you saying I'm brain-damaged?"

Her mind clicked. "We had our implants removed before they malfunctioned, but perhaps yours began to degrade while connected to your neural tissues." She made a mental note to get her own brain rescanned for any signs of decay.

"What won't you do to hold on to power." A statement, not a question. "The implant experience merely opened my eyes. I prefer being the puppet master, not the puppet."

"Henry, your brain is clearly malfunct—"

"And even if it is," he said slowly, "what will you do?"

"I can have you committed to the Center."

"On what grounds? Will you tell them that we had our brains implanted with a stolen device, that we were planning to wrench away control of the Council by making the others our slaves?"

Shoshanna had no answer to that because he was right—she wouldn't give up everything she'd achieved just to turn him in. "You need to get medical assistance."

"No, Shoshanna, I don't think so. And don't try an assassination—I know all your tricks. I was connected to your mind, remember?" With that, he walked out of the room.

I was connected to your mind, remember?

Yes, he had been, but she'd been certain she was the controlling entity. Now, it appeared she'd made a gross miscalculation. Henry was a pure telepath—she had no way of knowing what he'd plucked from her brain, or embedded within it. As she had no way of knowing how much damage had been done to Henry's neural tissues . . . or what he'd do now that he was operating free of any normal constraints.

CHAPTER 50

When you take Aleine, make sure you leave behind evidence that implicates the Council. With their blood riding high after the assassination attempt, the leopards won't stop to question things. Play them.

—*Secure e-mail sent from unknown individual in Venice to unknown number of recipients in San Francisco*

Dorian had decided to keep being rational—hell, he wasn't going to throw away the miracle of his mate and child—but his cat wouldn't settle, even though it appeared that Ashaya was now untouchable as far as the Council was concerned. In fact, according to Anthony, the Council was actively *protecting* her, and had even reined in Pure Psy on the matter.

The irony of it might've been rich had Dorian's cat not been so aggravated at having been cheated of a target on which to vent its rage. Dorian had always known he was a little more leopard than other changelings in human form—his cat seeking to get out whatever way it could—but he'd expected the savage nature of his need to lessen after mating.

It had only gotten worse—as if the cat knew it would never be stroked by its mate, never be admired as was its right, never even be *seen* by the woman who was everything to it. The leopard was dying a little each day and all that distressed anger was now being channeled into a pounding need to blame someone.

His meeting with Anthony Kyriakus didn't help matters. The rebel Councilor was blunt in his choice of words. "Ashaya needs to stay out of the limelight. Anything she does from here on out would just put her in danger, while contributing nothing to the cause."

"Because she feels?" He barely kept his tone civil.

"Yes." Eyes of cool brown met his. "Silence is beginning to crumble at the edges, but the ones who've broken the chains make our imprisoned state far too obvious—people aren't ready to see the truth, to go out into the unfamiliar darkness."

Dorian looked at Anthony, and wondered at the strength it took to play the double-edged game the other man had been playing for longer than any of them knew. "So, they're all safe?"

"Yes. Amara's been written off—she was already unstable and if they get a chance to hit her, they will. But she's not an active target."

"Keenan?"

"Was only useful as a way to control Ashaya. He's not a uniquely powerful Psy in his own right, and no one seems particularly concerned about what happened to him."

Dorian's hackles lowered. "Thanks for the intel."

Anthony gave a slight nod. "If I ever find out who ordered the hit, I'll tell you."

"Good. I can't wait to tear his heart from his chest." Even if it took years, Dorian would finish this. Patience was simply another side of stubborn, and Dorian had stubborn in spades.

But now, as he stood outside the cabin while Ashaya and Keenan slept inside—Ashaya in his bed, Keenan up above in a hastily but carefully erected addition to his home—his cat was anything but patient. It wanted to make someone pay. For being trapped, for being unable to protect its mate, for being goddamn latent. Claws shoved inside his fingernails, cutting and tearing. But never coming out. It fucking hurt. Until the pain and the anger left him unable to think.

And then the enticing scent of wild honey and woman heat wrapped around him. An instant later, he felt Ashaya's cheek press into his bare back as her arms slid around to lie palms down over his chest. The man leaned back into her hold and even the cat settled a little under the petting. The pain faded.

"This bond," she said, "it's so deep, I can hear you in my heart."

Smiling, he put his own hands over hers. "Good."

Lips on his skin, soft, gentle, possessive. "No more blood, Dorian." A whisper. An order. "The need for vengeance in you—it's destructive."

He turned to tip up her chin. "It's who I am. The cat wants retribution."

"No," she said, passion in her eyes, "you're a beautiful, charming, dangerous leopard. But you're not ugly in your anger. I'll allow you to keep us safe—I won't get in the way of that—but if you begin to obsess over this until it burns a hole in your psyche"—she stabbed a finger into his chest—"I'll tie you up and teach you exactly what an angry M-Psy can do to the man she loves."

He blinked, taken completely by surprise. The leopard, too, was chastened enough to retreat from trying to dig its way out of Dorian's skin. "Shaya—"

"No." She kissed him. And kept doing it until he groaned and thrust his hand into those incredible curls of hers. "Enough," she said. "The threats have all been neutralized."

Something niggled at him, something he'd seen. A flicker of an image—a dark car with opaque windows. "I'm not sure that's—"

She nipped at his lower lip, breaking his train of thought. "Forget vengeance. It's time for us to learn each other."

He retaliated with a kiss that left her breathless. "I already know you." In his heart, in his core, to the depths of his changeling soul. "I just want to play with you now." It was another kind of bonding, a kind that spoke to the cat even as it seduced the man. Maybe it would even be enough to heal the leopard's broken heart.

"Why are you sad, Dorian?"

He couldn't lie to her. "The leopard wants you to see it."

"I see it every time you look at me, kitty cat." A kiss pressed to the hollow of his throat. He shuddered under the caress. "But I'm working on the DNA. Give me a little more time. Tonight, let's play." A husky whisper that spoke of sex and hotter, richer things.

He slid his hands under the tails of the shirt she'd pulled on to cup the smooth warmth of her buttocks. "What about—?"

"Keenan sleeps like a log, and I'll know the instant he wakes." She nibbled at his lips. "Don't you want me?"

He knew when he was being handled. He decided he liked it when it came from his beautiful mate. "You're definitely a fast learner, Ms. Aleine." Grinning, he tugged her away from the cabin and into the dark blanket of the trees. "Now, where was I?"

She shivered as he cupped her bottom again before trailing his fingers down to stroke over her cleft. "That's . . . nice."

"Nice?" He rubbed lightly, gratified to hear her moan. "I think you need an education in how to talk to me in bed."

"Oh?" She was standing on tiptoe now, trying to escape his fingers but rubbing back against him at the same time.

"Hmm." He nipped at the line of her neck, taking his time teasing the dampness of her. "Lesson one—use words like 'magnificent,' 'amazing,' 'mind-blowing.' "

She pretended to bite the line of his jaw. Almost purring, he slipped a finger into her. "Be good."

"Make me," she gasped as he pushed one hand up under the front of her shirt to cup the heavy weight of her breast. Ashaya was shaped like a woman should be, he thought, all curves and softness. As far as he was concerned, she was his own personal sensual banquet. And right now, she was hot and wet around him. He moved his finger with slow precision, coaxing her to ride him.

Her muscles clenched as he stroked a second finger into her liquid heat. He grazed her ear with his teeth. "Now would be a good time to use 'mind-blowing.' "

She was melting around him but she didn't surrender. "You have a high opinion of yourself."

He brushed his thumb over her nipple. "The truth's the truth, beautiful. Let me teach you all about it."

Ashaya had seen flashes of Dorian's charm during the course of their unusual courtship, but that night, out in the soft dark of the forest, she found out exactly how indulgent he could be with a woman he considered his. There was husky male laughter as he teased her, lashings of the most incredible pleasure, and tenderness, such exquisite tenderness.

When he withdrew his fingers from inside her, she whimpered. It got her a kiss. Then he opened her shirt and pushed it off her shoulders and to the forest floor. "Mmm." A sound of complete satisfaction as she stood bathed in moonlight.

He licked the curve of her collarbone, making her shiver.

"Did I tell you I want to see you naked in the sun?" His hands squeezed her buttocks. "All smooth and pretty and mine." Those strong hands stroking up over her back, then sliding down again. "Definitely mine." Another bite along her neck, this one with a teasing flick of tongue.

Her breath was already coming in gasps, but she somehow managed to speak. "You seem to have a strange fascination with seeing me naked in daylight."

"It's my fantasy." He shrugged, unrepentant. Then he dipped his head and bit her nipple.

She jerked, her hands clenching in his hair. "Stop that."

"Why? You like it." He did the same to her neglected breast.

Her heart felt as if it would thud out of her chest. "Dorian, I don't have your control."

"Baby, as I recall, I came with a single touch," he said, between nibbling kisses. "It's your turn." Making a sound incredibly akin to a purr, he bent his head to suck at the pulse in her neck, even as he thrust two fingers deep inside her. Once. Twice.

And that was all it took.

She shattered.

The pleasure was incredible, but what was even more so was that she felt him with her all the way. And when she opened her eyes, it was to the openly pleased curve of his lips, his arms holding her tight. "Magnificent," she whispered, teasing him because she'd learned he liked it. So did she. "But I would rather have you inside me."

Feline delight in those blue depths, the dark edge of sorrow and rage pleasured away. Ashaya was no expert at passion, but if that was what it took to keep Dorian from the edge, she'd play with him night and day. Because he was hers to care for, as much as she was his. "Please, Dorian." She smiled. "Come inside me."

He chuckled. "I like the way you say please. I think I want to hear it again."

"Please, Mr. Christensen." Wrapping her arms around his neck, she hooked one leg over his waist. "Pretty please."

He scowled. "It's not begging if you smile."

She leaned in until her lips brushed his. "You make me want to crawl all over you."

"That'll do." He was inside her an instant later, a hot, hard intrusion that was somehow the most perfect of joinings. "Up." His hand went to her bottom, urging her to wrap her other leg around him. The second she did, he backed her against the smoothness of a moss-laden trunk.

Then he proceeded to show her exactly how magnificent he could get. There were no hard, fast thrusts, nothing that might cause her back to bruise. No, tonight, he was determined to drive her insane with slow rotations that touched her every sensitive spot over and over . . . and over again. The orgasm hit her hard, and rode her in long lush waves, wringing her dry. Her bones turned molten.

It took a while to find the brain cells to say, "Mind-blowing." His oh-so-satisfied smile of pure male delight followed her into her dreams.

And perhaps it was that smile that unlocked the knowledge in her mind.

She woke at dawn to find her cat watching her. He was on his stomach, the sheets barely covering his buttocks, all golden hair and bright blue eyes. "What?" he asked when she stared at him.

She went to tell him, but stopped herself at the last instant. Until she was sure, she had to keep this to herself. "Blondie?" she asked instead.

He grinned. "That was her revenge for me calling her Carrot. What're you going to call me?"

She took a moment to think. "Mine."

He gave her a startled look. "Possessive."

"So?" She stole the answer he'd given her so many times.

"Nothing." A meek look but his voice was filled with laughter. "I'm not going to argue with a sexy woman who wants to make me her poor, overworked love slave."

She found herself laughing, even as part of her mind obsessively considered the implications of what she'd discovered in Dorian's genetic structure. She was still working on the problem that afternoon as they drove to Talin's home. It seemed the—

"Mommy, look!"

She glanced into the backseat to see Keenan making the strangest face. "That's very interesting, baby."

Satisfied, he nodded. "I'm a leopard."

"Of course you are." She looked at Dorian to see him biting

back a smile. "Are you excited about seeing Noor again?" she asked Keenan.

"Yeah! We're gonna play tag."

She was excited herself—Jon was going to be there today, too. Turning to the front when Keenan became engrossed in a handheld game, she touched Dorian on the arm. "Are you sure Jon won't have psychological issues with seeing me?" She'd been part of the lab where the teenager had been tortured.

"Kid isn't ready to be your best friend," Dorian said bluntly. "But he knows you got him and Noor out and he wants to say thanks."

"I'm—" Ashaya never got to finish her sentence as gunshots came out of nowhere, hitting both the engine casing and the tires in rapid-fire bursts. Belching smoke, the car spun out of control. She turned to grab Keenan, but he was too far to reach. "Get down!" she told him, trying not to panic. "Baby, listen to me. Get down." She reinforced the vocal command with a telepathic one.

He curled low in the seat, eyes huge.

"Good boy," she soothed, just as Dorian managed to get the car straightened and said, "Hold on, kiddo." He activated the hover-drive.

The vehicle lurched drunkenly but kept going. "Come on, come on." He raced down the road and swung into a heavily forested area the instant before the car's computronic engine began to splutter. "Get out." Braking to a complete halt, he reached into the backseat to release a silent Keenan from his child seat. The boy wrapped his arms and legs around him as Dorian got out of the car and ran around to her side.

"Where?" she asked him, fear making her brain act with cold efficiency.

"Telepath Sascha," he ordered as he gave Keenan to her and opened the trunk to take out his rifle, stuffing extra ammo into his pockets. "Tell her we've been ambushed."

Ashaya didn't tell him she wasn't a strong enough telepath. Instead, as Dorian took Keenan again, and told her to follow him as he ran into the trees, she opened her mind to the Web of Stars and sent out a generalized distress call. She would've never done the same in the PsyNet, but this web was much smaller, filled with . . . family.

Amara's mind responded first, though she was living and working in Sierra Tech's mountain headquarters. *I'm calling for reinforcements.* A message sent through the Web.

Unable to hold the contact, given the intensity of the run, she dropped back out and tried to match Dorian's pace. It was brutal, but she knew he was holding back so she could keep up.

He stopped just as she was beginning to fear she'd be unable to go any farther. They were in the midst of a grove of sorts but from the low density of the trunks, she had the feeling civilization lay not far ahead.

"Here." Dorian's voice was a command as he walked around a tree and nodded at the hollow created by its massive roots.

She sat down inside, holding out her arms for Keenan. Dorian's eyes met hers as he bent to hand Keenan over. "I'll be on the other side of the tree, in the branches. You're safer here—whoever it is will expect me to stash you above." He nodded at Keenan.

She understood the message—if anything happened, Keenan would hear it. So she'd have to ensure he didn't. Using the maternal bond, she wrapped him in a cocoon that promised safety. He relaxed immediately. "The Council?" she dared whisper.

His mouth was a grim line as he shook his head. "Human." Bending, he brushed his lips over hers in a fleeting kiss, his hand lying protectively on Keenan's hair. "Don't move." He took a small gun she hadn't seen him retrieve and put it in her hand behind Keenan's back.

She slid her fingers through the grip. "Be careful." Pressing her back into the tiny cave created by the roots, she curved her body over her son's, aware of Dorian moving away. She heard a footstep or two, and then nothing.

Her leopard had gone hunting.

Dorian was furious with himself. He'd been so focused on the Council that he'd forgotten the other threat. No, he'd *disregarded* it because the threat came from mere humans. If he survived this, he'd have to fucking shoot himself for his arrogance. Hadn't Tally taught him anything? One small woman and she'd managed to put fear into the heart of a Psy killer. Humans might not have changeling strength or Psy mental abilities, but they were no less strong . . . and had the capacity for as much evil.

Lying in the branches of a tree only a small distance from the one where he'd hidden the two most important pieces of his heart, he calmed down his heartbeat and focused, eliminating everything from his consciousness except his awareness of the intruders. The first thing he realized was that they'd planned this very carefully. *Shit.* He was moving back down the tree even as the curse passed through his mind.

Ashaya looked up in surprise when he returned. He took Keenan, holding a finger to his lips. "Grab on to me, K-Man." When the boy obeyed, Dorian quickly scaled the tree and put him in the crook of a branch. "I'll be back with your mom."

A nod, not as much fear as he would've expected. Trust, he thought, his heart clenching, the kid trusted him. Going back down, he found Ashaya already halfway up. She let him help her the rest of the way. Once beside Keenan, she put her arms around their son's tiny figure, and gave him a questioning look.

He made a circle with his finger. *Surrounded.* Unlike the Psy, these humans weren't so egotistical as to come into leopard territory expecting easy prey. They'd brought a small army.

He watched as Ashaya settled Keenan more firmly into his little spot, then put her back to him so he'd be protected by her body. Holding the gun awkwardly in one hand, she lifted the other to show Dorian three fingers, then five.

Fifteen minutes until backup arrived.

Dorian mentally counted his ammo, the number of hunters out there, and knew he couldn't take them all out, not with his gun alone. It might come down to hand-to-hand combat. He bared his teeth—no one was getting up here. Nodding to Ashaya, he moved quickly away and lower down the tree.

Finding a good spot, he lay along the branch, put his rifle in position. And waited.

The first man showed his head a minute later. His brains exploded over the forest floor an instant after that, the shot silent, the kill precise.

Everything stilled and he could hear them break their radio silence and talk for several seconds. Then nothing—as if this army was organized enough to get itself under control. They were more careful after that, but he was a cat, and this was his territory. Despite their camouflage gear, he picked off three more before getting up and moving.

Ashaya's worried eyes met his as he climbed up to take a position along her branch. He took out four more men before they realized he'd changed position. They got wary after that, and his job got harder. He moved again, only managed to take out one.

He knew they were going to be able to pinpoint which tree he was in, very soon.

He put his lips to Ashaya's ear. "Regrouping. Few minutes' grace."

She nodded. "Ten minutes." It was more the shape of her lips than sound.

He gritted his teeth, knowing he wasn't fighting amateurs. These people wanted Ashaya, and they clearly wanted her alive. If they rushed the tree, he'd certainly manage to kill most of them. But not all.

Not all.

CHAPTER 51

Stop worrying, sweetheart. Hell, yeah, I'd like to shift, but I stopped wishing for the impossible a long time ago. Far as I'm concerned, being latent gives me an edge—I'm the most experienced weapons handler in either pack. Even that assassin you call a mate can't outshoot me.

—Excerpt from instant-message conversation between Dorian Christensen and Brenna Kincaid, three months ago

Making another quick decision, Dorian swung the rifle over his head and onto his back and pointed upward. Ashaya's eyes went wide, but to her credit, she gave him Keenan and began to climb, displaying the lithe skill that had saved her life from the lynx all those weeks ago. "Dorian?" A boyish whisper against his ear.

"Yeah?" He followed Ashaya, Keenan clinging to him like a monkey, not a tear in sight. Dorian was fucking proud of the boy's courage.

"I want a gun."

He winced, wondering what Ashaya would say to this new development. She'd been "rather surprised" to wake up the other day and find Keenan trying to copy Dorian as he went through his martial arts workout—the memory of those small legs kicking determinedly was almost enough to make Dorian smile even now. "We'll talk about it later."

Seemingly satisfied with that, Keenan kept his silence as they continued the climb. When Ashaya took a seat on a branch a

ouple of meters from their previous position, he nodded. Hand-
ıg her Keenan, he jumped up beside her, shifting so his back
ɔrmed a protective wall. "Makes it harder for them to rush us."
'rom here, he could pick them off one by one. Even the best hu-
ɪan climber wasn't leopard-fast.

He could hear Ashaya's heart thudding behind him, the
ɔcent of her sweat fresh and clean. She leaned onto his back
ɪnd, to his surprise, pressed a kiss to his nape, tucking the spare
ʒun into the waistband of his jeans at the same time. "After this
ɔs over," she whispered, her confidence in him a vibrant beat in
ɪis heart, "I'll lie in the sun for you." Grinning despite the dan-
ʒer, he leaped lightly onto the branch below theirs and began
ɪunting again. This time, he moved after each shot, scattering
ɪheir attackers' defenses.

The scent of blood and flesh drifted up. Then the gunshots
ɪtarted. Every time he made a hit, that position was riddled sec-
ɔnds later. They were reacting quicker and, with the fifth kill, he
ʌvas nicked in the arm. Swearing lightly, he told himself to
ɪnove faster. It would be at least seven more minutes until
ɔackup arrived.

He checked his ammo again and realized he'd have to stop
ɪhooting if he wanted to keep something in reserve. Teeth
ɔared, he crawled along the branches until he was in prime po-
ɔition to protect Ashaya and Keenan. The hunters began moving
faster the instant they realized he wasn't picking them off anymore. Probably thought he was down.

The first ones who attempted to climb the tree found their
faces shot off. The others drew back and he heard low-voiced
conversation. Not low enough. A mistake at last.

"Can't have much more ammo."

"Who's gonna volunteer to find out?"

"Shoot into the tree."

"And kill the target? Genius."

*"Why the fuck didn't anyone know we were dealing with a
sniper? He's supposed be fighting with claws and teeth."*

"Shut up, all of you." A furious voice. *"Maintain silence.
He's a cat."*

The men obeyed. Resisting the urge to swear, Dorian spread
out his senses again and waited for their next move. Several
shots were fired into the trunk.

"We want Ashaya Aleine alive," a male voice said. "That all. We don't want to harm her."

Then you fucking shouldn't have shot at her and our chil Dorian used the speaker's voice to get a lock on his positio without the benefit of a sightline.

"Give her to us and we'll let you—"

The voice cut off as Dorian shot through the tree and hit hi target. The sound of bullet meeting flesh was close. They'd su rounded the tree.

"Fuck this," someone said. "Shoot!"

And suddenly the tree was a war zone. Dorian move swiftly up. They weren't aiming high enough yet but sooner o later they'd figure it out. He put his body in front of Ashaya's intending to tell her that they'd need to move. There was a pos sibility he could jump them to another tree. But before he coul get to that, he caught a familiar scent on the breeze. His leopar snarled, but the man grinned. "Damn wolves."

Ashaya made a questioning face. "Wolves?"

"Wolves." Knowing backup was on the way, he leaped bac down to a lower branch and began to pick off the attackers onc more. They were close to getting a fix on him when the firs scream sounded. He hoped to hell Ashaya had Keenan's ear blocked, because the wolves were being noisy about their work Then the cats arrived.

In spite of the fact that the fight was now over, Dorian didn' lower his guard. It was a good thing he didn't. One of the hu man hunters had evaded everyone. Dorian caught the man' scent from his left, and realized he'd climbed over from neighboring tree. Not wanting to chance a shot going haywire he stalked the man with quiet leopard focus. A whisper of ai was the last thing the man heard as Dorian snapped his neck The body crashed through the branches and to the ground.

A few minutes later, a whistle rang out. "All clear, Boy Ge nius."

"Ice-fucking-cold water," he muttered. "I've got Keenan up here."

"Give us a couple of minutes."

When he climbed up to Ashaya, she said, "Is Boy Genius an other nickname?"

"No. It's a way to get my temper going."

Her lips curved slightly, despite the white-knuckled grip she
ad on Keenan. The kid gave him a pleading look. Dorian kissed
Shaya and reached for him. "We're safe. Give the K-Man to me."

Keenan came without hesitation. "I want a *big* gun like yours."

Trying not to smile, Dorian dropped an absent kiss on
Keenan's hair. "Did he . . . ?"

"No. I shielded him." She looked down, eyes worried. "Will
there be anything down there . . . to see?"

"They're tidying up." The bodies would be hidden away, the
blood covered up, by the time he came down with Keenan.
Since the boy didn't have changeling senses, he wouldn't smell
the carnage.

Ashaya touched his cheek. "You protected us."

He wondered how she'd known to say exactly what he needed
to hear. "It was my own stupid—"

"Shh." A feminine finger on his lips. "If it was your fault, it
was mine as well. No ifs, no buts. You did good."

Strangely, that simple sentence did more to soothe him than a
thousand flowery words. "Come on, beautiful. Let's go home."

But it took a while for that to happen. After stashing Ashaya
and Keenan in the Tank, the large vehicle Clay had driven to the
location, he left them under Rina and Barker's careful eyes, and
returned to the scene of the kills.

The instant he saw the wolves, he realized the reason for the
amount of noise—the boys weren't juveniles, but only by a year
or two. "Tai, what were you doing down here?"

Tai looked a little green as he shrugged. "Kit, Cory, and the
others pulled a stunt in our territory, so we were, you know, paying them back."

Dorian wondered what the DarkRiver boys had done. "Do I
need to talk to them?"

"Nah." He shook his head, swallowing as a wave of scent
rose up in the shifting air currents. "We were just playing stupid
games. Kid games."

"You didn't act like a kid today. Thank you." Dorian held out
his hand.

Tai gave him a shaky smile as their hands met. "We've never
killed. Not people."

Dorian glanced at Clay. "You called Hawke?"

"He's on his way."

Knowing the wolf alpha would take care of the boys, he told Tai and his friends to grab a seat on the forest floor a good distance away from the carnage. They obeyed without argument leaving Dorian to walk over to the bodies. "Any ID?" he asked, crouching down beside Clay.

"No. But we found this." The other sentinel pulled up the pant leg on one body, revealing the back of the shooter's calf. The tattoo was simple. The letter *A* bordered by two straight lines. Except Dorian knew that that wasn't what it was. It was an *A* overlying an *H*.

"Human Alliance." He'd guessed as much, but it was good to have proof. "The others?"

"Yeah, ones with their legs undamaged." Clay's tone was predator-quiet as he said, "Two of them didn't have bullets in their guns, but some kind of a dart."

"Tranquilizer?"

"Probably. I'm going to send it up to Sierra Tech for tests, have one of our people run it." To Dorian's surprise, he leaned in to lift the dead male's hair away from his neck.

Dorian spotted the reason why an instant later. "What *is* that?" The man had some kind of tiny metal device embedded at the top of his spinal cord.

Clay drew back his hand. "Maybe Ashaya can figure it out—they all have them." He tapped a finger on his knee. "Important thing is, I don't think we have to worry about another attack."

"I'm not letting my guard down again." He felt a sharp sense of disapproval along the mating bond. Ashaya, refusing to allow him to give in to guilt. It almost made him smile. "Why do you think this is over?" he asked Clay.

"There were fifty of them. All are dead." Clay shrugged. "Whoever is running this would have to be an imbecile to send more people in now that we've been forewarned. And judging from their prep, I don't think he's that moronic."

"No, he's not. If I hadn't had backup, they would've got what they wanted. Still, we make sure the word gets out that Ashaya's got no info worth this much death." Dorian didn't kill easily, and he hated this fucking waste of life. But these men

...ad come in with the intent to attack a predatory changeling's
...nate and child. They'd made their choice.

"I'll get the Rats on it," Clay said, eyes narrowed as he began
to go through the man's equipment. "It's time we began paying
serious attention to the Human Alliance."

It took Ashaya most of the next day to settle her thoughts
enough that she could talk to Dorian about his latency. Even then
she had to wait until Keenan was in bed and Dorian had returned
from a meeting with Lucas; Hawke, the SnowDancer alpha; and
several others.

"Can I talk to you?" she asked as he came out of the shower
and collapsed facedown on the bed. Naked. This cat had no
shame. Lucky for her, she thought with a smile.

"About the chips we found on the humans?" He all but purred
as she straddled his back and began to knead his muscles.

"No. I'm still working on that. It's a complicated piece of
technology—some kind of a neuroinhibitor."

"Mmm."

She pressed a kiss to his nape. "Don't go to sleep. This is important."

"I'm awake." He yawned. "Mostly."

"I think I did it, Dorian."

Something in her voice cut through the drowsiness, making
Dorian turn onto his back to look up at her. "What, sugar?"

"I've figured out how to correct the mutation that makes you
latent."

He froze. "Shaya?"

"I've run and rerun simulations. I think . . . I think if it works,
you'll be able to shift. Gene therapy isn't as rare as it once
was—this one is a complex and very, very fine genetic change,
but I'm ninety-nine percent sure of success."

Not since his father had explained to him that he was
different—at age two—had Dorian ever allowed himself to
think about this. "Jesus, baby. How?"

"I don't think I could've done it without being mated to you,
not even with my abilities." Her eyes filled with the devotion of
a strong woman for her man. "It gives me a connection to you
that's so deep, the work's intuitive. It's like my gift recognizes

you on a primal level. Once I stopped trying to think and let in stinct guide me, it was almost easy."

He blew out a breath, trying to make sense of the chaos in his brain.

"You don't have to decide now." She put a hand on his chest. "It's okay if you don't want to do it. I just wanted you to know the option was there."

"Would it matter to you?"

"Of course not, Dorian." A bright, beautiful smile that knocked out his heart. "I'd love you even if you were a damn wolf."

"Now you're learning." But despite his teasing words, his mind was pure turbulence.

CHAPTER 52

In a large room in the sunken city of Venice, several people sat silently around a long table and considered the abysmal failure of their most recent operation.

"We wipe Aleine from the target list and go under," the man at the head of the table said. "And we stay under until the furor dies down."

A slow murmur of agreement. Some of them were grieving the loss of friends and colleagues. But not one, *not one* suggested that perhaps they'd taken the wrong path, that blood and death wasn't the right way.

In truth, it was likely that the idea hadn't even entered their minds. They were too blinded by the knowledge that the Psy Council was beginning to falter in its totalitarian rule, that the changelings were slowly gaining ground. Things were in flux, as they had not been for centuries. For a race that had spent eons in the shadows, it was a heady time, a time when empires might be felled . . . and power might be taken.

CHAPTER 53

Perhaps I shouldn't have told him. But how could I lie to him, to my mate? His hurt is a bruise inside of him, his beast forever trapped. To me, he's perfect, but I know that in his soul, he feels torn apart.

—*From the encrypted personal files of Ashaya Aleine*

Dorian was sitting outside the cabin in the middle of the night, drinking a beer and attempting to get his head around the gift Ashaya had offered him, when a black panther prowled out of the forest. Dorian had caught Lucas's scent long before his alpha appeared before him, and now waited as Lucas shifted to human form.

Changelings weren't particularly concerned with nudity, but since Dorian's cat got snarly at the idea of Ashaya walking out and seeing Luc that way, he went back into the cabin on silent feet and found a pair of sweats. Lucas pulled them on with a nod of thanks, and took the beer Dorian threw him, continuing to stand while Dorian sat.

"Let me guess," Dorian said. "Sascha sent you after me." He adored Lucas's mate, but Sascha's empathy tended to make brooding difficult.

"Actually, I figured this one out all on my own." Lucas took a drink. "I think my first clue was when Nate called you Boy Genius this afternoon and you didn't threaten to throw Tally in a lake."

Dorian grunted, staring out at the forest. "Where's Sascha?"

"In the aerie."

"You left her alone?"

"As my mate would say—she's a cardinal, fully capable of protecting herself."

"So you left at least two others on watch."

"Of course I did." Lucas took another swallow of beer. "Why am I here in the middle of the night?"

"I didn't call you."

Lucas just waited.

Dorian was a sniper. He could've outwaited his alpha, but the truth was, he needed to talk. "Shaya's figured out how to fix the misfire in my body, so I can shift."

Lucas's face went very quiet. "Well, hell."

"Yeah." He dropped the hand holding the beer bottle between his raised knees.

"You don't want to?"

"I don't know what the fuck I want." He thrust his free hand through his hair. "All this time, I've done everything I could to be better, deadlier, faster." Talin called him Boy Genius because she thought he was a compulsive overachiever. She was right. "It wasn't enough that I was good at computers, I had to become a top-level hacker. Not enough that I got into architecture —I had to ace every exam. Hell, I even became a fucking pilot because it was a skill none of the other sentinels had. That drive—it was because I couldn't shift."

"Made you one tough son of a bitch, even as a kid," Lucas agreed. "Now you're wondering if you'll lose that drive if you gain the ability to shift?"

"Yeah, I guess."

"Dorian, that's pure bullshit. We both know you're too fucking hardheaded to ever be less than the best." Throwing Dorian the empty beer bottle, Lucas folded his arms. "You're scared, man."

Dorian's leopard growled. "And you know shit, Luc." He got up and went into the house, closing the door behind him. He felt Lucas shift back into panther form and disappear a second later.

But as he slipped into bed beside Ashaya's curvy body, soothing his beast with the lush warmth of her, the words of two very different men kept circling around and around in his head.

You're scared . . .

. . . people aren't ready . . . to go out into the unfamiliar darkness.

Turning, he propped himself up on his elbow and looked down at Ashaya's sleeping face.

Her eyes opened a second later. "You're thinking too hard." A complaint followed by a yawn.

"Sorry." Their bond wasn't telepathic in the true sense, but it had become obvious that they picked up thoughts from each other at random times.

"You're still worrying over the shift, aren't you?" Her eyes darkened. "I should've kept silent. You were hap—"

He pressed a finger against her lips. "When you want something so bad it hurts," he said quietly, "and you bury it, bury it so deep that you convince yourself it no longer matters . . . and someone tells you you can have it, it's terrifying. What if you take the chance and you're wrong? What if you let yourself feel the loss and it's this huge pain and you can't put it back in the box?"

Ashaya kissed his finger and moved his hand so it lay over her heart. "I'm not an expert on emotion," she said in her honest way. "Most of the time, I have no idea how to deal with the storm inside me."

"You're doing fine."

"But see, Dorian, I know one thing." She pressed her hand to his chest. "There are two huge hurts in you. You let yourself cry for Kylie but you've never let yourself face the other loss."

The way she'd simply accepted Kylie's memory as a part of their lives made him love his mate even more. "You accepted my sister," she'd said when he'd asked her about it one night, "how can I do any less for yours?"

His guilt, too, was gone. It had burned away during that same conversation—when he'd told Ashaya about Kylie's fierce spirit. "She hated bullies," he'd said. "She was ten years old when she saw some kids picking on another boy at school. She flew at them, scratched them up, got into trouble for fighting. But she didn't care. She made friends with that kid, stuck with him until his family moved to another town."

"Such a big heart she had," Ashaya had murmured. "Such a beautiful heart."

That was when he'd heard Kylie's laughter in his mind, seen her chiding face.

Of course I would've accepted her, big bro. Stop being silly and let her make you happy. Or I'll haunt you.

He'd finally understood that his sister, with her huge heart, would never have wanted him to feel guilty about this beautiful, perfect thing called the mating bond. That simple knowledge had given him a powerful kind of peace.

But Ashaya was right; as far as his latency went, he'd never even tried for peace. "If I mourn for it," he said to her now, releasing the vicious control that had allowed him to survive as a child without half his soul, "then I admit it's gone forever. I don't want to do that, Shaya. I don't want to tell my leopard that it's going to be trapped inside me until death. I don't want to think of it as a separate being. I want to be complete."

Ashaya nodded, eyes shiny. "I've got it almost ready to go. I thought I should be prepared in case you—"

"Let's do it. Soon as you've finalized everything." The decision was made. "That way, we'll know quicker if it doesn't work."

A burst of panic in Ashaya's eyes. "Dorian, I'm so sure but what if—"

"Then I go on," he said. "At least we'd know that we tried. No regrets."

A jerky nod. "No regrets."

And he knew that the words were true. No matter what happened with the trapped animal inside his body, both cat and man were one in this moment, in this truth. Ashaya Aleine was his. And he was hers. Leopard and man. Man and leopard. All of him.

EPILOGUE

It's been three months. Dorian has forgiven me, and I'm trying to believe that it doesn't matter—he managed to make me say those very words last night. I'm blushing as I write this. The things he comes up with . . . it's enough to shock a scientist.

I think I hear him. Better turn this off—he keeps trying to steal it so he can read my secrets. Silly cat. He is my biggest secret.

—From the encrypted personal files of Ashaya Aleine

Dorian was not in a good mood. The cat still trapped in his body was clawing at him, his mind was full of growls and other leopard crap he didn't want to deal with, and his favorite rifle had just broken. "Shaya!"

His mate poked her head out from the tent where she'd been sitting. Taking her and Keenan camping had been his idea. Noor had tagged along. Oddly, of the two adults, it was Ashaya who was enjoying herself the most. Even the organizer only came out when she wanted to write about her experiences—in a journal she refused to let him read.

"Shh," she said, "our son is having a nap with his girlfriend." She took in his mud-splattered clothing. "Oh, dear."

He muttered a few choice words. "Towel." He'd dunked his entire body, clothes and all, in a nearby stream, washing off most of the mud, but he was soaking wet.

Making an expressive face at his tone, she grabbed a towel

from one of the packs and came out. "Stop giving in to your mean side." She began to dry his hair while he used the other end of the towel to wipe his face.

Dropping the towel the second it was done, he snaked out an arm and slammed her to his chest. "Put me in a better mood then."

She rolled her eyes. "Fine. I'll strip naked and lie in the sun once we get home and our son is out visiting his friends. Happy?"

He grinned, his bad mood disappearing at the speed of light. "Hell, yeah."

Her lips twitched. Ashaya was still learning to laugh but he knew when his mate was happy. Leaning in, he stole a kiss. "What if I get naked and lie with you?"

Her lips parted. "Oh, then I'd *definitely* be ready to do you all sorts of favors."

God, he loved the way she reacted to him. Bending his head, he stole another kiss before she pulled back and glanced down. "You made me wet." Her nipples stood out hard and tight against the fabric of her T-shirt.

He felt like purring, he was so damn pleased with himself for having this sexy woman for his mate. "Maybe you'd better hang it up to dry."

"One-track mind."

"Thank you very much."

Smile widening, she wiggled out of his arms. "Children, remember?"

"They sleep soundly." He thought back to the previous night, to how she'd snuck out with him. The interlude had been a whole lot of fun.

It had also been a chance to talk. Ashaya's guilt had been eating *him* alive. He'd finally loved her into exhaustion and told her to stop it. "We tried, Shaya. It didn't work. I'm disappointed but I didn't lose anything."

"Your hopes," she'd begun.

"I have you. I have Keenan. I'm happy." It was the truth. Damn but she made him happy.

"You hurt," she'd insisted.

"I did," he'd acknowledged, because he couldn't lie to her. "It hurt like a bitch when I realized the therapy wasn't working, but then I got over it. I'm not the moping kind."

Her face had softened. "No, you're not. You just get out and find a way to deal."

Looking at her now, he could tell that she still wasn't feeling completely okay with the way things had turned out, but time would fix that. "Is there any coffee?" he asked as she grabbed clothes for him from inside the tent.

"I'll make you some while you change." She threw him a sweater and a fresh pair of jeans.

He was reaching out to grab the clothing when a spasm hit his body. It was so unexpected and violent that it doubled him over. His vision shifted, the world swimming before him. He was vaguely aware of Ashaya crying out and running to kneel beside him. Her frantic hands felt odd on him, not quite as they should. His senses were so acute, everything too sharp, too bright.

His first thought was that the gene therapy had gone terribly wrong. His second was that he had to let Ashaya know he didn't blame her. It wasn't her fault. Just fucking fate. But he couldn't get the words out, his vocal cords all wrong. He couldn't even reach for her. His hands wouldn't cooperate.

"Give in!" he heard Ashaya scream. "Stop fighting it! Dorian, please!"

Give in? What was she talking about? He had to fight, fighting was how he'd survived.

"Baby, please. Please. Please."

Ashaya never used endearments, a part of him thought. She was still learning. He liked to tease her by saying— A pulse of need, of love, came down the mating bond. It had the wet saltiness of a plea.

He couldn't deny her. He could never deny her.

He gave in.

Agony and ecstasy, pure joy and shuddering pain. It was endless and the firefly flicker of a bird's heart. Then it was over. He blinked but his vision remained all wrong, his eyes too low to the ground. He opened his mouth to ask Ashaya why she was crying . . . but what came out wasn't human.

Ashaya began laughing at the look on Dorian's face. "You are so beautiful." A leopard with puzzled green eyes and the cutest expression she had ever seen. "Oh, I could just . . ." She reached out to stroke her hand down the fur of his back.

He made a rumbling sound that vibrated under her fingertips.

"Mom!" Keenan skidded to a stop beside her, Noor gasping beside him.

Dorian looked up and immediately lost his balance. Ashaya slung an arm around him, keeping him upright. "Slow, slow. You have to get used to it."

Keenan bent his body, braced his hands on his knees, and looked sideways at the man he usually followed around like a solid little shadow. "Dorian? Is that you? You're a leopard! Noor, look, Dorian's a cat!"

Ashaya felt shock ripple through the mating bond as Keenan's innocent exclamation finally cut through the confusion blinding Dorian. "You're magnificent," she whispered, cognizant of his keen hearing. "Amazingly beautiful."

"Dorian's a cat! Dorian's a cat!" Keenan, her previously silent son, began running around them in circles, a giggling Noor attached to his hand.

Laughing at their antics, Ashaya pressed a kiss to Dorian's brow. "Try to walk."

He wobbled dangerously.

Shit! Dorian thought. He was like a cub, all lack of coordination and paws out of order. Okay, he thought, he was still a man inside. He could work this out.

Strokes on his back, through fur. The sensation was so different, so luscious. And then the whisper in his ear. "The leopard knows. You don't have to cage him anymore."

It was as if he'd just needed to hear it. The leopard took over, the man retreated. Then the two combined for the first time in his life. He felt Ashaya move away even as his body straightened. Turning his head, he leaned forward and closed his jaws very gently over her wrist.

It was a kiss.

Her face lit up in understanding. "I love you, too. Now go, run. Play."

He released her, stopping to snap his teeth at the kids simply to hear them laugh and scamper off. Then he ran. The forest took on a thousand new colors clothed in scent, and when he chased prey, it was for the sheer joy of it. Hours passed. Night came and stars lit up the sky.

But the best part was going home . . . because she was waiting for him in front of a small fire. He walked out of the forest on four feet, thought about wanting to hold her in the arms of a man, and that quickly, he was kneeling naked on the forest floor. "Hey. Kids asleep?"

She nodded and ran to him. "Oh, Dorian!"

Her joy blazed along the bond until it pulsed golden inside his heart. "God, I love you," he whispered. The words came from the heart of him, a heart that held the wild fury of a changeling—there was no man and there was no leopard. Only Dorian.

Turn the page for a sneak peak of
the first book in a thrilling new series
from Nalini Singh

Angels' Blood

Coming in March 2009
from Berkley Sensation!

Elena's instincts were screaming at her to grab the knife in her boot, do some damage, and get the hell out, but she forced herself to stay in place. The truth was, she wouldn't make it more than two feet before Raphael broke every single bone in her body.

It was exactly what he'd done to a vampire who'd thought to betray him.

That vampire had been found in the center of Times Square. He'd still been alive. And he'd still been trying to scream, "No! Raphael, no!" But his voice had been a rasp by then, his jaw hanging on by stringlike tendons, his flesh missing in places. Elena—out of the United States on a hunt—had seen the news footage after the event. She knew the vamp had lain there in agony for three hours before being picked up by a pair of angels. Everyone in New York, hell, everyone in the country, had known he was there, but no one had dared help him, not with Raphael's mark blazing on his forehead. The archangel had wanted the punishment witnessed, wanted to remind people of who and what he was. It had worked. Now the mere mention of his name evoked visceral fear.

But Elena wouldn't crawl, not for anyone. It was a choice

she'd made the night her father had told her to get on her
and beg, and maybe, maybe, he'd accept her back into the fa

Elena hadn't spoken to her father in a decade.

"You should have a care," Raphael said into the unnatu
silence.

She didn't collapse in relief—the air continued to hang heav
with the promise of menace. "I don't like to play games."

"Learn." He settled back in his chair. "You will live a very
short life if you expect only honesty."

Sensing the danger had passed—for now—she unclenched
her fingers with an effort of will. The force of the blood rushing
back into them was painful. "I didn't say I expected honesty.
People lie. Vampires lie. Even—" She caught herself.

"Surely you're not going to practice discretion now?" The
amusement was back but it was tempered with an edge that
stroked like a razor across her skin.

She looked into that perfect face and knew she'd never met a
more deadly being in her life. If she displeased him, Raphael
would kill her as easily as she might swat a fly. She'd be smart
to remember that, no matter how the knowledge infuriated her.
"You said I had to do a test?"

His wings moved slightly at that instant, drawing her attention. They truly were beautiful and she couldn't help but covet
them. To be able to fly . . . what an amazing gift.

Raphael's eyes shifted to look at something over her left
shoulder. "Less a test than an experiment."

She didn't twist around, had no need to. "There's a vampire
behind me."

"Are you sure?" His expression remained unchanged.

She fought the urge to turn. "Yes."

He nodded. "Look."

Wondering which was worse—having her back to an enig-
matic and highly unpredictable archangel or to an unknown
vampire—she hesitated. In the end, her curiosity won out.
There was a distinctly satisfied expression on Raphael's face
and she wanted to know what had put it there.

Shifting, she turned sideways with her whole body, the position allowing her to keep Raphael in her peripheral vision. Then
she looked at the *two* . . . creatures who stood behind her. "Jesus."

"You may go." Raphael's voice was a command that awak-

absolute terror in the eyes of the one who looked vaguely man. The other scuttled away like the animal it was.

She watched them leave through the glass door and swallowed. "How old was . . ." She couldn't call that thing a vampire. Neither had it been human.

"Erik was Made yesterday."

"I didn't know they could walk at that age." It was an attempt to sound professional though she was creeped out to her toes.

"He had a little help." Raphael's tone made it clear that that was all the answer she was going to get. "Bernal is . . . a fraction older."

She reached for the juice she'd rejected earlier and took a drink, trying to wash away the stink that had seeped into her pores. The older vamps didn't have that ick factor. They—except for the unusual ones like the doorvamp—simply smelled of vampire, like she smelled human. But the very young ones, they had a certain rotten-cabbage/putrid-flesh smell that she always had to scrub three times over to get rid of. It was why she'd begun collecting body washes and perfumes. After her initial contact with one of the newly Made, she'd thought she'd never get the smell out of her head.

"I didn't think a hunter would be so disturbed at the sight of the just Made." Raphael's face appeared oddly shadowed, until she realized he'd raised his wings slightly.

Wondering if that implied focus or anger, she put down the glass. "I'm not, not really." True enough now that that first, instinctive flash of disgust had passed. "It's the smell . . . like a coating of fur on your tongue. No matter how hard you scrape, you can't get it off."

Open interest showed on his face. "The feeling is that intense?"

She shivered and looked around the table for something else to take the edge off. When he pushed a cut grapefruit in her direction, she dug into it with relish. "Uh-huh." The citrus fruit's acidic juices dampened the reek a little. At least enough that she could think.

"If I asked you to track Erik, could you?"

She shivered at the memory of those almost-dead/not-quite-alive eyes. No wonder people believed those stories about vampires being the walking dead. "No. I think he's too young."

"What about Bernal?"

"He's on the bottom floor of the building right now. In lobby."

Golden tipped wings spread to shadow the table as Rapha put his hands together in a slow clap. "Well done, Elena. We done."

She looked up from the grapefruit, belatedly aware she'd just proven how good she was when she should've flubbed it and gotten out of this, whatever "this" was. Shit. But at least he'd given her some idea of the job. "Do you want me to track a rogue?"

He rose from his chair in a sudden, liquid movement. "Wait a moment."

She watched, transfixed, as he walked to the edge of the roof. He was a being of such incredible splendor that simply seeing him move made her heart squeeze. It didn't matter that she knew it was a mirage, that he was as deadly as the filleting knife she carried strapped to her thigh. No one, not even she, could deny that Raphael the Archangel was a man made to be admired. To be worshipped.

That utterly *wrong* thought snapped her out of her dazed state. Pushing back her chair, she stared hard at his back. Had he been messing with her head? Right then, he turned and she met the agonizing blue of his eyes. For a second, she thought he was answering her question. Then he looked away . . . and walked off the roof.

She jumped up. Only to sit back down, a blush reddening her cheeks, when he winged upward to meet an angel she hadn't seen until that moment. *Michaela.* The female equivalent of Raphael. Her beauty was so intense that Elena could feel the force of it even from this distance. She had the startling realization that she was looking at a mid-air meeting between two archangels.

"Sara's never going to believe this." She forgot the stench of young vampire for the moment, her attention hijacked. She'd seen photos of Michaela, but they came nowhere close to the reality of her.

The other archangel had skin the color of the most exquisite milk chocolate and a shining fall of hair that cascaded to her waist in a wild mass. Her body was quintessentially female, slender and curvy at the same time, her wings a delicate bronze

...at shimmered against the richness of her skin. Her face . . .
"Wow." Even from this distance, Michaela's face was perfection given form. Elena fancied she could see her eyes—a bright,
impossible green—but knew she had to be imagining it. They
were too far away.

It made little difference. The female archangel had a face
that would not only stop traffic, it would cause a few pileups in
the process.

Elena frowned. Despite her appreciation for Michaela's
looks, she was having no trouble thinking straight. Which
meant the damn arrogant blue-eyed bastard *had* been fucking
with her mind. He wanted her to worship him? They'd see about
that.

No one, not even an archangel, was going to turn her into a
puppet.

As if he'd heard her, Raphael said something to his fellow
archangel and winged back down to the roof. His landing was a
lot more showy this time. She was sure he paused to display the
pattern on the inside surface of his wings. It was as if a brush
dipped in gold had started at the top edge of each wing and then
stroked downward, fading to white as it neared the bottom. In
spite of her fury, she had to face the truth: If the devil—or an
archangel—came to her and offered her wings, she might just
sell him her soul.

But the angels didn't Make other angels. They only Made
blood-drinking vampires. Where angels came from, no one
knew. Elena guessed they were born to angelic parents . . .
though, come to think of it, she'd never actually seen a baby
angel.

Her thoughts derailed again as she watched the fluid grace of
Raphael's walk, so seductive . . . so perfect.

Standing up, she sent her chair crashing to the tiles. "Get.
Out. Of. My. Head!"

Raphael came to a standstill. "Do you intend to use that
knife?" His words were ice. She felt blood scent the air and realized it was her own.

Looking down, she found her hand clenching on the blade of
the knife she'd drawn instinctively from the sheath at her ankle.
She'd never have made such a mistake. He was forcing her to
hurt herself, showing her she was nothing but a toy for him to

play with. Instead of fighting, she squeezed harder. "If you wan me to do a job for you, fine. But I won't be manipulated."

His eyes flicked over the blood seeping from her fist. He didn't have to say anything.

"You might be able to control me," she said, in response to the silent mockery on his face, "but if that would've gotten the job done, you'd have never gone through the farce of hiring me. You need me, Elena Deveraux, not one of your little vampire flunkies."

Her hand unclenched in a violent spasm as he made her release the blade. It fell to the ground with a *thud* dampened by the blood that had pooled below. She didn't move, didn't attempt to stem the flow.

And when Raphael walked to stand less than a foot from her, she stood her ground.

"So, you think you have me over a barrel?" The sky was a seamless blue but Elena felt storm winds whip her hair completely out of its coil.

"No." She let his scent—clean, bright, of the sea—settle over the lingering coat of vampire on her tongue. "I'm ready to walk away without a backward look, return the deposit you paid the Guild."

"That," he said, picking up a napkin and wrapping it around her hand, "is not an option."

Startled by the unexpected act, she closed her hand to help slow the bleeding. "Why not?"

"I want you to do this," he responded, as if that was reason enough. And for an archangel, it was.

"What's the job? Retrieval?"

"Yes."

Relief began to wash through her like the rain she could feel so close. But no, it was his scent, that fresh bite of water. "All I need to start with, is something the vampire wore recently. If you have a general location, even better. If not, I'll get the Guild's computer geniuses to track public transport and bank records, etcetera, while I hunt on the ground." Her mind was already at work, considering and discarding options.

"You mistake me, Elena. It's not a vampire I want you to find."

That halted her in her tracks. "You're looking for a human? Well, I can do it but I really don't have any advantage over a good private investigator."

"Try again."

Not vampire. Not human. That left . . . "An angel?" she whispered. "No."

"No," he agreed, and once again, she felt the cool brush of relief. It lasted until he said, "An archangel."

Elena stared at him. "You're joking."

His cheekbones stood out starkly against the sun-kissed smoothness of his skin. "No. The Cadre of Ten does not joke."

Her stomach curdled at the reference to the Cadre—if Raphael was any example of their lethal power, she never wanted to meet that august body. "Why are you tracking an archangel?"

"That, you do not need to know." His tone was final. "What you do need to know is that if you succeed in finding him, you'll be rewarded with more money than you can hope to spend in your lifetime."

Elena glanced at the bloodstained napkin. "And if I fail?"

"Don't fail, Elena." His eyes were mild but his smile, it spoke of things better not said aloud. "You intrigue me—I'd hate to have to punish you."

Her mind flashed to that image of the vampire in Times Square, that broken mess that had once been a person . . . Raphael's definition of punishment.

Nalini Singh's Psy-Changeling series
continues with

Branded by Fire

Coming in summer 2009
from Berkley Sensation!

"I'm going to kill you." It was more hiss than sound.

Riley bit her.

In the soft, sensitive place between neck and shoulder.

Mercy felt her entire body shiver from the inside out at the blatant show of dominance. "Stop it." It came out husky, nothing like the rejection she wanted it to be.

He took his mouth from her. "I've pinned you."

"That's wolf shit. I'm a cat."

"You're still trapped under me." He nuzzled at her throat. "And you smell all hot and wet and hungry." His voice was dropping, going wolf on her.

And the heat between her thighs was turning into a pulsing drumbeat. Her stomach twisted in a vicious wave of need. God she was hungry, so sensually hungry. And Riley had taken her, his hold unbreakable. At that moment, the leopard didn't care that he wasn't a cat. It just cared that he was strong, sexy, and aroused.

Read the full chapter excerpt at www.nalinisingh.com!